**RAVE REVIEWS FO**
**WINNER OF THE N**
**CHOICE AW**
***AFFAIRE DE COEUR* R**
**FOR BEST TIME TRAVEL OF 2000!**

"Ms. Plunkett exhibits "creativity and genius for characterization . . . unparalleled poignancy and an intimacy of both heart and soul."

—*Booktrees*

"Susan Plunkett . . . will entertain readers and make her mark as a true star of the genre."

—*Romantic Times*

"I have found a new, buy-on-sight, must-read author!"

—*Bookbug on the Web*

"Ms. Plunkett has created a new dimension to the genre that must be developed further."

—*The Literary Times*

"Ms. Plunkett you are the BEST!"

—*Bell, Book and Candle*

"Ms. Plunkett writes some of the best sensual romance sandwiched between two covers."

—*Booktrees*

"WOW! Ms. Plunkett knows how to draw readers into her story and keep them there until the end."

—*Old Book Barn Gazette*

## *ALICIA'S SONG*

"An entertaining time-travel romance that readers will fully enjoy even as they breathlessly await the upcoming stories starring the two siblings."

—Amazon.com

"*Alicia's Song* is very much a keeper."

—*Romance Reviews Today*

Other *Love Spell* books by Susan Plunkett:
**ALICIA'S SONG**

# A NEW POSITION

"Has no one ever said *no* to you, Mr. Gray?"

His sharp laughter startled her. Before she recovered, he caught her around the waist, lifting and spinning her to the table beside the box.

Her heart pounding against her chest, she was too startled to scream. His palms landed on either side of her hips, and Matthew leaned forward until they were practically nose to nose.

All she could do was stare at him. Good grief, other than her father, no one had ever picked her up like that.

"*No* is a word I hear all the time. Right now, I'd prefer not hearing it from you. I have made every concession you've requested. Now, how about a little compromise on your part?"

"I . . . don't understand." His warm, moist breath smelled of coffee and cinnamon. The faint aroma of bay rum wreaked havoc on all her feminine senses. His gaze lowered to her lips, which she unconsciously moistened with the tip of her tongue.

Great Gerty's ghost, he wanted to kiss her!

# Susan Plunkett

LOVE SPELL  NEW YORK CITY

*For my friend and a true pioneer, Phyllis Taylor Pianka.*

A LOVE SPELL BOOK®

November 2001

Published by

Dorchester Publishing Co., Inc.
276 Fifth Avenue
New York, NY 10001



ISBN 0-505-52463-5



Printed in the United States of America.

# Bethany's Song

# *Prologue*

"Let this one go on alone." Digger Phelps, the graveyard caretaker, barred the iron gate with his thin body. "She's a loner all her life and don't need anyone now. Besides, I heard she's a witch. If that's true there ain't no tellin' what'll happen iffen you ladies do your Christian-like service."

"People have been scaring each other with those old rumors for years," Alicia assured him.

"Yolanda D'Arcy deserves the same consideration and reverence as anyone else, Digger," Bethany said. She looked away, remembering the three children who had encroached on the old woman's privacy years ago. Instead of being a witch who turned them to stone, she'd given them flowers and asked them to sing for her when she died.

Since Bethany was old enough to walk, her mother had taken her to sing in the Drexel Cemetery. By the time she started school, she realized that she, her mother, and her two sisters were the only people who visited the cemetery when some people died; doing so was part of the James family's lives. Now, though their mother was gone, they were carrying on.

Bethany half-listened to Alicia cajole the caretaker into moving out of the way. As the eldest, Alicia had stepped into the leadership role when a drunk driver killed their parents.

"Your mama wouldn't sing fer a witch," Digger insisted.

Bethany pressed her lips together and remained silent. Alicia excelled at confrontation. Bethany shied away from such situations. And Phelps, trying to hide the alcoholic tremors wracking his hands by shoving them into the pockets of his bib overalls, was just the type of unpredictable sort that Bethany hated.

At last he opened the gate. Bethany followed Alicia into the granite forest of weathered headstones.

"I thought he was on the wagon," Alicia whispered.

"Last I heard, he was." Bethany brushed back a wind-whipped lock of hair. Then again, she didn't pursue gossip. Keeping track of twenty-nine fifth-graders through the end of the school year demanded all her attention.

"It feels like a storm brewing. Maybe that's why he's on edge," Alicia suggested.

"I, for one, don't believe in witches," their younger sister Caitlyn spoke up. "Besides, we made a promise to Yolanda we have to keep."

Bethany suppressed a smile at the girl's bravado, knowing from whence came its strength. The three siblings lent one another courage. Hand in hand, they could handle anything life dealt.

They walked until they found Yolanda D'Arcy's headstone. Clad in a straight skirt and heels, Caitlyn took the lead position at the foot of the grave. Bethany moved to the center, her long skirt billowing in the breeze and as shapeless as the flowing blouse and linen vest hanging almost to her thighs. She was the shortest of the trio.

Caitlyn offered the words to send this lonely soul on her way to the next world. She spoke of peace and the kindness of the human heart. Together the James sisters prayed Yolanda D'Arcy found harmony in the hereafter.

Because it was her turn to do the honors, Caitlyn prayed aloud for Yolanda. Then she ended the invocation abruptly. In the next heartbeat, her pure soprano sang the first strains of "Ave Maria."

Immediately, the breeze stilled. The birds silenced.

The sisters' voices carried through the cottonwood centurions flanking the graveyard's wrought-iron boundaries, their three-part harmony, in its beauty, rivaling that of the mountain birdsong echoing through the Tetons.

Bethany lost herself in the poignant words of "Amazing Grace."

" 'I once was lost—' " Dear God, she was still lost and unable to find the road to complete healing.

When Alicia's throaty alto led them in "Climbing Up the Mountain," Bethany thought of the application still sitting on her pile of year-end school projects. Going for her Ph.D. meant moving to Laramie for at least a year. Maybe two. It seemed so far away from Drexel, Wyoming, this place she called home.

Yet teaching was her life. Her students were her *children*—the only ones she'd ever have. She owed it to them, and to herself, to be the best teacher possible. Which meant getting more education.

The song ended. As though signaled by an unseen force, fog rolled out of the surrounding cottonwoods. Like a thick wave of clouds seeping from the ground it crept over the land, hugging the summer grasses just sprouting into life. It advanced with a will of its own through the still afternoon air, and as the final note of the James sisters' service faded, the mist swirled over Yolanda D'Arcy's grave and engulfed the trio.

The sudden change in the weather made the small hairs on the back of Bethany's neck prickle.

"We'd better go," Alicia said.

"Lead the way." With their obligation fulfilled, Bethany was ready. Perhaps over coffee the three of them could discuss her application to graduate school. "We're right behind you. Don't lag, Caitlyn."

"I'm right here," the younger girl assured them.

The atmosphere grew thicker with each step through the familiar graveyard.

"This is creepy."

"Stay close. I can't even see the stepping stones," Alicia warned.

Bethany decided this was one of the times it paid to be the middle child; she had a sister less than an arm's length in front and behind her.

Needing to touch her sisters, to take their hands for assurance, she reached out.

She found only darkness and fog. This was the end of the world.

# *Chapter One*

Strangely, the end of the world was green.

Mist the color of spring leaves swirled over Bethany. The strange air clung to her skin like damp satin, and its thickness caught in her lungs.

She wiped her eyes, but her vision remained blurred.

When she squinted into the soupy air again, she was alone in the eerie turbulence.

"Alicia? Caitlyn? Where are you?" Bethany extended her arms in search of her sisters. She encountered nothing more solid than ethereal wisps that sluiced through her fingers.

Confusion made her retreat. "Caitlyn? Don't mess around. If you trip in those stilts you call shoes, Alicia and I aren't carrying you down to the car."

Green-tinged vapor and a whispering in the obscured distance followed her movements as she cautiously turned around.

"Alicia? Caitlyn? Stop kidding around! Where are you?"

The sluggish fog grew thicker each time she moved.

Bethany completed her circle and stood still. This was weird. Really, really weird. She put her hand over the rapid pulse at her throat. If her sisters were within earshot, they'd have answered by now.

Dear God in Heaven, there were no voices, no winds, just the eerie hiss of something moving very fast, like water running over a falls, or steep series of rapids. She hugged herself against the clammy chill. The sound couldn't be water; there were no rivers or streams near the graveyard.

"Okay, you two. This isn't funny anymore. You win. I'm scared." Memories of childhood flooded back. *Bethany the wuss*.

She shouldn't be frightened; even disoriented by the pea-soup fog, it didn't seem possible to get lost in a place where she could name every marker and grassy tuft. This cemetery was such a place.

The vapor began to disperse into the luminescence of twilight.

Bethany spun—searching for anyone, anything—and nearly lost her balance. The tenuousness of her footing doubled her awareness. Using her left foot the way a blind person taps a cane, she groped for familiar headstones so as not to stumble.

The air cooled. Iridescent colors winked through the diminishing mists like swimming fireflies.

Around her, the grave markers had disappeared—right along with everything else, including the early summer grasses off the beaten path. Thick vegetation that usually swished around her knees had become spongy mountain ground that sprung back to shape whenever she lifted her foot.

Gingerly, she moved forward. The cemetery's spiky

wrought-iron fence was gone, too. Dusk swallowed even the old landmarks. The totality of her disorientation opened the door for the monster named fear. The beast emerged roaring in Bethany's temples.

"Alicia! Caitlyn! *Wait for me!*"

As though denying her, the remnants of the mist—a green swirl that mutated into a dark blue, then violet—evaporated fully. Thick, sullen gloom enveloped her.

Heart pounding, Bethany opened her eyes wide in a desperate attempt to see anything. She drew a chilly breath deep into her lungs. The sharp, unfamiliar scent of alpine forest and something she couldn't identify lingered in her nostrils and on her tongue.

Fear became a weight pressing on her lungs. Whatever was happening, she had no control, and no hope of gaining the upper hand. For the second time in her life, unseen forces dictated her fate.

Would this be a repeat of the past nightmare? Would she once again see the horror approach and be powerless to thwart death and disaster?

Here, she had nothing to lose but her own life.

And those of her sisters.

The realization shattered her paralytic trance.

Cold sweat broke out all over her body. *Oh, God. Oh, God.* "Caitlyn! Alicia!"

Struggling to hold herself together, Bethany clawed at the darkness, the air growing more oppressive and difficult to breathe with each rapid heartbeat.

The ground beneath her feet bucked.

Her arms windmilled for balance; the blood-curdling scream welling up from her toes never reaching her mouth. She half-fell, half-sat on the spongy, gyrating earth. This truly was the end of everything she knew.

Time lost all meaning.

Gradually, her surroundings became so quiet Bethany

heard the thunder of her heartbeat and the labored sound of her own breathing.

"Alicia! Caitlyn!" she yelled at the top of her lungs.

The ground shuddered, as though protesting her noisiness.

Self-control was the key to success, she'd told her students countless times. *Though you can't control anything or anyone around you, you can control yourself.*

She would not let fear win.

Not again.

She was strong, had survived a car crash that claimed four other lives. In the eerie gloom, the realization of being totally alone became an anvil weighing her down. As though reinforcing her isolation, the silence pressed against her with the force of a viable, relentless entity.

"Fear is the enemy. Do not embrace the enemy," she whispered, cradling her elbows in trembling hands and rocking back and forth.

Bethany fervently hoped that her sisters were at least together.

Alicia and Caitlyn were her mainstays, her backbone, her motivation, and the source of her happiness. Enduring this without them was terrifying. She hoped they were not suffering similarly.

A faint voice of twisted logic wormed into her awareness. If this indeed were the end of the world, why wasn't her life passing before her eyes? Or did that happen only to those who drowned?

But she was drowning—in darkness and in uncertainty. She pushed to her feet, her hands searching for something, anything solid. "*Alicia!*"

Without warning, the world tilted again. Caught off balance on the slippery slope, Bethany fought for purchase and lost.

The ground rippled, then fell away.

Tumbling head over heels, she caught flashes of light,

then green, blue, white, brown, until she closed her eyes. As a child, she'd learn how to fall from a horse, from haylofts, even fences and trees. But this tumbling, as if she were being juggled by invisible hands, struck terror into every cell of her body. There was no up or down, just a gyroscope of motion and movement.

With a sudden jolt, the ground solidified beneath her. Night turned into day.

Soft earth, splashes of color, and a fragrance she dimly recognized as flowers and ferns assaulted her. Trees so tall their tops blotted out the sunlight appeared in her vision. Her senses fought to assimilate the chaotic collage spinning around her.

Bright sunshine forced her to squint as she somersaulted down a grassy embankment. She caught glimpses of people. Gravestones. An angel . . .

Oh, God, she really was at the end of her life!

The angel extended an open hand to her.

Bethany wanted to reach back, but she was moving too swiftly.

Then there was nothing.

The sun peeked through clouds gathering in a blue sky. A lazy breeze played in the branches of a giant spruce. The tree had been ancient before Joe Juneau found gold in the Silverbow Basin in 1880.

Four men shared a buckboard with a coffin. The iron-and-wood wagon wheels rumbled over the worn road to the cemetery. Summer wildflowers hugged the markers poking out of the glassy ground.

Despite their divergent relationships with Old Man Gray, the foursome had a final, solemn duty to discharge. No one spoke. Each remained lost in his own thoughts.

Big, rawboned Henry Bittlehorn stopped the buckboard at the entrance to the cemetery. Sharing the seat with Henry, Matthew Gray gazed inside. As always, his eyes found the marker bearing his wife's and child's names, then found his mother's granite monument.

Today, two mounds of dirt obscured the marble lamb that distinguished Candice Temple Gray's final resting place. Today, the old lion in the coffin riding in the back of the wagon would lie beside that lamb.

And when the last shovel of dirt filled his father's grave, Matthew would have something he'd never dreamed of having.

*Freedom.*

Yet, the emancipation wrought by his father's death carried no joy. The most optimistic sensation Matthew could muster was keen disappointment, for himself and the old man. Experience had taught him the folly of expectation. Anything could change, even a father's love.

As a child, Matthew had regarded his old man as a god. For so many years they'd shared affection, laughter, stories. They'd had a unity, an affinity nothing could match.

Then a careless moment had ended Matthew's idyllic youth.

The death of his mother had been hard, but worse had been the emotional withdrawal of his father. It had left a hole inside Matthew that he'd sealed plank by hurtful plank over the years. Matthew's wife, Victoria, had planted a garden of joy over that empty place. The flowers of life had bloomed in ways he hadn't thought possible, then died just as unexpectedly. He'd buried Victoria and their son—and his heart—two years earlier.

He tore his gaze from his wife and baby Ethan's grave to his mother's simple headstone.

It read: CANDICE TEMPLE GRAY, 1845–1879, BELOVED WIFE OF GEORGE.

The inscription ought to have included: LOVING MOTHER OF MATTHEW.

The intentional omission served as another reminder

of the blame his father laid on his shoulders. A blame he accepted.

Matthew had killed his parents, plain and simple. His mother had died in his arms the day the carriage Matthew was racing along a rutted road overturned. His father had taken longer to stop breathing.

He'd promised his dying mother he would unite them in death. And Matthew always kept his promises.

"Let's get him in the ground." Matthew squared his tension-stiffened shoulders. The only positive aspect of his father's decree of no service, no ceremony, and no one in attendance was the swiftness with which they could accomplish the deed. This was the last time he'd have to do something his father's way, and one burial that wouldn't haunt him. Hell, no. Now maybe he and the old man would find peace. Certainly, they had finality.

Henry put the brake on the buckboard and secured the reins. The seat springs creaked as he and Matthew climbed down on opposite sides. At the rear of the wagon, Jeb, the strapping Irishman, and the big Norseman, Dall Lockner, slipped coils of rope over their shoulders. They slid the heavy pine box to the edge of the wagon bed.

Matthew shouldered the front, right corner of the coffin. After a bit of jostling, the foursome found balance and marched in step through the silent graveyard.

He hadn't been able to find a way to turn off what he felt for his father, though God knew he'd wanted to. Part of him wanted to believe Victoria's assertion that his father hadn't stopped loving his only son—right up until George Gray's final breath.

Even then, the old man's rheumy eyes had accused his son of murder.

His mother hadn't blamed him for the accident, just loved him unconditionally. God, one moment they had been laughing, feeling the wind in their faces, racing across the brisk morning; the next, they had been tumbling down the steep hillside. Matthew had been thrown clear. His mother had not.

Lost in hurtful memories, Matthew kept his gaze on the rocky dirt piled beside the pit awaiting his father.

The physical weight of the old man in his plain, pine coffin felt feather-light in comparison to the personal burdens Matthew had borne over the years.

He lifted his gaze to the sky above the western trees. An eagle glided in a lazy circle as though overseeing the quiet ceremony. His mother had loved the majestic birds, watching them ride the wind.

I fulfilled my promise, Mother, Matthew thought. *Here he is, beside you once again. I did my best. It may not have been good enough, but you and God know I tried. He's free now. And so am I.*

Gazing into the six-foot-deep hole beside his mother's final resting place, Matthew wondered when the sense of liberation he'd anticipated would lighten his spirits. He felt only disappointment and sorrow.

"Lay the ropes," Jeb called out, easing the coil from his shoulder and waiting for the others.

Behind Matthew, Dall and Jeb whipped the ropes they'd brought into two lines on the ground.

"Set him down." Dall's voice was barely a whisper on the lazy afternoon breeze.

As though they'd done it a dozen times, the four men positioned the coffin, the ropes, and themselves at the yawning grave. They were burying a legend, not just a man. This was the Devil—or a saint; it depended who you asked.

Other than his son, none knew the real George Gray. That man had died in Tacoma with his wife—only a bitter, vindictive shell remained. He'd become a husk with a heart as crippled as his left leg. And the change was all Matthew's fault.

The rope slid through his gloved hands.

*I've endured.*

The four men seesawed the coffin, widening a narrow spot constricting its descent into the rocky earth.

The old man had won the last skirmish. Now, the war was over. Matthew couldn't argue with a dead man. All he could do was bury him.

"Keep them ropes even or he'll tip," Henry Bittlehorn warned.

It would be just like the Old Man to pop out and deliver a final miserable memory to those loyal to him.

The coffin settled at the bottom of the hole. Clumps of dirt trickled from the walls as the men tossed their ropes down onto its top. The coils reminded Matthew of a ball of snakes.

How fitting. From his first glimpse into his father's study in years, that was exactly what he worried the Old Man had left him in the Gray Wolf Mine.

The sound of something moving through the brush caught his attention. Matthew glanced toward the tree line at the edge of the cemetery and reached for a shovel. He wanted this over, his father buried. The Old Man was gone, but no one would forget him. That was for damn sure.

"What was that?" Jeb glanced uneasily over his shoulder toward the trees.

"Nothing important. Let's get Matthew's papa into his resting place." Henry started shoveling dark, rocky dirt into the grave.

"What the—"

"Did you hear—"

"Oh, my Lord—"

"Shit!"

All four men leaned forward and peered into the hole.

Matthew was the first to look away. The source of the sudden moaning wasn't his father. Of that, he was sure.

"What was that?" Dall caught Matthew's gaze.

"An eagle," Henry said fiercely.

"You've have been standing too close to the stampers, Henry. I know the sound of an eagle," said Dall. The man worked as a tunnel foreman at the Gray Wolf and had no patience for silliness. "Before that."

"Don't know. Maybe some animal rootin' around for a meal?" Henry pulled a shovel out of the dirt mounded behind him and Matthew. "Or maybe the meal who don't want to be ate."

"Didn't sound like any animal I know."

Henry sank the shovel into the rocky dirt pile. "Acht. You know all animals and the sounds they make?"

Dall and Henry could go back and forth the rest of the day: Matthew wasn't in the mood to listen. "Maybe some animal's hurt. I'll take a look." He turned and walked in the direction of the sound, aware his three companions followed.

He skirted the section where miners were buried, moving quickly through the rows of graves. Some had headstones, others wooden cross markers, and a few had ornate statues. At the outer edge of the cemetery, not far from the wall of towering spruce, a majestic marble guardian angel stood over Baby Webster's resting place. Hands outstretched, the androgynous seraph cast benevolent, sightless eyes on the bundle lying against the base.

"What the hell . . ." The words trailed off as Matthew's astonishment grew. There was no injured animal here. He crouched beside the still form of a woman.

Curled into a fetal ball swathed in voluminous skirts, it was difficult to determine whether he was looking at a small woman or an adolescent. Long, wavy hair fanned over her face. The sun caught in the golden highlights of those auburn locks.

With a moan, the woman tucked deeper into what already seemed an impossibly tight ball.

Matthew pulled off the glove from his right hand and

moved forward onto one knee. Whoever this was, he figured she'd been here a while. They hadn't seen her arrive. Hell, they hadn't seen anyone.

"A woman? Who is she?" asked Jeb in a hushed voice.

"What's that she's wearin'? Her unmentionables?" Henry chimed in.

Careful not to add to their find's discomfort, Matthew moved the thick locks of hair away from the side of her face. The curls were unbelievably soft and warm, like spun honey. Long black lashes rested on her pale cheeks, her skin dusted with a fine sprinkle of freckles.

He swept her hair back, revealing small, shell-like ears pierced with three hoop earrings. A red welt ran across her temple, ear, and neck. This girl was going to have one heck of a headache. Sympathy curled his lip into a wince.

"Can you hear me?" Matthew didn't know where to touch her, as the extent of her injuries wasn't immediately apparent.

"Son of a bitch. It is a woman. Where'd she come from?" Awestruck, Dall leaned closer for a better look. His towering height and the breadth of his shoulders cast a large shadow over Matthew.

"We'll be askin' the lass when she comes around," Jeb answered. "No telling how long she's been here." He moved to Matthew's left side.

"Damn, but she's a pretty little thing. Wonder who lost her." Dall spoke with reverence.

Matthew raised his hand for quiet.

"Miss?" He touched her shoulder. There was nothing to her except clothing and hair. "Can you open your eyes?" His only answer was the play of the breeze on the fine strands of her hair and the ruffle of her skirt.

"Mebbe we ought to take her over to Doc Swenson's," suggested Dall.

"I don't think so," Matthew said. "Doc Swenson hasn't

drawn a fully sober breath in all the time I've known him. Whoever this woman is, she deserves some real help. Megan can do it, can't she, Jeb?"

"Me wife usually deals with birthin' children, but no matter. Me Megan knows all the healing arts. She'll take good care of this lass," Jeb said.

The flutter of the woman's long eyelashes accompanied another moan.

"That's it," Matthew encouraged. "Open your eyes." *Tell us you're fine so we can finish what we came to do.*

Her straight, delicate nose twitched against the grass. From what he could see, the woman had fine features and a precise arch to her thin eyebrows.

Her lashes stilled. Her brow furrowed as she opened her eyes into a squint, but still she did not look up. Tentatively, she straightened her left leg, only to freeze when she encountered Henry's big foot.

"Sorry, ma'am." Henry retreated to give her room.

Damn, it hadn't seemed possible for the woman to become more pale, but she had. The bloodlessness of her tightly pressed lips meant she was afraid. Matthew understood. "You're safe," he assured her. "No one will hurt you."

"Be you broken anywhere, lass?" asked Jeb in a calm voice. "She doesna look so good, Matthew."

"Broken?" she asked in a faint voice. "I, ah, don't think so." Eyes closing again, she reached up to the nasty bruise along the side of her head.

"If I help you, can you sit up?"

"No." Her eyes snapped open. Unmistakable panic set in when she caught sight of him and the three spectators towering behind him. "I'm fine. Just . . . Please. Please, don't touch me. Please." Her voice faded into the breeze combing through the nearby grass.

"No one will hurt you, miss." Despite his annoyance at her words, Matthew wanted to reassure her, to alleviate the fear darkening her eyes. They were stunning. Never before had he seen eyes the color of forest violets—but neither had he seen such deep-seated fear.

Alternately squinting and widening, her expressive eyes moved from him to Henry, then Dall, and finally to Jeb. She seemed to be waiting for something and began to scoot away. The base of the marble guardian angel blocked her retreat.

"You're safe." Matthew offered his hand. When she made no move to accept it, he changed tactics. "Step back, gentlemen. Let's give the lady a little room to put herself aright."

He himself took a step back. The others followed suit.

Still, she hesitated before attempting to sit.

"Take it slow," Matthew encouraged. "You've got quite a knot on the side of your head. Are you hurt anywhere else?"

She took her time, visibly gathering more than her physical resources as she pushed into a sitting position. Bracing against the stone base of the angel statue, she looked around with a dazed expression. She appeared small, defenseless, and frighteningly lost.

"The little toe on my right foot," she said softly.

Perplexed, Matthew asked, "You hurt your toe?"

"No. It's the only part of me not hurting at the moment."

The trio chuckled, and Matthew smiled. "At least you haven't broken your sense of humor. What's your name?"

"Bethany James." She leaned back and tried to peer around the men. "Are my sisters here?"

"You have sisters?" Dall's pleasure at the thought seemed misplaced given the group's situation and surroundings. "They're with you?"

The girl bit her lip. Her eyes shone with unshed tears. "I don't know where they are."

"What happened? An accident?" Matthew expected

the tears collecting on her lower lashes to spill any moment. Good Lord, but he wasn't in the mood to deal with a crying woman. He glanced around for some type of conveyance. Seeing nothing but waving grass, trees, and headstones, he frowned down at her. Had she walked here? Unlikely; it was over a mile to town. "Where are you from?"

"Drexel." Drawing her skirts around her, she bent her knees and rested her forearms on them.

"Drexel? I've not heard of it, lass. Where might that be?" Jeb looked around to see if anyone else knew.

For once, neither Henry nor Dall had an answer.

Matthew glanced at the disoriented woman, then ordered the men. "Search the woods. See if anyone else is around."

The three men scattered—Jeb to the wall of trees on the slope, Henry into the southern forest line, and Dall into the graveyard. When they were gone, he turned his attention back to the woman.

"Who are you?" she asked.

"Matthew," he told her. "Matthew Gray."

For a moment, she stared, entrancing him with her tear-drenched violet eyes. Then she dragged her gaze away with seeming reluctance and looked around. Her brow furrowed. She rubbed her hand across her forehead and blinked several times in open confusion.

"Great Gerty's ghost—"

# Chapter Two

*This isn't the Drexel Cemetery.*

"Who . . . how?" The questions barely reached Bethany's lips.

A bass drum pounded inside her head. Blurred vision interfered with her ability to analyze her situation. Considering she'd just survived something that felt like the very end of the world, she was lucky to have escaped with only bruises and a cracked skull.

Seeing eight men . . . or was that twelve? No, *four* men crowded around her had nearly stopped her heart.

Fear sluiced through her veins. Would this nightmare never end? She fought the urge to retreat through the stone at her back.

This was not, could not, be happening. She and her sisters were the only ones at Yolanda D'Arcy's service. Where had these men come from? She didn't recognize them as locals. And how was she now in a different cemetery?

For a few seconds, her eyes focused on the man crouched on one knee before her. Her wavering vision blended the multiple images into one.

This stranger, this rugged-looking man with dark hair, in need of a shave and a clean shirt, radiated authority. Instinctively, Bethany knew his sharp blue eyes took in everything. Her fear-heightened sense of smell caught the aroma of man, evergreen boughs, and damp earth. Strangely, the man crouched beside her seemed to be using up all the air, making it difficult for her to catch a full breath and even harder to think through the pounding in her head.

She wanted to believe his promise of safety. How could she? She didn't know him. To be honest, she wouldn't feel secure until she walked through the front door of her little house just down the street from Drexel Elementary School.

Matthew Gray blurred into two people, then became three fuzzy images.

Bethany turned away, squinting to bring her vision into focus. The perfume of wild roses wafted from flowers climbing a headstone she didn't recognize.

Her ears buzzed like a jar of shaken wasps; the noise corresponded to the throbbing in her head. To keep her skull from exploding, she closed her eyes and took several deep breaths.

What had happened after they left Yolanda D'Arcy's graveside?

Bethany had neither answers nor explanations for the multitude of changes around her. Whatever had happened, it seemed clear she wasn't anywhere near her home.

The sweet smell of summer grass, wild roses, and evergreen mingled with something she couldn't readily identify. The air was thicker here, more humid than the arid altitude of Drexel. This world was too green. Too lush.

She waited a moment—long enough to force the tremors in her throat down to her stomach, then said "Now what?" in a calm voice. Sounding vulnerable was akin to being helpless. And helplessness was a horrifying place she never wanted to visit again. She was a strong, competent adult, not a victim.

"Why don't you stay here and see if your head clears. We'll be close, shoveling dirt. We have something we have to finish."

"I'm not going anywhere for a while." Even if she could manage to get to her feet, she was certain the ebbing and flowing waves of vertigo would be too much for her. Things were awful enough without her collapsing at some stranger's feet.

"If you start feeling poorly or you need help, call out."

The concern in his voice sounded genuine. "I just . . . need a few minutes to . . . collect myself."

"No hurry. My task isn't going anywhere," he added dryly. "And don't worry, my men will look for your sisters."

The uncomfortable sensation of being watched added another layer to her uneasiness. *Oh, please, walk away. Go shovel dirt. Straighten a headstone. Do whatever caretakers do and leave me alone to figure this out.*

"Is it Mrs. James?" he asked with an odd solemnity.

"I'm not married." *Nor will I ever be.* That was clear. The only question in her future centered around graduate school.

When still he hesitated, she hugged her folded legs and rested her forehead on her knees. Eyes closed, she searched for the elusive inner calm she'd found through tai chi.

Gradually, she relaxed and focused inward. Regardless

of what happened in the exterior world, the solutions she needed most were there, inside of herself.

Bethany clung to the necessity of keeping her befuddled thoughts open to all possibilities. At the moment, discovering a glimmer of insight as to what had happened—and why—was all she could handle.

Drawing from a sense inside herself, she accepted she was alone. She didn't question how she knew, she just did—those men would not find her sisters.

Whatever had happened, for whatever reason, the detour into this verdant setting was for her alone. This was a life test, and she would meet it and triumph. Somehow, she would find where she was and return to Drexel.

A feeling of overwhelming anxiety swept her.

No! Fear would not rule her. If she gave in to that, turned her back on the logical voice she'd relied on most of her life, all was lost. She knew that from before. Once before life had administered a severe test. She had survived and had the scars to prove it. Some were physical; all were permanent.

How long she sat in a meditative state, lulled by the sounds of birdsong, the breeze through the trees, and the rhythmic crunching of a shovel, she had no idea.

"Miss James, are you awake?"

The voice disrupted her thoughts. When she opened her eyes, she was looking directly into Matthew Gray's blue irises. Her breath hitched at his nearness. The size of him. The unabashed maleness of him. The scant tranquility she'd struggled to achieve threatened to unravel.

His dark brows drew together in a frown. "Is your vision giving you trouble?"

Instead of answering, Bethany lifted her hand to keep a distance between them and shifted against the base of the guardian angel.

"How many fingers do I have?"

She stared at the wavering hand he held before her. "I

suppose you have four fingers and a thumb."

"You suppose correctly. How many of them do you see?"

"As many as you have raised." She looked away. She didn't know this man, didn't know what sort he was. Worse, she didn't even know her surroundings. No way was she going to advertise her impaired vision.

She smoothed her skirt over her curled legs as though his questions bore no consequence. A lingering dampness in the ground seeped through her clothing.

"Your eyesight is playing tricks on you, isn't it?" Insufferable man. Couldn't he let this go?

Considering her surroundings and the man giving her the third degree, double vision wasn't her only problem.

"The men found no signs of your sisters."

"I apologize for sending you on a wild-goose chase. That bump must have rattled my brains. When last I saw my sisters, we were in Drexel. I was thinking about them . . . when . . . you found me," she answered slowly, feeling her heart clench. Would she see them ever again?

"How many sisters do you have?" He sat on his heels in front of her, his forearms braced on his thighs.

"Is this like the finger question?"

"No," he answered with the hint of a smile.

"Two."

"How did you come to be here?"

"Here? In this cemetery?" She bet even Regis Philbin couldn't answer that for a million dollars.

The sound of shovels moving dirt filled the silence. "Here in Juneau."

"Where?"

"Juneau," he repeated in a soft, patient voice. It grated on her nerves. "As in, the city of. In Alaska Territory. You do know where you are, don't you?"

"Of course." *Not!* Lowering her gaze to her folded hands, Bethany tried to gather her wits.

*Juneau, Alaska? Territory? What?*

The body aches and headache seemed to preclude any possibility that she was dreaming. This was living, breathing, and inexplicable reality. And, unlike a nightmare, she doubted this would end.

She drew a deep breath, resolving to handle the situation the way she might handle a crisis at school; coolly, logically, and without emotion. Without betraying the quivering, lemon-colored Jell-O of her backbone.

"We haven't had any ships for several days. How did you get here?"

Prepared to look him in the eye and lie, she couldn't discern which of the three shimmering images was real. The unnerving experience made the lie shrivel on her tongue. Yet, if she told what seemed to have happened, it would make her sound crazy. Oh, no, she couldn't say she had no idea how she'd gotten here from Wyoming, could she? And it was that, or lie.

"I haven't a clue how I got here," she finally said. *But I want to go home now.* She rubbed her aching forehead. Maybe she could claim amnesia until she came up with something that sounded plausible. . . .

"I, ah, see."

Bethany looked around. Her blurry vision distorted everything beyond the angel.

"Where are you staying?"

"At the moment—here." At least until her head cleared enough for her to call a cab and book a flight into Cheyenne or Salt Lake City. Then, if she couldn't catch a puddle jumper to Drexel, she'd rent a car. First, she had to call Alicia and Caitlyn. They must be worried sick.

She assumed that they had made it home okay.

"You don't mean *here* here, do you?"

"What does it matter to you where I'm staying?" *Go away. Let me think.*

"It doesn't. Just, if you'll tell me where to take you, I

will. However, I won't leave an injured woman, one who can't see well enough to stand up, alone in a graveyard a mile from town. After you die, you can spend every night of eternity here, but not until." He spoke with the calm of a man with limitless patience.

She didn't recall "Matthew the Gravedigger" among the saints' names she'd memorized as a child. "Give me a minute, please."

"Your minute is up, Miss James. You've been sitting here for over an hour. You can't stay on this damp ground all day. It's time we get you to your family." His blue eyes searched her face. "Megan Calahan will have something for that bump."

"I hope so. I'm quite sure it feels worse than it looks." Wait. Had that come out right? Did he have to continue talking? She could use a nap. She felt battered, bruised, confused, and exhausted. Things might look better after a little nap.

"Do you remember anything beyond your name? Where you're staying? With whom?"

Bethany latched on to the excellent excuse he unwittingly provided for selective memory. As a rule, she clung to the truth like a raft in a tempestuous sea. But until today, she'd always known the truth. Suddenly, everything had turned to bizarre shades of gray. The only blacks and whites were in the dirty fabric of Matthew Gray's sweat-stained shirt.

Matthew didn't know what to make of the violet-eyed woman who'd disrupted the Old Man's private business. Upon reflection, he found a twisted sort of satisfaction in the fact that the burial hadn't gone quite as his father had dictated.

Perhaps because of that flicker of gratification Matthew took in Bethany James's intrusion, he felt doubly responsible for seeing her safely home.

The fine sprinkle of freckles along her nose scrunched as her brows pinched in concentration. She seemed afraid of something, or someone. Had someone physically harmed her and left her in the cemetery to die? A vengeful husband? A lover? Either might be a possibility, although he'd seen no one on the drive here, and there were no signs of anyone else. If Miss James knew the answer, she intended to keep it to herself.

What a strange little bird she was. Although here on the edge of civilization he saw women dress in everything from seal-hide leggings to Parisian finery, her wrinkled skirt of swirling colors was unusual. And when he'd brushed his fingers over her arm earlier, her shirtsleeve had felt softer than a well-worn handkerchief.

The girl moved to get her feet under her and Matthew assisted by taking her arm. The way she paused for a few seconds before continuing felt awkward, and he wondered about the severity of her head wound. His concern deepened when the sudden wildness of her unusual eyes focused on him.

"Shall I carry you?" She didn't look like she weighed any more than a sack of grain.

"No. I'll be fine in a minute."

He doubted that, and the swiftness of her denial rankled him; it betrayed her fear. Still, he understood that no words would change her feelings. Only deeds spoke in such situations. She'd soon realize he meant only to help.

"Let go."

Her arm flinched in his loose grasp. "Please, Miss James. I'd hate for you to fall and suffer additional injury."

"I don't need—"

He clasped her shoulders as she teetered. "I won't let you fall." He was sorely tempted to carry her despite her protestation. The wary glances she continued throwing his way warned she'd strenuously object.

"You won't let me stay here, either. Where are we going?" The quaver in her voice warned she was on the verge of panic.

"Not far. Just over to the grave." He indicated where his friends were patting down the last dirt over his father's grave.

"Is your head clearing?"

The sound from low in her throat could have meant anything.

He walked slowly, allowing her time to adjust and find her balance with small steps. Twenty-nine years as George Gray's son had taught Matthew how to read people, moods, and nuances. Out of self-preservation, he'd honed his ability to anticipate turns of events as they formed.

Today, those skills had disappointed him. Twice.

Yet he would figure this woman out, starting now. "Do you recall where you're staying?"

"Motel Six," she mumbled.

He frowned. "I don't know of it."

"You know. Tom Bodett's place. They left the light on for me."

"Bodett? Tom Bodett?" The day was full of surprises. "I thought I knew almost everyone around here. Never heard of him."

"That's impossible." She stopped and gazed up at him. Her luminous violet eyes twitched as though she couldn't decide where he was standing. "How can you say you've never heard of Tom Bodett or Motel Six?"

"Because it's true." And he damn sure wasn't accustomed to anyone calling him a liar! "Now, if you can give me directions to the Bodetts', I'll make sure you arrive safely—after Megan Calahan has a look at your head."

The way she held her jaw, then pressed her lips into a colorless line, said more than the words she suppressed could possibly say. He found himself annoyed. It shouldn't matter what this stranger with a bump on her noggin thought, but it did. Anything that impugned his integrity or called his character into question needed addressing. For years, he'd bitten his tongue and held his temper every damn time the Old Man assailed his integrity. He damn sure didn't have to put up with it from this little sparrow of a woman.

"Thanks for your offer. There's no need to go out of your way. If you'll call me a cab, I'll take care of myself."

"A cab." Where did she think this was? San Francisco? New York? London?

"Yes, please." She lowered her gaze.

"I'm afraid you'll have to settle for riding into town with us." One good turn deserved another. He refrained from adding the sarcastic remark dancing on the tip of his tongue. The woman had a head injury. *Patience*, he admonished at the same time he sensed he was losing it. Damn, he was tired of being patient.

The woman was addled by her injury. No doubt her present behavior didn't reflect her true nature. If it did, he'd make it a point to avoid further contact once he got her safely into town.

"Guess that's it." Jeb whipped off his hat and wiped his brow with the back of his forearm. "The marker will be fixed in a couple of days."

Matthew gazed from his father's grave over to the granite headstone atop his mother's. It would soon bear both their names and the dates of their deaths.

"Gonna say a few words?" Henry asked.

Matthew deposited Bethany against a secure headstone. "Are you clearheaded enough to stand here, or do you want to sit on the ground and lean against the headstone?"

"I'm fine."

He doubted it, but he wasn't going to argue.

Flanked by the others at the foot of his father's grave, Matthew cleared his throat. The words he wanted to say weren't for other ears, so he toned them down. "You were a hard man, George. I'd like to say you were a fair one, but I can't. You'll be missed." *Like a festering blister*. "One thing is certain. Things won't be the same without you. I'm sure of it." *Or intend to make sure.*

"Amen," concluded his companions.

"Not amen," Bethany said.

Surprised by the piquedness of her tone, Matthew turned to see the young woman rise, then approach on wobbly legs. Jeb stepped away, allowing her a place at the edge of the gravesite.

Matthew's surprise became amazement when she wound her fingers in his shirtsleeve as though anchoring herself.

"This man needs a real prayer," she said.

"He didn't believe—"

"In that case, he needs more than one."

"—in God. But if you'd like to say a prayer—"

"I would."

"—then go ahead," Matthew finished with a slight bow and a gesture toward the grave. If anyone needed honest-to-goodness praying for, it was George Gray.

Matthew and Jeb exchanged glances before he nodded at the woman. She was becoming stranger by the moment. "Pray," he said.

He'd expected a recitation of the traditional Lord's Prayer or a psalm. Instead, she astonished him by singing. And the quality of her voice left Matthew dumbfounded. With each stanza of "Amazing Grace," Bethany's voice swelled with power. She seemed to grow stronger as she sang.

Speechless, awed by the emotion packed into every note, Matthew stared at her. How was it that a man who did not even believe in an afterlife had merited an angel singing at the foot of his grave?

It made no sense.

Then again, neither did her presence.

The woman's face relaxed, and tears shone in her violet eyes. A trace of color sprang to life in her pallid cheeks and lips. Only now did Matthew notice the slight cleft in her chin. The sun caught the gold threading her wild, curly hair, formed a halo around her head and shoulders.

This woman possessed the voice of an angel—and had the face of the fairy queen from the book he'd kept hidden since his mother's death. That treasure was the only one he'd managed to rescue—for fifteen years he'd cherished it—from the fireplace in which his father had burned all the other mementos of his mother.

Matthew closed his eyes and listened to the crescendo at the end of her song.

Why hadn't someone sung like this for Victoria and Ethan or his mother? Why now, for his father? Life was definitely unfair, and sometimes it made no sense. George had been right about that.

The last notes rose to the heavens.

No one moved.

Bethany drew an audible breath and began again, a new song, in Latin.

Matthew let his mind drift with the melody and translated the words in his head: another prayer for a man who hadn't said one in fifteen years.

Yet he could not remain angry and listen to this music as beautiful as the land around him, this hymn from the little songbird clutching his shirt to stay on her feet.

When she finished, he looked into her eyes. Tears had spilled over the dam of her thick lower lashes and run freely down her cheeks. They continued as she returned his stare with a profound sorrow.

"The Old Man wasn't worth those tears," he told her.

She sniffed and blinked, more tears coursing down her cheeks. "What makes you think I'm crying for him?"

"Aren't you?"

She averted her gaze. He pulled a clean handkerchief from his back pocket and offered it to her. "Are you ready to go, Miss James?"

Bethany released his shirtsleeve and accepted the hankie. Swaying slightly, she dabbed her eyes and wiped her cheeks. "Yes." She paused. "If you would take me to a motel, I'll make my own arrangements to get back home." A deep blue discoloration spread from the bruise along her temple and disappeared into her hair. "I just need a little rest."

"Miss James, taking you to the hotel would be a disservice. Right now, the only place with available rooms is unsuitable for a lady. Considering the way the bump on your head is swelling, you probably shouldn't be alone, either." Hell, he could just see her stumbling around amid a bunch of horny miners. She wouldn't stand a chance. Where the hell was her man? Or her family?

What was he going to do with her?

"You think I need someone to watch this goose egg swell?" she snapped.

Jeb stepped forward. "Aye, lass, that and more. Me Megan is a midwife and a healer. She's a gift when it comes ta takin' care of injuries. She'd skin me alive if I didn't bring you home for her to care for."

"It's settled. Let's go," Matthew said, considering the matter closed. Jeb and Megan would care for this young fairy queen and keep her safe until her family appeared. They had to be out of their mind with worry.

"I, ah . . ." Clearly, Jeb's offer left her as speechless as the knock on her head.

"If yer worried about repayin' me, mebbe when yer feeling better, you might teach my Sorcha a wee bit about singin'," Jeb suggested.

Before she could object, or Henry could ask the same of her for his brood, Matthew took her elbow and gestured her in the right direction. "We're done here. Let's load up the wagon and head back to town while Miss James considers."

"Wouldn't get no rest at my place." Henry gathered the shovels from the men. "My brood'll wake the dead."

"Did you ever consider how much quieter it would be around your place if your wife didn't keep having kids two at a time?" Dall clapped Henry on the back, and the two led the way out of the cemetery.

"She can't help it. Now she wishes Hubert would've had a twin brother, too."

"Anytime you get tired of Hubert, send him over to live with me. He's a fine young man," Matthew called out. The middle of the five Bittlehorn children, Hubert was a fish out of water. Lord, how Matthew identified with the boy.

As they neared the edge of the burial ground, Bethany stopped in her tracks. What she saw made her sick to her stomach. "Ohmigod! Is that the *wagon?*"

The wagon was real. A wooden one. Not a Jeep. Not an SUV. Not even a red Radio Flyer. In the shade of a towering thicket, a harnessed team of horses waited patiently.

This wasn't happening.

In a flash, she understood her circumstances with brutal clarity. She'd fallen when the fog rolled in. Hit her head. Gone into a coma from which she had to awaken soon.

Please, God, very soon.

None of this was real, not the aromatic trees, the banter of these strange men, or their wagon and horses. The blue-eyed gravedigger at her side was a hallucination, too. She had nothing to worry about. This was simply a dream state, and none of these men posed a danger. Only her mind was taking this flight of fancy. Her body was safely ensconced in a St. Agnes hospital bed. When Bethany opened her eyes, Alicia and Caitlyn would be there. They were probably beside her now. Maybe they were taking turns holding her hand as they'd done two years ago.

Thank heaven something finally made sense.

Relief surged through her. The pounding in her head accelerated.

"Lead on, Macduff," she told the phantom gripping her elbow with very corporeal pressure. "I'm sure we've windmills aplenty to explore and tilt at."

"We have waterwheels and waterways, but no windmills." He lifted her onto the back of the wagon. "And I believe it was Don Quixote, not Macduff, who tilted at windmills."

The sudden movement made her head spin. "Only because Cervantes beat Shakespeare to the line."

"You know Cervantes?" he asked in a delighted tone.

"Not personally." Who knew? Maybe Cervantes and Will Shakespeare were strolling the streets of her imaginary Juneau right now. She almost smiled. "Now what?"

The wagon bounced as Henry and Dall climbed up to the driver's seat. Bench springs groaned in protest at Henry's weight, and the entire conveyance rocked with the movement of the men bracing for a bumpy ride.

"You scoot back here with me." Matthew settled at the front of the wagon behind Henry, his back to the sideboard. He folded two horse blankets and laid them over a canvas tarp.

Jeb offered her a hand, which she accepted. None of this was real, so what harm was there in taking things a step further and acting normal with these strangers?

Once on her feet, she held Jeb's hand tightly. The sway of the buckboard from the shifting weight and the jangling harnesses of eager horses added an element of very real-feeling danger.

"Ready to go, little lady?" Henry asked from the driver's seat.

"Uhhh . . ." Why, oh why, wouldn't her vision clear?

"Okay." Henry released the brake.

Her stomach lurched as she caught Matthew's outstretched hand and released Jeb's.

"Hey! Hold it!" Matthew called. "Give us a minute to get situated."

"Sorry, ma'am," came the big driver's sincere apology.

All that saved Bethany from falling on Matthew or over the side were his strong hands, catching her, turning her, then settling her on the pile of blankets between his legs.

"Just relax. Lean against me. I know this isn't proper, but believe me, I have your safety—and your comfort—in mind." His arms folded over hers and pulled her snugly against his chest and abdomen. His long legs cradled hers like hot branding irons.

The fright of nearly falling and the unconventional rescue shot adrenaline through her veins. Dazed, her head thundering and spinning with even greater vigor, she didn't care what anyone did. She was more than ready to chuck this coma state and return to awareness. Maybe they'd give her morphine for this headache.

" 'Twill be all right, lass. Matthew knows best." Jeb lent assurance from the opposite corner of the wagon, where he balanced on the balls of his feet and held on to the sides. "The lane roughens a ways from here."

"Thank you," she managed. Manners are free, she'd told her students countless times. The least she could do was practice what she preached.

The bounce and bump made her blurry vision worse, making the trip into a carnival ride. And closing her eyes didn't help shut out the world. A skateboard ride on a washboard seemed tame compared to this jarring expedition into the unknown.

"Where'd a wee lass like you learn ta sing like an angel?" Jeb asked. The Irishman's green eyes—all six of them—sparkled from beneath the shadow created by his hats.

"My mother," she answered softly. A serious rut bounced her like a jumping bean. Her left hand gripped the rolled shirt cuff on Matthew's forearm. With her right, she clutched at his trousers. She made several frantic tries before she gathered enough fabric over his rock-hard thigh to hold firmly.

"You have a lovely voice," Matthew said. "Mind telling me why you were so adamant about singing for a man you didn't know?"

"It isn't necessary for you to distract me. When my head rolls off my shoulders, you'll know the bump was too severe." *Wake up. Wake up and beg for an aspirin or six. This dream is the pits.*

Then his cool hand cupped her forehead against his shoulder. He lowered his chin, effectively bracing her. "I wasn't trying to distract you." He spoke into her ear, and his closeness made her feel something warm and tingly inside. If she didn't know better, she'd believe she was experiencing desire! Not that it would matter, awake or comatose. More likely, a blood vessel in her brain had ballooned and popped.

Intentional or not, he was definitely distracting her. And so was the wagon, bouncing her down the road—and against him—with a violence that could loosen the surgical pins in her knee. Why hadn't she hallucinated them riding in a slow-moving—very slow-moving—SUV with leather seats two-feet thick? And maybe an ice chest filled with raspberry slushy or peach tea. And perhaps a first-aid kit with a magic pill to slay her dragon-sized headache. Or how about—

"Are you going to answer me?"

"Huh?"

"Why did you sing for a man you didn't know?"

"Even people no one understands need a prayer and a song to send them on to the next world." Eyes closed, she relaxed against her dream man without giving up her grip on his clothing. "My mother taught my sisters and me about music . . . harmony . . . by singing in the Drexel cemetery. Her father was a mortician. Grandpa had been a minister, but back then, the town needed a mortician more."

"I suppose that's logical," he said, but his voice sounded wary.

She drifted in the silence, allowing him to cushion her against the worst of the dips and drops. "You didn't like that man you buried, did you?" she murmured after a while.

"Not particularly."

"You weren't alone, though. Four of you showed up at his graveside service." Thank heaven, it was happening. She was slipping into a place where her head throbbed less. Maybe that meant she was recovering. The pattern of shadows cast by the giant trees they passed under added to the darkness gathering behind her eyes. She found a comfortable spot for her head on Matthew's broad chest.

"That's the way he wanted it." Her pillow rose as Matthew inhaled deeply, and she heard the steady beat of his heart beneath her ear. "He always got what he wanted. Regardless . . ."

He stopped short, and even in her languid state, she felt a torrent of conflicting emotions in the sudden tension of his body, the movement of his jaw against the side of her face, and the twitch of his legs.

"Who . . . was he?" The words formed deep in her throat and emerged only with a concerted effort. The darkness was thickening, and this time she welcomed it. When it passed she'd awaken with Alicia and Caitlyn sitting beside her bed.

"My father."

# *Chapter Three*

" 'Tis a nasty crack she's got on the side of her head. We'd best put ice on it." Megan drew back the quilt on the bed reserved for expectant mothers.

"I'll see to it." Jeb hurried from the medicine room. "You'll be wantin' a cloth, too?"

"Aye," she agreed, turning her attention to the woman in Matthew's arms. "Do you know yer name, lass?"

Bethany snuggled against Matthew's shoulder, and his arms tightened instinctively. "Sleep," she said.

"You'll be sleeping like a babe afore long. The rest will be good for you," Megan said in her Irish lilt, which never failed to soothe her patients. A small woman capable of moving mountains with her generous heart and rigid determination, Megan had delivered a score of babies and helped mend countless injuries over the last six years. Those she'd helped considered her a healer. Doc Swenson's followers labeled her a witch.

"I'll be wakin' you every now and then to make sure you're not sleeping too deep."

"Sleep *here*," Bethany said, so softly Matthew wasn't sure Megan heard. The implied desire to stay in his arms wasn't nearly as surprising as his own receptiveness to the notion. The warmth of her body against his chest had stoked his sense of protectiveness. She seemed totally relaxed against him, marginally aware of what was going on around her. Her sudden trust in such a vulnerable state was very different from her initial wariness—not just wariness, fear.

"Who is she, then?" Megan fluffed the pillow, then stepped aside, twitching the coverlet with rarely idle hands.

The concern Matthew saw in the woman's hazel eyes deepened his own worry. He refused to analyze the irrational anxiety he had about the condition of this stranger.

"Her name is Bethany James," he answered. "That's all we know about her." But not all he wanted to know. Questions like, to whom she belonged, why she was out in the forest alone, and how she had struck her head on the granite guardian angel, all begged for answers.

The songbird in his arms fit as though she belonged there. But of course, she didn't. She was light as a feather, her skin alarmingly pale.

"Bethany James," Megan repeated thoughtfully. " 'Tis a lovely name. I've not heard of her. Where does she come from?"

"One minute we were burying George, the next we heard her moaning. Judging from her bruise's discoloration, I don't think she was there for long."

Nor did he think she'd be *here* long. Someone was searching for her—had to be. A beautiful woman like this, with the lithe body of a siren, a sharp wit, and the voice of an angel, was a prize most men would kill to win and turn the world upside down to reclaim.

At one time, it wouldn't have mattered to whom she belonged; he would have wanted to know such an intriguing woman better. But that was before Victoria. Now, even speculative interest in another woman felt like adultery.

"'Tis good you brought her here. I'll see she's tended proper, though in truth there may be little I can do." Megan looked away, leaving unsaid what both knew.

For his own perverse reasons, Matthew's father had placed his own life in the hands of the person who would do him the least good. Doc Swenson wasn't fit to treat a sick dog.

"I say, Matthew," Megan said with a smile, "you'll not be holding the lass in your arms all night, will ya? When ya get weary, put her on the bed and let me have a look at her."

Matthew laid Bethany on the bed, careful to turn her head so the pillows didn't touch the oblong goose egg darkening like an approaching winter storm.

Her thick lashes fluttered, then lifted to reveal her enigmatic eyes. She squinted, found him, and smiled. The unexpectedly sweet expression stole his breath, reached inside, and tugged on something he'd thought dead and buried.

Her eyes lost focus then and drifted closed. The smile faded. Her pale skin assumed a frightening translucence.

"Is there a potion, an herb treatment you can give her, Megan?"

"I'm afraid not. Head wounds are God's province. 'Tis best they're left alone. No laudanum. Nothing to interfere with her healin' from the inside out." The Irish woman bent to the task of removing her patient's boots. "Glory be. Will you look at this?"

"I thought the lass's head was hurt, not her legs. Have ya found another injury?" Jeb asked from the doorway. He held a bowl of snowy ice and some soft towels.

"I believe her legs are fine. 'Tis her boot fastenings that're of interest. Aye, they're like nothing I've seen before." Megan picked up the little metal tab at the top of Bethany's boot and pulled it down.

"It's a zipper," Matthew said, watching the way the mechanism slid down the seam and opened the tiny teeth that held her soft boot in place. The revolutionary invention had caught his attention during his last trip down to California. "Some say the zipper will replace button fastenings."

"You've seen such a thing before?" Megan asked in amazement.

"A form of it, though I hadn't considered its usefulness for footwear." He preferred boots heavy enough to protect a man's feet, and such boots would not be having such a fastener.

He shrugged. "While in San Francisco I saw a version of this mechanism. From the looks of it, Whitcomb Judson's invention has undergone great change from the hooks and eyes I saw."

He gathered Bethany's boots and tucked them under the bed, then stood and looked from Megan to Jeb, and finally to the sleeping woman. "Let me know how she fares."

"Aye." Jeb set the bowl of ice and towels on the nightstand. "Will you be going back to the house, or continue stayin' at Mama Johanson's?"

"Frankly, I hadn't considered living in my father's house again." Damn, getting out from under the Old Man's roof the first time had been the equivalent of an early prison release. Trouble was, it felt like he'd been on parole for fifteen years.

"Maybe you should think on it," Megan said. "The house belongs to you now. You helped build it, did you not?"

Only Megan or Jeb would dare point out such a blatant, sore truth. "You're right," he agreed. At seventeen, he'd helped erect the house from plans his father had brought from Tacoma. The effort had required sixteen-hour days from May through September. Still, it had never been his home, just a house he'd lived in for one miserable year.

With a parting glance at the sleeping woman Megan was tucking quilts around, Matthew left the room.

"I expect someone will inquire about Miss James," he told Jeb while crossing the parlor. Matthew retrieved his coat from the hall tree where Jeb had placed it.

"Aye. I canna ken someone not missing *her*."

The two men left the house and closed the door. "Nor can I."

"I followed the path she made comin' down the hill. It appears she fell outta nowhere," Jeb said solemnly, pulling his pipe from his shirt pocket. "If this were Ireland, I'd say the leprechauns spirited her there." He tamped tobacco into the bowl of his pipe, all the while watching Matthew regard him.

"Leprechauns, huh? You're the last person I'd expect to acknowledge the wee folk." Despite the seriousness of the situation, Matthew couldn't resist a subtle ribbing. "Except to Sorcha, of course."

"Aye, a man tells whatever tales his daughter wants to hear just to see her smile." Lighting his pipe sent smoke signals into the summer air.

Matthew donned his coat, his gaze never leaving his friend's troubled features. "I'm listening," he prodded.

Jeb tossed the match into a broken bowl on the porch. "There's precious little more to tell. I followed the trail of broken grasses up the hill. Inside the tree line, just where the shadows thicken, I found a small area of matted ferns and grasses. The space wasna much bigger than a washtub."

"She would have had to come through the woods.

We'd have seen her otherwise. What else did you find?" Matthew knew there had to be more.

"A snarl of flowering berry canes rife with bees and thorns. She couldna come through forest there, Matthew. The thorns woulda torn her fair skin to shreds. I checked along the tree line. Nothing larger than a fox left a mark on the summer grass.

" 'Tis as if she fell outta the sky." Holding the bowl of his pipe, he met Matthew's stare. "I wouldna tell this to any other man."

Unsure what to make of the story, Matthew nodded and clapped his friend's shoulder. "I've more questions than answers these days, too." He straightened his coat, then ran his fingers through his hair. "Perhaps she'll think more clearly when she recovers some."

"A bloody optimist, aren't ya?"

"You know better. I have faith in your wife."

"As do I."

Neither man wanted to take the conversation any further.

Matthew lifted his hand in silent farewell and descended the steps to the stone walkway leading to the street. He'd mastered the arts of patience and self-restraint under his father's roof. Nothing changed the past. Nor would worry change the events unfolding around him. Good or bad, what was, *was*. *Forever*.

Tomorrow, he'd delve into the nasty mire of his father's legacy. This evening, he wanted a bath, a hot meal, a stiff drink, and the oblivion of sleep.

Bethany dreamed of white glaciers, green trees, and blue eyes. The jagged peaks of the majestic Tetons had filled the western horizon her entire life. As a rancher's daughter, she respected nature's brutality, and loved its tough beauty. Was there anything as miraculous as wildflowers blooming in a late spring snowstorm or surviving summer heat? But the beauty of this new place in which she'd emerged, this dream Alaska, was something else entirely. Still, it was time to return.

Struggling up through her visions, she opened her eyes.

A wave of disappointment ran through her.

Neither of her sisters sat nearby.

Neither the bed nor the room resembled a hospital.

A wooden crucifix and a faded painting of the Madonna and child were the only adornments on the white, plastered walls. A scarred armoire stood in the far corner. Beneath the adjacent heavily draped window sat a matching chest of drawers. A plain linen cloth ran across its top. A basin and pitcher shared the surface.

Each discovery made her heart beat faster.

It wasn't supposed to be like this. She was supposed to have woken in a hospital bed with her sisters at her side.

She closed her eyes and tried to calm her racing heart.

The unfamiliar room was straight out of a museum. Good grief, whatever had happened was real; the graveyard, the blue-eyed man, even the God-awful wagon ride from hell!

She touched the side of her head and moaned, sure she'd never comb her hair again.

Oh, Lord. There was no room for denial or delusion.

*Suck it up. Let it all pass over, around, and through you.*

She could and would deal with whatever awaited outside the door of this strange little room. In preparation, she concentrated on the immediate details.

An oil lamp burned on the nightstand between the bed and the wall. Not a light switch or socket marked the walls.

A glass of water and a small pitcher sat beside the lamp.

Until seeing the water, she hadn't realized how thirsty she was, or how hungry. She moved to the edge of the bed, slid her legs off its side, then slowly pushed into a sitting position.

A surge of light-headedness came and went. She sat very still, her hands gripping the bedclothes.

Gradually, the world solidified.

How long had she slept?

Staring at the wall, trying not to think about anything, she sipped until half the water was gone.

How easy it would be to lie down again and sink into the oblivion of sleep.

Withdrawal wouldn't solve anything, though, so it was out of the question. Sighing, she left the idea on her pillow with the impression of her head.

Noting a robe draped over the ladder-back chair beside the armoire, she looked down at herself. Relief swept through her and ended in a small prayer of gratitude that no one had removed her camisole and tap-pants.

She scooted on her butt to the foot of the bed. Holding the short ball poster of the footboard for support, she stood.

A vertigo she feared would unhinge her balance danced at the edge of her vision like a clown ready to play a prank. Gradually, her focus sharpened.

She found a mirror in the nighttable drawer and examined the line of swollen discoloration running from her left temple to her neck. It felt as ugly as it looked.

By holding tresses of hair close to her head, she finger-combed snarls from the curly length and ends.

"That's as good as it gets," she said to the woman in the small mirror, but it was okay. Other than lipstick and occasionally some mascara, Bethany had left the cosmetics counter to Caitlyn. Calling attention to herself in any fashion wasn't something she'd even wanted. Men ignored plain-looking women in shapeless clothing, and that was the way she liked it.

Besides, finding the bathroom wasn't something she needed to look good for.

Smoothing the wedding-ring pattern quilt back on the

bed, she looked around. The quilt's precise handiwork represented countless hours, and the braided rag rug at the bedroom door reflected the same colors and prints. The wood floor showed signs of many scrubbings, and it needed refinishing. Although scrupulously clean, its weathered surface seemed at odds with the pristine freshness of the rest of the room.

As ready as she'd ever be to face what lay on the other side of the door, Bethany drew a deep breath, then slowly let it out. She opened the door.

Moving outside, she found herself in a small hallway. A hand-braided runner covered the center length of the hardwood floor. To the left, an archway led to the parlor, and from the aroma of fresh bread wafting in the air, the kitchen.

Delicate lace curtains filtered the light streaming through a window at the end of the hallway. Polished wood molding capping the darkly stained wainscoting gleamed in the muted light. Rose-patterned wallpaper reached to the crown molding at the ceiling. Sepia-toned portraits hung in ornate frames on the walls. Every detail bespoke the love and caring of this home's occupants.

"Oh, Toto. Where the heck are we?"

Matthew stood at the end of the dock and read the letter from Phineas Montgomery a second time. All around, stevedores unloaded cargo and equipment from the *Golden Glory*. The smell of raw lumber, emptying bilge tanks, and workhorses filled the misty air.

"Bad news?" Jeb asked.

"Yes and no," Matthew muttered. "Apparently the Old Man couldn't resist meddling in the school's affairs before he died. He cancelled Mr. Montgomery's contract." The letter in Matthew's hand bore a neat script and several postage marks.

"We've got no schoolmaster?" Jeb asked with a frown.

"Things aren't as bleak as they could be. Montgomery is an astute man. He's written for confirmation of the contract's cancellation."

"He is still willin' ta come?" The surprise in Jeb's voice was reflected in his uplifted brows.

"Apparently so. He's cautious, but perceptive. My estimation of him increases. Seems he didn't like having his contract voided by a man who didn't hire him. Even so, the earliest we can hope for his arrival is another two months."

"Aye, and that's providin' his circumstances don't change," Jeb cautioned, then barked an order at one of his teamsters. The driver urged his dray horses into position on the wharf. Shouts and creaking wood blended with the jangle of tack and the rigs unloading the *Golden Glory*'s hold.

"Which could happen," Matthew conceded. Meanwhile, the school needed a teacher. Even if Montgomery came straightaway, they'd lose the two months when most of the children could attend.

"Is the lad from Tacoma, the one Lawrence favored, still available? What's his name?" Jeb divided his attention between Matthew and the stevedores loading cargo onto their wagons.

"Harold Sims. No, he accepted a job in Seattle." Even if he hadn't found Phineas Montgomery, Matthew would have passed on Sims. The boy's credentials lacked the hard science background Matthew considered essential.

"Young Sam will be waitin' for the last load. Walk back to the store with me." Jeb turned away from the wagons. "Think the Treadwell Mines would consider sharin' their schoolmaster for the summer?"

"For the children's sake, I'll approach him." What a distasteful thought. "I'll go with my hat in hand, my head bowed in respect and humility." And hate every damn minute of it.

"Kiss the Blarney stone before ya go. The Treadwell folks will enjoy having George Gray's son asking fer a favor. Iffen they agree, they'll be chargin' an arm and two legs."

"If they agree and the children get their schooling underway this summer, it'll be worth it. As for the money, I haven't gone over the books."

"Guess you'd best be doing that before Lawrence leaves." Jeb laughed sharply. "Yer a rich man, Matthew. You've not got any worries there."

He hoped not. "Lawrence Camden will remain as the mine superintendent until the end of the summer."

"Aye. Perhaps he'll stay on even after he's reacquainted ya with the mine operations."

"Not a chance. As soon as he can collect what the Old Man left him in his will, Camden will be off to see his wife in Seattle."

"Speakin' of families, Megan is askin' ya to dinner tonight."

The day had a bright side. "Ah, she's taking pity on me. I wouldn't miss it." And with that settled, Matthew left Jeb at the Golden Nugget General Store.

Although he preferred walking almost everywhere he went, time restrictions sent him over to the livery.

"I hear you found a little lady in the cemetery," Oscar Ludden remarked as he lifted Matthew's saddle from the saddletree outside his horse's stall. "Word has it she's a beauty. She gonna make it?"

"If Megan has any say, she will." Not in the mood for small talk, particularly not about a woman of whom he already felt protective, Matthew saddled his horse and rode out.

His first stop took him to the construction site of the Mortimer house on Fifth Street.

Randal Skinner, Matthew's partner at Gray & Skinner Architectural Design and Construction, shouldered the bulk of the firm's field supervision. The two men normally shared the office and administrative tasks. Both had agreed the settling of the Old Man's estate, the Gray Wolf Mine in particular, would temporarily change the balance of responsibilities. Part of the new scheme required Matthew to provide additional directions to the construction crew building the Mortimer house.

After he had done so, he headed for his father's. The residence, know simply as the Gray House, signified all that had been right and wrong between him and the Old Man. And there was so much.

Matthew had been a strapping fourteen-year-old when the two of them left Tacoma, Washington, to escape memories of the death of his mother. More than anything, he'd wanted to stay in the busy port city and continue school, but his father had needed to start fresh.

The Old Man had told him he was in for a different kind of education and gave him a stack of books. He'd sold everything they owned, including their beloved Tacoma home, and booked them on a ship bound for Juneau.

They'd joined the gold seekers. With an eye trained in geology, George Gray had selected a site, staked a claim, and set up a tent.

The hard labor of felling trees, then hewing them into tunnel supports, became Matthew's new schooling. By his sixteenth birthday, he'd learned how to set a directional explosion, shore up a tunnel, and follow a vein of gold. He became one of his father's best workers. Then it all changed.

Days before Matthew's seventeenth birthday, a miner named Charlie Roberts miscalculated the amount of dynamite needed for a charge. He'd compounded his mistake by prematurely igniting it. The explosion collapsed the tunnel in which Charlie, Matt, and a miner named Reggie Halleck had been working.

Charlie had died instantly.

Reggie hadn't been as fortunate. He'd died, suffocated, believing the hand he held belonged to his mother.

Matthew had met his rescuers on the third day of digging with a shovel, pick, and his bare hands. But nothing could get him to enter the claustrophobic hell of the mines again.

Once the Old Man realized his son's mining days were ended, he tapped into the boy's natural mechanical ability. Matthew became a one-person maintenance crew for the mine's stamper.

The intricacies of the machine fostered his interest in construction and, later, architecture. The following spring, the Old Man had wanted to build Gray House. The construction required brawn and brains. His father had brains, but Matthew had both.

Of course, having to rely on Matthew had added more gall to their relationship. The carriage accident that killed Matt's mother had crippled George's left leg and forced him to use a cane.

God help him, Matthew had tried not to succumb to the animosity the Old Man had fostered. He'd tried to focus on the good things. Building the house had been the best and worst summer of his life. By September, he'd known his calling. And one way or another, he'd sworn to become an architect and build things. And he'd done so.

He unlocked the front door of the manor. The interior gleamed where light filtered through the windows. Not a speck of dust marred the highly polished floor and furniture but, upstairs, the Old Man's study—the only room Doreen Feeney did not clean—looked like a whirlwind had passed through.

Matthew's gut roiled as he sank down to go over the books.

# *Chapter Four*

Bethany sank onto a ladder-back chair in the kitchen area. Her hands shook so hard, she dropped the carefully penned stack of invoices she'd picked up from the center of the table.

If curiosity killed the cat, as the old adage claimed, she would be dead at any moment.

The successive dates on the crisp pages confirmed the awesome truth. The papers rustling in her hands were working, current invoices, not antique documents someone had casually left on a museum table. Although the months and days changed, the year remained constant.

1895.

Those people, their primitive transportation and road, the bathroom—the entire house—all of it was out of sync with the twenty-first century world she knew.

Sweet Heaven on high, how had this happened?

A small sound escaped the back of her throat.

No. Right now, neither *how* nor *why* mattered. The

question was how to undo it. What steps must she take to go home to Drexel with her sisters? Was it even possible?

*Yolanda D'Arcy.*

The name came from nowhere, and with it an undeniable reality. She was in the past, and Yolanda was somehow involved.

"Oh, God, is this what she was trying to tell me?"

Bethany took several quick, sharp breaths.

Memories of visiting Yolanda as a child, then later, as a disillusioned, wounded young woman, flooded her mind. The realization the old woman had prophesied Bethany would end up alone and far from home struck her as hard as had the granite pedestal in the graveyard.

She recalled a snippet of conversation, Yolanda asking what Bethany thought of all the missing people in the world, where she thought they went. At the time, the question had seemed silly. But Yolanda had pushed forward, eventually mentioning something called the River of Time, how it moved across the past and the future in a continuous stream. She'd spoken of the way it breached the surface of the earth, caught the unwary in its current, and whisked them to times and places they'd never dreamed of seeing.

Everything in Bethany went still.

That was what had happened to her! What other explanation could there be?

She wasn't dead.

She wasn't in a coma.

She wasn't in Drexel.

Panic summoned again her thunderous headache. The pounding gained momentum.

"Dear God, please, I beg of you, don't leave me in this place and time. Let me go home." The whispered prayer hung in the silence, but nothing happened.

After several minutes, Bethany assumed her schoolteacher posture: shoulders squared, back straight, and feet flat on the floor. She sought composure through a series of long, deep breaths exhaled slowly through her parted lips.

Obviously, her prayer was not going to be answered. She reminded herself of the three things she needed to embrace.

*Acceptance.*

*Adaptation.*

*Survival.*

The clarity of what she must do quelled her worst fears of being alone in a strange place and time. She'd work on acceptance and adaptation together. Both were imperative to survival. But while she was trying to adapt to the new environment, she'd search for the elusive River of Time and a way home. There had to be a way.

Calmer, she mustered the courage she often bolstered with stubbornness. In an effort to find some normalcy, she stacked the invoices in the center of the table where she'd found them.

"No point in wishing things were different," she murmured. "They aren't." Perhaps she was supposed to learn a lesson from this experience. Why not? Wasn't life one big schoolroom?

Yeah. Sure it is, she thought with some anger. But I already have a classroom with my name on the door—in Drexel. And she was the teacher! This just wasn't fair.

"Well, let's get on with it." She forced an end to her lament. *Things are the way they are*. That was the first item in the litany that had sustained her through the Dark Times. She needed to remember it, to find acceptance.

Bethany turned at the sound of the front door opening, her thoughts interrupted. Footsteps approached the kitchen.

Her benefactors were home.

Braced for whatever came next, she stood beside the

table, her hands stacked at her waist, her shoulders back, and her spine straight. At barely two inches over five feet, and with a petite build, she knew she needed to project an air of self-sufficiency, of courage. She needed to move forward and make the best of a situation she hoped was temporary.

A woman in the process of removing her bonnet and blue woolen cloak entered the kitchen. She stopped short, her hazel eyes growing as large as saucers when she saw Bethany.

"Hello," the woman said. She removed her hat and patted her dark hair, neatly drawn into a bun at the nape of her neck. "Don't you think you're outta bed a wee bit soon?" She folded her cloak and handed it to a child who skipped in behind her. "Put these away, please."

"Yes, Ma." As the girl backed out of the room, her gaze remained fixed on Bethany.

"I feel much better," Bethany said. At least, physically she felt well. Mentally and emotionally, she wasn't so sure. "Did I sleep very long?"

The woman went to the sink, gave the pump a couple of saws, then washed her hands. "Aye. The clock 'round, and a few hours more."

That seemed pretty darned long to Bethany. "Guess I needed it. Thank you for your hospitality and your care."

In the midst of tying on an apron, the woman waved off her thanks. " 'Tis good Matthew and Jeb broughtcha here. Truth be known, I was startin' to worry. Each time I checked on ya, you were sleepin' like a babe. Strong breathing. Good heartbeat. Yet, I couldn't see what was going on inside your head."

"I doubt you'd want to." No point in sharing the bizarre truth of what was going on; if Bethany's knowledge of history served her well, the insane asylums of the 1890s weren't nice places.

"Please, sit. I hope you're hungry." Her hostess put the

water pump to work filling a blue-and-white speckled coffeepot.

"I am. I'd like to help."

"You'll help by sitting down, lass. It stands to figure you'd wake up just when I had to run down the road for Sorcha."

"Sorcha?"

"Me daughter," the woman said with pride.

"I'm Bethany James, and I'd—"

Her hostess threw up her hands and blushed. "Look at me. Forgettin' my manners." She quickly closed the distance between them, stopping so close that Bethany had to sit down or be bowled over. "I'm Megan Calahan, Jeb's wife." She thrust out her small, callused hand, her grip amazingly strong.

"Bethany—"

Megan didn't let her finish. "James," she interrupted. "Aye, so Matthew tells us. And this is my daughter, Sorcha." At a gesture, the girl reappeared through the doorway.

Bethany guessed the child's age at nine or ten, and yet the girl was almost as tall her mother.

Sorcha curtsied, her gaze darting to Megan for approval. "How do you do, Miss James? I'm Sorcha Calahan, and I'm very pleased to meetcha." A second glance at her mother, then her wide grin proclaimed the child's awareness she'd performed the introductory ritual correctly.

Bethany inclined her head and offered her hand. "I'm doing very well, thanks to your mother. It is a pleasure to meet you, too, Miss Calahan."

Beaming, the child took the hand extended in friendship, shook it twice, then released it. "Mr. Gray and my da say you sing like an angel."

"Really? Do angels sing in Juneau often?"

Sorcha giggled. "If they do, I haven't heard them. The

only time people sing is in church—and Da says they're all tone deaf."

Megan rolled her eyes. "Your da will be home for dinner soon. He's bringin' Mr. Gray, so set another place." She turned her daughter toward the sideboard, then pointed a finger at Bethany. "You stay right there."

Her heart gave a little jump at the mention of Matthew's name. Strange he should have any effect on her. "I'd better get dressed before they arrive."

"You've time to relax for a spell," said Megan.

Rather than argue, Bethany sat back and watched as the mother and daughter set to work. Memories of preparing a meal in the old kitchen at the ranch burst forth with astonishing clarity. She recalled her mother's clear soprano singing or humming as they worked, encouraging Bethany and her sisters to join in. When one of them sang, they all did.

Only now, looking back, did Bethany realize how calculating their mother had been. She'd timed many of those impromptu concerts to coincide with the start of a disagreement. It was mighty hard to bicker with a sister while harmonizing with her.

Bethany tried to shake off the memory and the pall it cast over her emotions. It was time to deal with what lay before her. Small-talk time. Maybe she could learn something useful. "I've never visited Juneau before," she said carefully. "What is the town like?"

Megan shrugged as she stirred the stew. "I suppose it is a mining town like most others. Across Gastineau Bay, there are times when the noise and smell from the stamping plants is enough to raise the dead. 'Twill surely turn those who live in Douglas deaf. 'Tis not so bad on this side."

"Stamping plants?" Funny how the history books mentioned gold rushes and mining in passing but made little mention of the industry surrounding it. "The men from the graveyard—those men who brought me here—they work at the mines?"

"Henry Bittlehorn and Dall Lockner work the Gray mine—the Gray Wolf." Megan handed five crisp Irish linen napkins to Sorcha.

"Gray? Is the owner related to the gravedigger?"

Megan disappeared onto the closed-in back porch and returned with a covered butter bowl and a jar. She handed the butter to her daughter. "What gravedigger?"

"The one who brought me here." *The bossy, handsome one.*

Megan's hazel eyes glistened with amusement; she opened the jar. "Gravedigger? Matthew Gray doesna make his livin' digging holes for the dead; he draws plans and builds fine houses and buildings. But with his own da buried in the ground, I'm supposin' he'll be running that mine, too. As if he doesn't have enough to do, what with the tinkering he does on those gadgets he's always building. Or those books he's always reading. Did you know how many he has stashed in his office?" Obviously, it was a rhetorical question, for Megan continued solemnly, "I hope you like fish chowder, Miss James. 'Cuz that's what we're having, with bread and a dried-apple pie for dessert."

"Please, call me Bethany. And the chowder smells wonderful. How do you make it?"

"You've never had fish chowder?" Surprise pitched Megan's voice an octave higher.

"In Wyoming, we're pretty loyal to beef." And pizza, and half a dozen franchised eating places.

"We seldom have beef. Venison. Elk. Moose. Once in a while, someone shoots a bear. But I reckon wild game is your regular fare in Wyoming."

"Oh, sure." Right. Nothing like a bear burger with mustard, tomatoes, onions, and a side of fries. Maybe that would catch on big at the Mighty-S drive-in chain.

The lilt of Megan's voice as she explained how to make fish chowder enthralled Bethany. Though she doubted she'd ever concoct such a meal, she was pleased to know what she'd be eating.

Shortly before dinner, Bethany excused herself. She wanted to look as nice as she could.

In the bathroom, she splashed water on her face again and made another attempt to work out the snarls in her hair before a sudden dizziness forced her to grip the basin. Swaying, she held on with a ferocity that turned her knuckles white. The exertion of fighting off the bout of wooziness made her perspire despite the cool air.

Slow deep breaths and sheer determination kept the vertigo from overwhelming her. The silent battle seemed to take forever.

At last, she lifted her head and eased her death grip on the basin top. Perspiration beaded the face in the mirror. Fatigue bleached the color from her skin.

Her around-the-clock sleepfest apparently hadn't cured the mayhem in her brain.

"Figures that nothing about any of this is easy," she snapped. Pumping at the top, she cupped her hands to catch the cold water and splash it onto her face.

She supposed there was no reason she should expect to have a clear head in the midst of the worst displacement in history, but she needed to find a way. The cold water had the appropriate effect, and it made her gasp with its chill.

At last steady on her feet, her head clearing, Bethany went to her room and found her clothes. No way was she going to the dinner table with a bunch of strangers while dressed in a borrowed robe.

She quickly changed, then returned to the kitchen. Inside, the men had arrived and were standing around, laughing.

Eyes bright with mirth, Megan glanced from her husband to Bethany. "Are you feelin' ill, my dear?" Her smile faded as her brow furrowed in concern.

"Should she be out of bed?"

Matthew's voice made her turn in his direction. The sudden motion robbed her of equilibrium again.

"I just need to sit down."

"You mean lie down. You look ready to swoon." Despite his sharp tone, his grip on her arm was gentle—though it was firm, too. "I'll help you to your room."

"When I need to lie down, I will." If she spent any more time in bed, she'd develop bedsores. The nausea would pass soon enough, and she needed food. Even fish chowder sounded appetizing. And freshly baked bread and butter was always wonderful.

"Miss James knows her own mind, Matthew. Leave her be. You go wash up." Megan smiled up at her husband. "You, too. Sorcha will help me serve."

"Are you sure you're all right?" Matthew asked softly.

"I'm sure I'm not going anywhere until I eat every crumb of my dessert." No way would she show weakness. Strength and fortitude; those were her middle names. She stared deliberately at the man who'd brought her here.

Boots polished to a high shine, a razor crease in perfectly tailored black trousers matching his jacket, a black brocade vest, a crisp white shirt with a tie and a tiepin, Matthew Gray was certainly a vision of strength and fortitude, and a well-dressed one at that. Now that her vision had stabilized, she wondered how she'd missed the aura of power surrounding him. How had she ever thought him a gravedigger?

How, indeed?

Matthew Gray owned this time and place.

It was Bethany who didn't belong.

The guest at the Calahans' dining table inspired a rigid attention to table manners. Surprisingly, conversation was the usual open discussion of events and ideas. Still, for the millionth time that day, Matthew found his thoughts absorbed by the assorted papers in his father's study. He'd spent half last night and all day today poring through account ledgers and files.

"You've a quiet tongue tonight, Matthew," Megan remarked as she rose to clear the table. "Uh-uh. You just sit there, Bethany. 'Twill only take a moment to bring out the pie I baked this morning."

With casual efficiency, Jeb's wife made short work of clearing the dishes and serving her sumptuous dessert. "I'm waiting to hear your answer, Matthew."

He couldn't help smiling. "For a wee Irish lass, you've the tenacity of an English bulldog."

"Bite your tongue." Megan reached for the piece of pie in front of him.

Matthew snatched it away, grinning. "You wouldn't let a man sit at your table with his mouth watering."

"He ate all his dinner, Mama," Sorcha defended. Her gaze met his with a conspiratorial twinkle. The girl, too, was an only child, and they shared an unspoken alliance.

"Please?" Matthew asked, enjoying the diversion from his business concerns. Few people were more fun to play with than Megan.

With mock righteousness, the Irish woman shook her head and wiggled her fingers. "You'll not be softenin' me up so easy, Matthew Gray. Give back me pie."

"If I apologize for the English part?" He gave her his most sincere plea, careful to keep his dessert out of her reach.

"Do ye?" she snapped.

"I do indeed apologize." He glanced at the pie, then met the impish, expectant rise of her left eyebrow. "From the very bottom of my stomach, I apologize."

He and the Calahans laughed softly. Across the table,

Bethany regarded him with amusement. He caught her eye and his smile faded.

Her laughter became a ghostly smile, and she looked away.

"We've asked around Juneau for your friend, Tom Bodett," Jeb said slowly, his Irish brogue minimal, as it always was when he spoke deliberately. "Henry Bittlehorn visited the mines on the Douglas side of the channel. He did some askin' among those miners but learned nothing. 'Tis strange no one has heard of him."

"Thank you for your time and effort," Bethany said, a strange expression clouding her features. "I'm sorry to put you through all the bother. I'm remembering some things much better now."

"How long have you been in Juneau?" Matthew picked up the thread of the interest he shared with Jeb.

"Not long." All expression faded from Bethany's pale features. "I'd like to tell you how I got here . . ." Her voice trailed off and she gave a small shrug. "But I honestly don't know."

"Memory loss isna unusual for a knock like you've received," Megan chimed in. "It'll come ta ye in good time. Not to worry. You remember the important things—your family and your home—do you not?"

"Yes, I do. Only the time between leaving Drexel and when you men found me is a blank. For now," she added quickly. Although her smile returned, a melancholy air lingered, and she lowered her gaze. "Megan, you're an excellent cook."

Matthew and Jeb exchanged glances. For the moment, it seemed best to let her change the subject.

"Thank you."

"You have sisters?" Sorcha asked. "How many?"

"Two. One older, and one younger. They are also my dearest friends," Bethany answered. Her entire demeanor brightened as she spoke to Sorcha.

The woman seemed accustomed to children, and while that wasn't odd, Matthew's thoughts leaped to another possibility. "Have you children of your own?"

Her big violet eyes turned to him in startlement. "No." Color rose in her cheeks as she hesitated. Sorrow darkened her eyes. "Nor am I married. I believe you've asked me that."

"Don't badger the lass, Matthew," Megan chided good-naturedly. "And there's no question, 'tis best ta have the husband *before* ya have the children."

"You've no intended?" Jeb reached for his coffee, but Matthew caught the Irishman eyeing his reaction.

"No. And no intention of marrying," Bethany answered with apparent vexation.

"Oh, Miss Bethany, you *must* find a husband. There are many men here. Surely one will be to your liking," Sorcha blurted. "Who will take care of you if you don't have a husband?"

A strange look passed over the woman's face, then came a reassuring expression. Bethany touched the girl's hand. "*I* will take care of me. I've been doing it for a long time. There is nothing written in the heavens stating a woman must marry. For some of us, it's best to remain unwed and pursue fulfillment through our careers."

"And what might your career be, Miss James? Are you a troubadour?" Jeb asked softly with a devilish twinkle in his eyes.

To Matthew's surprise, Bethany laughed. "I wish. Though if I made my living by singing, I'm afraid it would become a job and I'd lose some of the joy it gives me. Nor would I want to undertake such a pursuit without my sisters."

"Do they sing as beautifully as you do?" Matthew asked, unable to put his finger on why the woman was candid one minute and hesitant the next. A patient man, he would wait for the right time to press for answers.

"I thank you for the compliment," she said, placing her fork beside her partially eaten pie. "Alicia, my older sister, sings alto. Caitlyn has the purest soprano voice you'll hear outside the Metropolitan Opera. I—well, I sing second soprano." She squeezed Sorcha's hand. "That means in the cracks. My sisters have better voices than I."

"I would have to hear them to believe it," Matthew spoke up. In the cracks? He doubted it. Unlike most of the residents of Juneau, he'd had the benefit of attending the San Francisco Opera—and the theaters of Tacoma, Spokane, and Seattle. He knew a trained voice when he heard one.

"Aye," agreed Jeb. " 'Tis difficult to imagine, lass."

"Will they come here? Will they sing with you?" Eyes bright with excitement, Sorcha turned in her chair and took Bethany's hand in a double-fisted grip.

"If they come here, I doubt you could *keep* them from singing."

"I'm curious, Miss James." Matthew pushed his fork and empty plate aside. "If singing is your avocation, what is your job: this career you intend to work at for the rest of your life in order to take care of yourself?"

"I'm a teacher, Mr. Gray."

"A singing teacher?" Sorcha asked, her face shining with hope.

"No, I've never given individual singing lessons," she answered. "However, if your parents wish, I'd be glad to work with you. I noticed a piano in the parlor. Do you play?"

"No doubt she'll be more interested in doin' so now," Megan said with open enthusiasm, collecting the dessert plates. "If you want to spend your time learning music, I think it's a favorable enough pastime, Sorcha. But music comes after your daily school lessons. I'll not have you fallin' behind."

To Matthew's surprise, Bethany perked up. "Oh, I think we can combine the two very well."

"A singer and a regular schoolteacher, eh, Miss James?" Jeb asked.

"Yes. I graduated *magna cum laude* from the University of Wyoming with a major in education and a minor in science."

"What does *magna cum laude* mean?" Megan's hands hovered over the dishes she'd stacked in front of her.

"With highest honors," Matthew said, intrigued by the possibilities Bethany presented.

"It's recognition for my grade-point. I graduated at the top of my class."

"You mean you were the smartest one in teacher school?" Sorcha's eyes grew wide with awe.

Bethany smiled. "I doubt I was the smartest; I just had the highest grades. Working hard and avoiding distractions were most likely the reasons."

"Science?" Matthew asked. Science? Could she be the answer to a prayer? "Where were you last employed?"

"Drexel, Wyoming. I taught fifth grade."

He found his hopes being raised, but abruptly Miss James pushed away from the table. She turned to them all and said, "Please excuse me. My head is spinning like a top. If you don't mind, I'm going to lie down."

"I'll go with you." Sorcha looked to her father who nodded permission. She eagerly pushed away from the table and took Bethany's hand.

"I can't thank you all enough for your help and hospitality." Bethany drew a deep breath.

"Miss James. Bethany," Matthew began as he left the table. Damn, the woman was going to go crashing to the floor any moment. This time she'd take Sorcha with her and they'd both end up with bumps on their heads.

"I'll be fine." The woman raised her right hand as a

signal not to touch her. "Thank you. I'll be fine. I just got up too quickly."

He wanted to pick her up and carry her to the bed waiting in the other room, but her expression froze him, kept him from doing anything except watch her totter across the parlor and disappear into the hall.

He found himself thinking, Who the hell are you, Bethany James?

# *Chapter Five*

Bethany stared at the ceiling and thought of the spring two years before. It had been the worst year of her life, a year of losses: her parents, a large chunk of her dreams, two months in a hospital bed, nearly her life . . . When she'd recovered sufficiently to walk, she'd wanted to crawl into a hole. Instead, she'd ventured into the mountains in search of an old woman from her past.

Despite rampant speculation, no one in Drexel knew why Yolanda D'Arcy lived in isolation. Two years ago, Bethany had wanted to follow the same solitary path. Her visit to Yolanda had been as much for understanding the woman's need to withdraw from society as it was for insight. To be honest, Bethany had hoped for a modicum of guidance in finding the most expedient way of leaving it all behind. The old woman had listened, empathized, and in the end sent her back down the mountain to reconstruct her life anew—with new dreams and goals.

To this day, no one—not even Bethany's sisters—

knew she had paid that second visit to Yolanda's mountain home. But she herself recalled it perfectly.

*"You can't stay here, child. I'll not be the one who allows you to hide from life."*

*"It's too painful. I fit nowhere. Let me stay."*

*"It isn't your time."*

*"Time for what?"*

*Yolanda gave her a lopsided smile, her cornflower-blue eyes bright with a mix of wistfulness and excitement. "The fullness of life is ahead of you, child. Dust yourself off and live the way destiny dictates. The time will come—"*

*"No amount of time can change what happened!" Could change what would never now be.*

*"Do not be so sure. Time is a river without banks. Its waters cleanse the deepest wound, smooth the sharpest pain, and soften the hardest heartstone. You'll discover your destiny at the River of Time's end. You've only to embrace it to find happiness."*

The old woman had been partially right. Time had made a difference, but it hadn't changed *her*. Neither had the therapist, the psychologist, or the group sessions she'd attended.

In fact, she couldn't say whether any of it had really done any good. What she knew was, her sisters had helped pull her through the knothole of loss and set her on the right track. They had taken her to the locked area of the junkyard reserved for impounded cars. They were the ones who made Bethany see the mangled SUV that had almost become her coffin.

Recalling the obscene twist of metal, plastic, and leather made her shiver. Her parents hadn't had a prayer of surviving the head-on collision.

Had she not opted for the rear seat, been poring over catalogs for new teaching materials, chances were she wouldn't have survived, either. As it was, she'd hung upside down for two agonizing hours before "Jaws of Life" freed her. The paramedics had extracted her carefully, but the pain had been excruciating. And there'd been nothing she could do. Now, years later, although grateful to the EMTs who had saved her life, she fostered an unreasonable abhorrence of any stranger's touch.

She'd been told it was impossible to remember pain, but she didn't believe it. Whoever said that hadn't seen what a head-on collision at seventy-plus miles an hour could do to a twenty-four-year-old body.

During the infinity between the accident and the first faint whine of sirens, Bethany had come to understand being "alone" in a way that touched every cell in her body.

Strange, yet she felt the same detachment from the world now. When the shock wore off, would she start screaming again?

"What are you doing?" Lawrence Camden stood at the door of his office at Gray Wolf Mine.

"Looking for the rest of the company books." Matthew glanced at the mine manager, then deliberately closed the file drawer. "Where are they?"

"They're here." The man's brown eyes flashed with dark emotion, but his expression remained noncommittal. "I'd expected you to come for them yesterday." Camden rounded the big desk and settled into his padded leather chair. The rich mahogany paneling, baroque visitors' chairs, an executive desk, and the size of the office befit the managing head of the Gray Wolf Mine.

A portrait of George Gray occupied a prominent position behind the executive chair. A bright electric light softened by a silk-and-brass shade flaunted the prosperity of his mine. On the polished desktop, a tintype of Patience, Camden's socialite wife, occupied a prominent spot.

"For me, the mine is a priority only as far as the people

who work for it. My own business had demands and a client who couldn't wait." Matthew crossed the office to examine a photograph of Camden and his wife with the Old Man; it was arranged in an ornate frame atop a bookcase. "Have you considered staying on? I'm going to need some time to find your replacement."

"I promised your father I'd stay until you took over the operation. My wife awaits me in Seattle. However, George being George, he put a kink in my plans. You know as well as I, if I want to claim the fifty-thousand-dollar bonus detailed in his will, I have to stay until the first of September."

Matthew nodded, aware of the surprise the Old Man had sprung on his employee. "That gives us some time."

Camden pulled two enormous ledgers from the bottom drawer of his desk. "These are what you want." He dropped them in front of him with a loud boom.

Matthew eyed the ledgers with distaste. They were nothing beyond a commitment he didn't want. "Well, I have no interest in taking over this operation. I'm an architect, not a mining executive—nor do I wish to be." Matthew leaned on the back of the padded chair facing Camden. "I'll need to hire someone if you won't stay. Any recommendations?"

"Let me think on it. Your father made some unwise choices and investments the last few years. I attributed it to his illness. No amount of reasoning put him off.

"I assume you're well aware of how closed-minded George became once he made up his mind on a matter." With a look of annoyance, Camden pushed the ledgers across the desktop. "If you can make sense of the top one, let me know. He insisted on keeping the books himself. It was his way of knowing what went on with the mine.

"However, the last year . . ." Camden shrugged in resignation. "You'll see for yourself. His handwriting turned to chicken-scratch."

"Did you know he used to be an accountant?" Matthew asked, clearly surprising Camden with the revelation.

"No, I did not," the man answered slowly, his gaze fixed on the books.

"Well, he was. He liked to be in control of everything. And you're right: Once the old man made up his mind, he didn't change it," Matthew agreed. *No point in confusing him with facts.*

He was digressing, reminiscing, resenting. He shook off the heavy cloak woven of past misdeeds, misunderstandings, and missed opportunities and nodded at the books. "What kind of financial shape is the mine in?"

"It's solvent," the mine manager said slowly. "There's money enough for operating expenses, payroll, and the like. But it's been close to the red line these past six months. Too close."

Camden straightened and met Matthew's probing gaze. "I have no idea what his personal accounts look like. Perhaps you can tell me, should the need arise."

"Do you think it might?" Perhaps Cyrus Tidwell had the answers. He'd acted as the Gray Wolf's attorney for years. Trouble was, he and his wife had sailed to San Francisco for the birth of their first grandchild.

"We're all right this month," Camden answered slowly, his gaze dropping.

Dread knotted Matthew's stomach. How in hell could the mine be even near the red numbers? "But . . . ?"

"As I said, he made—"

"Give me the truth."

"You've got a couple of big loans due."

Matthew shook his head. It made no sense. The mine had turned hefty profits for years. "What's the debt for?"

"New furnaces for the smelting operation. Additional stampers and improvements." Suddenly, everything about Camden seemed as wooden as the paneling lining the walls. "I'm sure it's all in the books. Not a dime was spent your father didn't authorize with his signature."

Matthew drew a heavy breath, skirted the chair, and picked up the ledgers. "Run a supplemental book until I bring these back, will you?"

"Sure. Have you walked through the operation since your father—" Camden leaned back in his chair and laced his fingers across his chest.

"No." Matthew wasn't eager to revisit the memories he had of the mine. "Maybe next week." Maybe never.

A knowing half-smile accompanied Camden's slight nod. "If I can be of help, call on me."

Matthew lifted the books. "Count on it." As he left the office, he dreaded what he'd find in the tomes tucked under his arm.

By her third day in the Calahan home, Bethany conceded the collision with the granite angel had given her more than a concussion. She'd wound up with a bizarre form of insanity.

Nothing else explained the irrationality of Matthew Gray intruding on her thoughts at odd times, and even worse, invading her dreams. She hadn't given any man a second thought in well over two years, certainly not in a sexual way. Now, in the midst of inexplicable chaos, visions of the blue-eyed man haunted her in ways she'd never experienced.

Raw excitement charged her, lingered in the aftermath of her dreams. She'd read about such breathless excitement, seen it in movies, but she'd never experienced the sensation first-hand.

It made her tingle with anticipation.

It made her shiver with fear.

It was ridiculous!

Especially since the caprice responsible for her presence in the nineteenth century might return her to the twenty-first at any moment. At least, she fervently hoped so.

Finding the River of Time was a top priority.

Meanwhile, she had to find a way to make a living. She'd start by taking stock of the town.

"Let's go see what we have to work with." A deep breath fortified her resolve. Hand on the doorknob, she envisioned herself as Rosalind Russell in Gypsy.

"Curtain up. Light the lights."

The song—complete with orchestra—running through her head lifted her determination and her chin. Dressed in a high-collared white blouse, comfortable blue summer-wool skirt, and matching sculpted woolen jacket, she looked good. The darker blue velvet trim on the skirt hem and jacket collar and cuffs actually complemented the absurd plume hat and gloves Megan had insisted were mandatory.

Bless the Calahan woman for being the same size. And doubly bless Jeb for buying his wife the latest fashions at every opportunity. Consequently, Bethany had inherited a small fortune in "outdated" clothing.

"Ready or not, world, here I come." Pumped up to tackle 1895 society, Bethany swung the front door of the Calahan home wide open—and walked straight into Matthew Gray.

"Good grief!" Startled by the wall of black suit and white shirt blocking her exit, she stepped back, caught her heel on the edge of the rug, then fumbled for the doorknob to keep from falling. Her momentum sent the door banging against the wall.

A strong hand closed firmly on her upper arm and steadied her until she regained her balance.

The unexpected disintegration of her composure brought into question her readiness for the world beyond the Calahans' porch, let alone the entire town.

"My apologies, Miss James." The sincerity of Matthew's tone meant nothing when she saw his eyes twinkle with amusement. "I didn't mean to startle you."

Flustered, her face warming with embarrassment, Bethany tugged at the hem of her borrowed jacket.

"Just because you're holding me like a wet cat is no reason to think you caught me by surprise." She looked at the fingers curled around her arm. "You can let go. I'm stable."

She was many things, but stable? A slight exaggeration, she admitted. Adjusting the velvet-trimmed cuffs of her blue woolen jacket gave her a few seconds to gather her wits and slow the drum roll of her heart.

Matthew released her and leaned closer, obviously indulging his curiosity. He cupped her chin in his large palm and carefully tilted her face to see her bruise. "Your injury has developed an interesting hue over the last few days. Do you still have headaches? Dizziness?"

"I'm rarely as clumsy as I seem to be." Still flustered, she looked up at him. The concern evident in his slight frown and scrutiny sent a strange curl of anticipation through her. No, not anticipation. Embarrassment. Yes, that was it; embarrassment for being on the defensive when all he'd been, so far, was kind. Concerned.

A blush heated her cheeks, and she stepped back. His hand dropped away, leaving a cold spot on her face. "I'm fine. Really. I was deep in thought and didn't expect anyone standing there. Here. On the porch, that is."

Did this newly developed mental imbalance include sporadic inarticulateness, too? Great Gerty's ghost, she was in worse shape than she'd thought.

"What I mean is, I've managed to walk around for three days without a slip. Until now, when . . ."

The sight of his mouth twisting from a frown to an inquisitive half-smile shut her up. Maybe chivalry and manners were still alive and only terminally ill in this era. "Thanks for the hand. Sorry, but Jeb is at the store. Megan took Sorcha with her to the Bittlehorns'."

"I came to see you."

Surprise rattled her fragile underpinnings. "Me? Why?"

Amusement lit his eyes. "Is that so surprising?"

"Well, yes." Flustered, she didn't know what else to say.

"What if I was coming to court you?" A dimple in his left cheek gave away his playfulness.

Court? As in . . . date? Too bad he wasn't taking her *to* court. The prospect of a lawsuit wasn't nearly as daunting as Matthew Blue-eyes asking her out. She covered by being brusque. "Am I supposed to get all gooey-eyed and gushing?"

"Good Lord, I hope not." He lost the battle to tame his impish smile. The dimple deepened in his right cheek.

The man was devastating and much too likable. "Then, your hopes have been realized. I don't do gooey-eyed. I don't gush. However, I also don't date—or court—Mr. Gray." With a sideways glance, she searched for a way out of this increasingly uncomfortable situation.

He stood so close, she caught a whiff of bay rum aftershave lotion. The tight weave of his white shirt gave the impression it needed no starch. A gold watch fob crossed the lower portion of a black woolen vest that fit with the same perfection as his suit. It struck her that his clothing was tailor-made; no off-the-rack suit of clothing would fit those long legs, slim hips, and muscular shoulders.

The longer he loomed over her, the more he seemed to heat the air around them.

"In that case, may we have a conversation about your past experience in teaching? Or would another time be more convenient?" He took a step back. "You appear to be on your way somewhere."

Teaching? "I . . . ah . . . was just going for walk."

"Alone?" The dimples disappeared.

She looked to the left, then to the right. "Since we're the only ones here, and I don't have a mouse in my pocket, it's safe to assume that was the plan."

"I try not to assume anything where women are concerned. However, it isn't a good plan unless you know where you're going and what areas of town to avoid."

She wouldn't argue that. "And you know everyone here, which areas are unsafe?"

"I don't know everyone, but a fair number of folks here and in Douglas."

Douglas? Good grief, where was this Douglas town he and Megan were always speaking of? "I hadn't planned to go to Douglas." At least, not today.

"Good."

"Anywhere else I should avoid?"

"Yes."

"Where?"

"Anywhere beyond this porch until your head heals. These hills can tire you out, especially if you aren't accustomed to climbing them regularly. And in your condition . . ."

In a manner so smooth she barely noticed, he guided her away from the door—toward the street. There, a buggy reminiscent of Doc's from late-night "Gunsmoke" reruns sat. A hitching post at the front of the yard held a loosely tied rein, and the brindle mare didn't show the slightest interest in wandering.

"It isn't necessary for you to be a tour guide. We can talk about teaching either way."

"Good."

"What, no more objections to my going beyond the porch?"

"You're with me, and we'll be riding. I'll make sure nothing happens to you."

The volume of Bethany's petticoats and skirts swayed like a heavy drape when she walked. The velvet-trimmed jacket fit too well; it accentuated the smallness of her waist and the fullness of her breasts, but the gloves and the feathery hat Megan insisted she wear in public made

Bethany feel like Miss Kitty's best friend at the Longbranch Saloon.

She accepted Matthew's help into the buggy. Settling in, she understood why women wore so many petticoats in this era. The seat was hard as a rock. In fact, it was little more than a board with a leather cover.

Circumstance dictated she play the role; she might as well enjoy it. Ironically, the scenario appealed to the bookworm, movie lover, and queen of her own fantasy world dwelling in the core of Bethany's soul. Ever the vigilant spectator, she watched Matthew climb onto the buggy. His easy, smooth grace brought him onto the seat beside her with barely a jiggle of the traces.

"Settled?" he asked.

Looking over the horse's rump at the hilly topography sloping to the sea, she wished for a seat belt. "All right. Show me the town, Mr. Gray."

He took the reins in his callused hands. The gentle but firm manner in which he held the leather ribbons over his long fingers fascinated Bethany. His clean, closely trimmed nails seemed to belong on a less-callused hand. Matthew Gray became more difficult to categorize with each encounter.

"What parts of town are you familiar with?" He flicked the reins. The tack jangled, and the buggy creaked with the first roll of the wheels. Bethany slid her right hand around and grabbed the seat beside her thigh. Suddenly, this seemed a very unsafe mode of transportation. And any answer she might give would make the situation more dangerous.

"None," she finally answered, gazing up at a tree tall enough to snag clouds out of the sky. Never a good liar, Bethany opted for diversion. "That's the tallest I've ever seen."

"It's a spruce. There are larger trees around, but not many left in town."

"Incredible." Looking about, she wanted to tell him to slow the buggy so she could examine the eclectic houses built along the road. The history segments she taught her students chronicled the hardships the pioneers faced crossing the country, but little more. This was a chance to examine history in the flesh!

With a growing appreciation for the country's stalwart builders, Bethany assessed each home as they passed it. Most were whitewashed houses with a second story under roofs pitched for heavy snowfall. Smoke curled from their cookstove chimneys, which doubled as heating sources—regardless of the temperature outside.

Few of the residences boasted any formal landscaping. Cords of wood lay stacked near their doors. Mottled gray canvases covered the piles in some yards, others had open lean-to structures to keep the rain and snow off the split wood being stockpiled for winter.

Looking up, Bethany saw a line of heavy clouds hanging over the western horizon. Snow-capped mountains surrounded Juneau on three sides. A short distance north, the Mendenhall glacier crept into the sea. A delta of silty, pale aquamarine ice-melt stretched into the darker seawater before blending.

She found herself wondering, where was the River of Time? What course did it run through this wild land and time?

"Has your memory returned?"

She caught herself before answering honestly. "You mean about how I got here?"

"Yes, and the whereabouts of your traveling companions."

She turned and found Matthew regarding her. Concern, rather than curiosity, darkened his somber air.

If only her sisters had accompanied her. Their personalities were so much better suited to this sort of situation. Alicia would have walked down that hill into the graveyard, her head high and her shoulders back as if she were royalty. The confidence she exuded would have made anything she said believable—even the idea of traveling through time.

Caitlyn, on the other hand, would have remained at the top of the hill and had transportation come to her. A crook of her finger would have brought all those men, especially Dall, on the run. Just the thought of tall, willowy Caitlyn in her typical short skirt and high heels, standing with her hands on her hips and looking down on the small graveyard, made Bethany want to smile.

Lord, how she missed them. If the River of Time somehow appeared, Bethany would run to it willingly. The chance to return to her sisters and her life in Drexel was worth any risk.

Staring up into Matthew's darkening gaze, she wondered what she could tell him without sounding crazy. "I was traveling alone."

Surprise widened his eyes. Disapproval set his mouth in a frown. "You're sure?"

"Fairly sure. Until recently, I've only traveled with my sisters. Believe me, if they had accompanied me, everyone would know." *Especially the townsfolk watching Caitlyn adjust her miniskirt.*

"Word of mouth travels quickly here. Thus far, no one has mentioned other female visitors. Nor has anyone inquired about you."

She couldn't recall whether it was acceptable for women to travel alone in this era. No matter; she couldn't change her situation. "That doesn't surprise me, but I can't say why. Frankly, it feels as though I went to sleep in one place and woke up in another. If you have a better theory, I'd love to hear it."

He turned his attention back to driving the "Gunsmoke" buggy. "I've considered a number of scenarios, but none of them like Rip Van Winkle. You didn't arrive by ship. You sure as hell—You didn't come overland. The Tlingit didn't bring you from down south." He shook his head. "You may as well have dropped out of the sky."

Dread yawned in the pit of her stomach. He had no idea how close to hitting the nail on the head he was. "Who was asking questions about me?"

"Mostly me. Henry's made some inquiries in Douglas. Dall spoke to the miners at the Gray Wolf and the Treadwell. Jeb asked a few questions of his customers. No one has heard of you or your friend, Mr. Bodett."

"Mr. Bodett"—*is a voice on the radio*—"is the only person I know who lives in Alaska." *Decades from now.*

Matthew adjusted the reins and the horse turned down a street busy with pedestrians, carts, and other conveyances.

The strange activity drew Bethany's attention. Part of her hung on Matthew's every word; the other part felt ensnared in a marvelously realistic movie set.

Mentally, she shook herself. It wasn't a movie. She was neither the star nor a voyeur. This was real.

Much as she liked Jeb, she hadn't considered tact or subtlety his strongest assets. Imagining him asking strangers about her made her nervous. "I assure you, this situation . . . finding myself here . . . well, it mystifies me." It scared her to pieces, and she had to find her way back to Drexel.

"I suppose it will come back to you in time. Until it does, we have no other option than patience."

*Time*. That concept sure had assumed new meaning over the last few days.

"How long have you lived here?" she asked, desperate to change the subject.

"My father and I were among the first to follow Joe Juneau and Richard Harris up here in Eighty. We staked a claim and worked fifteen hours a day through the first winter. Longer in the summer. It paid off." He raised a hand in greeting to a couple of hard-rock miners talking in front of the Decker Building.

"You must have been very young. What? Ten? Twelve?"

"Fourteen and big for my age. The old man had a bad leg. There were things he couldn't do." Matthew's voice assumed a detached quality. "He needed me."

Curiosity overrode her discretion. "Did you resent it?"

"No, but he did."

She bit her tongue to keep from asking why. "So, the two of you built Gray Wolf Mine from the ground down, so to speak."

The barest hint of a smile eased the tension from his mouth. "So to speak. Yes. And I built his house from the ground up, too."

"*His* house? Wasn't it your home, too?"

The tension returned. "I own the house now that he's gone, but I've never called it home."

"Ah, look, Mr. Gray, I don't like walking on eggshells, and I'm a little rusty on conversational etiquette. If you would like to switch the subject, please do so." She made a checkmark in the air.

"What are you doing?"

"Making a double list. On my side, we would do best to avoid my memory lapse and how I got here. On your side, I won't ask questions about your father. That leaves us the topic for which you came to the Calahans' house. Teaching."

"Fair enough. We need one for the children here. Tell me about your experiences."

Bethany laughed. "Which ones? The serious ones? The funny ones? The ones that tug at your heart when a child overcomes obstacles and rises beyond anyone's expectations?"

Matthew made a mark in the air with his index finger.

"What was that?"

He gave a devilish smile. "A mark on your side. I need to be clearer. I should have asked about your qualifications."

Bethany smiled, enjoying his sense of humor and amazed by how comfortable she felt beside him. Maybe what she'd needed all along was a bump on the head—and to be catapulted back in time—to let someone get close. "I take it you mean my *academic* credentials?"

"Are there other kinds?"

She shrugged and looked in the new direction he was driving the buggy. The steep hill required her to brace both feet on the shallow rim of the floorboards and tighten her fingers on the edge of seat. "Some people are natural teachers. They have plenty to offer of their own knowledge. Megan is such a person, I'll bet. Other people have the desire to teach and follow through by learning how to convey others' knowledge, making it easily understandable to all."

"I hadn't considered the distinction. Which are you?"

"The latter."

"And you always wanted to be a teacher?"

"Yes, and I'm good at it." She drew a heavy breath. "Credentials: I graduated from Drexel High at sixteen and received an academic scholarship to the University of Wyoming." *The same year my older sister Alicia started.*

"I finished college and my teaching internship in three and a half years." *Because I was the kid and had no social life.* "My world consisted of books, study, and pupils but the hard work paid off. The Drexel School District offered me a position at the Elementary. I jumped at the opportunity, and loved teaching fifth grade. The classroom was my life." Good grief, she sounded like she was in a confessional. The man in black beside her listened with the somberness of a priest.

"Was?"

"This isn't Drexel, is it? And I don't have a classroom, do I?"

"No. We've come full circle, haven't we?"

"I wish," she murmured. If so, she'd be tending the garden in the backyard of her little house.

"Pardon me? I didn't hear you."

"Apparently you're looking for a teacher. Well, it just so happens that I'm looking for employment. The next question is whether we have a fit." How difficult could the differences be between the years? She'd have to watch her history lessons, but other than that, reading, writing, and arithmetic probably hadn't changed.

Okay, arithmetic and basic science hadn't changed, if she didn't count New Math, or the technological advances in the past hundred years.

For a moment she got excited at the idea of speaking with true Civil War survivors. Then reality raised its practical head.

Some fit she'd be. A size-twelve foot of knowledge crammed into a size-six clog.

"How many students?" Heaven knew she needed a job to ensure her autonomy. She couldn't stay with Megan and Jeb indefinitely.

"Fifteen."

Delighted by the small class size, her optimism returned. "What grade?"

"First through eighth." He pointed down a side street and said out of the corner of his mouth, "Stay out of there."

"That street? Why? What's down it?" But before he could answer, his previous words struck. Fifteen children, eight grades? Great Gerty's ghost!

A clear tenor voice suddenly rose above the sound of the traces and the *chip-clop* of the horse's hooves. Bethany followed the sound to the Blue Whaler Saloon.

" 'Keep her impurity
In dark obscurity,
Only remember the good she has done.' "

"What a beautiful song," Bethany exclaimed. "Who is that man singing about?" This town was a veritable cornucopia of new experiences.

"One of the miners is singing Mollie May's eulogy," Matthew answered.

"Who is she?"

"She was a sporting woman from a mining town in Colorado. If Mollie May was still around, and here in Alaska, she'd work on this street."

"Oookkaaay." Bethany studied the conglomeration of one- and two-story buildings behind the planked sidewalks. So this was the equivalent of a red-light district. The temptation to ask Matthew how he knew the history of Colorado "sporting women" danced on her tongue, but she didn't.

Sex was something she wanted to avoid discussing. Still, it brought up the classroom curriculum. Sex education classes probably weren't acceptable in 1895.

He interrupted her musings by asking, "How strong is your math and science background?"

"I'll match calculus and physics problems with you any day." She looked over and met his gaze with a smile she couldn't suppress. "As for hard sciences, if an eighth-grader learned everything I could teach, she'd be ready for Harvard."

He laughed. "Harvard doesn't accept women, but I get the picture."

"They will. One day." She looked away. Women had come a long way in the twentieth century and would go even farther in the twenty-first. So what was she doing in the nineteenth?

# *Chapter Six*

"What happened to the last teacher?" Bethany's upturned face and serious question caught Matthew unaware. Good God, she had the thickest, longest eyelashes he'd ever seen. A tingle ran up his spine.

The sunlight emphasized the fine sprinkle of tiny freckles over her nose and the redness of her full lips. As he'd suspected, her curly hair had an independent streak and refused to remain coiled—even in the confines of pins, combs, and her hat. Fine, curly strands had worked loose and played in the summer breeze, shining golden in the light.

"Excuse me?" he asked, having missed her question while imagining his lips on hers and testing their sweetness, their softness.

"The former schoolmaster?" she prompted. Then she gave a dazzling smile.

"Ian McKenzie had excellent references. His former employer, the Couther School in California, provided him with a glowing letter of recommendation. Unfortunately for us, he remained only a few months. He developed a bad case of traveling leg."

Sitting beside her in the buggy rekindled the sense of awareness he'd experienced while holding her in the back of the buckboard, and later when carrying her into the Calahans'.

"Traveling leg, huh?" Bethany laughed softly. "Is wanderlust contagious?"

Wanderlust. He hadn't ever heard the traveling yen described in one word.

He thought about the way in which his plans for the future had changed. At one time, he'd hankered to return to Spokane, to make his name as an architect and builder. Time and circumstances had blunted that desire. Instead, he'd developed a solid reputation as an architect here. His partnership with Randal Skinner, an exceptional builder, had benefited both of them and provided a booming business that had grown steadily.

"It may be," he answered, wondering if she was already thinking of moving on. "I've gotten over the small case I had. Besides, I have a good business here." One he and Randal intended to expand as soon as he resolved the management of his father's mine. "However, come winter, more than a few folks around here will be thinking about Ian McKenzie exploring the Sandwich Islands."

"Ah, I see. Traveling leg is the same thing as 'Rippin' blood.' "

" 'Rippin' blood'? Is that what they call the need to see over the next horizon, where you come from?" Damn, this woman had an intriguing way about her.

"Yes. And right around February, when the snowdrifts reach twelve feet, Hawaii looks good from Wyoming, too."

"Hawaii?"

"Another name for the Sandwich Islands." Bethany's

eyes flashed and she looked away—as though guilty about something. He found himself even more intrigued as she added, "One that I'm sure will endure because of its Polynesian roots."

"Are you, now?" he mused. Her intellect was damn near as appealing as the delectable curves he'd held in his arms at the Calahans'. "So, how did you come by this treasure trove of knowledge?"

She gave him a look that was half-amused, half-perplexed. "Is this some sort of teacher qualification test?"

Her defensiveness caught him off guard. What was wrong? Did she not like knowing more than other people? "Absolutely not," he assured her. *That comes later. Along with some inquiries of a more personal nature.* He'd already penned a request for confirmation of her credentials to the University of Wyoming in Laramie.

"Did Mr. McKenzie leave lesson plans and progress reports for the students?"

"Yes. He was quite thorough. I have his reports and plans. Despite his short tenure, he was dedicated to the children's education. He spent long hours helping the Bittlehorn girls with math. We were all sorry to see him go, but we understood his desire to see the world." He gazed down at her tightly folded hands, the way they were pressed into the blue wool of her skirt.

"Ian had no obligations, no family. I saw no better way for an educator to learn about the world than through first-hand observation and study." Matthew owed no explanations for another man's actions and had no idea why he felt compelled to provide one.

"You're quite right, though it is unfortunate he didn't remain until his replacement arrived. Children thrive on routine and continuity."

Matthew recognized the statement for what it was: a probe for problems in the school or students. "He had no contract, and he'd made his intentions clear. I began our search for a new schoolmaster right away. Phineas Montgomery was supposed to arrive this week."

Bethany looked at him. "Mr. Camden is the Gray Wolf Mine superintendent, isn't he?"

"Yes." Had she learned all this from Megan?

"And this school is supported by and intended for children of mine employees and affiliates, right?"

"Yes. And Sorcha, too. Jeb's Golden Nugget acts as the company store for the miners." He wasn't sure what she was getting at, but clearly, Ms. Bethany James was like a dog with a bone once she sank her teeth into a topic.

"So, are you the educational advisor for the Gray Wolf?"

"Ah, I understand," he said, more to himself than her. "Why am I involved when I have nothing to do with the mine? Or *had*."

"Yes. How do you fit into all this?" She waved a hand in the air. "You own the mine, but why don't you leave this sort of thing to the mine manager?"

"When the Old Man and I came here, I had to quit school. It took a while, but eventually I got an education. The one concession he made when I returned from Spokane was a school for the Gray Wolf kids. I pushed for it to be built. Truth is, if he hadn't founded the school, he'd have lost several key employees, including Henry Bittlehorn, to the Treadwells. Henry wanted his five children educated.

"I agreed to set up the school, build it, and make sure it was staffed if the Old Man kept his nose out and funded it properly." He tried to keep his tone light.

"I see," she said, staring off at the trees rising off the steep mountain behind the town.

"I've written Mr. Montgomery and assured him the position is his, should he still be interested." Had she stiffened at those words?

"So we aren't talking about a permanent position, are

we? Unless, of course, Mr. Montgomery is no longer interested?"

"We received his request for confirmation of his contract cancellation shortly after the old man died. I penned a response and sent it immediately. We'll know in a month or two if, or when, he's arriving. I should have explained the position might be temporary. Do those circumstances affect your decision?"

She bit her lip and nodded. "Actually, a temporary position suits me fine." She paused. "Yes, just fine." Then she looked up at him with those violet eyes that damn near hypnotized him. "Why *was* Mr. Montgomery's contract canceled?"

"Nosy, aren't you?" He gave her a playful wink.

She lifted pale, slender hands in mock surrender. "Hey, I'm just trying to figure out what I'm getting into here. I mean, if you hire me, what prevents someone else—Mr. Camden, perhaps—from coming right out and firing me?"

"Me. I'm the owner now, remember? I have final say on everything." *Whether I want it or not*. "As for the contact cancellation, the Old Man stayed out of the way until shortly before he died. Guess he couldn't resist putting his finger in the pie one more time." *And complicating things a final time*.

What a dichotomy Bethany James was! She spoke with casualness contrary to any schoolmarm he'd ever known, yet there was no doubt about her learning.

He found himself drawn in by the woman, and yet something bothered him—the gaping holes in her memory perhaps. Her appearance in the graveyard at the precise time they were burying his father was strange, too. He didn't believe in coincidences, and he was now a very rich man—at least, he was the owner of a gold mine. Still, nothing about Bethany's arrival, her injuries, or her origins added up to any situation he could fathom.

He wasn't the trusting innocent when it came to the

opposite sex. Despite his attraction to the mysterious Miss James, Matthew was determined to reserve judgment until he found some answers. If she was up to something, he couldn't imagine what.

He had to figure out why she was here and all alone. If she wasn't hiding a shameful history, where were her traveling companions? On a more nefarious track, perhaps she'd been abducted and left for dead in the graveyard. But by whom? And why?

Questions and rationalizations rushed through his mind in an endless stream.

She might be a fugitive from the law. Then again, she might simply be someone wanting to start a new life. Few people here in the far north asked questions about a newcomer's past. And fewer answered them. If she was seeking a new start, she had come to the right place.

If she was looking for a rich man to fleece, she might have the right place, but she had the wrong man. He'd had his share of women and no one could hold a candle to his beloved Victoria.

Matthew knew good con artists put their marks at ease, made them believe the most preposterous tales, then sank their stingers into unsuspecting flesh.

Only time would tell which Bethany James proved to be.

He halted the buggy at the schoolhouse, a wooden building sorely in need of a cleaning and painting. He tried viewing the small structure with fresh eyes. A chimney pipe rose from the shingled roof. Rectangular windows flanked the porch. To the left, someone had begun stocking the woodpile for the inevitable harsh winter months.

A table with attached benches sat in the yard. A pair of rope swings hung from an ancient spruce branch.

"It could use a little paint, but it's a sturdy building," he explained. "The . . . privy is in the back."

He pointed to a covered box at the end of the porch. "The well has good water, and I don't think you'll have to worry about the pump freezing."

"Because the pump won't freeze or because you don't expect me to be here in the winter?"

"We haven't determined whether you'll be here at all, Miss James." She sure as hell kept him off balance with her honesty. It seemed fair to answer in kind.

"No, we haven't, Mr. Gray." She started to climb out of the buggy.

"Just a moment." By the time he set the brake, climbed down, and secured the horse, Bethany was on her way to the schoolhouse door. "Or you can get down by yourself," he added to her back.

"It's all right. I really prefer doing things myself."

"Stubborn," he muttered. And *intriguing*. Was the red in her hair indicative of a hot temper? A capacity for fiery passion?

"Independent," she corrected, then smiled. "I've been taking care of myself for quite a while and plan to do so for the rest of my life. I'm not your typical Eighteen-nineties female, Mr. Gray."

No argument there. Thus far, nothing was typical about Bethany James, particularly the way he reacted to her. "I never would have guessed."

She slanted a teasing glance at him and withdrew her hand from the doorknob. "I tend to forget myself on some things. I'd be most pleased if you opened the door."

He met her gaze and nearly laughed, sure she was the most confounding woman in the Northwest. "Why, thank you, Miss James. I'd be honored to open the door for you."

The hint of a smile tugged at the corners of her soft lips. The ride had put color in her cheeks and sparkle in her eyes. He didn't dare look at either them or her lips for long. An old, familiar sensation in his loins tightened each time he succumbed to temptation and let his gaze wander. The pain and pleasure of this burgeoning desire reminded him that he was still alive in ways he'd thought buried. Yet desire he could cope with; it was the unexpected tug at his heart that Matthew found disconcerting.

Bethany fisted her hands at her waist. "May I assume you have the key?"

"As a matter of fact, I do." He dug into his trousers pocket.

"Good, because when it comes to this job, I'll try not to assume too much." But despite her acerbic words, she smiled.

Touché.

He opened the door and stepped back, not quite sure what to think of their possible new schoolteacher. If she was what she seemed, he was in trouble. Big trouble.

Thank heaven Matthew couldn't see her face. Bethany kept her shoulders squared and tamped down her shock at the schoolroom's appearance. *"Little House on the Prairie" meets the Stainless-Steel Woman.*

Inside the main door, a cloakroom with pegs for coats, hats, and mufflers separated the entryway from the schoolroom. Wood floors that might have once known a coat or two of Marine varnish showed the wear patterns of countless children's feet.

Six long tables and eighteen chairs faced the teacher's desk, which was made of oak and was flanked by two framed blackboards on wheels. The whole set up was straight out of the Smithsonian.

A half-filled wood cradle and potbellied stove sat toward the left front of the room. The smudged windows invited little daylight inside, where wooden pegs held thick, faded draperies away from the glass, and dust motes danced in the sunbeams.

The room smelled of chalk, dust, and damp clothing. A globe filled the corner of the teacher's desk. Bethany ran her fingers around the leather orb. Curious, she picked up a square ink bottle from the top of a low, crowded bookcase. She stroked her thumb over the cool glass as she perused the titles on the shelf. *Eclectic Readers* from first-through sixth-grade level filled half the top.

"Thank you, William Holmes McGuffey," she breathed.

"Did you say something?"

"Just a thank-you to one of my favorite clergymen and teachers—the author of these little books." A lingering of her fingertip over the spines of the books added to her reverence. "His little books have helped more people learn to read than he could have imagined when he put them together."

Tomes on science, mathematics, history, geography, and an assortment of novels filled the rest of the case. "This is it for textbooks?" she asked.

"Make a list. I'll order whatever you need." From the scowl darkening his features, Bethany deduced a story behind the paucity of books. Suspecting it involved Matthew's father, she refrained from pursuing the matter and instead continued her exploration.

The enormity of the task facing her was prodigious even without the challenge of teaching under nineteenth-century conditions.

Slowly turning, drinking in her surroundings, she comprehended the changes she'd need to make in order to teach fifteen students of varying levels in one room. The prospect staggered and excited her. It represented an enormous test of her creativity and teaching skills.

She suddenly couldn't wait to get started.

Matthew pulled out a math book. Thumbing through its pages, he walked to the closest blackboard. The sound of his chalk screeching and clacking on the slate offered a familiarity Bethany savored. If she closed her eyes, the smells and sounds might return her to the familiarity of her classroom at Drexel Elementary—but that was hardly where she was.

*Talk about back to basics*. "I'll never complain about the broken microwave in the teachers' lounge again." Bethany tried to temper her excitement, but she couldn't quell the sense of adventure growing by the minute.

"What's broken?" Matthew looked at her over his shoulder.

"Nothing. Who cleans this place?"

"The teacher."

"All of it? The floors and windows?"

"Yes."

"Do you furnish the firewood, or do I have to chop it?" If necessary, she would do just that. "I mean, it's not that I don't know how or haven't chopped my share in the past." She needed this job—even with any strange duties it might encompass. "I just need to know what I'm expected to handle on my own."

"The wood is furnished."

Nodding, Bethany crossed the room and picked up a piece of chalk, then indicated the book in his hand. "Are you giving me a math efficiency test?"

"I consider math and science crucial." He let her take the book.

"Okay. Teacher testing in Eighteen-ninety-five. Hmmm." She flipped to the last lesson, found the most difficult problem, and wrote it on the board; then she smiled. "If you want to test my math skills, do it with something that pretends to present a challenge."

Her chalk grated against the blackboard. Fine pieces drifted to the tray as she wrote the solution and steps. "Something like advanced calculus or quantum physics would be more appropriate."

"Quantum physics? What is that?"

She'd slipped again. "An advanced form of physics based on . . . energy sources."

Without hesitation, she finished writing the answer to the problem on the blackboard. "I agree math and science are critical. They're my strong suits; but they're only rungs on the education ladder. Grammar, history, spelling—and art and music—are important, too."

"Art?" Obviously, she'd shocked him with the concept of a rounded education.

"*Art*. And I don't see any art supplies or art history textbooks. Are they somewhere else?" A short cupboard in the back corner caught her eye.

"Music?" If incredulity were life threatening, he'd need life support soon.

"They're all essential. Unfortunately, my Latin isn't strong enough to teach without a book." She dropped the chalk in the tray and went to the desk. A quick inventory of the drawers produced nothing more than a small stack of dog-eared paper, a broken pencil, a fountain pen with a broken nib, and five dust bunnies breeding in the corners.

"Ian didn't teach the kids anything about art or music. None of the previous schoolmasters thought those subjects critical." Matthew settled one thigh on the corner of the desk and folded his arms across his chest.

"I'm not questioning their curricula. I'm merely stating what courses *I* think should be taught." She looked past him to the tables and chairs the children would occupy. "I'd be shortchanging my students, their parents, and my employer if I gave less than my best."

"But art and music? This is mining country. Alaska Territory. The Tlingit carve and paint all the art you could want."

"I'm sure they sing well, too. Their culture is steeped in the land, and every outsider should learn about their legends, customs, and beliefs." The zeal to teach these new pupils burned inside her. Ending up in 1895 Juneau had just delivered the perfect opportunity to implement her own style of education. For once, no bureaucracy stood in her way.

Well, none other than Matthew Gray.

And the fact that she didn't have the job, yet.

"You went away to school, right?" she asked.

"Yes, to attend university." He gestured toward the empty seats. "Most of these children won't receive education beyond what they get here. So what they learn has to be substantial and comprehensive."

"No education is enough to last anyone an entire lifetime. Learning is an ongoing process. A good teacher instills the hunger to continue learning independently. Art and music created by the masters—Mozart, Liszt, Beethoven, Rafael, da Vinci, Michelangelo—foster curiosity and awe. That kind of exposure opens doors to worlds beyond the classroom and the community."

And, as she spoke, Bethany realized that sometimes opening doors revealed new worlds to the teacher, too. Her next challenge would be to learn what drew her to Matthew Gray with the undeniable force the moon exerted on the tides. At the moment, that magnetism was as frightening as it was exhilarating.

Of course, nothing could come of it. Even if she dared abandon reason, anything beyond friendship was impossible. A woman with her scars and secrets couldn't afford any kind of intimacy. "Not all learning is found in a classroom," she added.

"I'll not disagree with you on that point." He stood, sunk his hands into his trousers pockets, and looked around. "I'll arrange to have the place cleaned. Maybe I can wrangle a work detail to do something with the outside, too. The children will help."

She grinned. "Nice try. Slapping a coat of paint on a building in desperate need of one does not qualify as an art class. Sounds to me like free labor." Ready to leave, she stood and pushed her chair back into the desk hollow. "Child labor, at that."

He looked annoyed. "These children aren't coddled. This is a harsh land. They learn early what's needed and expected of them. They learn how to survive." The sharp sound of his boot heels walking across the wooden floor to the door, then its slam, indicated the end of their conversation.

Bethany stood at the desk after the door closed. She drew a deep breath. "Miss Kitty meets Little Schoolhouse on the Tundra." Now all she had to do was convince Marshal Matthew to hire her.

# Chapter Seven

The afternoon with Bethany left Matthew restless with an unwanted sexual awareness. He might have successfully ignored the awakening of desire if not for the mental challenge Bethany also evoked. Since Victoria's death, he hadn't given another woman a second look, let alone a second thought.

Bethany James was different, though, and she was a diversion for which he had no time.

He had a business to resume, a mine to run, a large home to decide whether to make his or sell, and a financial conundrum in the Gray Wolf Mine.

Trying to make one of his decisions, Matthew approached his father's house and looked around. The Old Man hadn't skimped on the maintenance of the buildings or grounds. A variety of ferns and some flowers Matthew couldn't name grew beneath the two spruce centurions flanking the main walkway. Manicured bushes blazed with red flowers directly in front of the long porch supported by Doric columns. Dark gray shutters flanked the four dormer windows ensconced below the sharp pitch of the roof gables.

The men his father had hired to keep up the white two-story colonial had earned their wages.

Two blue jays lectured from the porch rail.

"I'm coming," Matthew told the bossy birds.

A recent coat of varnish on the heavy carved front door completed the house's perfect facade—like that of the Old Man himself.

Long ago Matthew had accepted the enigma of his father. Everything neat, pristine, perfection to the outside world. Only the inner sanctum, the Old Man's second-floor study, which he used as a personal library and office, reflected his true soul. There, a strange form of organized chaos bloomed. Only two people were privy to that special room, the Old Man, and now Matthew.

He dug into his pocket for the key, musing on the origins of this house.

In retrospect, the style and layout had not been a source of disagreement between he and his father. The two men had built Matthew's mother's dream house with relatively little discord—for them. In many ways, the house was a benign ghost of a past that never was. The four upstairs bedrooms awaited the children his parents had wanted but never borne.

What irony that the child who had destroyed their dreams had built this monument to them. Yet the stunning achievement hadn't lessened the disdain and disappointment with which his father had regarded Matthew.

Matthew had built something very different for his beloved Victoria: an English Tudor-style home. By then, he'd wanted nothing remotely similar to this relic from the past.

A seamstress with a flair for color, Victoria had selected

the wallpapers and coverings, and the little details that had made the big Tudor their home. But the house he and Victoria had planned to fill with love and children belonged to the Bittlehorns now. After her death, Matthew couldn't live there with the memories.

Without Victoria and Ethan he couldn't walk into the nursery next to their bedroom. For a month he'd tried to drown in a whiskey bottle, but it hadn't done anything except give his father more room to point out his weaknesses and shortcomings.

And the whiskey hadn't helped anything. Eventually, he sobered up and nothing had changed. The memories were just as sharp and painful. The loss cut just as keenly. And the hole in his heart yawned just as large.

Worse, his understanding of what his father experienced when his mother died assumed a stark clarity.

There was no going backward, only forward.

A month after burying Victoria and Ethan, he'd sold their home to Henry for a month's wages and moved into Mama Johanson's boardinghouse. Last year, with her blessing, he'd added an outside staircase to allow him the freedom to come and go from his room at will. In addition, he'd arranged to have two more rooms built onto his quarters.

The jays squawked again, as though admonishing him for languishing in the past.

He unlocked the door.

Entering, he found the air inside had a fresh scent. Evidence of a recent visit by his father's housekeeper, Doreen Feeney, showed in the gleaming wooden furniture. The house was being maintained beautifully—all except the old man's study. There would rest all his difficulties, such as the venomous ball of snakes he'd inherited: the Gray Wolf Mine. Yet there was only one way to proceed—begin by defining the nature of the problem.

Steeling himself, he set the account ledgers on the

foyer table and headed for the nearest window. The Westminster chimes of the big parlor clock struck ten. One by one, he secured the drapes away from the underlying lace and opened the windows, letting in the long summer twilight.

Another difference between himself and his father was a love of fresh air. The tunnel cave-in he'd survived had left him with a craving for the freedom of the outdoors. Only in the coldest snaps of winter did he close all his windows. And he abhorred closed-in spaces.

Methodically, he lit every lamp in the rooms he planned to use.

The mystery of Bethany James flooded his brain. At the moment, he didn't want to contemplate any responsibilities, either his own or those thrust on him by the old man. For a moment, he let go, gave way to thoughts of the little schoolteacher who had invaded his concentration like spring flowers in the snow.

"Not wise," he chided himself. "You have work to do." How she had ended up in the graveyard, and why, nagged at him.

An unproductive hour later, he abandoned his father's ledgers and took stock of the pantry and larder. Canned goods lined the shelves. He opened the icebox. Milk, cheese, and a concoction he couldn't identify, were inside. Tomorrow he'd speak to Doreen about cooking for him. Tonight he was on his own.

A sense of dread gripped him when he thought about the additional ledgers and the mess of papers stacked in the old man's study, waiting for him. The only way to get a picture of the financial condition of the mine was to sort through that clutter.

He piled a plate with bread, cheese, mustard, and an apple he'd found in a basket stashed in the coldest section of the pantry.

Each time he closed his eyes he saw Bethany at the

schoolhouse, riding at his side in town. Something was out of kilter, but he couldn't put his finger on what. It was a manner about her: he'd swear she was looking at everything as though seeing it for the first time in her life.

She had an awesome innocence, a vulnerability that pervaded all she did, drew him in. The way her lips parted just enough to invite a kiss whenever she was amazed by a new sight enthralled him. Damn, but she was an enigma.

He wanted her.

Why the hell had his loins decided to come alive after all this time? Why now? Why with *her*?

Surely he had more character than to even consider seducing a defenseless woman, one without the alliance of close friends or family. Didn't he?

Bethany James struck him as a forever kind of woman. A woman a man would have to make promises to, and keep them. Like Victoria. But he hadn't been able to keep them to her. He'd promised Victoria forever, not three years. He'd promised her a family and half a dozen children, not an agonizing death during childbirth.

Hell, he didn't want another marriage. After two years of celibacy, his awakening loins wanted sex. And sex had inherent physical dangers, particularly with a petite woman like Bethany. A man would have to be out of his mind to risk having a child with her. She'd never survive the birthing.

Memories of Victoria's bloodcurdling screams as she tried to bring Ethan into the world sent shivers up his spine.

Yet he couldn't deny his desire for Bethany. She was intelligent, educated, delicately beautiful, and had a body he yearned to explore inch by soft, luscious inch. She made him smile and occasionally laugh out loud. He liked her humor, her gumption, and the way she argued for her beliefs.

He had to fight this attraction. He didn't like the mystery surrounding her. It made him nervous. No, Bethany was not for him. He'd keep telling himself that.

Even so, he knew he'd dream of the way she laughed, the arch of her throat, and the tantalizing curves of her compact body.

Oh, yes, he would look to his heart's content. And dream. But he couldn't, wouldn't touch her, wouldn't let her into his heart. He'd lost—no, destroyed—too many women already.

"Time to work." He forced himself upstairs. On the way, he stopped in the parlor and looked out the window. Beyond the trees, the faint glow of a nearby house's lights winked on and off through the swaying branches—the Calahans'.

He couldn't do much about Bethany or the questions multiplying around her like mosquitoes on a summer pond, but he could tackle the ledgers in his father's study.

"May I join you?" Megan asked Bethany after Sorcha had gone to bed.

An oil chandelier lit the kitchen. A second lamp burned brightly in the center of the table. The lingering aromas of the wonderful dinner they had eaten a few hours earlier and the heat of the wood stove gave the room a cozy feel.

Absently, Bethany pulled the chair beside her away from the kitchen worktable. "Not at all. I'm just making a list of the things needed for the schoolhouse—whether Mr. Gray hires me or not."

Two sheets of paper, one a list, the other a bunch of scrawled notes, lay in front of Bethany.

Megan sat and arranged a stack of invoices, a pen and ink, and a ledger in front of her on the worn oak table.

She peered over at the list Bethany was reading. "Hmm. 'Tis a long list. Did you find a pot o' gold in the schoolyard today?"

Bethany laughed. "I wish."

"While yer wishin', how about wishin' me a fairy to keep up Jeb's account books for the Golden Nugget? When he gets behind, he asks my help and I canna say no, especially knowing he's busy 'til the middle of the night stocking the shelves with his latest deliveries." Megan filled her fountain pen from its ink bottle.

Bethany set the school supplies list aside. "Oh, call me the numbers fairy and let me grant your wish." She gave Megan her most sincere smile, and then mimicked her hostess's brogue. " 'Tis the least a lass can do fer her keep."

The lilt of Megan's laughter warmed Bethany from the inside. For the first time in years, perhaps ever, she had a true friend outside of her sisters.

"Ya do plenty around here," Megan protested. " 'Sides, you dinna need to do anything for your keep. The piano lessons you give Sorcha are golden to me, Bethany. The lass has a fresh enthusiasm for music, thanks to you."

Bethany shrugged off the praise and took the ledger. "Today is my day for math problems. I'll enjoy helping you, Megan. Besides, even if I get the schoolteacher job, it's temporary, just until Mr. Montgomery arrives."

"Not ta worry. Matthew places a premium on the school." Megan gave her a wink and a smile. "He'll not pass an opportunity to put a teacher in it. This love of his for education is fortunate for our children."

"He did seem inordinately interested in the curriculum," Bethany agreed. The Golden Nugget's neatly kept books bore evidence of two distinct types of penmanship.

Megan leaned close and spoke in a conspiratorial voice. "Matthew had no formal schoolin' from the time his Mother died 'til the Jesuits accepted him at Gonzaga.

Though he doesna speak of it, I understand his uncle put a word in fer him."

"His uncle?" Bethany flipped through the ledger, noting the account structure.

"His mother's brother." Megan folded her arms on the table. "He got the callin' and became a Jesuit. He also had the good fortune ta teach at Gonzaga. Without his intervention, I doona think Matthew wouldda gotten his schoolin'."

"Interesting," Bethany mused. "I wondered what drove him. I suspected it might have had something to do with his father."

"Aye. The Old Man seldom had a kind word fer anyone, and never for his son. In a good week, they dinna speak at all."

Megan took the ledger and flipped the pages to the last entry. "I ken ya know numbers, ya being a schoolteacher. But how do ya know of bookkeeping?"

"I helped my younger sister become a certified public accountant. It was a major achievement for her. Caitlyn wanted to be an actress. However, she would have had to leave Drexel."

Wistfulness dampened Bethany's smile. Even if Hollywood had beat down her door, Caitlyn would have dug those spiked heels of hers into the ground and stayed on familiar ground. Her sister looked like a cover model but was even more of a homebody than Bethany. "Caitlyn's roots in Drexel reach all the way to the center of the earth."

"Ah, ya miss her sorely." Megan's brow pinched in sympathy.

"Yes, so let me fill the hours. Show me how I can help you here."

"Ye'll not need to twist my arm." Megan pointed at the ledger and embarked on an explanation of how Jeb had organized the accounts.

These weren't the same accounting practices used in twentieth-century America, but Bethany followed the logic easily enough.

"Let's sort these invoices and receipts so you can read them off and I'll enter them," Bethany suggested.

"Aye, 'twill take a fraction of the time that way."

"What other sorts of jobs might a woman find to support herself?" Bethany noted the way Megan sorted the paperwork, and followed suit.

"You could keep Jeb's books. That'd make all three of us happy. And perhaps Matthew and his partner, Randal Skinner, would be for turnin' theirs over to you, too.

"We'll speak with Matthew and Jeb. Between them, they know most everyone in town."

"It always comes back to him, doesn't it?"

"Him? Oh, Matthew," Megan said, and nodded. "Aye. He is a rare and fine man, Bethany. Iffen he calls ye 'friend' he'll not think twice about givin' you his last nickel." She paused. "From the way he talks about you, I think he'd like ta call ye more than 'friend,' but he doesna want to admit it to himself. He's a man with demons, Bethany, demons he doesna deserve."

"Who does?" Bethany asked.

"Oh, I ken a few," Megan answered with a laugh.

"Come to think of it . . ." Bethany grinned and let her voice trail off, then handed the first stack of invoices and receipts to Megan. "All right. Check the orders, then call 'em off, and the numbers fairy will make the entries."

"We'll be startin' with the Gray Wolf miners. Their section is in the second part of the ledger."

Bethany flipped to the second tabbed section. "Ready."

"Adams, Clarence."

"Got him."

After several episodes of laughter, discussions about accounts and clients, and two pots of tea, they finished. It was shortly before midnight, so both women excused themselves to sleep.

Bethany lay in bed, her left arm folded and propping her head while she stared at the ceiling. Thoughts of Matthew, the school, Megan, and the enormous changes in her life hopscotched through her mind.

She needed facts. Barring facts, she needed a few certainties—especially in her current circumstances. For starters, Matthew had to give her his decision concerning the teaching position.

*Matthew.*

The man was crucial to the resolution of so many of her problems, not to mention the instigator of the strange tingling, aches, and titillations of her traitorous body.

Yet, regardless of the seemingly mutual attraction, there couldn't be anything between them. Not now. Not ever. The jagged scars created by the accident, the car metal biting into her flesh, the straight cuts from the surgeon's scalpel, had not faded after two years. She loathed looking at them. What man could look at her without feeling revulsion? As if those scars weren't enough, the greatest changes lay hidden beneath them. The surgeries that had saved her life and rebuilt her legs with stainless-steel rods and a new right hip had taken a kidney, her spleen, several feet of intestine, and her uterus.

Her dreams of a husband and children had died with those four other people on a rural Wyoming road. She'd been lucky to survive at all. But Lady Luck was fickle.

Still, until Bethany found a way home, perhaps the Lady would take pity and smile on her, let her try to construct a new life here. And maybe, just maybe, Bethany would be fortunate enough to count Matthew Gray as a friend. She fervently hoped so.

These temporary jobs Megan had suggested, and the schoolmistress position, would buy time for her to adjust to her new culture and a society far different than she'd seen depicted in history books. And all the while, she'd continue watching, searching, and waiting for any mystic signs of the River of Time.

Reflecting on how she'd fit into the social fabric of 1895 Alaska once the new schoolmaster arrived, she lost track of time. Only faint whispers in the hall outside brought her attention back.

A faint laugh she recognized as Megan's, followed by a masculine growl and another muffled giggle, preceded the snick of a closing bedroom door.

Bethany turned her face to the wall, pulled a pillow over her ears, and closed her eyes. Her heart ached. She doubted she'd ever know such joyful intimacies.

She had to find a way home.

Soon.

Things were happening so quickly, falling into place as easily as if she were supposed to be in this time with these people. But she wasn't.

She was supposed to be home in Drexel, painting her bathroom, weeding her garden, collecting supplies and material for the start of the next school year.

She was supposed to be laughing with and teasing her sisters; singing at the cemetery; subjecting herself to their culinary adventures.

*Hiding*, added a small voice from her past.

*Safe*, she argued.

# Chapter Eight

The lamps in the Calahans' parlor blazed after supper the following evening. Bethany and Sorcha shared a bench at the upright piano tucked in the far corner. Megan occupied the nearest of two matching Queen Anne settees. A Mortlake tapestry representing sprays of cut flowers made the upholstery a work of art. A pair of sturdier chairs occupied a separate place near the hallway door; a pie table holding a lamp separated them.

Elegant crown molding framed the white ceiling, and over the white wainscoting was a duplicate pattern. Soft, pale blue watered silk filled the space between.

"You're doing very well reading the notes," Bethany told Sorcha.

The girl gave a puzzled smile. "But it doesn't sound the same as when you play it."

Bethany stroked the girl's hair. "Music is something you have to feel in your soul to make it come truly alive. Right now, you're in what I'd call an exploratory stage.

You're learning to read and play more complicated pieces. If you have a genuine passion for music, the emotion will come. You won't be able to stop it from flowing through your fingers to the keyboard and delighting everyone who hears."

"Oh, Miss James, I truly, truly have a passion for music. I want to play the piano and sing like you."

Bethany laughed softly, imagining the reaction of the town if she taught music the way she had learned it: in the graveyard.

"Can we sing the hands song? I'll play the top."

"Deal." Bethany squared herself on the bench and counted down.

" 'I'd like to teach the world to sing . . .' "

They belted out the first verse and chorus. The second time they sang the chorus, they started a round.

Bethany stole glimpses of Sorcha and suppressed her laughter. The child's green eyes were narrowed with intense concentration to get the notes and words right.

With the last word, Sorcha's fierce determination dissolved into the grin of an exuberant ten-year-old. Laughing, Bethany hugged her. Sorcha returned the hug and laughed.

A knock on the front door interrupted. Megan answered it, and Matthew Gray stood in the archway.

"I wondered if I might have a word with Miss James," he asked when Megan bid him enter.

Megan flashed a mischievous smile at Bethany. "Most certainly."

Once the formal pleasantries were concluded, they took seats on opposite settees.

"Despite your lack of references and my reservations concerning your background, you're hired," Matthew told Bethany. "If you still want the position, that is."

She'd known he had misgivings and now found great delight that he'd overcome them enough to give her a chance. Excitement and immense relief surged through her. A slow smile curled her lips as she gazed across the Calahans' parlor.

Once again she had purpose, employment, a means to sustain herself—the keys to autonomy and independence. Although this was a temporary job, the prospect of working with children grounded her in familiarity.

"I spoke with Lawrence Camden this afternoon. He understands the school is separate from the mine, and he has no authority. The only one you answer to is me. I've arranged a budget for the school with the understanding that we need to replenish the textbook inventory." His tone was conciliatory and fraught with unsaid meaning.

"You won't regret hiring me." *Or trusting me, because I'll show you what a wise decision you've made.* "When would you like me to start?"

"Monday. We have some groundswork to do, but you're hired as of today."

"Today?" Surprised at his generosity, Bethany wondered why he was willing to begin paying her before she started teaching. In Drexel, she prepared for the school year on her own time. However, because Matthew intended to pay her, she'd accept and not question his motives too diligently. She needed the money.

"It's only fair to pay you for preparation," he explained, gesturing to the valise on the floor. "I don't expect you to simply donate your time and effort."

"Thank you for taking my needs into consideration." Matthew's insight warmed her heart. She suddenly wanted to touch him, to smooth the errant lock of hair from his forehead. The impulse burst over her with a force difficult to restrain.

"I want this arrangement to work for all of us." Sincerity burned in his unwavering gaze.

"So do I, Mr. Gray." Especially for the miners' kids, because most of them wouldn't receive additional education beyond her little schoolhouse. For herself because for the first time she was standing alone, making her own way, finding her own limits under adverse conditions. And also for Matthew, because he was the man who cared enough to make this happen.

"Monday. That gives me almost a week," she said more to herself than to him. Perhaps the ugly bruise along her temple and jaw would have faded by then. With a little luck, the panicky feeling of impending doom would lessen, too.

Matthew shifted, visibly uncomfortable on the formal Queen Anne settee. "Our visit to the schoolhouse made clear the need for a few modifications." He withdrew a tablet and pencil from inside his suit coat.

"Are the previous schoolmaster's records in your valise?" The prospect of working with children of a variety of ages energized her.

"Yes." He patted the leather case beside his foot. "I thought a great deal about our visit. A teacher should teach. You'll have your hands full without being a cleaning woman or a handyman."

"I can do anything—"

An abruptly raised hand cut her off. "I've hired Doreen Feeney. She does an excellent job, and she'll give the schoolroom a thorough cleaning once a week." He ticked off an item on his list. "That arrangement should take the biggest part of the housekeeping burden off your shoulders."

"Thank you. It will. Doreen Feeney? Her name sounds familiar. Does she have a child attending the school?"

"Doreen is a widow. She's the housekeeper at Gray House," he said casually. "This weekend, we'll have a work party paint the school inside and out." Another tick mark. "We might even get a few volunteers who don't have children in the school."

Instead of pursuing her question concerning Doreen

Feeney, Bethany asked, "What color is the paint?" Later, she could find out about Doreen from Megan.

"Red outside. White inside."

She thought about that. "White reflects light. It's excellent for the interior. How about painting the back outside wall white, too?"

"What? You want to make it hard for the kids to find their way back after a trip to the privy in a snowstorm?"

"No, I—" She laughed, realizing he was making a joke. "Red will work fine. Weather permitting, I thought the kids and I would paint a mural on the back wall. We could get to know each other in the process. I'll learn how they interact with one another in an informal environment."

Matthew put down the list and pencil. He regarded her without blinking for so long that she became uncomfortable.

"What?" she asked.

"There you go with the art stuff again."

"We're not talking anything too fancy—a Rembrandt, a Renoir, or Picasso—just a well-planned mural. If there isn't paint available for the project, I'll think of something else." She wouldn't push. His generosity was unquestionable, but the fine arts were a touchy topic with him. She wondered why.

"The works of Rembrandt and Renoir I know. Who is Picasso?"

Uh-oh. She'd slipped up. Picasso was only a teenager in 1895. "We had a Carnegie Library on the Town Square. Pablo Picasso was the librarian's favorite artist." She tried shrugging off the mistake. "You know how it is when the town librarian develops a fondness for someone's art. She got the prints at a good price . . ."

Clearly, he didn't have a clue what she meant. Instead of elaborating, she took the advice her father had given most of his life. She remained silent. If Matthew Gray thought her a fool, so be it. No point in proving him right.

"I'll see what I can do about getting the paint for your project," he said slowly. His odd, unblinking expression gave the impression he could see right through her defenses.

"If you can't, really, it's okay. It was just a thought." Good grief, it wasn't as though they had a twenty-four-hour Home Depot around the corner. Where would they get the paints?

"What colors would you need?" As though coming to a decision, Matthew squared his shoulders and picked up his list and pencil.

"The primary colors. I can mix shades and hues from the basics." She smiled at him. "And you realize blending the paint to make additional colors will be an excellent practical application of math ratios. Such hands-on lessons are fun for kids. It gives them a chance to see how facets of education apply to the real world." Her enthusiasm grew, her head spinning with ideas.

"Math ratios," he said thoughtfully. "All right. Jeb will help get the word out." He continued making notes.

"Wonderful. How do you handle school supplies? Does Gray Wolf Mines furnish them? Do the children bring their own?"

"In the past, the students brought their own." He flipped the page and kept writing. "That'll be changing. The mine is furnishing the supplies this year. Tomorrow, you and I are going to Jeb's store for whatever he has. We'll order what you need. Stock the schoolhouse with paper, slates, whatever you think you'll require for your curriculum. You'll have an account at the Golden Nugget."

If anyone at Drexel Elementary had offered her free rein, Bethany would have passed out from shock. She'd never been in danger of that, thought.

Absently, her hand slipped into her skirt pocket. The wish list she'd worked on the previous evening had just moved closer to becoming reality.

"We haven't discussed compensation," Matthew added smoothly.

Helping Megan with the bookkeeping had provided insight for the cost of living, so Bethany did not feel totally in the dark. Still, she had no idea what a teacher made in 1895. Well, she doubted she was in jeopardy of being overpaid—regardless of how well she negotiated.

She straightened and folded her hands in her lap. "I'll take the same wage you've agreed to pay Mr. Montgomery." Her heart skipped a beat. "Plus twenty percent, because I'm a temporary worker with no job security." Her daring plunged her into uncharted waters. She hoped she wouldn't drown.

Astonishment was the only way to describe her new employer's wide-eyed reaction. He cleared his throat. Silence stretched between them like a rubber band threatening to snap. He thumbed through his notes. "You have an interesting estimation of your abilities, Miss James."

Fate had handed her a new start in a new place and time. As with the position of schoolteacher, Bethany had the opportunity to shape her life any way she dared. She seized the chance with two-fisted determination. There was no way she would again become the shadow she'd been since leaving the hospital two years earlier.

"This better not have anything to do with my gender. If there is another reason you believe I shouldn't be paid the same as Mr. Montgomery, please, I'd like to hear it."

"I hadn't thought of your gender."

"Then what is your difficulty?"

"I've seen Phineas Montgomery's credentials. Yours aren't available."

"Credentials don't teach children; people do. I'm here and ready to work. However, if you prefer to wait until you can verify my background or Mr. Montgomery arrives . . . which would you prefer, paper qualifications or a warm, capable body?"

Everything about him stilled, including his heated gaze. It took him longer than usual to answer. "I'll concede the availability point. You're here and Mr. Montgomery is not. Therefore, I'll pay you what I'd pay him. But twenty percent more—"

"Good." *Thank you, Megan, for telling me how important schooling is to him!* Her confidence bolstered by his quick concession, she drew a steadying breath and continued. "I'm prepared to compromise on the twenty-percent differential." *Strike while the iron is hot. The worst he can do is say no.* "You may hold the added amount until Mr. Montgomery takes over the school. If, in his opinion and yours, the children have not made substantial progress in comparison to the reports you have from Mr. McKenzie's tenure, I'll forego the differential."

Surprise became admiration shining in his eyes. A slow smile revealed his dimples. "You have a great deal of confidence in your ability."

"Yes, I do." She returned his smile, unable to suppress her exuberance. "Count on paying the money. I'm an excellent teacher."

He rose from the sofa and tucked his list and pencil into his pocket. "All right. We have a deal, Miss James."

Bethany offered her hand to seal it.

With a small smile and a barely masked flicker of surprise, he accepted her hand.

Her fingers closed around the curve of his palm. The warmth of his flesh against hers became a familiar heat traveling through her. Amazement over the depth of her enjoyment at even the brief, formal contact with him shot up her arm and down to her toes. She didn't want to release his hand, and for just a moment she reveled in the guilty pleasure of flesh on flesh.

# *Chapter Nine*

The following morning Bethany accompanied Matthew to Jeb's store. As they entered, a bell on the door jangled loudly. She smiled back at several men who tipped their hats to her.

Viewing the Golden Nugget General Store from the outside didn't do it justice. Standing on the wooden floor, it felt as though she'd stepped into yet another world. Neatly organized tables with crates of apples, potatoes, yams, and nuts surrounded her. Bananas hung from a chain fastened to the ceiling.

The store held a profusion of interesting aromas, each arousing in Bethany a different memory.

A long counter at the far end of the room held a cash register, scales, and two rolls of differently sized butcher paper with cutters. Tall, square glass jars showcased peppermint sticks, jawbreakers, caramels, and a variety of chocolate and other confections. Decorated tins of cookies and exotic bonbons rested on the top shelf of the glass display cabinet.

Boxes and glass cylinders of cigars, tobacco products, and cigarette paper occupied the space in front of a tall mirror between the sweets and the work counter. Shelves reaching to the ceiling held artistically arranged varieties of canned goods.

The store was a far cry from Safeway.

Clad in a white shirt, thin tie, vest, and black work apron, Jeb tallied a customer's purchases. He acknowledged their entrance with a wave.

"This way." Matthew indicated that she should move toward the back.

There she found an organized collage of sporting goods, hardware, furs and blankets, and groceries. Talk about one-stop shopping, she marveled. At the end of one aisle, a staircase connected to the second floor.

"Upstairs," he said.

She led the way, their footsteps loud on the bare wood of the risers. As she reached the top, she saw bolts of fabric, thread, and spools of ribbon covering a long counter with a yardstick nailed along its edge.

Matthew directed her to the last aisle of several rows of shelves. "We'll find what we need about halfway down on the right," he said. "I'll be there in a moment." He disappeared, then returned with several wooden boxes. A ledger and a pencil rattled in the top one. "You write. I'll count, load, and carry."

Marveling at the marriage of complexity and simplicity attributable to Jeb's organization, she took the ledger and pencil. How on earth did anyone know everything that was in this store? Without a computer, inventory must be a nightmare.

"Slates." Matthew counted out several and stacked them into the box.

Starting with those, Bethany catalogued the items Matthew called out and arranged in his crates. So much to learn! Sure, she would miss simple things she'd taken for granted in her Drexel classroom, like crayons, markers, binders, and three-hole lined paper. Even so, she hadn't felt this invigorated in years.

She couldn't wait to examine the textbooks in the schoolhouse and compare them against the achievement records and her lesson plans. For the first time in her teaching career, she believed she could make a difference. Given the short amount of time she'd have with the children, she'd have to work hard and fast. There was so much ahead of these kids!

"What makes you smile so?" Matthew switched his boxes around to place the final empty one on top.

"I'm happy. Excited." She folded her pencil into the ledger and tucked it under her arm. The gleam in his eye reflected genuine interest.

"Good. I'll take the supplies up to the counter and get Jeb started on them. Meanwhile, two aisles behind us you'll find what passes for fashionable working attire. Pick out some clothing."

"That isn't necessary." Good grief, for the first time in her life she had no money, no credit cards, and no relatives to fall back on. She hadn't wanted to think about her financial dependence, but it was unquestionable. She compensated for her room and board by tutoring Sorcha in music. Other than that, she was completely penniless. At least, until she received her first teaching paycheck. "I *have* clothing, Mr. Gray. Besides, my finances are a bit . . . stressed."

"You don't need money. Consider a modest wardrobe a gift from the school board." He picked up the first of his three crates.

He was determined to humiliate her. Megan's generosity was necessary for the moment, but Bethany had been raised as a caretaker. Being a recipient of charity sat uncomfortably—regardless of the reason. "I don't need more clothing, Mr. Gray. Even if I did, I couldn't accept—"

"Sure you can. Go over and pick out what you need. Believe me, we're talking neither fancy nor expensive." He carried the box down the aisle to the stairs as though her objection had never reached his ears.

The man exasperated her. She tossed her ledger into the nearest crate of supplies they'd selected, bent, and picked it up. His long strides made him difficult to catch. Her heels clacked on the wooden floor and clunked on the stairs as she trotted after him.

"Mr. Gray—"

"You shouldn't be carryin' such a heavy load." Jeb rushed around the counter as she descended into the main room. " 'Tis not fitting."

"I'm accustomed to heavier." Because she had no choice, she let him take the box. "Thank you, Jeb."

Matthew had placed his burden on the long counter and returned for the last container.

Determined he wouldn't ignore her, she hurried after him. "Mr. Gray, please. I understand you think you're being generous, but I can't let you buy my clothing." *Or be indebted to you for yet another consideration.*

"Why not?" Good grief; he moved with the swiftness of a marathon runner.

She followed him up the stairs. "Because I refuse to allow it. What I wear has nothing to do with the caliber of teaching I'll do."

"Are you going to wear Megan's clothing every day? Don't you want a few outfits of your own?" He hefted the final box and started back to the stairs.

Fingers gripping the newel post, Bethany blocked his way. "I'm not chasing you all over this store to make you stop long enough to listen to me."

"Fine. You have my attention." He placed the box on

a tabletop. The hint of the dimples in his cheeks unnerved her. Leading her on a merry chase might amuse him, but he had enough savvy not to laugh out loud.

"Look, you're not going to dictate what I wear or bully me into doing something I neither need nor want. If I determine I need new clothing, I'll get it. Thank you very much."

"I'll lend you the money."

Bethany shook her head. "While I appreciate the offer, I can't accept."

"Why not?" he demanded.

"I just can't."

"Every woman wants and needs a wardrobe, even from Jeb's meager off-the-shelf selection."

"Has no one ever said *no* to you, Mr. Gray?"

His sharp laughter startled her. Before she recovered, he caught her around the waist, lifting and spinning her onto the table beside the box.

Her heart pounding against her chest, she was too startled to scream. His palms landed on either side of her hips, and Matthew leaned forward until they were practically nose to nose.

All she could do was stare at him. Good grief, other than her father, no one had ever picked her up like that.

" 'No' is a word I hear all the time. Right now, I'd prefer not hearing it from you. I have made every concession you've requested. Now, how about a little compromise on your part?"

"I . . . I don't understand." His warm, moist breath smelled of coffee and cinnamon. The faint aroma of bay rum wreaked havoc on all her feminine senses. His gaze lowered to her lips, which she unconsciously moistened with the tip of her tongue.

Great Gerty's ghost, he wanted to kiss her!

He drew an audible breath. "Compromise. You give a

little. I give a little. Before you know it, we have a peaceful agreement."

"Are you looking for détente?" *Or something more personal?* Her lips burned. She wanted to taste him, know the feel of his mouth on hers, to slowly explore the fiery desire raging inside her.

"Whatever détente is, I am probably looking for it."

The electricity crackling between them erased all deniability of the attraction drawing them closer each day. A tendril of trepidation coiled around her heart.

Matthew's senses burned with awareness. The clean scent of Bethany's clothing mingled with the faint citrus aroma of her auburn hair. Shiny curls peeked out of the edges of her felt hat, which always appeared on the verge of falling off.

God, he wanted to taste those ripe lips she moistened with the tip of her pink tongue. He'd never encountered anyone who possessed vulnerability and strength in such dynamic proportions; she had the ability to lure him as the sirens of Greek mythology had enchanted unknowing sailors.

What the hell was the matter with him?

Even if he weren't aware of other difficulties, he knew the premium beautiful women placed on themselves. Youth and beauty—especially in Alaska Territory—were commodities. Love had little place in the equation. The memory of Delphinia Crutchfield surfaced, a young girl in Spokane with whom both he and Dall had fallen in love before they'd both ended up out here in Alaska.

He had been burned before. The voice of experience warned him not to be burned again. Looks were no guarantee of virtue or anything else. A natural beauty like Delphinia, one who traded love for money, had no place in his life—other than as a lesson.

He'd chosen Victoria, a woman whose beauty lay in her heart, who gave her all without reservation.

Memories flooded his mind until he was drawn back by the sound of men talking downstairs, the smell of yard goods, and the taste of disappointment. Bethany's quizzical look nearly undid him, then it turned hard.

"Get out of my way, Mr. Gray." The warning in her voice revealed her anger. Her violet eyes darkened with indignation. Her full, red lips pressed into a line warning she was indeed vexed.

He caught her around the waist and helped her down from the countertop.

"If you're done attempting to intimidate me, I believe we've finished here." Without another word, she marched purposefully down the stairs, her hat bobbing on her highly held head, her back as rigid as a broom handle.

Was that what she thought he was doing? Damn! When had desire-turned-caution become intimidation?

A primal need in him reawakened with a ravenous appetite. He tamped it down.

The voice of experience lauded the way he'd protected his heart. Being with Bethany wouldn't just be sex. It couldn't be. She'd already wormed her way into his thoughts and dreams, his heart. An image of her dying in childbirth hit him with the impact of a sledgehammer.

No. What was he thinking? He had kept her at a distance!

With more force than necessary, he picked up the last box of their supplies. It seemed heavier than when he'd placed it on the countertop.

Bethany wasn't waiting at the downstairs counter with Jeb, nor was she exploring the aisles of merchandise. He asked where she was.

Jeb raised an eyebrow and his head as his hand stilled over a ledger written in neat script. "So now it's Bethany, is it? You've gotten intimate with the lass?"

"Miss James," Matthew corrected, assuring himself with a glance around them that no one had heard his mistake.

"And no, we're not on intimate terms. She's a vexation. Where did she go?"

"She dinna say where she was going. She just left."

Matthew swore under his breath.

"You'd best go find her. She doesna know these streets. I'll tally your bill and hold the supplies."

"I need a favor."

"If it's in my power, you have it."

"Ask Megan to pick out some clothes for Miss James and put them on my bill. The woman is stubborn beyond belief."

"Now, that is the one favor I canna grant. You want something from Megan, you'd best ask her yourself. She's a mite particular about what I agree to in her name." Jeb turned his attention back to the ledger. "As for Miss James being stubborn, I've not seen evidence of it myself. You, yourself, can be a wee bit mule-headed sometimes—when you've set your mind on something."

There would be no help here, Matthew realized, then slapped the countertop. "Mule-headed," he muttered, "my ass." He headed for the door.

"Aye," was the Irishman's reply.

# *Chapter Ten*

Matthew hurried out of the store and checked the boardwalks. Down the muddy street busy with mule-drawn wagons and miners in grimy duck trousers and heavy boots, he caught sight of the white plume feather of her felt hat.

He stayed well behind, but kept her in view. Passersby greeted her with a tip of their hats or an inclination of their heads as they wished her good day. She responded with a tilt of her own head, but Matthew could not hear what she said, if anything. In her wake, men stared after her.

Between the wind and her accelerated gait, she needed to hold her hat to keep it from flying away. Regardless of how she tried to stabilize it, the hat bobbed precariously on her sea of auburn curls.

Following, Matthew found himself annoyed; he didn't have time to play watchdog for a moody schoolteacher, no matter how intriguing she was.

However, he had to put his mind at ease and be sure she arrived at the Calahans' safely. If he didn't, she'd weigh on his thoughts even more than she did already.

He sidestepped two men loading a wagon at the feed store. When he looked up, her pace had slowed as she climbed the hill. If she turned around, she'd realize he was following her. And there was no telling how she'd respond to that.

Damn. What a paradox she presented. She didn't act or react as he expected.

Bethany James intrigued him more every day. He couldn't pinpoint a specific reason she got under his skin. It was a problem, a big one, and growing daily. Maybe her dogged determination, her intelligence, and her candor touched something inside him. Regardless, the chemistry between them had become more potent with each contact.

She slowed near the crest of the hill.

*Damn-fool woman.*

She held her hat to her head and bent into the slope. Why did she have to get all pusslejawed and walk home?

*Stubborn? Independent.*

She turned down the final street, took a visible breath, then quickened her pace.

*Tough and determined.*

No wonder she attracted him—and most likely every other man around.

A wagon bearing the Treadwell name on the side sat in front of the Calahan house.

Good, he thought. Having one of Megan's patients around would keep Bethany busy helping out. He'd count on her curiosity to get her involved.

Just as he was about to assure himself that she was home safely, she continued walking past the house.

* * *

All the pieces for building a new life in this time and place were falling together as though orchestrated by an unseen director. But Bethany didn't want a new life. She liked her old life just fine, thank you very much.

Home, safety, familiarity, and family—those were her priorities.

"I want to go home," she murmured. "I'm not supposed to be here." She drew a shivering breath and held back tears. "I belong in Drexel with Alicia and Caitlyn. I want my own house, and my own clothes, and my own stuff."

A left turn at the next corner put her on the road to the cemetery. Once out of sight of the town, she removed her floppy hat and opened the form-fitting coat Megan had insisted she wear.

What she wouldn't give to wear her own loose, comfortable clothes; to putter around in her own kitchen; or to go online and find new teaching materials.

Oblivious to the towering trees flanking the rutted road, Bethany pushed herself to keep walking. The road rose steadily, seldom dipping for a respite.

The more she contemplated everything wrong in her life, the faster she moved. By the time she reached the graveyard, she was out of breath and her headache had returned.

Fighting the thrum in her temples, irritated that it had returned, angry at everything about her situation, she moved amongst the grave markers. A quick glance was all she afforded the mounded dirt over George Gray's grave.

She didn't slow until she reached the angel that had been her first contact in this new world. It looked different today, smaller than when she'd curled on the ground and looked up into its benign marble features.

With her skirts gathered into her lap, she sat at the feet of the six-foot statue. Arms folded over her spiked knees, Bethany put her head down. The only motion about her was the wind playing with her disheveled hair and tugging at the floppy hat in her hand.

Gradually, the pounding in her head eased and her hearing focused on the sounds of nature around her. A chill rode the soft current angling in from the northwest. Stray cotton-puff clouds rolled in on the horizon.

Bees noisily gathered nectar from the fragrant roses climbing the arbor beside the marble angel. Birds called from the tree line. The grass whispered secrets.

A myriad of busy insects rushed about their daily business. Twice, an eagle called from high overhead.

Yet the sounds she ached to hear remained silent.

Here was where the River of Time had deposited her. But what if its course had changed? Or what if it was always changing? How would she find it? How would she go home?

Oh, dear God in Heaven, what if she was stuck here forever?

Panic welled up inside her.

The only reason she'd survived after the gruesome car crash that put her in the hospital for nearly three months was because of her sisters. They'd pulled her through. If she had died, their heartbreak would have haunted her into her next life.

Where were they now?

Did they know how far away from them she was? How could they?

Surely they were looking for her, worried sick something horrendous had happened.

A ball of longing as big as Alaska filled her chest. She wanted to cry out where she was, to call them to her. The futility of such a notion oppressed her further.

Her thoughts returned to their departure from Yolanda's grave: the thickening of the air, the sound of water rushing down a mountain creek that wasn't there, the way she'd lost sight of her sisters. She'd walked between them.

What were the odds—that something would pluck her from the middle and sweep her into Yolanda's prophesied River of Time?

A choking noise escaped her.

The odds? *Give me a break.*

She lifted her head, sat up, and sniffed.

It took a few seconds to realize she was staring at Matthew Gray's crotch.

Was there no escaping the man?

"Bethany?"

"I'm not speaking to you at the moment. Besides, I'm busy." *Busy indulging in nostalgia and self-pity.*

"I'm not even going to pretend to know why you are so angry with me."

"Why? *Why?*" Good question. "Because . . . because you're being too damn nice. And I don't know how to cope with all these changes," she blurted out. *And feelings. And sexual attraction. And not knowing when or if I'll ever be swept back to my own time.*

He hunkered down on the balls of his feet, which put him at eye level with her. "I meant to help you, not offend you. I wasn't being nice. I was being practical. If you weren't so prickly, you'd see the difference."

His attempt to buy clothes for her was the tip of the iceberg of what bothered her. She didn't know what to say and remained silent. For reasons she didn't understand, chaos seized her emotions whenever she was around Matthew. Her palms turned sweaty. Her stomach felt like the aftermath of food poisoning. And she became short of breath. As her students in Drexel often remarked, the whole situation sucked big time.

Gazing into eyes as blue as the deep ocean, she knew she was looking at another woman's dream, one she'd never experience. Oh, sure. Matthew Gray was a hunk, the first and only man whose name appeared on the "Turns Me On" page of Bethany mental scrapbook. However, relationships, intimacy, hope for having a family belonged to other women, *whole* women capable of having children. Not her.

She couldn't afford involvement in this hopeless situation—not physically, emotionally, or mentally. Dear God, especially not in this here and now!

"You're making this damn difficult," he said softly, his gaze never wavering from hers.

"What do you want me to say? It's okay to let you give me charity? To let you run my life or indebt myself to you? I don't think so. Not now, not ever."

"I don't want you to say anything. I damn sure don't want you to feel indebted. And just to put things straight, the last thing I want is to run someone else's life."

The flash in his eyes and the unyielding set of his square jaw reinforced his conviction.

For a long moment, neither spoke. Finally, Bethany drew an audible breath and released it. "Go home, Matthew. I've got a lot on my mind. I really need to be alone." *Don't be nice. Don't show concern. Don't make it so difficult to turn my back when I know it's the right thing to do.*

He looked around, his gaze catching in the far corner of the cemetery for a moment before he met her gaze. "Do you do your best thinking in the graveyard?"

His attempt at levity didn't even dent her armor. "Yes," she answered flatly, resigned. He was going to make this difficult after all.

"This is where we found you," he said softly, breaking eye contact to gaze at the distant corner that had drawn his attention earlier. "Are you looking for memories?"

Living a lie, even by omission, imposed a new kind of burden. Rather than dig the selective-amnesia grave deeper, she tried diversion. "When I was a little girl, we went to Cheyenne. My parents told us that if we got lost we should go back to the last place we'd all been together and stay put."

"Sounds like a good plan. Did you get lost in Cheyenne?"

"No. I've *never* been lost." She met his gaze, and then added, "Until now."

He nodded, and stood. "Take your time. When you're done thinking, I'll walk you back to the Calahans'."

She appreciated his not calling Megan and Jeb's her home. Although, it was far easier to build a safety wall around her emotions when he was surly or overbearing. "Go home, Matthew. I can take care of myself."

She folded her arms over her knees and put her head down again to listen for the River of Time.

Matthew waited at the first turn in the road, out of sight but within earshot of Bethany.

What a strange little bird she was.

He leaned against a tree and listened as she started to sing. Good God, the sorrow in her clear, perfect voice damn near ripped out his heart. Whatever tormented her had roots wrapped around her soul. Mesmerized by the anguish in strange songs, he remained motionless.

She sang of love lost, love never meant to be, love forever denied. From the sound of it, the woman hadn't learned a happy tune in all her born days.

The despondency of the words and haunting lilt of her voice stirred a ghost from his past. Victoria appeared in his mind's eye, and after a moment he realized the sharp details of her face were fading from his memory. Horrified, he felt a sadness overwhelm him. Listening to Bethany made his heart break all over again.

Her songs evoked a slew of razor-sharp emotions. Today, he saw the folly of his first romance, the first and last time a woman broke his heart. He hadn't questioned

Delphinia Crutchfield's love, nor doubted his for her.

Like him, Delphinia had shouldered family responsibilities. She had sisters to marry off, a mother to support, a hundred other reasons for marrying old Archibald Moore for his money instead of a young and poor Matthew Gray. Had she preferred Dall Lockner and married him, it might have hurt less. At least then, he might have convinced himself it had been for reasons other than wealth.

A young woman of beauty, grace, and elegance, Delphinia Crutchfield Moore had fit into Spokane society with an ease that no one questioned. Her sense of responsibility demanded she barter her youth for the financial security of her mother and sisters, regardless of the cost of her heart or the hearts of the men who loved her.

The old memories were reminders of needing to be more, to have more, and to want more than he was.

Then, in Alaska, the seamstress Victoria Whitman had altered his life. She had loved and accepted him for himself, not his father's newfound money, which he didn't want. She had loved his creativity, shared his curiosity for invention, and laughed easily. During the three years of their marriage, she had filled every waking minute with a joy he hadn't believed any man capable of experiencing.

God, how he'd loved her.

Matthew drew a deep breath and pushed away from the tree, suddenly suspecting he understood Bethany better than she thought.

Someone had broken her heart.

Whether through deceit or death, it didn't matter. The pain of having a heart ripped out wasn't moderated by cause. It just *was*.

The soul-crushing lament he knew too well seemed to echo in the timbre of her voice. No doubt she was wounded.

But she was a fighter, too. She had claws and an iron

backbone beneath her borrowed clothing. And pride. God, the woman had pride.

In truth, it was no greater than his own. He, too, needed to stand alone, to rely on no one and allow no one to rely on him.

He checked the time. Nearly an hour had passed since he'd hidden himself to watch Bethany in the care of the granite angel. Several minutes later, the final notes of her songs faded on the afternoon breeze, and she walked out of the graveyard and down the road to town. Not once did she glance back his way.

The ramrod straightness of her spine conveyed a determination he wasn't going to challenge.

*Put yourself back together and carry on, songbird.*

He followed at a discreet distance until she reached the Calahans' house.

Three hours later, after a meeting with the foreman on two of his firm's construction projects, he returned to his office. There, he dispatched Hubert Bittlehorn, their part-time errand boy, with a message to Dall.

Matthew forced himself to finish the changes to a certain project, then went to Gray House. There, he once again faced the daunting disarray of his father's study—and the jumble of account books and files pertaining to the Gray Wolf Mine.

Every time he opened those books, all his instincts prickled in warning. He couldn't put his finger on why, but neither could he ignore the sensation. Still, an accounting problem would be much easier to solve than his feelings concerning Bethany.

At seven o'clock sharp, Dall knocked on the door. "I got your message."

Matthew opened the door wide. "Thanks for coming over."

Dall looked around. A wry smile curled his lips. "Seems strange to walk into this house and see you."

Matthew shrugged. "Don't get used to it. I don't live here, and I haven't made up my mind whether I will or not." *Or have I?* There were too damn many things happening at once and not enough time to sort through them all.

He led the way into the downstairs study, hearing Dall's boots on the marble floor behind him. "Tell me about the air-exchanging equipment Camden had installed in the mine last year." He poured each of them a neat drink from the crystal decanter on the marble bar.

"There are six of them and they make one helluva difference. They're exactly as you designed them." Dall took the drink and settled on a comfortable leather couch. "Your old man never knew you engineered them and had 'em built." He took a sip. "Or sold them to Gray Wolf Mine from your Spokane operation, did he?"

Matthew settled into the closest wing-backed chair and nodded thoughtfully. "You are the only one who knows."

A grin lit Dall's Nordic features. "Henry?"

Head shaking, Matthew sipped his drink. He and Dall had met in Spokane during Matthew's first year at Gonzaga University. They had sarcastically attributed their instant friendship to "the commonality of nurturing home lives." After graduation, Dall had returned to Bloomington, Indiana. Two years later, labeled as the black sheep of the family, Dall left the family quarry and joined Matthew in Juneau.

Perhaps the best secret Matthew had kept from the Old Man was his friendship with Dall. Had the Old Man known of their closeness, Dall would be working for Treadwell.

"Henry doesn't know about the air feeder to the smelter or the modification packages to the stampers, either." Matthew set his drink aside. "And I plan to keep all this between the two of us for a while longer. I need your help, Dall."

"You got it."

"Not so fast. I want you to take Camden's job."

The silence in the den stretched for several minutes before Dall downed his drink in one gulp. "Don't know if I want that much responsibility. My history isn't too great on that score." He rose and poured another drink. "You're really not going to take over the mine yourself?"

"No." If anyone alive knew the formidable depths of his fear of dark, closed-in places, it was Dall.

"Does this have anything to do with those nightmares you used to get?"

Matthew nodded. The admission cost him some pride. He was still tormented, still dreamed of dying in a cave-in. The torment returned sometimes, kept him up in the middle of the night.

And no power on Earth would get Matthew back into his father's tunnels.

However some good had come of it. He'd invented equipment to better conditions for those who did venture into those dark, confining spaces. He recognized his endeavors as a form of atonement.

"I don't want anything from the mine, Dall. I'd sell it to Treadwell, but he doesn't pay his workers well enough. I don't want my father's men to suffer."

"Treadwell doesn't maintain his mines as well as the Gray Wolf, either," Dall added. "No air exchangers and feeders, for starters. And they're less concerned with safety than George was."

Left unspoken were the other countless little improvements Matthew had designed and had manufactured in Spokane. With Dall taking the innovations to the Old Man, everything had worked splendidly. George had believed Dall a conscientious foreman interested in the productivity of his miners. Matthew's role in the development of the improvements and equipment never came into play.

The two men sipped their whiskey in contemplative silence for several minutes before Dall spoke again. "Have you considered selling it to the men themselves?"

"Yes. But not until I work out the financials. There's a lot of debt—"

"Debt?" Dall's foot slid off his knee and dropped to the floor. "What the hell are you talking about? The amount of gold we put through the smelter ought to make you the richest man in Alaska Territory, if not the entire West Coast all the way down to South America. Unlike Treadwell, you've got no partners."

Now they were getting somewhere. "That's what I thought, until I saw the books and talked with Camden. The Old Man apparently has a mountain of debt piled onto the mine's operating costs. The rich vein you're mining isn't sufficient—"

"Not sufficient, my ass. Do you have any idea how much we're pulling out of that mountain?"

"I *thought* I did." Dall's anger underscored his gut feeling something was terribly wrong. But who was the culprit? He needed to know before he acted. "I damn sure didn't expect to be facing a bank take-over. Particularly not by Moore Mercantile Bank."

"Ah, the love of Delphinia's life. Why the hell did your father choose *his* bank?"

"I have no idea," Matthew answered. The Old Man couldn't have known about Delphinia's association with his son, not without knowing about Matthew's friendship with Dall, too. "A strange twist of bad luck, I suppose."

Dall stood and went to the window. With a callused hand, he parted the delicate lace undercurtains. "Do you suspect shenanigans?"

"I'm trying like hell to keep an open mind." Matthew joined his friend. Both stared across the town toward the mine. "It's getting harder by the minute."

"Don't bother. Either Camden's a crook or your father

found a way to stick you after his death. My money's on Camden."

"Why?"

"Your father loved the mine too much to try to fit it into the coffin with him."

Pleased, Matthew clapped Dall on the shoulder. "Thanks."

"For what?"

"Your no-bullshit objectivity."

Dall turned to him. "I'll take the job."

"Good. I'll have papers drawn to give you full authority. But I won't execute them until we get this other stuff cleaned up. If Camden siphoned off the profits, we're going to find 'em. I won't be satisfied with just putting his ass in jail.

"When you take over the operation, it'll be with a clean slate."

The approval in Dall's hard expression was all the concurrence necessary.

"I think I'll go pay Mr. Camden a visit," Matthew said, his gaze shifting from the mine to the Calahans' house, and then back again. He had to remind himself: he had too much to take care of for the complications of a woman.

# Chapter Eleven

Bethany awoke in the same bed in which she'd gone to sleep. Okay. Another day in Alaska. Oh, well, a girl could hope.

Determined to make the most of her difficult situation, she devoted her time to preparations for her students.

By midafternoon, she sat at the Calahans' kitchen table and reviewed student records. There was a great deal more to take into account than the diversity of the children's ages and educational levels! Reading Ian McKenzie's lesson plans for the fourteen-year-old twins Harold and Harvey Bittlehorn gave her pause.

Boy, oh, boy, things had sure changed in the last century.

Her elbow braced on the tabletop, Bethany rubbed her forehead. "Incredible. Why didn't I know this?" she mused.

The requirements for graduating eighth grade in 1895 Juneau, Alaska Territory, appeared more stringent than most twenty-first-century graduation requirements for high school.

She wanted a challenge. Well, she'd gotten it.

And a challenge it was. The fifth-grade curriculum she'd known by heart was woefully inadequate in this era.

When she tossed out the advances of the twentieth-century, she had holes in her information big enough to drive a Mack truck through.

Concerned, she arranged the records in the valise. After penning a note to Megan, she placed it in the center of the table.

No point in disrupting Megan and the young woman discussing the advanced stages of pregnancy in the parlor. The talk of labor and childbirth provided a reminder of her own inadequacies. She considered it fortunate that her presence in Megan's "mother's room" hadn't interfered with her hostess's work.

Yet.

Bethany shivered at the thought of her inevitable transition from guest to inconvenience.

It wasn't as if the newspaper had columns of vacant apartment advertisements. She'd yet to see an apartment complex anywhere. Such living arrangements were still far in the future.

But there were boardinghouses. Perhaps there was one with a room to let.

Lost in thoughts of living arrangements and class curricula, she made her way to the schoolhouse. The key she'd found in the side pocket of the valise Matthew had given her fit the front door.

Evidence of Doreen Feeney's hard work registered immediately. The room smelled strongly of lye soap and sunshine. Naked windows sparkled behind scrubbed sashes. Worktables lined the walls, their benches inverted on top. The scents of pine and damp wood filled the air.

At the front of the room, the teacher's chair sat beside

the oak desk. The aroma of beeswax and lemon oil wafted off their fresh gleaming surfaces.

Not wanting to waste a minute, Bethany tested the top of the desk and the chair. Both were dry. Next, she retrieved a lamp from atop the side bookcase and lit the wick. Just that quickly, she was at home at the big oak desk.

With meticulous precision, Bethany dissected one textbook after another. Her notes nearly filled the journal Megan had given to her. She analyzed the differences between what she knew as history and the contents of the books.

Luckily for her, Matthew's interest ran toward math and science. If he'd asked the number of states in the Union, she'd have fumbled for the correct answer of thirty-eight.

Student by student, starting with the eldest Bittlehorn twins, Bethany assembled the pieces of individualized lesson plans. The hours slipped away. The picture in the giant jigsaw puzzle began to slowly take shape.

"What are you doing here?"

Bethany let out a yelp as she jumped in startlement. Her pencil flew into the air and she bolted to her feet. The chair skittered backwards and banged against the wall.

Matthew stood in the middle of the room—legs apart, arms balancing two of the crates they'd filled at Jed's store the previous day—scowling.

Flustered, Bethany put her hand over her thundering heart. "Great Gerty's ghost, you scared the life out of me."

"I didn't expect you, either. You didn't hear me come in?" he asked, incredulous.

She shook her head and tried to catch her breath. The adrenaline surging through her veins made her as jittery as a drop of water on a hot frying pan. "Obviously not."

He carried the supplies to her desk and balanced the

two crates on the corner. "I didn't mean to frighten you. You'll be needing these supplies Monday." He pushed the crates forward, all the while studying her. "With the work party and picnic tomorrow, I thought I'd better get these over here. If you need help sorting and putting away their contents, let me know."

Apparently satisfied she wasn't going to keel over, he shrugged and turned away. "I'll be right back with the rest of the supplies. Should I make loud noises when I come in again?"

"It wouldn't hurt."

Bethany gathered her composure and fixed her chair. By the time Matthew stomped back with the last crate, her heart was beating normally—at least as normally as it ever did in his presence.

He openly assessed her for a moment. "Good, you have your color back. From now on I'll make more noise before coming into a room unannounced. Maybe I'll whistle."

"Yes, whistle a happy tune."

"Let's not take it to extremes." He nodded at the crates brimming with supplies. "Once you decide what you want up front, we'll stash the rest in the cloak room . . . well, as soon as we paint it. Looks like you'll need another bookcase or cabinet to hold the books we ordered." He set the crate on the floor beside the desk. A fine sheen of perspiration beaded his forehead. The cuffs of his fine white shirt were rolled halfway up his tanned forearms. His tie wilted around his open collar. Smudges marred his snowy shirt.

"You've been working." The inane comment slipped out. "I mean, doing . . . dirty work." Too bad Yolanda's River of Time couldn't change course and whisk her from the schoolhouse before she made a complete idiot of herself.

"Yeah, you could say I'm doing someone's dirty work. The question is, whose?"

"I'm sorry." She rubbed her temple, wondering if her social skills had dribbled out of her ear while she concentrated on plans for her students. "I know that was all said in plain English, but obviously my mind isn't quite working."

"Let's clear it. Did you bring a coat?"

"Uh, yes. Why?"

"Grab it and let's go."

Bethany snagged her coat from the coat tree in the corner. "Where are we going?"

"Someplace vast and open," he murmured, helping her into the garment. He fastened the buttons as through she were a small child. When his hands brushed her throat, they lingered.

Bethany's eyes met his.

The back of his knuckles stilled against her rapid pulse. The way he looked at her increased her body temperature by at least forty degrees. She didn't need a coat; her skin tingled and felt on fire with the now familiar spell of desire.

Thirsty for what she couldn't, shouldn't, have, she licked her lips.

"Is it cold where we're going?" God, she hoped so. Being this close, feeling his hands gently rest against her skin . . . spontaneous combustion was a rare occurrence, but it was about to happen right here.

"You'll like it," he promised in a rough, soft voice.

"You're that sure of what I like and don't?" She sincerely hoped not. She'd curl up and pray for death if he knew how badly she wanted him, particularly since it was never going to happen.

His restless demeanor accentuated the tension enveloping them. It seemed he had the weight of the entire continent on those broad shoulders.

The afternoon's busywork had nearly erased Bethany's irritation from yesterday's disagreement at the store. At the moment, her concern for his unsettled state overrode the offense she'd taken for reasons that now seemed trivial.

"I'll button my own coat the rest of the way." She liked him touching her way too much; she had to stop it.

"It was an innocent pleasure." Reluctantly, he stepped back and jammed his hands deep into his trousers pockets.

Without his warm breath fanning her face, the cold he'd mentioned descended. She wanted to tug him back and ask what was disturbing him so deeply. No, she wanted to pull him close, feel his mouth against hers, and his strong arms around her. "Was it?" she asked instead.

"A pleasure? Most definitely." The look in his eyes warned there had been nothing innocent about it.

"Fresh air sounds like a good idea. Let me turn this off and we can go." She broke free of the place where her feet were rooted to the floor, and she attended to her desk lamp.

They left the schoolhouse together, not touching but keenly aware of one another.

Bethany sat on the buggy seat determined not to steal a glance at Matthew. Warmth rolled from his body in waves, and she soaked it up like the sun.

She took careful note of the turns and landmarks as they rode. To the east, the mountains rose out of the ground like granite bastions. Would that the barriers around her fragile emotions could be as strong.

The horse kept a steady pace over hills and just as slowly down the slopes. Bethany set aside the tumult from earlier in the day. No amount of emotion changed her situation. The rhythm of iron horseshoes on the ground and the long afternoon sun soothed her. The sheer beauty of rugged, snow-capped mountains, the silt-laden aquamarine sea, a blue sky pocked with cotton-puff clouds, and ledges of towering trees contrasted and shaped the landscape. Nature's tapestry depicted the toll of harsh winters, gloriously long and colorful summers, and the beauty of survival.

Matthew stopped the buggy beside a grassy slope and set the brake.

"How about a short climb?"

Bethany eyed the wildflower-dotted knoll a short distance from the carriage. "Sure."

With the grace of an athlete, Matthew bounded to the ground. In one deft motion, he tethered the horse to a boulder.

She turned to climb out of the buggy. Matthew's hands became velvet vises closing around her waist. A week ago, she would have found a way to avoid his touch. Today, whether because of her frazzled emotions or she'd grown accustomed to him, she let him help her down.

"Why are we here?" She straightened her coat to avoid looking at him. The heat her body generated while near Matthew rendered the coat superfluous. The sudden warmth coaxed her into unfastening its buttons.

"Come."

He took her hand and led her toward the hill. The brisk wind rushing over the crest caught her coat and cooled her off. Walking up the knoll, her hand in his, felt right—despite the chaotic uncertainty of her stay here. Matthew was big and solid, like an anchor in a storm.

Climbing the embankment and stretching her legs provided an outlet for her restless energy. The crisp air carried odd, distant sounds.

"Because I intruded on *your* thinking place, I thought it fair to show you where I come to ponder the world and my problems." Matthew glanced at her, held her gaze briefly, and then looked away. "You might like it better than the graveyard."

Something about him was different; he was more somber, perhaps. He wasn't smiling. In fact, his expression reminded her of a prairie thunderstorm. "I take it this isn't a simple matter of 'I showed you mine, you show me yours.' Want to talk about what's troubling you?" She wondered if his dilemma had her name on it.

He didn't answer.

They reached the top, and still he held her hand. In a heartbeat, she forgot everything except the vast, entrancing wonder at her feet. The crackling and snapping she'd heard belonged to Mother Nature.

How could she have missed seeing the vast majesty of this ice field that stretched for miles?

"The Mendenhall Glacier," Matthew said with reverence.

The enormity of the sight captivated Bethany. The sheer magnificence and power of the ice river flowing inexorably to the sea left her speechless. Instead of rapids and waves, great fissures of white and blue ice yawned into black depths. Dark stains of pulverized granite coated the glacier's sides. Ribbons of the dark stuff made marks as irregular and unpredictable as its surface.

"The reason I come here when I have something on my mind is for comparison. It's like looking at the open ocean. Here, it's frozen snow from God knows how many eons ago."

A breeze blew across the glacier and chilled Bethany's exposed skin. She closed her coat and folded her arms. "Thousands and thousands," she breathed.

"Watching the glacier puts my problems into perspective. It reminds me how insignificant they are in the scheme of the world." He looked away. A self-deprecating smile curled the corners of his mouth. "Glaciers carry the message of *patience* to all those willing to see it."

*Patience*: a quality she'd cultivated out of necessity. She hadn't had a choice. Like the glacier eroding its granite bed, stretching from lofty mountain peaks to a sea stained pale aquamarine from pulverized silt, the ice river moved at a constant pace. No amount of fretting made it move slower, no amount of anticipation hastened its spill toward the sea.

Standing on a precipice overlooking the ice, Bethany whispered, "Sometimes patience isn't enough, though. Sometimes, regardless of how long you wait, how hard you look, or how many ways you look, there are no answers. Sometimes . . . there aren't even any reasons."

The ice had a mesmerizing effect. In its own way, the glacier was a River of Time. Frozen time. If stepping out on the ice could carry her back to Drexel . . .

Her ears strained to hear the whisper of passing years.

"Don't get too much closer. The glacier erodes the underside of the hill here."

"Getting too close" summed up the reasons for her present circumstances. Yolanda D'Arcy had warned her of this—all of it. Bethany hadn't understood. Once again, she'd zigged in life when she should have zagged.

She was lucky the experience hadn't killed her, only changed her life.

"Hypnotic, isn't it?" Matthew caught her arm and gently tugged her away from the edge.

"Yes, very." The firm grip on her arm drew her attention from the parallel between Mother Nature's enigmatic rivers. Then she glanced up. The distress she saw in his features shamed her for contemplating her problems in his thinking place. "Does what's troubling you have anything to do with that grave back at the cemetery, the one apart from the rest?"

He released her and turned away.

"Was Victoria Gray your wife?" *Are you still in love with her? How did she die?*

"Yes. She and my son died in childbirth." The finality of his tone indicated that he had no desire to discuss them. "I've answered your question, how about answering mine?"

"I suppose turnabout is fair." Mentally she braced, sure he'd ask something she didn't want to answer.

"Why were you crying in the graveyard? And don't tell me it was because I offered to help you buy your own clothes." He shoved his hands into his trousers pockets.

"I was feeling sorry for myself and missing my family." That safe, truthful answer let her continue walking the tightrope stretching to the breaking point around her secret.

The chill of the wind off the glacier swirled through the open plackets of her coat. "My turn. What's bothering *you*, Matthew?"

"You're sure something is?"

"I can't read your mind; your face says it." These days, she could barely read her own mind. "I'm an excellent listener."

"If I ever need a listener, I'll keep that in mind." A cracking, breaking groan echoed out of the blue-white fissures below.

"What was that?" Bethany scanned the jagged glacier, half expecting to see the thing move in its enormous trough.

"The ice is calving into the sea. There's a place closer to the outwash where you can see the big sheets fall. The glacier is noisier in the summer, when the sun heats the surface against the water." As though drawn by the sound, he moved toward the brink.

"You like being close to the edge." The words spilled without thought.

"You don't," he answered without turning around.

"Been there. Done that. Got the T-shirt."

"What?"

"Never mind."

"Tell me what you mean."

Bethany shook her head. "I mean I have no desire to stand on the edge of anything. You never know when something might pull the ground out from under you." Hugging her arms against a sudden chill, she turned away. "I'll wait for you at the buggy."

"Stay."

Surprised by the vulnerability packed into the single word, she hesitated.

"Please," he added softly.

Her curiosity kept her there. "Why did you bring me up here, Matthew?" she asked.

"I wanted company."

"But you didn't want to talk?"

"Yeah."

"Oh. I understand."

"Do you?"

"Yes. Oh, yes." The number of times one of her sisters had spent an evening or an entire day with her, neither of them speaking, the two just being together, were etched firmly in her memory. Those precious gifts of time and understanding were beyond price.

She hunkered down on a huge boulder smoothed by ice and weather, picking at the buttercups and forget-me-nots growing nearby. Watching Matthew, listening to the wind and the glacier, she braided the wildflower stems into a pattern. The activity reminded her of summer picnics in the meadow with her mother and sisters. Childhood. Family.

"Long ago and far away," she whispered. Gradually, the wildflowers formed a fragrant crown. An examination of the lavender and yellow petals made her smile. Alicia would know the names of everything growing around her; Bethany was content to appreciate the simple beauty of the flowers. For her, inhaling the crisp mountain air had a calming, cleansing effect.

Whatever effect it had on Matthew was hard to discern. He hadn't moved. The problem he wrestled with made him impervious to the chilled breeze. He stood like a statue, legs apart, his white shirtsleeves rolled halfway up his forearms, his hands in his pockets, the breeze toying with his thick hair.

Good grief, but he was handsome—in a rugged sort of way. Strangely, the better she got to know him, the more facets she saw of his character, the more she liked him and the better-looking he became. Dangerous, she knew. But a woman couldn't help the way a man made her feel, or how she felt about him. She just had to be smart enough not to let it show—and strong enough not to act on it.

But was she smart or strong enough? Her feelings were so strange and terrifying.

There hadn't been many opportunities for dating during her high school and college years. Her youth had made her less appealing to her peers. The first few years of college she bore the nickname "Jailbait." And by the time she'd turned eighteen, the second semester of her junior year, she'd built a routine that left little time for a social life.

Recalling the lost opportunities and confronting the pain of what she couldn't have was a bitter pill. Nevertheless, she was grateful for her life. Her parents had not been as fortunate.

"Here, let me help you up."

She set the flower crown aside and accepted the assistance Matthew offered with his extended hand. Considering his shirtsleeve attire, his hand was warm against her cool fingers. She brushed her skirts clean of wildflower stems, leaves, and petals as he retrieved the laurel.

"Beautiful," he said, examining the way the flower steps braided into one another. "Where did you learn to do this?"

"When I was a child, my mother would pack a picnic

basket. We'd saddle the horses and ride to the high meadow. 'Ladies Day,' as Mom called it, became a tradition we counted on every spring before roundup." One she and her sisters could not repeat—at least not while she was separated from them, trapped in the past. "It wouldn't have been spring without a meadow picnic."

Carefree memories of happier times made her smile. "After we stuffed ourselves with all the special goodies Mom packed, we'd sit on the quilt and make flower crowns." She took the floral halo from his hands and smiled. "I learned early not to use purple clover, though. Bees love it." She stood on tiptoes and placed the flowers on his head.

Without thought, she swept his hair from his forehead. The thick strands were soft as a mink pelt. The feel of his warm skin under her fingertips warmed her entire arm.

She met his blue eyes and felt more lost than ever.

He seemed to be waiting for something, letting her make the first move. She lowered her hand and stepped back. Much as she wanted to know if his lips were as soft as they looked, if his kiss would rob her of her fears, she refused to risk finding out. Her emotions had softened to mush around him. Just the thought of his touch left her weak in the knees, melted her resolve to protect herself. It wasn't him she didn't trust; it was herself.

Great Gerty's ghost! One look at her scars and not only would his desire wilt like a violet in the Sahara, but he'd have a bazillion questions.

Silence stretched between them for a long moment before she looked away. His disappointment was palpable, yet was no worse than her own.

Apparently, he didn't want to let it hang there. "I need a favor," he said. "I'll pay you for your time, too."

"I thought we were friends," she said, wondering what kind of favor he wanted to pay her for.

"We are. It's a big favor, one I don't want anyone else to know about."

"Is it legal?"

"What the hell kind of question is that? Of course—" He whipped the flower crown from his head and approached her. He gave her an odd look. "You mean you'd do something illegal for a friend?"

Oh, the ice was thin up here. "Depends on the friend and the circumstances. Chances are excellent I'd come up with an alternative. I'm not really the brave sort. However, it's a moot point. Right?"

His eyes sparkled. "Apparently."

"So, what's the favor?"

"I understand you're quick and accurate at basic bookkeeping, logging accounts and such things."

"Word gets around fast. Did Megan tell you that I'd helped her?"

"No. Jeb did."

"Okay. So what do you want me to do?"

"I'd like you to go over some account books and sort some files."

"Whose?"

"The Gray Wolf Mine."

"Why?"

He placed the flower circlet on her wind-whipped hair. "Beautiful and curious, too?"

Bethany felt her cheeks heat. "Definitely curious."

"I need an impartial assessment. You're good with numbers, the best I've seen. You know little or nothing about the Gray Wolf, so you've no preconceived notions. Frankly, Bethany, I'm after your objectivity."

"And my silence."

"That too."

"I'll do it on one condition," she said slowly.

"Which is?"

"You help me find a place to live. It's only a matter of

time before Megan needs her spare room for one of her new mothers."

"Easy enough. You can use Gray House. All the papers and books are in the Old Man's study. You can work there undisturbed."

"I couldn't live in your house. How would it look—"

"It'll look fine. I considered living there, but I've changed my mind. I'm going to stay at Mama Johanson's. I'll speak to Doreen. She's an excellent cook and—"

"What will people *think?*" In her own time it might have been okay, but here it was a different matter.

"People who know us won't have a negative thought. Those who don't might talk, though." He almost smiled when he stared off at the long glacier climbing the lofty mountain slopes. "But those people will gossip regardless."

That made sense to Bethany. "So, what is the rent on Gray House?"

"A dollar a month."

"Bull-pucky."

His eyebrows rose. "Bull-pucky?"

"Right. Not even in this day and age does a house like that rent for a dollar a month."

His amusement hardened into a stony expression. "You're an expert on rent—in this day and age?"

Everything in Bethany froze. Once again, she'd slipped, and he'd picked up on it. No doubt he had each one catalogued and categorized. "No, I'm not."

"You can stay with Megan and Jeb, if you'd prefer the company. I understand you might not want to live alone in a big house."

"That isn't it. I—"

"There are few places for a respectable woman to live unless she has her own home. By living in Gray House you'll have space to spread out. For now, it makes the most sense for you to stay there. All the paperwork and the old Gray Wolf accounts are in the study. After you've gone through it all, we'll discuss different arrangements. Deal?"

"Do you have to make this sound so logical?"

"It *is* logical. And practical."

"And over the top, Matthew. But I'll do it. I don't do windows—"

"Doreen Feeney does. She also cleans, cooks, and does laundry." He grinned. "She's part of the deal."

"I hope you run your business more shrewdly than you manage your property. If not, you'll be living on that dollar a month—and it won't go very far."

"The only thing hurting my business these days is the amount of time it's taking to settle the Gray Wolf Mine. That's where you come in, and I'm figuring you're a bargain."

She hesitated, and indulged in a final look at the awesome glacier.

"Make any changes you want to make to the house," he continued. "There's nothing there but sad memories. I don't suppose you have a sideline as an interior decorator?"

"I'm a woman of many talents," she murmured and returned her gaze to his.

Matthew's smile disappeared. He ran the pad of his thumb along her jaw and over her lower lip. "I don't doubt that for a moment."

# *Chapter Twelve*

"Take these, too." Megan pushed a box of clothing across the parlor rug. "I'll never wear them."

"Oh, Megan, this is too much. I can't begin to repay your kindness," Bethany protested.

Hands on hips, the woman paused before her. " 'Tisn't charity on my part, Bethany. 'Tis selfishness. Me husband likes ta buy me clothes, whether I want or need them. You and I are the only women around of our particular height and fit. Now, I'm tellin' you to take them. I've no place to put more."

"But—"

"No buts. Iffen you don't, I'll have ta cut them up as rags, and mighty poor ones at that."

A knock on the door interrupted further protest.

Megan opened the door and grinned. "I thought I heard ye and your buggy outside. Ye dinna disappoint me, Matthew.

" 'Tis a noble thing ye're doing," Megan said, opening

the door. "Though 'tis nothing for a strappin' man, Bethany canna carry these boxes up the stairs of Gray House."

"No, she can't." He'd come dressed for physical labor in denim trousers and a soft blue shirt open at the collar and with rolled up sleeves.

"Take this box, will ye now?" Megan gestured to the objects of controversy. "There's another packed in her room."

Bethany tried not to stare at the shadow of silken chest hair peeking through the vee of Matthew's shirt. She glanced up and found him watching her. He seemed not at all put off by her probing gaze. A faint smile enhanced the sparkle in his eyes.

The sudden awkwardness of being caught looking at him quickly passed. Absently, she rubbed her fingertips over the pad of her thumb, wondering if his chest was as muscular under his blue chambray shirt as it appeared. And if his dark, glistening chest hair was silky-soft to the touch.

"We'll be at the schoolhouse in an hour or so, soon as my pies cool."

Matthew picked up the nearest box. "Now you're talking bribery, Megan. You know there's not a man in town who wouldn't do anything for a piece of one of your pies."

"I'll be savin' a whole one just for ye. Consider it a thank-ya for takin' these boxes off me hands. Jeb received another catalog just last week, so I'll be expectin' new clothes in a month."

Bethany noted the affection with which Megan spoke of Jeb's proclivity of showering her with fine clothing. From what she could tell, his need to lavish his wife stemmed from the poverty they'd endured in Ireland. Conversely, Megan preferred simple, utilitarian clothing and wasted nothing.

"Would ya like Sorcha and me to bring the bread ya baked?"

Bethany picked up the apron Megan had folded and set aside. "Yes, please. I'd like to take a few moments after Mr. Gray drops off the boxes to look through the house. That way, if I have any questions, I can ask him at the schoolhouse."

Matthew lifted the second box. "I'll answer, anything you ask."

"You don't say?" What a delightful prospect, if he really meant it—which she doubted.

The rise of his left eyebrow dared her to offer the same. She smiled back. Not a chance she'd reciprocate, but she had no compunction about taking *him* up on his offer. She had a lot of questions, but only a few she'd dare ask even with his open invitation.

With an agreement to meet up with Megan at the school, Matthew and Bethany set off to take her new belongings to Gray House.

"I still don't understand why you're doing this for me," Bethany said when they arrived. The magnificence of the Victorian was unquestionable. Later, she'd have time to examine the little details of the woodwork on the porch.

Matthew opened the door, pushed it wide, and handed her the key. His avoidance of any explanation encouraged her fear that he'd put her exactly where he wanted her—under a microscope. And it was one with his name on the brand plate.

"Take a look upstairs and pick a bedroom. I'll be up shortly with your boxes."

Wary, yet amazed by her new, albeit temporary, home, her gaze swept the exquisite lines of the stairway angling to the second floor. The banister, newel post, and spindles gleamed from years of care. A faint aroma of beeswax and lemon oil hung in the still air.

Crown molding framed the ceilings. A matching pattern formed the wainscoting cap. A rose-patterned runner stretched up the center of the stair risers. Brass rods stretched across the crook of each stair and secured the plush carpet on the oak.

Oils paintings of seascapes artfully decorated the stairwell walls.

The second floor provided a testimonial to the size of the house. A sitting area at the top of the stairs broke with tradition. The open design seemed far too modern for the time, but blended with the rest of the house.

The master bedroom on her right made her eyes pop out. George Gary's personal effects still filled the bureau drawers, closet, and armoire. And it was terribly decorated. Disturbed, Bethany closed the door on the obnoxious red, watered-silk walls.

"I'm bringing up the first box," Matthew called from below.

She hurriedly scanned the four upstairs bedrooms and selected one. It had soft blue and yellow tones that imparted a warm, sunny feel, and the window faced south, allowing the maximum light in the winter.

"I'm back here," she called to Matthew. *And I'm absolutely amazed by the stupendous house you built*, she admitted silently. For reasons she couldn't fathom, everything about the house—with the exception of the horrible burgundy-colored master bedroom—spoke to something inside her. Never mind that such whispers made her imagine a future here in the past. She knew better.

The sense of unreality she'd experienced since tumbling out of the River of Time returned full force. For the tenth time since he'd rented her this house, she wondered why he had. Surely he wanted something from her—more than an objective look at his father's books of account.

If that turned out to be the case, he'd have to learn to live with disappointment. Like she had. It was survivable. Inconvenient, occasionally painful, but survivable.

Matthew's footfalls in the hall stopped short of the

room she'd chosen. When she looked out, she saw him frozen, statuelike.

Before she spoke, he set the box of her stuff down in the middle of the hall. Although he cast a hollow-eyed glance her way, Matthew offered no explanation, and his dour expression warned her not to ask. He disappeared into a bedroom.

Curious, Bethany waited at the door for long minutes until he returned with a folded quilt. He stroked the faded fabric with a reverence she found hypnotic.

He laid the quilt on the box, then picked up both and carried them to the room she had selected. Without offering an explanation, he laid the quilt on the bottom of her bed. Then he turned around and went back out.

Five minutes later, both boxes sat at the foot of the bed.

"Do you need help unpacking these?"

"No," she answered. "I can do that this evening."

He picked up the quilt he'd brought and lovingly smoothed the folds over his forearm. "If you'd like a ride to the school, I'd be glad to drive you over. I have some business to tend. I'll be at the school in an hour or two."

Whatever significance the quilt held, he planned to keep it to himself.

"You built an impressive house, Mr. Gray. Why don't you show me the books you want me to review before you go."

It was time to see the reason for her bargain-basement rental deal on a palace.

Blue skies and warm summer temperatures added vigor to the already enthusiastic workers at the schoolhouse. The project was well underway when Matthew entered the schoolyard. He touched the brim of his hat and nodded to the ladies setting food on the long tables his construction crew had assembled for the occasion.

He'd watched for Bethany the moment the schoolhouse came into view, hoping to observe her with the children. Her concepts of education were foreign to him, but that didn't necessarily mean they were wrong. They were just . . . different. Like Bethany. He wanted to see her in action.

After greeting the men and acknowledging the ladies, Matthew found a paintbrush and went to work beside Henry Bittlehorn.

" 'Bout time you showed up," Henry said. "The women wouldn't let us have anything to eat 'til you got here."

"You worried about starving?"

"It never hurts a man to eat when he's workin' hard. Now, you go up on the scaffold. I like having solid ground under my feet."

Matthew nodded, preferring to work the top quadrant. Henry was a man of abundant talent. He could hold the ladder, paint, talk, and, given the opportunity, eat, simultaneously.

After numerous trips up and down the ladder, Matthew finished painting the upper portion of the east side of the schoolhouse, and climbed down from the ladder for a break. He stretched and accepted a beer stein from Henry. His German friend brewed a potent beer.

"I brought a keg of the good stuff," Henry said, leaning against the ladder and lifting an ornate stein to drink.

"Where are the kids?"

"Miss James has them painting the back side of the schoolhouse." Henry polished off half his stein of beer. "She says nobody should look there until they're finished." Henry peered at the end of the building amusement. "Yesterday, when she was rounding people up, she asked the children to wear their oldest, ragged clothing. Acht, but she wouldn't say why. She and those kids are protecting whatever they do back there."

"She's doing art," Matthew murmured. With a smile he

added, "Next, she'll be teaching them opera." His admiration for Bethany moved up another notch. The woman not only talked, she followed up.

"What?"

"Nothing. Good beer; thanks." He drained his own beer stein and handed it back. "Let's finish off this side and do the front."

"Ja, then we can eat." Henry's priorities seldom changed. "Hulda brought sauerkraut and bratwurst."

"Ya bring Hun food to a hungry Irish worker?" Jeb called out in passing. "Now, cook some corned beef and cabbage, then we'll really feast."

"I'd sooner eat whale blubber," Henry called back. "And complainer or not, I bet you'll eat Hulda's blueberry strudel."

"Aye, and before you finish your cabbage."

Myriad aromas mingled with fresh air and paint. The laughter of women preparing tables for the afternoon meal and the voices of men settling into the enormous task rode a soft breeze. Ladders, brushes, and men with pails of paint attacked the schoolhouse with a communal frenzy.

Gossip and anecdotes flew like leaves in autumn.

Laughter, shouts, and excited calls came from the back of the schoolhouse. Two dozen adults exchanged glances, all eager to know what was happening between the teacher and her students.

"My boys took a new interest in school after Miss James visited the other day. Whatever she said to 'em lit a fire. They finished their chores before breakfast and couldn't wait to get here." Henry cast a narrowed gaze toward the rear of the building.

Matthew knew exactly what the boys were going through. Bethany James had captivated them. She was the damn Pied Piper of Juneau, leading its children in a new, unexpected direction. He just hoped it was a good direction.

At lunch, the younger kids skipped from behind the schoolhouse. From the rainbow of colors straining their clothing, it looked as if they had used their bodies to apply the paint.

Matthew marveled at the messy youths rushing past. The smaller the child, the more paint he or she wore. Indeed, Bethany and the children had mixed every shade imaginable from the primary colors he'd provided.

At last, Matthew saw Bethany herself round the end of the building. She was flanked by the elder Bittlehorn twins, and the lanky adolescents towered over her, their red hair stained with blue and white paint. The boys were obviously smitten with their new teacher.

Bethany glowed with vivacity and joy. Bright-eyed and laughing, she appeared not to have a care in the world.

He found himself annoyed. How the hell did she expect to teach the children anything if she laughed and joked with them? The good professors at Gonzaga University in Spokane and the best teachers in the schoolrooms of Tacoma would never have tolerated the kind of familiarity Bethany James permitted.

"Excuse me," came a voice from behind him. "I'm looking for Mr. Matthew Gray."

Despite his annoyance, Matthew was reluctant to give up the sight of Bethany laughing with abandon and the adoring gazes she elicited from the children. He continued watching her, wondering at her intentions as he motioned for the man to approach him.

"You are Mr. Matthew Gray?"

The formality sounded out of place in the festive gathering. Matthew turned to see who it was who sought him.

The dapper young man interrupting Matthew's observation of Bethany's methods carried himself in a manner as stiff as his speech. Though a head shorter than Matthew, the man was dressed in a black three-piece suit, starched wing-collar white shirt, and silk tie. Not a hair on his blond head gave in to the breeze skimming over the center part in his pomade-sculpted coif. The clear spectacles perched on the bridge of his straight nose made his eyes appear even closer together than they were. He carried a polished leather valise in his left hand.

There was something disconcerting about a stranger who showed up uninvited to a work picnic in a suit and boiled collar.

"I'm Matthew Gray. If you wish to see me on business, please stop by my office on Fifth Street." Matthew finished scrutinizing the man and decided the only description that fit him was *toady*.

"I apologize for the intrusion, sir. All I need is a moment of your time. I'm Millard DuBois." The man gave his name with a slight bow of his head. "I'm Mr. Cornelius Lassiter's secretary." As though by magic, he produced a calling card and handed it to Matthew.

The way DuBois announced Lassiter's name implied the man was royalty, but Matthew had never heard him. He examined the card, debating whether to keep it. At least DuBois wasn't seeking employment. "Who is your employer?"

DuBois's golden eyebrows lifted in unabashed surprise. "A businessman. A successful one with an eye on the future."

The way Millard DuBois watched the workers gathering behind Matthew suggested further conversation would be better conducted in private. Matthew nodded and indicated a tree a short distance away. DuBois fell into step beside him.

Matthew scoured his memory. He seldom forgot a name or a face. Millard DuBois's expectation of recognition for his boss spoke volumes. Lassiter was a bigwig somewhere, if not in Matthew's circles.

He leaned against the tree and regarded the visitor. "I've never heard of Cornelius Lassiter. What can I do for you and your boss?"

The smile stealing over DuBois's thin lips held a secret amusement. "I don't believe you comprehend the importance of my visit, Mr. Gray."

"Apparently not. Unless your boss wants a house or building designed and built, I doubt we have much to discuss, Mr. DuBois."

"Please don't be hasty. Granted, the timing and circumstances are somewhat at odds with Mr. Lassiter's usual mode of conducting business; I normally wouldn't approach you on a Saturday. But, at the moment, he is the guest of a mutual friend."

"Yes, and . . . ?"

"Mr. Lassiter has business he'd like to discuss with you. If it is convenient, he'd like to pay a call to your home or business on Monday."

"About what?"

"I'm not at liberty to discuss the details of Mr. Lassiter's interests, but accept my assurances you'll want to hear what he has to say."

"I see." Wonderful. Another skeleton was rattling in the Old Man's closet. And likely he couldn't ignore it. "Tell Mr. Lassiter the soonest I can see him is Wednesday at three—at my office on Fifth Street."

Hell, whatever this Lassiter character wanted, it likely involved the Gray Wolf. That was the only explanation.

"Mr. Lassiter will arrive promptly at three on Wednesday. Good day, sir." With a curt nod of his head, Millard DuBois turned on his heel and walked to the street.

Another young man dressed as crisply as DuBois waited in the man's buggy.

Matthew watched them leave. "Even the lackey has a toady. This ought to be good," he murmured.

The sensation of his father's hand rising from the grave,

reaching across the threshold of death and grabbing him by the throat chilled him. It also made him angry. Eyes closed, Matthew swore he heard the hint of laughter in the breeze.

How did a man undo a careless adolescent moment? How did one find redemption when one couldn't change the past?

The answer was simple. One couldn't. And though nothing could bring his mother back to life, the Old Man had punished his son even after his death. And leaving Matthew an unwanted mine was just the latest. Its financial entanglements were what would really hurt.

Apparently, his father had known Matthew far better than Matthew had known his father. The old man had known he wouldn't walk away from his father's achievement. And he'd known damn well that his son would take every measure possible to keep the mine going for the workers whose livelihoods depended on it.

And before he could even *consider* selling the Gray Wolf to a reputable buyer, he had to prove its worth. The old man had thwarted him there, too.

The financial mess grew stickier by the day. How many vultures were there in addition to Cornelius Lassiter?

The sound of happy voices and the laughter of his friends and neighbors buoyed his sinking mood. Behind him, children called to one another and parents barked orders. It was a wonderfully normal day now that the toady had departed. As long as he didn't speculate about what awaited in the shadows.

Matthew ran his fingers through his hair.

One thing at a time. Right now, he had a schoolhouse to finish painting. If everything else went to hell, he'd keep the school going—even if the money came out of his own pocket.

Ready to rejoin the group, he pushed away from the tree and turned around.

Bethany stood in a no-man's land between him and the work crew. Their gazes locked as he closed the distance between them. Her earlier mood of hilarity and joy had faded into a seriousness reflected in her lavender eyes.

God, sometimes she saw so much, too quickly.

"How are the children doing with your secret project?" he asked as he approached.

A flicker of a smile returned to her mouth. Her gaze never wavered from his. "They are good kids, every one of them. I wish I could tell you how . . . how truly special this is."

"This? You mean your project?"

"All of it. The respect the children accord their elders. Their eagerness to learn. Their willingness to help one another and work together." A veritable glow surrounded her. "I feel like I've stumbled into the Garden of Eden's playground."

Bethany's ebullience struck deep. Despite his dour thoughts of a moment before, a smile tugged at Matthew's lips. This woman had a way of keeping him off balance, of lifting his spirits when he least expected it. Hell yes, he'd keep the school open. Treadwell didn't give a damn if these children got an education, but he did, and so did Bethany. "Does that make you Eve and me Adam?"

A spark in her lavender eyes flared before she tore her gaze from his. "They had a very different . . . friendship than we do."

She surprised him by taking his arm when he offered it and leading him toward the makeshift picnic tables. "Are schoolchildren in Wyoming so different from here?" he asked. What had she expected? A band of snarling timber wolves?

"No." She answered slowly, turning her head away from him completely.

Once again, his gut told him that she was hiding something, or hiding from someone, and the dishonesty of it hit him with the force of a punch. Rather than pursue information he knew she would not divulge, he changed the subject. "Things are changing faster than I expected. I need the information from the books you're reviewing as quickly as possible. How soon can we go over what you've got?"

Her brow furrowed in contemplation. "Well, you were right about the mess in your father's study. But Mrs. Feeney promised to leave dinner in the warmer this evening, so I can work tonight. By the way, Gray House is exquisite. The woodwork alone is an art form beyond measure." She glanced up at him, gratitude shining in her eyes. "And although your father's books look like a great deal of work, I think you're being extremely generous by letting me stay there."

"There's a lot to do," he said. "But I know you'd earn your keep."

She turned and looked behind her at several children, avoiding his eyes. "Let's eat," she proposed, taking Laurie Craddock's hand. The six-year-old child, who'd had little to smile about since the death of her mother last winter, lit up with a gap-toothed grin.

If Bethany James was running from a dissolute past, conning everyone into believing she was Miss Sweetness and Light, she was damn good. These kids were hard to win over, and she'd done it in a single day.

And when he wasn't thinking clearly, she won Matthew over, too.

The last of the scaffolding lay in the bed of a buckboard bearing the words GRAY & SKINNER ARCHITECTURAL DESIGN AND CONSTRUCTION.

"Take it over to the Sixth Street project," Matthew told the driver. "They'll need it by the end of the week."

"Right, boss. Ain't gotta move it twice." The driver snapped the reins. "Yah! Git up, there."

The harnesses jangled and the wagon groaned, then the team of horses pulled their burden through the deserted schoolyard.

Bethany gathered the last of the paint rags and dropped them into a bucket.

Satisfaction buzzed through her. This project had unfolded beyond her wildest expectations. In one day, she'd gained insight into her school's children, their interests, and formed a rough assessment of their group dynamics. The mural had been a bonus. Stealing a glimpse of it while finishing the cleanup in the yard made her smile.

What had begun simply had evolved into a picture the entire width of the wall: the glacier spilling down the mountain and into the sea flowed with changing colors into the Gastineau Channel separating Juneau from Douglas Island. She'd begun by sketching out a mining town and its wild surroundings. The children, as a group, had then decided on changes and made them. Bethany's eyes landed on a highlight: the Orca whale pod Sorcha had pleaded to include, which now swam in the Gastineau Channel.

Matthew approached. "Everyone expressed amazement over the mural you and the children painted. How in seven shades of heck did you get fifteen kids to create this masterpiece?" He stood back from the center of the mural, his arms folded across his chest, his legs apart.

"I have a gift." A smile escaped her as she basked in his approval. She was glad to have been able to manage the kids and help them produce something so precious.

"A gift? You're far too modest. Each time I look at what you've done here, I'm more impressed." He winked. "You didn't tell me you could control kids' minds—make them all artists."

She laughed. "I can't." She joined him in his appraisal of the mural. Then she looked up into his eyes. "I have to admit, I cheated."

"You painted the mural in the dead of night and let the kids paint each other today?"

"Not exactly," she said with a laugh. "I sketched the mural on the wall yesterday afternoon, then color-coded it. For the children, it was more of a paint-by-numbers project."

"Paint by numbers? I believe I missed that lesson when reviewing the Grand Masters."

"We mixed the paint in various hues and shades—"

"The likes of which most of us haven't seen," Matthew mused, tilting his head.

"—then I labeled each of the mixes to match the proper numbers on the wall. It provided a little guidance. The creativity part was theirs. The older Bittlehorn twins have real artistic talent."

She pointed out two sections in the upper corners. "See the two circle tableaux on the top right and left sides? Harold painted the mining scene; Harvey did the loggers. It was an incredible sight, Matthew. They painted those scenes, including all the details, in a couple of hours. And they did it freehand."

"They come by their talent naturally. Their mother paints."

"Really? Perhaps she'll come to the school and share a bit of her knowledge on colors, textures, and perspective." Each new resource for the little school seemed the equivalent of a gold nugget.

"No. Teach them to read, write, and do mathematics. Teach geography and science, civics and history. Art and music are—"

"Necessary for a rounded education!" Oh, he was stubborn!

"—gravy," he finished. "They need the meat and potatoes."

"Well, sometimes a little gravy makes the main course

more palatable, not to mention more exciting. There is no substitute for enthusiasm."

"Nor is there a substitute for the things these kids will use the most in their lives."

"Give a little, will you?"

Perplexity knit his bow. "I could have sworn I had."

"I'm not talking about money or time. How about a little compromise?" She couldn't help grinning. "The kids want to paint the privy."

"Inside or out?" he asked, as though contemplating.

"Yes." She could be just as unyielding as he.

"If their parents don't object to them doing it *after three*, I see no problem. . . ."

"Fine." She'd just lengthen the school day by fifteen minutes. Then she could get music and art into the curriculum.

That settled, Bethany and Matthew returned to Gray House. Pleasantly tired, satisfied beyond measure with the fruits of the day's labors, Bethany led the way to George Gray's private study.

Inside, they lit lamps, then found their way to the desk. The faint aroma of pipe tobacco leaked from the rich wood paneling and the spines of countless leather-bound books lining the south wall of the room.

Paper stacks of varying sizes filled the floor, chairs, credenza, worktable, and desk. A number of the heavy tomes pulled from the bookcases acted as paperweights. Each had a slip of paper sticking out of the top.

Matthew seemed surprised. "What are you doing?"

"Categorizing and sorting. I finished early this morning."

Bethany pulled a handful of papers into the center of the desk. She settled in the big leather desk chair while Matthew drew a leather wingback close enough to look on.

A tablet filled with notes corresponding to indicators

of questionable entries rested in front of her.

"For the second time in the same day I'm impressed with what you've accomplished. Do you sleep?"

The genuine admiration in his voice became "gravy" on the meat and potatoes of the week's accomplishments. Little in Bethany's life gave her the joy and satisfaction of a job well done, a problem solved, and the sense she'd helped. But his appreciation came close. "When I'm tired. This"—her hand swept the expanse of the study—"is a big jigsaw puzzle. Solvable, but some of the pieces are missing."

"No surprise there."

The magic of the day began slipping away. "We need the bank summaries for this past quarter. The further back I went, the better they matched. Up to a year ago the numbers added up with very small variances. This past year, though, there are holes big enough to drive . . . a herd of horses through."

She looked up at him. "There's a deeper story here, Matthew, but I'm not sure what it is because I don't know the mining business."

"That's partly why I asked you to do this. If the money isn't buried somewhere in the books, I need to find out where it went. Thus far, I've no idea why the mine is so heavily encumbered by debt." He studied the papers she handed off with cryptic explanations of their contents.

In truth, she'd slept little since accepting this task. Now, after seeing Matthew's reaction to the stranger who sought him out at the schoolhouse, it seemed worth the sacrifice. "I've done only a cursory review."

Matthew reached in front of her and flipped the edges of the tablet. "Given my schedule, it would have taken me two weeks to get this far."

"Well, I didn't know what you were looking for, and it has taken me a little while to figure out the methodology." She bit her tongue to keep from explaining the difference between the methods employed now and the standardization in twenty-first century accounting practices. Good grief, she'd nearly overdone it again. She couldn't count the number of times her sisters had accused her of starting with the first atom during the creation of the universe when delving into a problem.

"What's your initial impression?"

"I don't want to rush to any conclusions." She hated to be the bearer of bad news.

He scooted the ledger she'd created around to examine it. "No one will accuse you of jumping to conclusions. And I assure you, I'll go over every note and reference you've made."

He retrieved a folio he'd carried in from the buggy. "I've made my own list of observations and questions. Let's do a quick comparison and see if we're looking at the same things."

The room assumed a close, crowded feeling. Logically, she knew the walls weren't moving; it was sitting so close to Matthew that made them feel that way. It was being in the same room, alone with him.

The battle flags of the war she waged between reason and desire flapped at full mast. The quicker she retreated or drove him away, the better. Her detailed notes were self-explanatory and easy to follow—or as easy as something as complex as the Gray Wolf Mine ledgers could be.

"Would you like to take my notes with you to Mama Johanson's?" she asked. "You know where to find me if you have any questions or need my help."

"Yeah. You've made amazing progress." He sorted and stacked the files and papers on the desk.

Bethany scooted back in the big leather chair and folded her hands on her lap. "I noticed your marks all through some of the files and ledgers. Let me ask you straight out: Is there someone within the Gray Wolf Mine you suspect of embezzling or diverting funds?"

He gave her a tight nod and remained silent.

"Then I'm sure you've already started comparing every invoice with what was ordered, checked them against the payment schedules and bank statements." Her heart skipped a beat. "And checked how many times each invoice was paid," she added softly.

"You think that's how he's doing it?"

Raising a hand in protest, she hurriedly answered, "I don't know. Without bouncing the purchase orders and invoices against the books and bank statements, I can't say. It's just a thought. A possibility. There seem to be a number of terribly repetitive entries, particularly for timbers and explosives. Given the cost of shipping, the cost of—"

"I thought you didn't know anything about mining."

"I don't. But I know a little about the fluctuating costs of doing business of any kind. I didn't see those cycles reflected in the books. That's all I'm saying." She pushed her final stack of files at him and stifled a yawn.

Matthew gathered his things and stood. "Time to let you get some well-deserved rest."

"I am tired." She slid out of her chair. "I suspect you have a great deal of work ahead of you." He had to go. Now. The longer she watched the way his body moved beneath his blue chambray shirt, the weaker her defenses became. At the strangest times she imagined slowly unbuttoning his shirt and running her fingers through his silky chest hair. If she wasn't careful, she'd lose herself in such thoughts.

She waited for him at the study door, then led the way down the stairs. By the time she reached the foyer, her back was on fire from the heat of his gaze. Flustered, she stopped at the door and faced him.

He stood a few inches from her. A slight frown darkened his expression. Desire blazed in his blue eyes.

"You picked a helluva time to show up in my life, Bethany James."

"I didn't pick the time or the place," she answered, breathless. This close, she noticed flecks of black in his eyes. Bittersweet longing coursed through her. Her heart hammered in anticipation of his kiss.

Just when she raised her hand and rested her fingertips on his chest, she didn't know. The heat of his body, the cadence of his heart, each seeped through his soft shirt.

A lump formed in her throat. She didn't want to think about what was happening. With Matthew, one kiss was one too many, but a million wouldn't slake the desire racing through her. She didn't want an affair—and wasn't that all she could have in an era where her presence was so tenuous?

He set the papers on the corner of the foyer table, his gaze never leaving hers. His big hands framed the sides of her head. "Let me kiss you," he whispered.

Captivated by his movements, which were drowning her rationality, she couldn't answer, couldn't move. He kissed her.

The light pressure of his lips on hers turned her bones to jelly. She inhaled sharply, drawing the scent of him deep into her lungs and indelibly imprinting him on her memory.

He drew back and she leaned forward, as though pulled by an invisible cord.

Staring into his passion-dilated eyes, she ran the tip of her tongue over her lips. How could a man taste so good?

Matthew breathed a word she didn't understand, then lowered his head and kissed her again. This time his arms engulfed her, steel bands. His tongue invaded her mouth, explored its soft interior, and dared her to soar into mindless passion with him.

In response, her body squirmed against his. Bethany was very aware that each movement pressed her against the erection straining at his trousers, yet she was powerless to stop herself. She was lost, more lost than when the River of Time carried her away from Wyoming. For the moment, she didn't care where she was swept as long as Matthew Gray never stopped kissing her.

# *Chapter Thirteen*

Matthew held the curtain aside and stared out his second-floor window at Mama Johanson's. A summer storm rolled over the trees, bending branches and sending conifer needles skittering along the ground. A faint drizzle caught the wind and splattered pin-sized droplets against the glass.

He shouldn't have kissed Bethany.

He wasn't sorry he had, nor did he delude himself into thinking he wouldn't do it again. Given the opportunity, he would taste Bethany's sweet, hot mouth again—if she allowed. But that was all.

Even if she were to want more, he wouldn't take the chance of planting his child in her womb.

It didn't matter that women gave birth without complications every day, he was still afraid. And logic had nothing to do with fear. And as much as he wanted to be with Bethany, to make love to the enigmatic school teacher, the idea of some mishap, some unwanted pregnancy killing her was a shadow that loomed in his mind.

Victoria's bloodcurdling screams during the final hours of her life filled his ears. Nothing kept away the agonizing sounds, the screams that had faded into moans as her energy and her life bled away.

He'd stayed and done anything he could to help her, but it had been for naught. Had a man ever felt so damned useless?

*Felt useless?* Hell, teats on a boar had more purpose than he'd had the night Victoria and Ethan died.

Things might have turned out fine if Victoria hadn't contracted influenza during the final month of her pregnancy.

*If* the illness hadn't left her tired and weak . . .

*If* Ethan hadn't tried to enter the world feet first . . .

*If* Megan could have stopped the bleeding . . .

*If* the cord hadn't become tangled around his fragile neck . . .

*If.*

A thousand *ifs* changed nothing.

The day he laid Victoria and Ethan in their grave, he'd vowed no other woman would die because of him. He didn't need children—or another wife who could only hope to expect them.

He'd put all thoughts of sharing his life aside. He'd spent his time expanding his business and inventing machines to improve life in the mines.

The diversions had worked until Bethany James's unexpected arrival. Unknowingly, she had touched his heart and reminded him of a future he'd once planned with a very different woman, a future that, like Victoria, belonged in the past. He was a different man now, with different goals. But his dreams were haunted.

Bethany was a test. God, she was that and so much more. Her small frame would surely split in two if she had a child, particularly a baby the size of Ethan.

Bethany enticed him in the same fashion the mythical sirens lured unsuspecting sailors to their fate. Yet, she seemed as affected as he, and unaware of the deep water their desire swept them toward.

Matthew suspected the powerful kiss they'd shared had stunned her as if had himself. Damn, no woman kissed the way she did—hungry, naïve, assertive, fearful, daring.

In the space of a heartbeat, he'd experienced an epiphany. He hadn't thought it possible to experience such an overwhelming sensation twice in a lifetime. With Bethany in his arms Matthew felt complete.

Yet everything was wrong. Caution demanded he close his mind and heart to her. The woman had more holes in her background than a cold-water miner's screen. She was great with kids, but she had strange ideas and was entirely unknown. She was too dangerous.

And yet, caution was a cold companion.

Her origins and reasons for venturing to Juneau had made no difference during their kiss. Logic held little sway against the genuineness of her giving nature and the heat of her pent-up passion.

A flood of hope salted with trepidation and desire surged in him. He fought to keep the wild sensation under control, but the very existence of his growing feelings for Bethany unnerved him to the point of distraction.

He turned back to the papers she'd prepared.

Try as he might, concentration on the growing problem of the Gray Wolf's finances was hard to obtain. Starting at the waves of numbers in the small hours of the morning, he sorted out what bothered him.

A feeling of completion, of being whole, had soothed his soul for the brief time he'd held her against his heart. But the aching emptiness was back. He'd endured it since leaving her, and it grew with each passing moment.

He hated missing Bethany, thinking about her, wanting her at all hours of the day and night. He had no time for personal involvement, but the way she pervaded his every thought wouldn't allow him to ignore the effect.

As he pondered, morning rolled in with clouds and the threat of rain. He went to his office on Fifth Street before breakfast. The mountain of work waiting on his drafting table couldn't wait for a resolution to the Gray Wolf Mine's financial conundrum.

He worked steadily until early afternoon, when he stopped long enough to eat a quick meal at the Blue Heron. Leaving the drafting table freed his mind to toy with the mine's problems.

He'd begun to doubt all the answers lay hidden in the ledgers. Something was missing.

Bethany had flagged a dozen subtle inconsistencies in the entries, and her findings had dovetailed with his and pointed out additional discrepancies that raised even more questions, but it all pointed toward a missing element.

Lawrence Camden had to know more than he'd revealed. The last few months before his death, George Gray hadn't left the house; the final month, he'd spent in bed. Yet the questionable expenses had continued well after the Old Man's illness had confined him.

Matthew donned his rain gear and set out for Camden's office at the mine, sure if he didn't find him there, he'd find him at home.

An hour later, unable to locate the mine manager and feeling the press of time, Matthew settled behind the executive's desk at the Gray Wolf and pored over a stack of files.

He was missing something important.

Bethany put the last calligraphied nametag into place. Tomorrow morning, fifteen students would file in, find their names and places, and gaze at her with expectant eyes. A slate, chalk, and soft wiping cloth waited at each student's assigned seat. Ink bottles, pens, pencils, and paper lay in orderly fashion over the top of the front bookcase.

She clasped her hands and took a final look around. A sense of satisfaction fueled her anticipation of her first day of school. She smiled at the thought of being the teacher of this Little Schoolhouse on the Tundra. Okay, not the tundra, but certainly the frontier.

The blackboard on the left side of the room had two lines of the alphabet printed at the top. The chalk crutch she'd found in the supply bin at the back of the room had helped create the three evenly spaced lines defining the boundaries of the letters. The successive letters of the cursive alphabet ran neatly above the top of the board on the right side of the room.

With a hammer in hand and two nails clamped between her teeth, Bethany dragged a stool to the front wall.

The back door of the schoolhouse opened, startling her. Palm flat against the wall, she braced herself and balanced precariously on the low stool. A gust of cool, moist air raced into the room and coiled around her ankles.

She cast a concerned glance over her shoulder, wondering who would venture out in a summer storm so late in the day.

It was Matthew Gray. He shucked his slicker without breaking stride through the cloakroom, and rain spiked the front of his disheveled hair along his forehead. He approached, himself like a thunderhead. A thunderous scowl reflected the lightning in his eyes.

Bethany's palms began to sweat. Butterflies returned to the pit of her stomach. All her senses were ratcheted into hyperawareness. The power of him overwhelmed her.

Her fingers curled against the wall. The flat, unyielding surface helped maintain her balance on the stool and keep her focused. What she needed was a handle for stabilizing her internal excitement. For the first time since she knew the rest of her life would be doomed to celibacy—and decided that it would be for the best—she dared to imagine a different possibility.

Then she rethought.

Real intimacy, particularly with Matthew Gray, carried its own punishment. She did not intend to subject herself to that kind of misery.

Even at best, he'd ask questions about the torturous scars running from between her breasts to her pelvic bone and from hip to hip. After two years, the incisions had faded from angry red lines to blend with the pigment of her flesh, but they were still there.

She tore her gaze from Matthew's and shuddered. If the scars weren't the ultimate turnoff to lovemaking, the explanation he'd demand would be. And they would destroy everything else, including her employment.

Instead of giving in to the flood of emotion threatening to overwhelm her, she resorted to the survival tactic responsible for redirecting her life. She sought detachment. Later, she'd deal with her feelings.

Yes, later.

When she was alone.

Determined to postpone the inevitable emotional chaos approaching, she hammered the first nail into the wall. The vehemence of each blow bolstered her conviction to cling to the straight and narrow. She had refused to play the victim two years ago; she would make the same refusal now. So, life wasn't fair. She'd managed to overcome worse.

Matthew's silent presence in the center of the room drew her eyes.

Bethany paused, determined to concentrate on one thing at a time, to ignore the tantalizing man watching her every move. She took the second nail from between her teeth and hammered it in.

"Would you please hand the map to me?" she then asked.

Her heart accelerated with the sound of each step he took across the hardwood floor. She had a thousand things to say to him, none of which would cross her lips. Each translated to *You drive me out of my mind with want, but we're racing down a dead-end street.*

"You shouldn't be climbing on things, particularly when you're alone." His softly spoken admonition sounded at odds with the storm she'd seen in Matthew's expression. Well, at least she wasn't the only one hiding her feelings.

"The stool is sturdy enough."

"What if you fall?"

Too late. *I've already fallen—for you. The trick now is to keep from self-destructing.*

"Give me the hammer," he demanded.

With her left hand bracing her against the wall for balance, she put the hammer in his palm. "Please," she said. "Hand me the maps and I'll hang them."

He placed the hammer on her desk. Instead of fetching the map, he caught her at the waist and lifted her from the stool.

Startled, she let out a muffled cry and quickly reached for stability, which turned out to come from the ledge of his broad shoulders.

The world around her ceased to exist. Secure in his arms, her body sinuously gliding down his, she felt each wrinkle in their clothing. The heavenly experience lasted until her tiptoes reached the floor. He smelled of rain, evergreens, and the faint hint of bay rum.

Her pulse pounded for a repeat of yesterday's kiss. Her head cried out against indulging this passion with inevitable disastrous consequences.

Staring into his emotion-filled blue eyes, she saw a yearning that reached into her core, and she didn't think it possible to want his arms around her and his mouth on hers more than she did at that moment.

Anguish forced her to look away. "I can't have you," she whispered, her hands sliding down his tension-coiled shoulders.

"Yes, you can." He lowered his head. Then, obviously fighting with something, he said, "All you have to do is want me."

A hollow laugh wrenched from her nightmarish past escaped. Summoning all her courage, she pushed away. "It isn't so simple."

He didn't release her.

"Please, Matthew," she begged in a whisper. The torture of his desire made her voice break.

Reluctantly, he eased his hold, his fingers trailing along her flesh to prolong their physical contact.

She retrieved the map roll propped against the side of the oak teacher's desk. "I need to hang this."

"I'll do it."

"I'm used to fixing my classroom by myself." *And it would be so easy to get used to having you around. And so very, very dangerous for both of us.*

Gazing steadily at her, he took the map. "You try so hard to be an island. Why?"

"I don't know what you mean." She turned away, wanting him to know the truth—yet not wanting it.

He hung the map roll, tested it, then added the security of two additional nails. "That should hold it." He set the hammer on the desk. "Why is it so hard for you to accept the smallest assistance?"

She felt his gaze burning into her, so she answered. "I've leaned not to take anything—or anyone—for granted. Self-sufficiency is the cornerstone of independence." *That's me. Miss Independent.*

"A woman should have a man around she can rely on," Matthew said from where he stood at the desk. "And I don't necessarily mean a husband."

"A woman should have a lot of things," she agreed. "However, a man—husband or not—isn't essential." Those adolescent, romantic dreams she'd rejected with the prospect of marriage and a family two years ago. She drew a heavy breath. "I think this conversation is over." Poised for whatever tack he might take, she gathered her work tools and carefully put them in a satchel.

He gave a tired smile. "A conversation needs a minimum of two participants, so apparently it is." He offered her hammer back to her but held on to it until she met his volatile blue gaze.

"What do you want to discuss, Matthew? A kiss that should never have happened?" His scowl assured her that she was right to put an end to the false impression she'd created the previous evening. This was a man she could not afford to love. With great effort and a quickening heart, she tore her gaze from his.

Strong arms spun her toward him. The next thing she knew, she was staring up into an anguish-filled face. Her heart cried out, but her voice remained silent.

"You're going to deny what we felt?"

"No," she whispered. "I have no doubt we both know lust when we experience it."

"Lust? Is that all that was?"

"For me." The acid lie scorched her mouth. With every fiber of her being she wanted to break the hypnotic trance of his predatory gaze, pull away from the restraint of his embrace and flee. Her muscles refused to do anything but melt against him.

Lightning flashed outside. Thunder boomed with the force of metal drums rolling across the roof. Rain beat against the little schoolhouse. The air crackled with anticipation.

"Liar," he said with a growl low in his throat.

Before she could protest, he cradled the back of her head and covered her mouth with his.

The surprise of his gentle, tantalizing kiss crumbled her armor like a sand castle attempting to hold back the tide. Everything in her cried out to abandon reason.

The strength of his arms kept her from dissolving into mush as all Bethany's senses screamed with awareness. Matthew's sensuous heat overwhelmed her, obliterated the chill of the room.

Her nostrils filled with the tang of fresh paint, floor varnish, and the unique aroma of the man probing her lips with the tip of his tongue.

Of their own accord, her arms lifted and entwined behind his neck. Being in his embrace felt so right, so perfect.

A defense mechanism in the back of her brain clicked off. The hunger for his kiss, for the magic of his touch, took over. She responded like a starving woman offered sustenance for her body and soul. Every inch of her reveled in the awareness of his thighs pressed against hers, the undeniable proof of his desire against her abdomen, and the quickening of his heartbeat.

Tiny pinpricks of pleasure danced along the places where their skin touched. Uninhibited, lost in the moment, she explored his mouth and inhaled the aroma of his rain-soaked skin.

The pressure of his fingers moving back and forth against her scalp drew her into a rhythm of lovemaking. The subtle motion hinted of an erotic dance, slow and sinuous, flowing from deep within and leading to an inevitable joining.

Even as she stole the brief moments of connecting on this intimate plane with Matthew, savored the brief glory of his kiss and touch, she knew it wouldn't last. And dear

God, as much as she wanted it to never end, she knew it must.

Before losing her entire mind to the desire burning her flesh, she pushed away. The dark passion she glimpsed in his expression spurred her to speak.

"I can't do this," she managed, hating the shakiness of her voice. "I can't . . ."

Without another word, she grabbed the satchel and hurried across the classroom. On the way through the cloakroom, she snatched her slicker and rushed out into the storm. Not until the door closed behind her did she pause long enough to pull on the garment and secure her heavy valise within its oilcloth protection.

Lightning flashed, followed by another round of booming thunder. Wind snagged the hood protecting her head and blew it back. Rain pelted her curly hair, matting it to her scalp and forehead.

She did not attempt to protect her head. The rain mingled with the tears flowing down her cheeks.

With a mood as foul as the storm outside, Matthew locked the school and dashed to his waiting buggy.

Bethany had managed half a block before he caught up to her.

"Get in," he demanded. "You can't walk home in this weather."

"Sure I can." She didn't even look up.

"Please, let me drop you off in front of Gray House."

She stopped.

He halted the horse.

"Don't get down," she said, scrambling up to the seat even as he rose to help her.

Neither spoke during the wet, tense ride.

"Bethany . . ." he started when at last they stopped in front of the porch at Gray House. He wasn't sure what to say.

"Thanks for the ride." She bolted up the steps to the front door.

Moments later, he was staring at a closed door.

He'd lost his mind. Nothing else explained why he'd thrown caution and logic to the winds.

He knew better.

Aside from all his complex personal reasons to avoid her, there was still the matter of the mystery surrounding Bethany. She held a great many secrets that she did not want to share with him.

No question she'd lend a hand with damn near anything asked of her. She was a hard worker, and creative ideas and innovative ways of viewing a problem flowed from her generous nature.

But on a personal, private level, clams could learn a thing or two from her.

Sitting back in his seat, he couldn't figure out which was greater, his anger that she'd refused them both the completion of their kiss or his relief that she wouldn't allow anything between them.

The woman made him crazy.

*Wanting her* made him crazy.

But he had to be half out of his mind to extend her a single thought outside their business dealings.

He returned to his office. When he lifted his head, Lawrence Camden stood under the eaves.

Matthew stopped in his tracks. The elusive omine manager had picked a helluva time to surface. Until this moment, Matthew would have wagered that Camden had been purposely avoiding him.

"Mr. Gray." Camden touched the oilskin cover on the brim of his hat. "I received your message."

Matthew didn't bother asking which message, as he'd left several in various places. "Thank you for braving the storm."

"It is a nasty one," Camden agreed, stepping away from the main door.

If subsequent findings confirmed Matthew's suspicions, this storm was nothing compared to what would happen inside his office.

He opened the door, removed his slicker, and hung it in the mud alcove. He led the way through the outer office where his assistant oversaw the work schedules and correspondence, and into the rear area. He lit a lamp on his desk and picked up a pencil that had fallen from his drafting table.

"I understand you spent a great deal of the afternoon rooting through my files."

"When did they become your files, Camden?" On edge from the frustrations of the day, Matthew couldn't help but indulge his desire to be rude to the other man.

An easy grin, so much a part of his charm, lightened Camden's somber expression. "I guess when you've spent as much time building a mine and worrying over its financial aspects, you develop a proprietary attitude."

"The files you take such jealous responsibility for are incomplete. A number of invoices for the last year are missing."

"They aren't missing. Misplaced or misfiled, perhaps. Unfortunately, your father's accountant, Howard Cantwell, returned to the States three months ago and I haven't found a suitable replacement. As you've discovered, some of our bookkeeping has fallen behind since his departure.

"My successor will undoubtedly have his own preferences and hire someone he trusts. He'll be working closely with whomever he selects."

Camden's patronizing tone added to Matthew's irritation. "Where are the latest bank summaries?"

"I gave them to your father."

Years of conditioning to utter nothing negative concerning his father kept Matthew silent. Certainly he'd speak no ill of the dead to this man. He leaned against the edge of his desk, folded his arms, and studied Camden for a moment. "You do realize it behooves you to find those records. In good conscience, I can't bring in your replacement until this is straightened out."

Camden's affable smile melted. "Until *what* is straightened out?"

"The reason the mine is heavily in debt. The books aren't readable. Who is going to sign onto the outfit willingly, Camden? It's a bed of snakes. Would you?"

"No, I wouldn't. However, you cannot hold *me* responsible for decisions your father made or actions he took. He tied my hands. I'll not allow you to do the same.

"I'm leaving no later than September, with my bonus. Try to interfere and we'll end up before a judge." The man's smile returned, and there was a sinister glint in his eye. "I assure you, you won't have a prayer of prevailing."

"The sooner we get this mess straightened out, the sooner you can head to Seattle." Matthew straightened. "With your bonus, of course." He was as anxious to get rid of Lawrence Camden as the man was to leave. But not before he got to the bottom of things. "All I'm looking for is a little cooperation."

"You have my cooperation. Exactly what is it you're looking for?"

"I want all invoices for the last two years, and all equipment orders."

"Any particular reason?"

"I intend to compare them with the books." *Thank you for the suggestion, Bethany James.*

"I'll see what I can find," Camden snapped, then started for the door. "Anything else?"

"Not at the moment."

Matthew continued leaning against the edge of his desk

long after the other man's departure. The adversarial bent of their conversation rankled him.

This inheritance of his was beginning to stink worse than a whaling dock in summer, and Lawrence Camden seemed the source.

# *Chapter Fourteen*

Bethany had never worked harder as a teacher than this first week of school in Juneau. Each night she fell into bed exhausted. In the morning, she hurried to her classroom. She remained vigilant for any signs of a way back to her own era.

From the first day, brown-eyed Laurie Craddock captured her interest. Although Bethany was far removed from Drexel, some things remained unchanged—like the presence of unhappy children or Bethany's desire to nurture them. Sadness enveloped the quiet Laurie, small for her age, and so vulnerable that the other fourteen students protected her. Nothing in the records Ian McKenzie left provided insight into the child's background. And Laurie volunteered nothing, not even when delicately questioned.

Thoughts of the freckle-faced six-year-old weighed heavily on Bethany's mind as she walked home from school Friday evening. Certain something wasn't right in the child's home, she decided to ask Megan or Matthew about the Craddock family. Most disturbing was her fear that she would find Laurie had a history of bruises that could stem from physical abuse.

Tired and nervous, Bethany entered the gate to Gray House. She slowed at the sight of Matthew sitting on the steps, reading the paper.

Her heart skipped a beat.

And here she'd thought she was doing so well at conquering her preoccupation with her landlord!

His scowl increased as she approached, but her gaze feasted on the sight of him.

"Is the lemon you're sucking really as sour as you look?" she asked from the bottom of the porch steps.

He folded the paper and rose. "It seems so."

They'd managed to avoid one another for five of the shortest days and longest nights Bethany had known. Next week would be different, less stressful, but nonetheless exciting, with the challenge of her diverse students. She'd already settled into a kind of routine, but she wondered if it would even dispel the allure of her employer.

"Are you here to scold me for extending the school day fifteen minutes for those who wanted to sing at the Fourth of July festivities?" She figured the best defense was a good offense.

"No. Though it comes as no surprise you found a way to circumvent my concerns." He tucked the folded newspaper under his arm. "I need to search the study."

"For anything in particular?" She was pleased he respected her privacy enough to wait for her to let him into his own house.

"Something we haven't found yet. I've checked every damn nook and cranny at the Gray Wolf offices and haven't found the records I need to make sense of all this." He pushed the big front door wide after she unlocked it, then followed her inside.

Out of habit, she locked the door and set the key on the foyer table. "Mmm. Smell that? Mrs. Feeney has made something wonderful for dinner. Go on up. I'll be there shortly."

A side trip into the kitchen made her grin. As promised this morning, Mrs. Feeney had made crab cakes. The pie cooling on the sideboard was a bonus. Bethany inhaled the aroma. Of course the pie was her favorite—it had crust.

Upstairs, lamps blazed on every surface in the study. The desk's drawers sat atop the desk.

"What on earth are you doing?"

Frowning, Matthew barely afforded her a glance. "The only thing I know left to do; take this room apart one piece at a time."

Bethany stood on the business side of the desk and peered into the drawers brimming with papers.

"And we're looking for?"

"Anything that might explain the mine's heavy debt."

Bethany grabbed a handful of pillowcases from the linen closet. "Why don't we use these to sort things?"

"Good idea. You finish with the desk. I'll go through the bookcases and cupboards."

"Did he hide things in his favorite books?" Bethany asked.

"My mother read prodigiously. She loved fiction." He pulled a book from the shelf and examined the spine. "I can't say whether or not my father's preferences changed in that direction the last few years of his life, or if he collected all these books as a tribute to her."

"Was he a non-fiction reader?" Bethany began sorting through the highest stack on the desk. Correspondence, statements, and notes interspersed old periodicals and newspapers.

"Yes." He turned the book over and fanned the pages.

Paper money soared through the air and fluttered to the floor.

"Son of a bitch," he whispered, his gaze meeting hers.

"Great Gerty's ghost." Bethany peered down at the bills settling around his feet. "Did he always hide money in books?"

"No." His gaze traveled the breadth of the bookcases. "My mother did."

Bethany wondered if George Gray hadn't adopted a number of his wife's idiosyncrasies and preferences as the time to join her shortened.

"Forget the desk." He riffled the book's pages a second time before returning it to the shelf. "Start at the other end of the room and check the books on any shelves you can reach."

"Don't mock my height," she said with feigned indignation.

"Why would I do that?"

He appeared so stone-cold serious, she didn't know whether to laugh. Rather than guess wrong, she tossed a pillowcase at him. "Clean up that mess at your feet."

"When I'm done."

She grabbed a second pillowcase and headed to the far side of the room. "Trick or treat," she said, checking the first book on the shelf she'd chosen. The crackle of the binding when she lifted the cover indicated that the book had not yet enjoyed a good reading.

Several bills floated to the floor.

A quick glance his way told her he was watching.

"Why would your father stash so much money in these books?"

"I don't know," he answered solemnly. "I don't know why he did many things."

"Like saving the quilt you found the day you helped move me?" Treading on thin ice, she spoke softly but didn't expect an answer.

"My mother made that quilt and gave it to me nearly twenty years ago. I thought he'd burned it." The book he slid onto the shelf hit the back of the case with a thud.

"Good grief, why would he burn—"

"Because he burned every memento I had of her. The only thing I have left, a book, *Grimms's Fairy Tales*, she used to read to me. I hid it from him. My first memories are of her sitting on the bed after tucking me in, reading that book until I fell asleep. The next night, she'd continue from the spot where I drifted off."

"My mother read to us, too, but not every night," Bethany mused. Alicia and Caitlyn had waited to sell the ranch until Bethany recovered sufficiently to agree to their plans. Sorting their parents' personal things had been a tearful, painful, yet healing experience. They'd relived memories and laughed and cried simultaneously during the week they spent clearing out the ranch house.

"My mother had a mauve sweater she wore all the time. It was her favorite. I slept with it for a year after . . ." Once again, she'd allowed her alligator mouth to run on. "The sweater smelled of her," she added, meeting Matthew's unwavering gaze. "And I have no idea why I told you that."

An almost imperceptible nod accompanied a softening of his features. "I understand."

The realization that he did understand struck her. And his seemed a level of loss she couldn't fathom. She had no desire to play victim or compare wounds.

She turned back to the bookcases. "Want to guess how much money is here?"

He checked another book and both watched several bills sail into the pile growing at his feet. "Sure."

"You first," she challenged, counting the bookshelves and guestimating the number of books.

The pillowcase she'd tossed to him earlier became useful. Sinking to one knee, he collected the money strewn across the floor. Before dropping the bills inside, he examined the denominations. "Based on what I've got here, I'd say close to forty thousand."

"Fair enough. But I'd say there is more than that. Fifty thousand, at least."

"Nothing the Old Man did would surprise me now," Matthew said, reaching for another book. "Keep an eye open for papers of any kind. He may have put the loan papers in one of these."

Bethany resumed the search and hummed as she worked. The hum blossomed into a soft song.

They worked for several hours, examining every book in the bookcases. The proliferation of paper money filled both pillowcases. At last, they went downstairs to eat.

They set a second place at the dining room table and shared the meal Doreen Feeney had left for Bethany. Although the crab cakes were melt-in-your-mouth delicious and filling, they delved into the berry pie as though they hadn't eaten in a week.

"Now what?" she asked Matthew. Both had maintained a safe distance while working in different parts of the study.

"You should count the money. I'll keep looking for the loan papers."

"Do they have anything to do with the august Cornelius Lassiter?"

"That's part of what I hope to discover. He's made quite a splash, hasn't he?"

"He strikes me as a man accustomed to swimming with the sharks and coming out on top." She toyed with the last crumbs of piecrust remaining on her plate. "I heard him talking to Jeb at the store yesterday. He's smoother than a snake-oil salesman at a county fair but dresses better. I'll bet his clothes wouldn't wrinkle on a hot day in Panama."

"Where the hell do you come up with your metaphors?"

He cut another sliver of pie and put it on her plate.

"You'd be surprised." She tilted her fork. Flaky piecrust crumbled. "Is he going to stay around for a while?"

"Are you interested in Mr. Lassiter's social life or his business with me?" His wry half-smile indicated he suspected the latter.

Bethany shrugged. "Him. He's the only one in town who seems more out of place than me."

"Now that you mention it, he is an obvious stranger. We're not accustomed to men who travel with a cadre of lackeys. Dogs, horses, work gangs, yes. Even the Northwest Mounted Police stop here on their way to some little settlement called Darwin or Dousham."

"Dawson," she corrected without thinking. "It's on the Alaskan border on the Yukon side." She finished the last crumb of her second piece of pie and reached for his empty plate to clean up. "Mr. Lassiter doesn't seem like a Klondiker. Besides, the gold rush won't start there for another year or two."

Strong fingers closed around her wrist. She froze, her gaze darting to his. "What?"

"How the hell would you know that?"

Staring into his stormy blue eyes, she realized what she'd said. The teaching mode of her persona kept running after she'd left the classroom. The hours of working with Matthew in the study had formed a false bond of camaraderie.

"Kn-know what?"

"About Dawson, to start with."

"It's on the map." The flicker of his left eyebrow made her question whether she'd just dug the hole a little deeper. "Isn't it?"

"No."

"I must have heard someone talking about it, then." Her forearm shook in his hand, just like the rest of her body. No wonder she never got away with anything; she was too easily shaken.

"Like they were talking about a gold rush a year from now?"

She wished he'd shout instead of speaking in such calm, lethal tones. The dismal thought of her slip turned the pie in her stomach to stone. She couldn't let him know how unnerved she was or he'd have even more questions.

Be cool. Divert him. Evade him.

The pie stones turned to boulders. She'd never pull this off. And now wasn't the time to reveal any secrets. After all, Matthew Gray was her landlord and her employer. If he thought she had a loose screw in her head, she'd be up the proverbial creek without a paddle. And out in the cold.

"I . . ." *have terminal foot-in-mouth disease*. As though in self-defense, her throat closed. Whatever she might have said remained locked in silence. A thousand things raced through her mind. None offered an out for the gaffe she'd committed.

"You *what*?"

She tried to swallow, but her throat remained locked tight. Instead, she stared at his hand gripping her wrist. Good Galloping Gerty, he could snap her arm.

He wouldn't, she knew, but his strength was awesome nonetheless. A long, tense minute passed before he released her. Bethany popped to her feet. "Do I need to leave, Matthew?"

He folded his arms over his chest. "Leave? Of course not. All I'm asking for is a few answers."

"I thought that's what we were doing, looking for answers in the study."

"I'm not going to get any about you, am I?"

It took all her courage to look him in the eye and remain silent. She'd never been good at playing a role.

Her loathing for deception hadn't allowed her to lie. Where, oh where was the River of Time? She had to go home. Soon. Before it was too late. The razor-thin edge she balanced on seemed to be growing narrower by the moment.

"What are you hiding, Bethany?"

"Not nearly as much as your father," she answered with a lightness she didn't feel. If she kept the focus on his problem, he might not create more for her. "Speaking of him, I'm going to count money." She fled.

He didn't follow her to the study right away. She heard him rummaging through the parlor and downstairs office.

From her place in the middle of the floor and flanked with piles of money, she barely glanced in his direction when he returned. "Any luck downstairs?" She stretched another rubber band around a stack.

"No, but I didn't expect to find anything. I just needed to make sure." He was apparently resigned to her silence, for he simply returned to the tornado-stricken desk and began sorting.

"Why did your father want two offices?"

"He didn't like people coming to his house, but he liked working at home. According to Doreen, he spent most of his time in here or in his bedroom. He reserved the downstairs study for rare business callers." He glanced over the mess on the desk. "All that's down there is basic stationery."

Bethany finished counting the last of the bills. One by one, she dropped all the stacks into a pillowcase. "I win."

Matthew looked up from behind the desk. "How much?"

"Fifty thousand on the nose. Feel free to double-check."

"Fifty thousand is the amount of the last loan."

She nodded, wondering if George Gray had hidden the cash from the other loans throughout the house.

"Why don't I start looking through some of the other

rooms? From what we've seen, he might not have been thinking clearly the last few months before he died."

Where would a disoriented, sick man too weak to go downstairs hide loan papers and nearly a half million dollars?

"Go ahead. Start in his room. Use the mirror on the dresser to check the underside of the drawers. My mother used to put her important papers under a drawer," Matthew said.

Considering the way George Gray had worshipped his dead wife, it made sense for him to adopt her practices, particularly when he was preparing to meet her again in the next life.

Leaving Matthew in the study, Bethany drew a deep breath and entered his father's room.

She lit a lamp and looked around. It wasn't that she had avoided exploring Gray House; she hadn't had the time. Now, she had orders to snoop and examine to her heart's content.

She began with the armoire and moved through the room.

An hour later, Matthew ducked his head in the door and showed her a large sheaf of papers. "It's getting late. I'd better go. I may have found something. Then again, maybe not. I'll come back for the money later, when the bank is open."

"Good night, then. I'll finish this room before I turn in."

"Bethany . . ."

"You might consider donating your father's clothing to one of the churches."

"Going through his personal things is very low on my list of priorities," he said with finality.

When she glanced at the door again, he was gone. Both relief and disappointment washed over her.

* * *

The sun rose long before the town awakened. Unable to sleep and weary of trying, Bethany straightened her room and prepared for the day.

On the way downstairs, she paused at the study door. Pillowcases laid on their sides held paper stacks. The one stuffed with money sat upright in the desk chair.

George Gray was certainly an eccentric.

Matthew hadn't finished his quest for the loan papers. Not by a long shot. He'd return to the house and continue, but she wouldn't be there.

She dashed out into the bright morning without so much as a cup of coffee. The urge to flee this place and time, but most of all Matthew Gray, was irrepressible.

Watching every word she said, worrying about slipping up and giving away her predicament was too tiring. Last night she'd literally let the cat out of the bag. What if she slipped like that during school?

She wouldn't, she assured herself. In the classroom, she worked from an outline for each group of children and did not deviate. The method kept her grounded and didn't allow the students to lure her into irrelevant discussions.

The classroom wasn't the real problem, though.

Matthew Gray was—or rather, how she felt about him. It still blew her mind that she'd slipped into enough of a comfort zone to slip as she had.

Morning dew clung to the grass. It collected on the bottom of her skirt as she crossed the cemetery on her way to Baby Webster's guardian angel.

Once again, she stood at the base of the monument and listened, hoping, praying to hear the distant whispers of the rushing River of Time.

The tang of a fresh day filled her nostrils. The rising sun and scrubbed air carried promise and possibilities. Her father had loved the dawn, particular during roundup. It had been a special time shared by the two of them.

They'd sat at the campfire while the coffee brewed.

Her father had made special coffee for her, with hot chocolate mixed in. God, how she wished he was here to talk to now. His long, drawn-out stories had always made her laugh, but they had always held wise answers.

Oh, what should she do?

If her present situation carried a lesson, she wasn't sure what it might be. The irony of her predicament was that even if she had listened, and believed, Yolanda's prophecy about the River of Time, she'd be in the same predicament. She'd given her word she'd sing for the witch. Hell would freeze over before she negated her integrity. And that's what it would have been.

"I kept my word, Yolanda; I sang for you! Is this my reward? Being stranded thousands of miles from home in another century?"

Her shout loosened something inside her.

"This *sucks*, Yolanda!"

The only response to her outburst was silence. It seemed even the birds awaited Yolanda's response.

Movement on her right sent her heart into her throat.

Oh, dear God in heaven. Why oh why hadn't she checked the whole graveyard before opening her mouth? At barely six o'clock on a Saturday morning, she'd expected to have the cemetery to herself.

"Who is Yolanda?" Matthew asked from beside the headstone of his wife and child.

"I'm not going there this early in the morning." Oh, *expletive!* Why couldn't she be sharing this corner of the graveyard with anyone except Matthew?

If it weren't for bad luck, she wouldn't have any luck at all.

"Who is Yolanda?" he asked again.

"I do have a life that has nothing to do with you." She patted the angel's hip, then leaned against the statue.

"Answer the question, Bethany."

"A woman I knew in Drexel."

"And you are . . . talking to her?"

Spontaneous laughter bubbled from Bethany. "Don't worry, Matthew. I haven't hit my head again." Something new washed over her.

He remained as immobile as the headstone hiding him from the waist down. As usual, he wore a white shirt, but this morning he'd forsaken the tie, vest, and suit jacket.

Staring at him, she wasn't sure whether she'd lost her mind or found it. A glimmer of the intrepid woman she'd been prior to the car crash was reemerging in this Alaskan frontier town. The mouse hiding in her clothing faded more each day. The niggling fear she'd awakened in the hospital with was gone.

She'd survived when everyone else had died.

She'd survived in spite of the odds stacked so high against her. Yes, she'd lost part of her self—physically and emotionally. Now, she stood on the brink of blending who she'd been with the woman she'd become. Fate had forced her hand.

"I've realized something." A sense of personal freedom soared through her. The lingering shadows of uncertainty fled.

"About Yolanda?"

She laughed. "Great Gerty's Ghost, Matthew! You're like a bulldog. Once you've sunk your teeth into an idea, you don't care about anything else."

"So now I am a source of amusement for you?"

She studied him as he approached. What was there about this man that made him better-looking and sexier every day? Had she less to lose, she'd completely disarm him by throwing her arms around his neck and giving him a juicy kiss. "Not you. *Me*."

"You think you amuse me?"

"Do I?"

"Not at the moment."

"That's too bad, because for the first time since my arrival—" A glance up the hill to the flowering snarl of thorny berry canes reminded her that she could have wound up with more than a bump on the head. "I feel whole."

She straightened and gave the granite statue beside her a friendly pat. She'd had another angel watching over her the last couple of years. Two of them, in fact. Her parents.

"Is that a physical assessment?"

"Oh, Matthew, I'll never be whole again physically, and I can't do anything about that. I don't know why, or what triggered it, but today I've found myself."

"Yolanda is the one who's lost?" His confusion was hardly reflected in his stony expression.

"Yolanda is dead, and I've no intention of discussing her with you—now or ever." And that was the beauty of recapturing her former self—she didn't have to explain anything.

"I don't expect you to understand," she continued. "Yesterday, you might have intimidated me, or laid a three-mile-deep guilt trip to pressure me to explain. Today . . . today, things are different. *I'm* different. It's like a switch turned on in my brain."

"Has this sort of thing happened to you before?" he asked in a soft voice he might use to calm a wild beast.

"Yes. Once, only in reverse," she answered and couldn't stop grinning. She shut her mouth before explaining she'd gone from Mighty Mouse to Minerva Milquetoast and was now regaining her inner superpowers. Oh, she'd never leap tall buildings in a single bound, but she could now surmount some emotional wreckage incurred on a rural Wyoming highway.

"Let me get this straight. You think you're two people and one of them is Yolanda?"

Hands on hips, she looked at him from head to toe. "Are you intentionally obtuse or aren't you listening?"

"I've listened since you got here. However, I've yet to make any sense of your babbling."

"Is that what I'm doing? Babbling?" Of course it seemed that way to him, she realized. He wasn't the one experiencing an epiphany.

"It seems so."

"Things are not always as they seem." Unable to stare into his troubled blue eyes another moment, she turned away. "I have a million things to do today and I never leave a graveyard without singing." She glanced over her shoulder; he hadn't moved from beside the granite angel. "Have you any preferences?"

He hesitated for a moment before answering, then spoke with an odd solemnity. "Sing for my son."

"I'd be honored."

He joined her at the headstone bearing the Gray names. Its polished surface of black granite held a simple elegance, and white-marble sculpture of a sleeping woman holding a baby to her breast stretched the width of the marker.

Megan had explained the details, but Bethany could not imagine the depth of Matthew's loss. Although she had wanted to ask more questions, she'd refrained. Two years hadn't blunted Megan's pain over the loss of her dearest friend and her child.

At the foot of Victoria and Ethan Gray's grave, Bethany closed her eyes and imagined her sisters beside her. A lullaby from their childhood began as a faint hum in her and grew into a song. The words and notes poured from her soul.

After she ended her songs for Ethan Gray, she sang for his mother. This time, she chose a song she'd written while in the hospital. It seemed appropriate because she'd written it for her own mother.

She and Matthew stood unmoving for several minutes after the notes drifted away.

"That was beautiful. More than beautiful, Bethany. Thank you," Matthew whispered, his head bowed.

"You're welcome." Then, she left the graveyard without a backward glance.

Today, she was brand-new, or at least well on her way to being her old self. Not until the sensation of having the world lifted from her shoulders registered had she understood the weight of her self-imposed burden. Maybe it had been almost dying, or actually dying and being resuscitated.... Whatever had raised the fear that had turned her into a cowering mouse was gone.

Strangely, she'd always thrived on stress. Now, it had brought back her old self. "Right," she said, whacking a tree limb with a stick she'd picked up. "I O.D.ed my mouse persona on stress. Good Lord, what was I afraid of?"

*Everything*, came a swift answer.

Suddenly she realized she'd been waiting for a white knight to ride out of the forest and rescue her. But he wasn't going to come. She'd have to do it herself. But that was fine.

If the River of Time had forsaken her, she'd have to build the best life possible with what she had—which, when she pondered the matter, was quite a bit.

Thinking of her college days, she laughed out loud and twirled around with her arms and stick extended. "And they said an American History minor was a waste of time. *Time*," she repeated. "Talk about hidden assets."

Right now, she had to go see a man about preparing for a gold rush in the Klondike.

# *Chapter Fifteen*

The clock Jeb Calahan had donated to keep time in the schoolroom chimed softly.

Where had the last few hours gone? The grumble of Bethany's stomach at the thought of Doreen Feeney's cooking and generous portions prompted her to finish the final entry in her teaching journal.

Two weeks as Juneau's schoolmarm had settled all her misgivings. Never in her wildest dreams had she believed teaching so many children of different ages, all in the same room, could be so challenging or exhilarating. And she would use the entire weekend to put the final touches on her preparations for the next week's lessons.

Time to go home to the culinary treat waiting for her in the warmer. Not having a microwave oven wasn't nearly as bad as she'd thought it would be—as long as she had Mrs. Feeney to cook for her.

The daily tasks she needed to perform before leaving the schoolhouse were becoming a ritual she barely thought about. With the lamps out, the windows closed, the assignments posted on the blackboards, papers graded and lying facedown at each child's place, she was ready to go.

The warm summer day was too nice for a coat, the breeze too unpredictable for her hat, and she was looking forward to getting out into it. When she was halfway across the schoolroom, the door opened.

For a fleeting moment she thought Matthew had come to see her. They had managed to avoid one another since Saturday morning in the graveyard, but they couldn't continue the tactic forever, though it was undeniably the smartest way to handle their attraction.

Instead of Matthew Gray, a young woman in an advanced stage of pregnancy emerged through the cloakroom door. Her big brown eyes scoured the schoolroom. Wisps of sweat-dampened blond hair hung from her chignon and clung to her neck. She carried a valise in one had and a carpetbag in the other. Her advanced pregnancy made the buttons on her suit jacket impossible to fasten.

"Hello. Can I help you?"

"I . . . I truly hope so. I'm seeking the schoolmaster, Mr. Ian McKenzie."

"Mr. McKenzie has left Juneau. I've taken his position here, Mrs. . . ." She let the inquiry hang for the young woman to finish.

Both pieces of luggage hit the floor with a bang. "Ian *must* be here. He . . ." Color drained from her face as she swayed.

Alarmed, Bethany tossed her hat and coat on the nearest chair in her rush to help. Her heart sank. This was a *child* having a child. "Hey, don't you faint on me."

"He must be here." The girl, a full head taller, clutched Bethany's shoulders in a desperate grip. Her trembling reverberated through Bethany's small frame and nearly knocked her off balance.

"Come. Let's sit you down." She pulled the closest chair into the aisle and turned the young woman until she settled onto the seat.

"When will he return?"

"I'm sorry, but I know next to nothing about Mr. McKenzie and even less about his travel plans. There is someone, Mr. Matthew Gray, who might be in touch with him." She withdrew her handkerchief and patted at the perspiration on the girl's face. "My God, you're burning up."

"I am not well. I need Ian. . . ."

"What's your name?" Bethany opened the high collar of the woman's blouse. Perspiration soaked the fabric.

"Mary Katherine . . . McKenzie. Mrs. Ian McKenzie." The way her glassy brown eyes flickered with uncertainty, Bethany deemed her a poor liar. Mary Katherine "McKenzie" was as alone here as Bethany—but not for long.

Whether sensing a kindred spirit or just softhearted, she wanted to help this girl. "How did you get here?"

"Oh, dear, my head is spinning." Mary Katherine reached blindly for something to hold. Her fingertips slapped the tabletop, groped, and found the edge. Her knuckles whitened under the pressure of her grip.

"Is there anyone I can contact for you? Have you family or friends I can fetch?" The girl seemed on the verge of collapse.

"What? Uh, no. Just Ian." She swayed in the chair, her free hand moving protectively over her distended abdomen. "I don't know what to do. I thought once I arrived, Ian would . . ."

Bethany developed a sudden, intense dislike for Ian McKenzie, former schoolmaster and soon-to-be-father. The gut-level suspicion Mary Katherine's last name wasn't McKenzie added to her antipathy.

"Tell you what, Mary Katherine. Why don't we get you situated on the floor so you won't have far to fall if you pass out. You need help and I'm going to see you get it."

Mary Katherine cooperated, seeming relieved that someone had stepped in to shoulder the burden.

Together, they situated her on the floor, her back against the wall, and her sides braced by her luggage.

"Oh, God!"

Alarmed, Bethany caught Mary Katherine's fear-stricken face in her hands and forced the girl to look at her. "What? What is it?" Her widened brown eyes made the woman's terror contagious. Gooseflesh rippled across Bethany's arms.

"The child . . ."

"Tell me you're not in labor. Forget it. I'm going to get help." *Megan, please, please be home.* She started to rise. Mary Katherine grappled for her hand.

"Don't leave me. I'm so scared, and I don't know what to do." Mary Katherine's fingers dug into Bethany's arm. "I'm so weary of being alone."

"It's okay. Really. I'll come back—with help." She brushed aside hair from Mary Katherine's damp forehead. The woman was burning up with fever. "I won't be gone long." She dropped to one knee. "I won't abandon you, Mary Katherine. I'll return and I won't leave you until you're out of the woods. Okay?"

"Promise?"

"I promise."

Suddenly, Bethany was free. The girl slumped against the wall and closed her eyes, her hands settled on her stomach. "That's what he's done, hasn't he? Abandoned me."

"Perhaps he's made plans to return. Right now, we need to concentrate on what's most important: you and your child."

A faint nod conveyed Mary Katherine's resignation. A

profound sorrow filled her eyes when she opened them. "Thank you."

Choked with emotion, Bethany nodded and then hurried out, leaving her coat and hat behind.

Fueled by anger, energized by purpose, she gathered her skirts and ran. With each pound of her feet on the road, she prayed Megan was home. Oh, dear God, she needed Jeb, too.

Someone had to fetch a buggy, then help get Mary Katherine out of the schoolhouse and into the bed Megan reserved for her patients. Even together, she and Megan couldn't get the stricken woman into a buggy safely.

The woman's fever was worrisome.

Women in labor perspired from pain and exertion, but they didn't normally have a high fever unless they were sick.

She stumbled, and barely caught herself before falling flat on her face.

She hadn't thought about the primitive medical conditions of 1895. Or the number and types diseases eradicated since that time. Or the vaccines developed.

And it was too late to consider the ramifications now. *As though she'd had a choice, anyway.*

Bethany was out of breath by the time she rounded the Calahans' gate. She burst through the door without knocking.

"Megan!"

"Glory be. What is it?" Wiping her hands on a towel, Megan rushed from the kitchen.

"Is Jeb here?" Hands on her knees, Bethany tried to regain her breath. Proper or not, she had to start jogging again and get into shape.

"Aye. What's the matter?"

"A girl is having a baby at the schoolhouse." She gasped for a half-breath. "She's sick, Megan. Feverish. I didn't know who else to come to for help." Two more gasps filled her lungs. "I promised I'd get her help."

"Sorcha," Megan called. "Get your overnight things. Da will take you to the Bittlehorns'." Megan darted into the kitchen and barked orders at her husband and daughter with the authority of a boot-camp drill instructor.

"I heard ya," came Jeb's voice from the kitchen. A chair grated on the wooden floor. "Not to worry about Sorcha. We'll get a buggy and meet you at the schoolhouse."

Precious minutes later, Megan had her medical bag. Bethany didn't have time to fully catch her breath before she and Megan were on their way to Mary Katherine's side.

The lamps in the mother's room of the Calahan home burned brightly. Outside, a storm pounded the night with its fury. It seemed Mary Katherine's labor would go on forever. Bethany wrung out the cooling cloth and swabbed the girl's face. Not even ice packs had lowered her fever.

By dawn, Bethany was nearly as exhausted as the expectant mother. Megan had slept for several hours, but Bethany had stayed awake. Had anything about Mary Katherine's condition changed, Bethany would have awakened Megan. Luckily, nothing had changed.

"I'll stay with you for a while," Megan told Mary Katherine as she entered the room. "Bethany should have a bit of breakfast."

Bethany started to protest, then thought better of it. A cup or six of coffee was just what she needed.

"I'm going to die," Mary Katherine said, her voice a raspy whisper.

"Aye, lass, ya are, but not today." Megan rinsed the mopping rag in the bowl of icy water beside the bed.

At the bedroom door, Bethany stopped in her tracks. Dear God in heaven, please help this woman-child, she prayed. Shaken, she followed the aroma of fresh coffee.

To her annoyance, Matthew shared the kitchen table with Jeb. Tired as she was, the last thing she needed was a confrontation.

"Sit," Matthew ordered as he rose.

"Can I fix something for you to eat?" Jeb asked.

Bethany shook her head. Food was the last thing she wanted.

"Megan will have my hide if ya doona eat something."

"All right." She reached for the bread in the center of the table. Almost instantly, Matthew put a plate and a steaming cup of coffee in front of her.

She looked up into his stern face. "Thank you." *Please don't be nice to me. Keep your distance—for both our sakes.*

"You need some rest."

"Not any more than Megan and not nearly as badly as Mary Katherine." She slathered butter on a piece of bread. "Did you know about this?"

"This what?"

"Ian McKenzie's wife and child." She slapped a spoonful of berry preserves atop the butter.

He resumed his seat at the end of the table. "He said he was unmarried." He met her gaze.

If Ian McKenzie had not married Mary Katherine, let him return and state his denial in person. Mary Katherine and his child didn't need the stigma of *illegitimate* branded on their foreheads—and they could avoid it until proven otherwise.

"Excuse me. I've got to get to the store today. Send word if you've need for me." Jeb returned his chair to its place at the head of the table. "I'll bring ya lunch at midday," he said to Bethany, then he took his coat from behind his chair and pulled it on. "Stop by the store later, will ya?" he added for Matthew.

"Before noon," Matthew agreed and raised his hand in farewell.

After Jeb left, Bethany asked, "Why are you here?"

"I'd like to talk with you."

"So you hunted me down here." She bit savagely into her bread.

He sat back in the chair with a casualness she envied. Yet, he didn't appear any more rested than she felt.

"Must we talk now?" she asked in a low voice. She was exhausted. "I'm tired. There's a woman in the other room who needs me. She's my priority today." She drained her coffee, poured a fresh cup, then, when he said nothing, she started out of the kitchen.

"Bethany," he called.

She stopped at the door, and felt the heat of his gaze on her back.

"Ignoring something doesn't make it go away."

"Tell me something I don't know."

Mary Katherine screamed. Megan shouted for Bethany to come quickly.

She set down the coffee and ran.

"Jesus, Mary, and Joseph, help us," Megan prayed as Bethany entered the room, trying to lift Mary Katherine's limp body.

"What are you doing? How can I help?"

"She stopped breathing."

"Let me in." Thinking only of Mary Katherine and the child struggling to come into the world, Bethany pushed Megan aside and felt for a pulse. Nothing. She whipped back the perspiration-dampened sheet and pounded Mary Katherine's chest, listened, then started CPR.

"Breathe, damn it. Breathe!" She administered mouth-to-mouth, then returned to pushing on Mary Katherine's chest.

After four repetitions, her efforts paid off.

Mary Katherine gasped for breath.

Relief so profound she became light-headed swept over

Bethany. She had to grasp the headboard to keep her balance.

Megan tugged at her and pointed to the chair they'd positioned beside the nightstand. "Ya must teach me that when this is over."

Bethany sat, her gaze fixed on the young girl on the bed. For the first time, she realized this woman might not survive the birth of her child. A sudden rage at the unfairness of life and death rose within her.

His concentration waned as the morning turned into afternoon and a fresh round of summer storms darkened the horizon. The drafting table in front of Matthew held a half-finished rendering, the last in a series. The stately home his new clients wanted built on an acre plot three blocks away would be one of his best jobs ever, but despite his enthusiasm for the project, his thoughts strayed to Bethany.

He hadn't known what to think after the graveyard incident. Was she off kilter, or was he?

Or, had his scant understanding of women diminished further during the last couple of years?

He was thinking in circles again, which seemed to happen a lot where Bethany was concerned. The woman got involved in the damnedest things. She attracted complications like a magnet.

Shortly before dinnertime, Matthew finished his work. Monday, the Wilkinsons would return from Europe with expectations of reviewing their house's plans. Confident they'd have minimal changes, he rolled up the prints and laid them in a labeled drawer.

Twenty minutes later, he knocked on the door of Gray House. When he got no answer, he went to the Calahans'. Thunder rolled through the leaden sky and the first raindrops fell as he ducked under the porch overhang.

Jeb acknowledged him with a nod and lift of his pipe

as he continued to slowly rock in the nearest of three rocking chairs.

"Ya doona want to go in there," Jeb said. "And if Ian McKenzie shows his face here again, I may have ta have him killed—though I'd prefer to do the deed myself. At the very least, I'll be rearrangin' his nose. No man should leave a lass he's loved and made a child with."

"You may get your chance. I gave a letter to the captain of the *Jenny Laura*. Ian sailed with him to the Sandwich Islands. He'll hand deliver it."

"Good." Sorrow clung to Jeb like a second skin. "Mary Katherine'll not be seein' another dawn."

"Is she . . ." The word refused to form on his lips. He leaned against the house and studied the porch boards. Even being within hearing distance of a woman struggling to bring a child into the world was too close. He didn't want to relive the night Victoria and Ethan died.

"No, but it doesna look good. Father O'Sullivan spent the mornin' at her side and gave her the last rites. Three times her heart's quit beating. Each time, Bethany did something to bring her back. Me Megan thinks her a saint."

"What do you mean, 'bring her back'?"

Jeb rocked a little harder in his chair. " 'Tis somethin' she does by pumping on the lass's chest and breathing into her mouth. I tell ya, Matthew, that woman knows more about a lot of things than any other schoolmaster in Alaska Territory."

He'd give him no argument on that score. She had a lot of explaining to do. "Is there anything I can do for Mrs. McKenzie? Her luggage may still be at the wharf."

"Nay. I fetched her trunk last evening. And her last name isna McKenzie. It's Murphy."

Not once had Ian McKenzie mentioned Mary Katherine Murphy. "Where's she from?"

"She was a student at the Couther School until they

asked her to leave. The lass had to find Ian and prayed he'd take care of her and the babe." The Irishman clamped his teeth on the pipe stem and created a series of smoke signals. "So what brings ya here?"

"They gave him an excellent reference," Matthew said, sickened.

"They didna know of his tutelage of Mary Katherine Murphy at the time, or I doubt that would be the case."

"Her family?"

"Dead. She had a trust fund. No doubt that motivated the bastards at the school ta keep her until they couldna deny her condition."

Matthew swore under his breath. Was there no end to the misery selfish people inflicted on the innocent or unknowing? "I hope Ian does return," he said softly.

"I asked what brings ya here, Matthew."

"I was looking for Bethany."

"She may not be happy ta see ya, considering neither she nor Megan have slept—"

The door burst open. Ashen-faced, Megan stuck out her head. "We need help."

Jeb bolted from the rocker, tossed his pipe into the flowerpot, and reached the door in three strides.

Matthew hesitated. The same agonizing sense of helplessness that had swamped him the night Victoria died moved through him like a tidal wave.

The sound of the rocker continuing to move on the wood porch became a metronone marking time.

He had two choices: Leave and once again prove his ineffectuality, or swallow the bolder emotion in his throat and stay. If nothing else, he knew how to boil water.

Unable to walk away from trouble regardless of personal pain, he followed Jeb into the house.

"Remove your coat, roll up yer sleeves, and scrub yer hands with lye soap," Megan called over her shoulder. "In the kitchen."

His heart in his throat, Matthew obeyed the petite dictator and joined Jeb at the sink. He rolled up his sleeves as ordered. Following Jeb's example, he used plenty of soap and water to scrub his hands and forearms.

He took a clean towel from the stack on the table. "What can I do to help?"

"We do whatever the women say. We're here for the heavy work and the runnin'. If either one of them tips the scale at more than a hundred pounds—"

"Damn you, Mary Katherine! Don't you die before you give this baby life." The desperation in Bethany's voice froze Matthew in his tracks. Every nerve in his spine tensed in warning.

"Jeb!"

"Come on."

Matthew forced himself to move. He eyed the front door as he crossed the parlor behind Jeb, but there was no running from his horrific memories.

This wasn't the home he'd built for Victoria. It wasn't Victoria in the birthing bed. No, this was another woman—a child—in need, and he couldn't walk away.

He stopped cold at the bedroom door, loath to enter. The smell of camphor, sweat, and alcohol filled his nostrils.

It took a moment to register the activity in the small room.

"Stop!" Megan ordered. "She's gone."

"Goddamn it, you may not want this baby, Mary Katherine, but I do. Don't you dare give up." Bethany stopped rhythmically pushing on the woman's sternum and bent to her head. For a split second, she appeared to kiss the woman.

Matthew tightened his fists.

"Breathe," Bethany hissed.

Mary Katherine's head rolled to the side. Her sightless eyes stared out the door and directly at Matthew. Oh, good God, she was young. Not more than what? Fifteen? Sixteen? And never getting a day older.

"Matthew," Jeb called. "Lend a hand or leave."

Without hesitation, he crossed the threshold into hell.

Tears spilled down Bethany's cheeks. What a waste of life! Mary Katherine had needed antibiotics to arrest whatever had caused her fever, an I.V. to replace the fluids lost to feverish perspiration, and a good surgeon to perform a Caesarean.

"We're taking the baby," Megan announced. She tossed a sheet at Matthew. "Cover her from her head to her abdomen.

Bethany retreated to give them room to work.

"Matthew and Jeb, pack fresh linen around the poor lass. Bethany, get ready ta take the baby." Megan opened an enamel sterilization container and withdrew a scalpel.

With the steady hand of a surgeon, Megan made an incision across Mary Katherine's distended abdomen. The coppery bite of fresh blood mingled with the myriad of smells. The whisper of Irish praying was the only voice in the room. The seconds ticking by felt like hours.

Then everything happened at once.

"Take the lad," Megan snapped.

Bethany reached out with a fresh linen draped across her forearms. She clutched the small infant around his left thigh and shoulder. Megan tied and cut the umbilical cord.

"That's it. Hold him tight and turn him. Let's clear the mouth." Megan spoke softly while she worked on the child.

Bethany couldn't look at Mary Katherine, only at the child. She prayed, promising God anything and everything for the child's life. Although she'd learned long ago that God didn't barter, it seemed worth one last desperate try.

"Hold the babe feet up. We've got ta clear his wee airway."

The seconds dragged like days.

"Ah, yes, wee child. That's it. Let the world know yer here."

The baby took a shuddering breath and began to cry.

"Aye, that's a good lad. Clean him up, Bethany. Matthew, ye help her. There's water heated in the bathroom."

Awe, joy, and gratitude filled Bethany to the bursting point. "Child, you are a miracle." She led the way down the hall to the bathroom. With each step her fatigue fell away.

The precious child in her arms was as close as she would ever come to birthing one.

"We need some light," she told an uncharacteristically silent Matthew.

He obliged and returned to look over her shoulder.

"Do you want to hold or clean?" She hoped he'd want to clean because she loved holding the baby. "What do you say, little guy? How about a sponge bath and your first shot at making a fashion statement?"

As though in answer, the baby stretched.

"I know nothing about these matters," Matthew confessed. "Good God, he's little."

"Not for long. They grow up in the blink of an eye, or so parents tell me all the time." Clearly, Matthew knew even less about newborns. She reluctantly placed this one in his big, capable hands.

In awed silence, they cleaned the baby and marveled when he expressed his displeasure. His fingers balled into a fist he shook as though railing at the world for the death of his mother.

"Look at the perfection of this little guy," Bethany said. She ached to hold him close and never let him go. "Patrick." She said the baby's name with awe.

"There was so much blood," Matthew whispered.

"Megan did the right thing. She saved his life." Bethany wrapped the baby in a clean towel and kissed his head. "Mary Katherine wanted her baby to live." Her gaze met Matthew's. "If Ian McKenzie returns, I will personally flog him to within an inch of his life, then I'll see him castrated."

For the first time since the ordeal began, the shadow of a smile crossed Matthew's face. "Think you're big enough?"

"There isn't a woman in Juneau who won't help hold him down. So, yes." She kissed the baby again, breathing in his special, clean scent.

She diapered Patrick, then dressed him in clothing she'd found in Mary Katherine's bags. The child's mother had planned on taking good care of him. Bethany yearned to fill the void created by her death.

Already, she contemplated how she might adopt the child. It made such perfect sense. Patrick needed a mother, a protector, and a guardian. Who better than she—a woman who wanted, even needed him? A woman who already loved him. A woman who could not have a child of her own.

"Let's go in the kitchen, next to the stove," she suggested. The baby nestled against her shoulder.

"Wait." Matthew tucked a small quilt around the child. Although a bit awkward, they managed to wrap him.

"Why don't you hold him while I take care of the bathroom mess?" The bathroom cleanup was far easier than Megan's task.

Matthew sat in a kitchen chair near the warm stove. Bethany placed the child in his arms and showed him how to support the head. Both tucked and folded clothing and the little quilt around him.

"Okay?" she asked.

Matthew nodded, his gaze never leaving the yawning

infant. "I've never held a . . . live baby right after he was born."

The awe in his voice twisted her heartstrings. She dropped down onto the balls of her feet and looked into Matthew's troubled blue eyes. "You'll be fine. If you need me, call out and I'll be right here."

It was painful, watching him struggle with memories of what might have been with Victoria and Ethan. She patted his knee, then used it to help her stand.

"I won't be gone long."

"Take your time." He didn't look up, and she suspected he fought tears.

Needing the busywork, she gathered the linens from the bathroom. With a bucket of soapy warm water, she scrubbed down every surface.

"There's a laundry bag in the second drawer of the bureau," Megan said, appearing from nowhere.

Bethany thrust the soiled sheets, pads, and towel into the bag, then tied off the drawstrings. "Where's Jeb?" She nabbed a second bag from the drawer for the linens on the bed.

"He's gone to fetch Father O'Sullivan. Afterward, he'll pay a call on the undertaker." Megan's hand shook as she put the last stitch into Mary Katherine's abdomen.

The two women washed and prepared Mary Katherine for burial.

"What happens to the baby now?" Bethany asked.

"I doubt I'll have much trouble findin' someone ta take the lad in."

"I want to adopt him, Megan."

"Ya have no husband, lass."

"Neither did Mary Katherine."

# Chapter Sixteen

"Will ya care for the lad while I fetch Sorcha?" Jeb asked Matthew.

"Yes. Go get your daughter." It seemed the least he could do. His plans to finish searching his father's study for the loan papers had lost their urgency. The sightless eyes of Mary Katherine Murphy would remain with him for a long time.

Megan had retired to her room, and Bethany had crawled into the spare bed in Sorcha's room. Both wanted to be near Patrick should he need them. The ordeal had taken an exhausting toll on the women.

As soon as Jeb left for the Bittlehorns', Matthew went back inside. He stood beside the cradle and couldn't take his eyes off the tiny baby lying on his stomach. A crocheted blanket softer than eiderdown covered him. Although a different pattern, the pale blue color was identical to the one Victoria had crocheted for Ethan—

the small blanket remained folded on the corner of Matthew's bureau at Mama Johanson's.

A shock of raven hair as straight as Mary Katherine's stood out against the white comforter upon which baby Patrick lay.

Had he lived, Ethan would have celebrated his second birthday the month before.

Patrick opened, then clenched his tiny fist, then opened it again. Crouched on one knee, Matthew noted the perfection of each finger, the tiny nails and cuticles.

What kind of man seduced a student in his charge? And why the hell hadn't he stuck around long enough to determine the consequences of his action?

"Because he is immoral," he whispered. "You deserve better, Patrick Murphy McKenzie."

A family. That's what the baby deserved.

Matthew couldn't give him a mother, but he could be his father.

Oh, yes, he could.

Thick clouds roiled over the graveyard. Bethany stood next to Matthew beside Mary Katherine Murphy's open grave. The Calahan family stood on the opposite side.

Father O'Sullivan prayed for Mary Katherine in Latin. A normally jovial man with a curly halo of gray hair, shocking blue eyes, and generous features, he spoke with solemn reverence.

The closure Bethany had hoped for eluded her.

Likely, all the naïve young woman lying in the coffin at the bottom of a cold, dark hole had wanted was love. Was such a dream for loving and being loved so universal? So elusive?

A voice inside Bethany cried out for justice, not just for Mary Katherine, but also for herself. For the children she'd never have. For the family lost to her by more than distance.

Where was the justice in Mary Katherine dying in childbirth?

How different medical science had made the world. Bethany contrasted Mary Katherine's plight with her own as a woman who couldn't have a child and should have died two years ago.

She wanted Patrick as her own. No child would know more love or a more secure sense of belonging than this one.

Adopting him meant keeping her feet planted in the here and now, though—even if the River of Time appeared, even if she could find a way home.

Choices.

Tough ones.

Dear God in Heaven, was nothing in this life easy?

The question required no answer.

If she found a way to become Patrick's mother, nothing could drag her from her son. Nothing.

Father O'Sullivan closed his prayer book and bowed his head.

Before lifting her voice in song, Bethany prayed for Mary Katherine and her son, the child Bethany already loved as her own. Eyes heavenward, she sang from the heart.

But this time, she sang alone. Her sister's voices had stilled in her memory.

Tears rolled down her checks. Sheer willpower kept her voice from breaking. Her songs were for the woman-child she'd come to know in her final hours.

When her songs ended, the undertaker's men began filling in the grave. Bethany stood unmoving until the gravedigger flattened the last shovelful of dirt.

"Can we give her a cross or a marker?" Megan asked no one in particular.

"I'll see to it," Matthew said.

"Thank you," Bethany whispered. "She was so alone." She hunkered down on one knee and planted a small pink rose cutting she'd brought from the back of Gray House. In time, it would grow, and flower, and draw admirers. Mary Katherine wouldn't be alone again.

"I want to adopt Patrick," Bethany said, patting the dirt into place.

"So does Matthew," Megan mentioned softly.

Her initial shock quickly gave way to reality. Of course he wanted the child. But Bethany's heart sank as she stood and faced him. "Why?" She looked at him and frowned. "What would you do with a newborn baby? Do you even know how to feed or change him?"

"Those things I can learn. I'll love him the same way I would have loved Ethan." His gaze roamed to the distant corner of the cemetery, where his wife and child were buried. "Don't start in on me. I know he's not Ethan. He's not a replacement. But I want this child, Bethany. I can build a life for him."

"So can I. This baby needs a mother. He needs me." *And I need him to love, to care for and nurture.*

"There is an alternative," Megan ventured.

Bethany looked at her. "What could possibly—"

"Marry the lass," Jeb said. "Marry Bethany and you'll have little trouble takin' on wee Patrick."

"No," Matthew answered. "I don't want a wife."

"Not an option," agreed Bethany. "And Mary Katherine wasn't married. Would you have kept the child from her for that reason?"

" 'Twas different, Bethany. She was the babe's mother. Yer not."

And that summed it up. In 1895, an Irish Catholic like Megan would never give her custody of the child unless she was married. "What will happen to him?"

"I'll not allow anything ta happen to him for the next

couple of months at the least. He'll be stayin' with us. Ye may come see him whenever ye've the chance."

She couldn't take him to school, and she had to work to survive. Had these people even heard of day care?

"Thank you."

"What happens then?" Matthew asked.

"I'd be supposin' that'll be up to the circuit judge when he comes through again." Jeb put his arm around his wife and gestured for their departure. "If we doona find a home for him here, Judge Wardell will take him down to Seattle or Tacoma and place him with one of the Catholic orphanages."

"Over my dead body," Matthew roared.

"No!" Bethany protested at the same time. In this they were in perfect accord.

"Then I'd suggest the two of ye find a solution ye like better." Head high, Megan accompanied Jeb to their buggy. Neither looked back.

"I can't marry you," Bethany said.

"Did you hear me ask?"

"No," she admitted, wanting to scream.

"Though God knows I want you, Bethany. And I suspect you want me." Hands in his pockets, he turned away. "Unfortunately, the solution isn't that simple; desire isn't enough."

*No kidding.* "You're damn right it's not simple. These days, nothing is." She gazed down at the fresh grave. "I promise you, Mary Katherine, your little Patrick will *not* end up in an orphanage."

"Amen," Matthew agreed. "We'll think of something."

"Yes, I will."

"*We* will. And I don't know how they do it in Wyoming, but here no one gives a child to a woman who can't support him."

She whirled on him. "Are you threatening me with my job?"

"Damn it, woman, you're impossible. You knew the job wouldn't last beyond Phineas Montgomery's arrival."

"But I have that long, right?"

"What kind of bully do you think I am? I'm not about to fire you or kick you out on the street over this."

"Good. Sell me Gray House."

"What? Why would I want to do that?"

"Number one, you don't want it. Number two, you don't have time to take care of it. Number three, it has to be a drain on your pocketbook. Number four, I'm an excellent credit risk. I can't run out on you." The birth of her idea was an exciting thing. The worst he could do was a flat refusal.

"You don't have any money." His eyes narrowed. "Or *do* you? Have you only been pretending you don't remember how you got here?"

"I haven't the foggiest idea of how I got here." *Or how the River of Time works*. It wasn't as though she could wait for a flood, then put a boat in the water and row home!

"So how the hell would you pay for Gray House?"

"You could give me a mortgage after Phineas Montgomery arrives." Oh, yes, it might work. It would work. All he had to do was say yes.

"And then?" Arms folded across his chest, he glowered down at her.

"And then I'd turn Gray House into a boardinghouse." Her heart thundered in her chest. This plan had real merit. If she had a job and a home, a judge might, just might, listen to her petition for adoption.

"Clever," he said in a voice that cut with the sharpness of a razor. "Tell you what; before we discuss this further, suppose I finish my work in the study. If I don't find the loan papers, selling Gray House to you or anyone else may become a moot point. The Old Man may have mortgaged it as collateral."

Okay; she could bide her time. She owed it to Matthew

to help him find the missing pieces of his legacy.

"All right. Let's get this scavenger hunt on the road." She started toward town.

"By the way," Matthew caught her hand and tucked it into the crook of his arm. "You're not the only one interested in buying Gray House."

"What? Who?" Alarmed, she saw her plans threatened by an unknown assailant.

"Cornelius Lassiter. He wants the house and the mine. He's under the impression they're tied together in a snarl of bank loans."

"We'd better find those papers." She lengthened her stride, eager to resolve the status of Gray House.

By eight o'clock that evening, Matthew finished counting the money they'd found among the pages of the books in the *downstairs* study. The amount fell shy of twenty thousand dollars.

A series of banging and thumps overhead sent him bolting up the stairs. The attic door yawned open.

"What the hell is she doing up there?" he asked himself. He rushed down the hall and took the stairs to the attic two at a time. A single lamp burned on a dusty trunk.

"Bethany?"

A muffled sound came from well beyond the lamplit area. Fortunately, she didn't knock over the lamp and set the place afire.

"Where the hell are you?" He raised her light and looked around. Where had all these filing cabinets and trunks come from? "Bethany?"

"Back here. I'm stuck."

Matthew moved a crate aside and found a neat aisle down the center of the attic. The smell of wood mingled with the dust motes whirling in the air.

At the edge of the lamplight, he saw her foot protruding into the aisle.

"I'm oh . . . sort of . . . wedged in here."

"Can you move?"

"Yeah, but I'm afraid the yellow crate will fall on me if I do. If it's filled with feathers, that's okay. But if it's crammed with books and papers like most of these others, I won't fare as well."

"Damn." He examined the jumble of boxes. Apparently, they'd sat on the dresser, protected by a blanket.

"I reached for a small box, lost my balance, and everything shifted and tumbled. Including me."

"Where's your left leg?"

"Attached to my left hip. Where else would it be? Just fix this stuff so it doesn't fall on me. Please," she added sweetly.

She seemed to delight in trying his patience. Even so, he couldn't leave her beneath these precariously stacked boxes and chairs. "Can you straighten your left leg?"

"Yes." Her left foot appeared beside her right.

"I'm going to pull you out by your ankles. I'll go slowly. If you get hung up anywhere, holler." Other than an invisible hand, he had no idea what kept the stack from collapsing.

He set the lamp on the opposite side of the aisle.

"Ready?"

"More than."

His hands closed around her delicate ankles and pulled slowly and steadily. A thick coat of varnish made the dusty floor easy for her to slide across.

"Feel around for anything you might knock over as I pull you out. Damn, I don't want this falling down on you."

"That makes two of us." After a few bumps and knocks, she continued, "I think if you pull me straight out, I'll clear everything. Whoa. Stop! Just a minute."

More clunks, and the furniture shifted. Dust billowed and he held his breath, sure he wouldn't get her out fast enough to keep her from injury. Without waiting, he pulled her straight out.

The boxes and furniture crashed into the space she'd occupied a split second earlier.

He couldn't drag his gaze from her exposed legs. Her skirt had ridden up and a jagged scar ran from just above her knee to under her drawers. Stunned by the extent of the mark, he said nothing, but he met her gaze and saw fear.

She scrambled to push her skirt down and get to her feet.

His protective instincts took over. "Goddamn it, Bethany. What the hell were you doing? You could have gotten killed!" Relieved she'd escaped such a close call, he pulled her against his chest. "You scared the hell out of me."

The little songbird quaked like an aspen in the wind. He held her tighter, wanting to save her from all the dangers in the world.

"I'm fine," she said against his chest.

"You're trembling." He smoothed the wild curls from her face and almost drowned in the emotion blazing in her big eyes. Drawn by her parted lips, he lowered his head until his lips gently grazed hers.

"Bethany," he whispered. She felt so soft, so warm and inviting. A man could drown in her eyes and die happy.

Lost in the moment, he felt the tentative motion of her hands sliding around his ribs and up his back.

Each time he touched her, the need to make love and protect her grew stronger, more alive and demanding.

The way her hands roamed his back and sides made him wish he was naked. The electricity of her touch ignited his ravenous desire.

He brushed her lips again with his own. It wasn't

enough. The tip of his tongue traced her lower lip. Soft. Sweet. Tantalizing.

Her fingers curled over his shoulders. She stood on tiptoes and claimed his kiss.

She was sweet and so willing to soothe the savage beast returning to life within him. God, he was hungry for her. Cradling her face, he explored her mouth with the thoroughness of a man who hadn't made love in over two years.

Her response encouraged his brazenness, though in the back of his mind he knew they were playing with fire. He wouldn't make love with her, not in the traditional sense, but damn it, he would please her if she'd allow it.

His questions found an answer when he started to break the kiss. Her fingertips dug into his shoulders. Her tongue followed his and demanded the same freedom to explore. All he could think about was loving her in every physical way possible.

"This has nothing to do with anything else," Bethany exclaimed in a rush. Her arms threaded through his and locked around his neck. "This is just something we both want."

He kissed her with all the hunger in his soul, loving the way her hands felt on his face and neck and reveling in the response of her body moving sinuously over his erection. He cupped her buttocks, lifted, and held her against himself.

Bethany's hold tightened and she moaned.

"Yes. Truce for now," he managed to say, kissing her and moving toward a fainting couch covered by a sheet.

"Turn out the lamp," she murmured, then kissed his throat and let her tongue linger in the hollow.

He didn't question her reasons, just reached over and turned down the wick stem. In the dying glow, he found the corner of the couch's dustcover and pulled it away in one sweep.

Bethany laid a trail of fiery kisses along his collarbone and freed his shirt buttons. "God, you taste delicious."

"I want you," he breathed, settling their bodies onto the fainting couch so that she was on her back and he lay on his side next to her.

She tugged on his shirt, pulling the tails from his trousers. "For right here and now, you have me."

How well he understood what neither of them wanted to acknowledge in the heat of passion. When their interlude ended, everything would go back to the way it was when they'd left Mary Katherine's grave. Wouldn't it?

"Make love to me."

Her plea became a knotted cord around his heart. He'd give almost anything to do just that. But even in his current state of arousal and after two years of deprivation, he wouldn't risk getting her with child.

He opened her blouse, following his fingers with his lips. "There are dozens of ways to make love."

He deftly freed himself of the shirt she tugged over his shoulders, then quickly found her breasts again. Unable to get enough of her, his mouth replaced his hand. God, she was so open, so sensuous, and so responsive—a woman a man dreamed of even while she was in his arms.

"You taste like roses and honey," he rasped against her breast. "Sweet beyond belief." His attention shifted to her other breast, suckling, tasting, nibbling, and nipping until she was breathing rapidly.

She made her point by opening his trousers. "I was thinking of having sex the more traditional way."

Matthew swore under his breath. "It's been over two years—"

"Good," she said, pushing his trousers down his hips. "It's been even longer for me. So, let's get it on before one of us comes to his or her senses."

He lifted her skirt and petticoat and unfastened her

drawers. With one sweep, he got them down to her ankles.

The perfume of her arousal drove him wild. He caught a nipple between his teeth. The sensitive bud became pebble hard with just a little teasing of his tongue. Lord, how had she kept such sweet, full, firm breasts hidden?

Her hand closed around his manhood, and he damn near stopped breathing. Not even his wife had been so wonderfully brazen.

"Bethany, Bethany," he breathed, wrapping his hand around hers.

The sensation and sound of her soft cheek against his chest excited him to a near-frenzy. She caught his free hand and moved it to her breast.

Caught between heaven and hell and on the brink of doing exactly what he'd sworn not to, he felt the tendrils of self-control slip away.

Almost caving in completely, he removed her hand and moved over her. Propped on his elbow, his hips nestled between her thighs, he kissed her with all the longing pent up since he'd first laid eyes on her.

She writhed beneath him, her back arched to fill his hands with her luscious breasts, her hips rocked, searching, seeking. Every fiber of his body wanted nothing more than to thrust himself into her.

"Please," she begged.

He cradled her face in both hands and kissed her into silence. "We'll have to improvise. I have no French letters."

"What do the French have to do with us having sex?"

"Contraception," he said through clenched teeth.

She relaxed beneath him. "Not a problem. It's safe."

Though he couldn't see her eyes, her body language provided a kind of assurance.

"Trust me," she whispered, pulling his head down and tilting her hips.

"I don't think . . ."

"Don't think," she agreed. She reached between them and rearranged her skirts. "Trust me, Matthew."

Despite the doubts he'd harbored about Bethany in so many other areas, her voice promised she was telling the truth. "Sweet Jesus," he said and slid into her. Warm, wet, and tight as a fist, she was. They both groaned.

Nothing and no one felt so damn good.

She reached her climax immediately.

Matthew had to withdraw to keep from doing so, himself.

When her breathing returned to a slower pant, he reentered her.

"Sorry about that," she murmured with a laugh that belied her words. Her hands glided from his buttocks to his shoulders, while her hips moved in slow, deliberate circles.

Withdrawing and entering her again was like being reborn.

The sense of being whole, complete as never before, scrubbed the stains of sorrow from his soul. Her legs locked around his waist. Feeling her build to a second climax put him over the edge.

"Oh, God, Matthew! Yes."

He took her hard, fast, and thrust all of himself into her, the intensity of his release almost pulling his heart out of his chest. The connection they shared in those moments would remain with him forever.

Her name escaped his lips with the hiss of air drawn deeply into his lungs—dark air redolent with their lovemaking. He readjusted their position on the narrow fainting couch. Lying on his side, barely able to make out her form in the fading daylight leaking through the rafter vents, Matthew moved damp tresses of hair from Bethany's cheek.

"Thank you," she said, and kissed his chest.

He couldn't help laughing at the absurdity of her thanking him. "This is not exactly what I hoped, the way I wanted to make love with you."

"You *hoped* for this?"

"This? The attic, the darkness, not taking the time to rid ourselves of our clothing? No. To make love with you, yes. But Bethany, this was beyond my wildest dreams."

"Well, I've got something even better for you."

The strain in her voice let him know the time for intimacy was over. What a strange little songbird she was. "I can't think of anything better than what we just did."

"How about a box of your father's most important papers?"

"Not even close," he said, and meant it. Before she could squirm away, he managed a final kiss.

Funny, she tasted like tears.

# Chapter Seventeen

Bethany refused to look back in regret. Their intimate interlude in the attic embodied the best and the worst about the changes in her life. It made not a bit of difference if Matthew thought her brazen, so be it. The incomparable, exquisite pleasure she'd experienced with him was worth any price.

After the crash, during the months of recovery and intense physical therapy, she'd come to terms with her future. A woman who couldn't look at her naked body without revulsion couldn't expect any man to find her desirable.

Yet all the expectations fostered by books, movies, and her college years paled in comparison to the bliss she'd experienced with Matthew—despite her fears of never finding fulfillment.

She soaked in the bathtub, grateful that Old Man Gray had indulged his fondness for "the latest technology."

The dusty black lacquered box she'd spotted atop the

furniture in the attic seemed just the sort of place to keep special papers. George Gray had apparently cornered the market on paper; he had enough documents to keep a recycling plant busy for a year. It seemed logical for him to put the loan papers in a special place. And she'd doubted he would file them. Her exploration of his files and crannies had only revealed one incongruity after another. It appeared that once George filed something, he was finished with it forever. With the exception of his desk, the contents of every other drawer in the house portrayed a neatness fetish.

Thinking about George Gray provided an ineffective diversion from the pleasure she'd shared with his son. Each time she closed her eyes she saw Matthew engraved on her inner eyelids. The heat of his kiss burned deliciously in all the places his lips had touched her skin. The pleasant aches lingering from their lovemaking were beloved souvenirs.

The realization of what she'd done made her smile. In all her life she'd never even contemplated doing anything so bold or reckless, so completely out of character.

Her smile became a giggle.

She couldn't begin to imagine Alicia or Caitlyn's reactions if she told them she'd seduced the man haunting her dreams and negating her good sense.

She laughed out loud.

Her sisters wouldn't believe she'd dared take such a risk.

She hadn't believed *herself* capable of seducing a man. Bethany, the barren now ex-virgin who dressed and undressed in the closet where she wouldn't encounter a mirror.

She laid back in the tub, lifted her feet, and arched her neck until the water covered her face. And still she couldn't stop laughing.

She'd done the impossible. Had sex with the most desirable man in the world and kept her clothing on. And most astoundingly, she'd kept her secret.

He'd never know about her scars, or about the womb she no longer had—or the ruptured spleen and kidney she'd lost at the same time.

Part of her still couldn't believe she'd seized the opportunity. . . . Seized? What was truly amazing was that she had recognized the situation as the chance of a lifetime.

The odds against her having sex again—she refused to call it making love because of the implications—were slim to none. But now she'd gotten what she'd wanted—and with a man she desired

She might have felt guilty if he hadn't shared her fulfillment and found his own satisfaction.

She finished her bath and dried herself with her back to the mirror, as usual.

"Tomorrow is another day, Scarlett," she said. And, with that, she turned out the light.

The next day, Bethany entered the Golden Nugget General Store shortly before closing time. She browsed the aisles while Jeb finished waiting on a group of men and closed the store for the day. His two clerks eyed her with open curiosity when she returned to the counter empty-handed.

Jeb organized the countertop as he spoke. "I'm sorry, lass. I know ya mean well, but I canna support yer cause for Patrick any more than I can Matthew's. Neither one of ya can care for the wee lad properly. He should have a mother *and* a father."

"That's not why I'm here." Before she had so much as a glimmer of hope for adopting Patrick, she had to secure a future and the means to support them. She couldn't count on Matthew selling Gray House under the conditions she'd offered. There was also the possibility the house had a mortgage tied to the mine loans and would wind up belonging to some nefarious, impersonal bank.

Jeb loaded a new spool of twine on the packaging spindle and threaded it. "Why are ya here?"

"I've a business proposition for you." She set her valise on the edge of the counter.

"Business, ya say? What does the school need?"

"This has nothing to do with the school." Bethany's hands turned damp from nervousness. "Can I trust you, Jeb?"

"Sure ya can." The pinch of his brow conveyed she'd offended him.

She began to pace. " 'Trust' isn't the right word." The butterflies in her stomach grew in strength and number.

"Spit it out, lass. What is it ya want?"

She paused at the end of the counter and eyed the candy jars. "A cut."

"A cut of what? You're not making sense, lass." He retrieved the trashcan from under the counter and set it on top.

On the verge of losing her nerve, knowing she'd already crossed the line, she moved closer to Jeb. "You're going to think I'm crazy, and I don't know what will convince you I'm not—other than time."

"Why don't ya say what ya came to say and let me decide?"

Bethany weighed her options: take the risk or walk out the door. "Suppose someone knew something," she started, forcing her words through the trepidation turning her insides to jelly. "Something no one else knew. Something they couldn't know."

"How would someone come inta possession of such knowledge?"

"Revealing my, ah, source isn't part of the deal."

"Exactly what sorta deal are ya proposin'?"

"Knowledge."

"The school—"

"No, no, no. Forget the school for now. This is business, pure and simple." She rubbed her palms on her sleeves in an attempt to dry them.

"I'm always interested in a good business deal." He dismissed his clerks, carried a pair of stools around the counter, and set them in the open space, then said, "Have a seat, lass, and speak. I'm listening."

She'd wanted his attention and she'd gotten it. She retrieved her valise and sat on the stool facing Jeb.

"Speak yer mind," he prompted. "It'll go no further regardless of what you say."

"Fair enough." She folded her hands in her lap and cleared her throat. "If I could tell you with absolute certainty about an event that would dynamically impact your business, would it be worth something to you?"

"I'd say it depends on the event and the impact. I wouldn't be buyin' a pig in a poke, now."

This was more difficult than she'd thought. "Suppose I became your inventory advisor, on a consulting basis."

"Suppose you explain what ya just said."

"Whoeee, boy, this is tough."

"Why not make it easy on yerself, lass? Spit it out."

Unable to hold still, she rose and began to pace. "Let me put it this way; if I told you that you needed to build an enormous inventory of a certain kind and you'd be able to sell it at an obscene profit, would that be worth something to you?"

"Is that what you're tellin' me, lass?"

"Answer the question." She turned near the front door and started back.

"I reckon that would depend on how ya came to know such a thing. Is this something comin' from the States? Canada? The Russians or the Orient? Or, God help us"—he crossed himself—"the bloody English?"

"None of the above," she answered, her excitement

sparked. "This event hasn't happened. In fact, it won't happen until next year."

"And you know about it?" Jeb asked so softly the small hairs rose on the back of Bethany's neck.

"Yes, Jeb. I know. Nothing I do can change that. What I'm offering you is an opportunity to prepare. In exchange, I want compensation." She added, "When Phineas Montgomery arrives, I'm unemployed."

"You'll have no trouble findin' a husband, Bethany. There's men askin' about ya daily here, but it seems Matthew has staked a claim."

A quick shake of her head dismissed the notion. "Like I said before; marriage is not an option."

"Ah, lass, it is if you want to mother the orphan boy."

This was a topic for another time and place. Right now, she had to get her proverbial ducks in a row and hope something came along to delay Judge Wardell from his next visit. "I understand if you need some time to think about what I've said, Jeb. It's a big hunk for you to bite off and believe. From your standpoint, you're taking all the risk."

"Aye. Supposin' I build inventory according to what ya tell me, and this momentous thing yer talkin' about doesna happen?" He stood and removed his work apron.

"This is the surest thing you'll come across in your life time. However, you have to operate in your own comfort zone."

He tossed his apron onto the counter and picked up the stools. "And if I say no?"

"Then I'll find a way to do it myself." She reached down and picked up her valise. "The bottom line is, in this instance, you have the business, I have the inside knowledge. No one other than me knows about this, Jeb."

"If I say yes?"

"Simple. I tell you. You stockpile. I get ten percent of your profits for two years."

"Yer daft, ya know that?"

"You'll sing a different tune in a couple of years." Bethany smiled sadly, seeing her last real hope slip away. "Shall I take that as a no?"

"Nay. Take it as, 'I'll think on it.' "

"Fair enough."

She went to the door and waited for him to let her out.

" 'Tis best we not speak of this with anyone until I sort my mind out," he said. A contemplative frown accompanied his wary glance, which Bethany met with a sinking heart. Had she misread Jeb completely?

"I-I understand. What I'm offering requires a great deal of faith on your part." Without revealing her background—and really lending credence to his skepticism—she doubted anything she said would convince him. "Could you let me know before Sorcha's music lesson on Tuesday?" If she couldn't enlist Jeb's cooperation, she'd have to find another way to earn a living to support Patrick.

"Aye."

"Thank you."

"Would ya mind not visitin' Patrick tonight? I'd like ta mull this over with Megan—if it's all the same to ya."

"Sure. I understand." *That I've blown it big time.*

Heavyhearted, fearing she'd further jeopardized her chances of adopting Patrick, she headed for Gray House.

Maybe time-travelers weren't supposed to capitalize on their knowledge of the era's future. All she could do was wait for Jeb's decision. Of course, he could have her committed. Or speak to Matthew and the parents who sent their children to the schoolhouse.

Great. In her zeal to build a future, she might have shot herself in the foot.

Regardless, if she wasn't careful she'd wind up as much of an outcast as Yolanda D'Arcy, and with far less reason and fewer resources. At least Yolanda had owned a chunk of land, for starters.

Anxious to ponder the scant alternatives for her future, she made a bee line for home. She barely noticed the changes along the street. A block from the Golden Nugget she found the Juneau City Hotel and a restaurant, but past there the reputable businesses gave way to seedier establishments. A ways ahead, she saw the caliber of the businesses improve. Thank Heaven.

Bethany looked down what she called Saloon Street, which sounded better than Brothel Boulevard. The post-dinner hour heralded increased activity everywhere.

Scantily clad women stood outside the saloons. Their poses and flirtations hawked their wares. A woman watched her from the boardwalk outside the Red Dog, her breasts threatening to spill from her camisole. A colorful, fringed shawl spanned her shoulders and disappeared behind her meaty upper arms. The breeze whipped the woman's tousled hair around her painted face, accented by kohl-lined eyes.

How many of the women working these bars and beds had a choice of occupation?

Bethany shivered and quickened her step. Just the thought of all that unprotected sex in an era before antibiotics made her shudder.

A burly man nearly as tall as Matthew brushed against her and almost knocked her off her feet. A miasma of old sweat and stale liquor surrounded him. He wore a brown suit coat over his stained duck trousers and brogans.

"You're a little one. Betcha don't charge as much as them buxom pieces of heaven."

"Is that one of your friends waving at you?" Bethany inclined her head toward the woman watching him from the Red Dog Saloon.

"She don't smell as good as you."

Wondering how he could tell, she looked squarely into

his rheumy eyes and hoped her revulsion didn't show. "Please leave me alone." She resumed walking, her grip tightening around the handle of her valise.

"How much?"

"I'm not for sale."

He matched her quickened pace effortlessly and reached for her. "I don't take long."

The steely fingers closing around her upper arm triggered her defense mechanisms. She swung the valise with all her might. The full impact caught him in the crotch.

He dropped to his knees and bellowed.

Bethany hurried from the man spewing the most colorful curses she'd heard in years. More angry than scared, she kept her head up and her ears open. She should have known better than to take a shortcut home from the Golden Nugget. Right then and there, she vowed not to do it again.

"Miss James," came a smooth baritone from behind her.

A clean getaway wasn't in the cards. She kept up her quick pace and didn't bother looking back. Although the voice had a familiar sound, she couldn't place its owner.

"Miss James, are you all right?" Lawrence Camden swept off his hat as he came to her side. "Did that lout harm you?"

"I'm fine, Mr. Camden. Thank you for your concern." *Where were you two minutes ago? Watching?*

"This is a dangerous part of town. I'm surprised Mr. Gray didn't warn you to keep a safe distance."

"He did. I was in a hurry to get home and disregarded his advice." Her urge to jerk her arm from his protective grasp stopped just short of action. She stole a glance at Camden. His looks were as smooth as his appearance. In a well-tailored brown pinstripe suit with a snowy white shirt accented by a tan brocade vest and tie, he was the epitome of fashion. Not a speck of dust marred the toes of his highly polished boots. The man was a study in earth tones right down to his ash blond hair and brown eyes. Everything about him implied perfection, including his evenly spaced, handsome features.

"I'm sorry we had to meet under such circumstances," he continued, reaching for her valise.

Although it went against her independent streak, Bethany allowed him to escort her and carry her valise.

Perhaps the misstep might become an opportunity after all.

"What brings you to this part of town, Mr. Camden? Or is it tactless of me to ask?"

His laugh held an unexpected warmth. "Most definitely not what you might think."

"And what do you suppose I'm thinking?" She hated guessing games with strangers, but it might pay to play this one. Anything she learned about Camden would help her divine his approach. Perhaps if he saw her as an ally and not a threat, he might let something slip. What, she didn't know, but like good art, she'd know it when she saw it.

"My lovely wife, Patience, has taught me to appreciate the mysteries of a woman's mind, and not to second guess." A chuckle low in his throat won another glance from Bethany. "I'm eager to be quit of Juneau and return to her in Seattle. And she is just as anxious for my arrival. We've plans."

"What sort of plans?" *Do they involve a lot of money? Perhaps from the Gray Wolf Mine?*

"We're traveling to Europe with Patience's parents. They're eagerly anticipating the voyage. The most opportune time to go, of course, is before I engage my next position." His voice softened when he spoke again, "The journey means a great deal to my wife."

"Sounds like a marvelous trip. What do you want to see most—London?"

"I'm fond of art galleries and historical buildings. The

Tower fascinates me. I must see it, though not from a captive perspective, thank you."

Bethany smiled, suspecting he had a valid reason to dread viewing the world from the wrong side of those steel bars. "Will you watch the changing of the guard at Buckingham Palace? I understand it's impressive."

"Of course. I have a number of histories from England and Europe, as well as maps, drawings, and even some lithographs. If you think you'll find them useful with the children, I'll give them to you before I leave."

"What a marvelous contribution to expand their horizons," she said, and meant it.

"I'll find some lithographs of paintings by the great masters, too. I'm sure such things would be beneficial—though I'm afraid Mr. Gray and I have bumped heads on the subjects of music and art as part of the school's curriculum."

"I'm well aware of his opinions regarding the fine arts. I've found a way to satisfy his demands for the content of a standard school day and provide some rudimentary knowledge of music, though. I believe we'll save the intricacies of art until the weather turns. Mr. Montgomery may have a different approach. By winter, *he'll* be in the classroom."

"Very true. However, I'll send whatever I can for the children. Schoolmasters have a way of leaving Juneau, as you may have noticed."

Oh, she definitely had. His veiled reference to Ian McKenzie and the unfortunate circumstances of his "wife" let her know the story had circulated throughout town. "That's very thoughtful of you."

They walked in silence for half a block before he spoke again. "What will you do when Mr. Montgomery arrives?"

"I'm exploring a few possibilities." *Like learning to live in an igloo and subsist on nuts and berries.*

"Perhaps I can help."

Surprised, Bethany nearly stopped in her tracks. "You? How? I mean, aren't you leaving as soon as possible?" And why? She barely knew him.

"Let's just say I have my reasons." A rich baritone laugh rumbled from deep in his chest. "Nothing nefarious, I assure you, Miss James. When I came here, the dearth of culture, save the resident Aleuts and their magnificent totem poles, gave my system quite a shock. However, in time I found like-minded individuals, well traveled, and educated. We get together and exchange ideas, discuss literature, and ideas. I'd be honored to introduce you. A woman of your reputed intelligence will fit comfortably. The group takes care of its own." He continued looking straight ahead and patted her hand in assurance.

"Sometimes, who you know is more important than what you know," she agreed slowly, her mind racing. How had he found out anything about her?

"You are an astute young woman, Miss James."

"Thank you, Mr. Camden. When and where will your discussion group meet again?"

"Next Wednesday evening. Why don't I escort you the first time? I'll pick you up at seven, if you're agreeable."

Gray House loomed ahead. Long shadows crept across its well-manicured grounds. "Thank you for your generous offer. I accept." If nothing else, she'd make a few connections. Who knew? This might be just what she needed. It certainly didn't seem as if she'd be going back to her own time soon.

"My pleasure," he said with a smile so sincere she wondered how Matthew could have doubted his integrity.

She said good-bye at the gate and felt his gaze follow her all the way to the door. After unlocking it, she glanced back, acknowledged his protectiveness with a wave, and went inside.

Dashing into the dining room, she peered through the lace sheers from a distance that thwarted detection. Lawrence Camden headed off toward town. "Something isn't right." Had Matthew been wrong about the man?

# *Chapter Eighteen*

"We've got trouble."

Yanked from deep concentration, Matthew looked up from his drafting table. Dall Lockner's grit-covered face and grimy duck trousers underscored the severity. "What is it?" Matthew set down his pencils. The chair scraped against the wooden floor when he pushed away from his work area.

"We've got rotten timber in Number Four. The last round of blasting damn near brought down the entire tunnel. I had men down there." Dall tucked his cap into his back pocket.

Matthew held a glass up to the light streaming through the window. Clean enough. He poured in water from the pitcher on the sideboard and handed the glass to Dall. "Who ordered blasting while you had men in the tunnel?"

"Camden. He's determined to squeeze the last bit of gold he can out of every tunnel. He claims we're running at a loss and wants to get everything even before he leaves. Dall finished the water and poured a second glass. "You know my opinion on that matter.

"Worse, this push to get the last bit of gold out of Number Four before he leaves has the men concerned abut their safety. A few are talking about going to Treadwell or Mexican Hat."

"That's just what we need. Rotten timbers, collapsed tunnels, a greedy manager, and a bunch of deserting miners. Cornelius Lassiter was right; and this mine is closer to going belly-up than even he suspected."

"What's Lassiter got to do with anything?" Dall asked, his impatience as evident as the dirt ground into his clothing.

"He wants to buy the Gray Wolf." Matthew eyed the proposal Millard DuBois had delivered several weeks before. A quick glance at the numbers reminded him Lassiter was offering little more than the amount of the loans encumbering the mine. That alone called into question how much inside information Lassiter had about the Gray Wolf.

Dall set the empty glass on the tray beside the water jug. "Are you going to sell the mine to him?"

"I suspect this is one of those cases where the buyer knows a helluva lot more about the financial intricacies than the seller does." He picked up the proposal and handed it to Dall. "Read it yourself. I may not know the subtleties of managing a mining business—"

"You didn't want to know."

"—but I know men like Cornelius Lassiter. He's a polished version of my father. And I understand *business*." He eyed Dall. "Has anyone been hanging around the mine and asking questions?"

"Not that I know of."

"Hmmm." Nothing went on around the mine Dall didn't know about—sooner or later. He made it his business to know everyone and everything about his men.

"I'll ask Henry if he's noticed anyone around the stampers or smelter. He thinks those machines are his."

Matthew nodded. The two men he trusted most cared about the mine and the men. He doubted Lassiter or Camden gave the miners a second thought after examining the bottom line he couldn't find.

"Tell me about the timbers." Matthew settled behind the desk and made several notes.

Dall pulled a chair away from the wall and sat. "Before coming over here, I checked my personal records. Last September I ordered those timbers replaced and signed the authorization myself. I was with Ellison when the work started. He'd assured me everything was taken care of. Hell, I had no reason to question Ellison or doubt his word."

"Sam Ellison?" Matthew asked, jotting down the name. "One of the foremen Camden hired from the Mexican Hat?"

"Yeah. He took over tunnels four and five during the time Murchison recovered from a broken arm." Dall looked out the window. "Remember? Murchison tried to stop an ore cart when it hit a bad patch of track and tipped. That bad rail was the first serious accident since the Old Man hired me. In light of our talk the other day, it could be something else is happening here."

"What do you mean?" Matthew had the sick sensation he knew exactly what Dall implied.

"Thinking back, Ellison never said he'd replaced the timbers, just that he'd followed orders. It's time for a heart-to-heart with Sam Ellison."

"Good God, what other shortcuts did Camden order?" Matthew wondered aloud. "No one else should ever override your orders to the men!" He glanced at the drafting board, realizing he wouldn't finish before midnight. Again.

A rapid knock on the door preceded its opening. Randal Skinner, Matthew's partner in the construction business, poked his head into the office. "Mueller's here and ready to get started. Did you finish the changes the Carters wanted in the kitchen and pantry?"

"Yeah. Get a time estimate for them, will you?" Matthew retrieved a journal from the bookcase behind him, selected a scroll from the drawing bin in the corner, then handed them off.

Randal touched the edge of the scroll to his forehead as a way of acknowledgment and quietly closed the door.

"Where were we?" Matthew resumed his seat.

"Ellison, Camden, rotten timbers," Dall said, eyeing the project books behind Matthew. "Are all those active?"

Head nodding, Matthew made a note on a separate sheet of paper. "Randal and I have done well the last couple of years."

"You really don't need the mine, do you?"

When Matthew looked up from his notes, Dall regarded him with an odd expression. He dropped the pencil on the desktop and tossed the paper into a nearly overflowing basket labeled ACTIVE. "Never wanted it. Never needed it. Never expected to inherit it. Did you ever think otherwise?"

"I thought you might have a twinge or two."

"My only concern with the mine is for the men and their families. Any deal I make for the sale of the Gray Wolf will have provisions for them."

"For how long?"

"As long as the gold lasts or they work for the new owner. At least long enough for them to find other employment if they want. Realistically, that's the best I can hope for." He leaned back and regarded Dall with new interest. "Are you interested in buying her?"

"Maybe. If she's for sale when I get ready to settle down."

"Don't know if I can wait that long." Matthew checked

his notes. "Meanwhile, what say we have a chat with Ellison and get to the bottom of this? If he's taking shortcuts or compromising safety, I want him gone." Matthew rose and reached for his coat.

"Could be he's doing both on Camden's orders."

"I need your help," Bethany told Matthew the next afternoon. She'd hurried to Matthew's office straight from school, not even bothering to grade papers or check over the assignments the elder Bittlehorn twins had turned in. Even her precious valise had remained beside her desk.

Today she'd find the underlying cause of Laurie Craddock's bruises. All Bethany's instincts screamed something was very wrong in the six-year-old's life. In similar instances, the cause was rooted at home, and bore the label: child abuse.

Bethany walked a thin line between intervention and interference. Children lacked the legal protection they'd have a century from now, but she had to do something. Visiting the parents was a start.

Matthew rose from his drafting board and turned around. "What do you need?"

"Laurie Craddock's address. The one in the files is wrong." Fiercely determined to confront the girl's parents, she'd already decided to follow the child home if necessary. But this way seemed easier.

Perplexity wrinkled Matthew's brow. "What do you need her address for?"

"I need to speak with her parents."

"Her mother's dead. All she has is her father."

"Then I want to speak with him."

Matthew reached for his coat. "From that look in your eye, he may not want to speak with you, Bethany. We'll go over there together."

"I've dealt with difficult parents before and don't need a baby-sitter. Besides, I know you're busy. Just give me the address and directions, and I'll find it myself." Judging by the barrels of scrolled plans and the orderly way every nook and cranny held papers, periodicals, books, or samples of building materials, Matthew had outgrown the office. The outer room was just as cramped.

"Bull Craddock isn't the sociable sort."

"This won't be a social call." Anger burned in her stomach. "And it really isn't necessary for you—"

"The hell it isn't."

His firm grip on her upper arm felt possessive. Worse, she wasn't sure she liked the fires his touch still ignited. They'd had sex, satisfied their curiosity, slaked the heated desire boiling between them, so why was it back? "Look, all I'm asking for are accurate records. You don't need to interrupt your day or get your shorts in a wad over a home visit."

"My *what?* Never mind." He spoke briefly to the men in the outer office.

Unwilling to argue in front of others, Bethany waited until they reached the neutrality of the boardwalk before digging in her heels. "Matthew—"

"You haven't met Bull Craddock."

She had to admit she hadn't. During their painting party Laurie was the only child without a parent in attendance. Bethany suspected she knew why.

"It's best if I introduce you. Bull is somewhat of a recluse. He goes from work to home and back. His life is his daughter."

She started to say something, then held her silence. Matthew would understand a man who'd lost the wife he loved and still grieved. But that didn't explain Laurie's bruises. More than ever she wanted to put a stop to the child's injuries.

"Why are you doing this?" she asked. But resigned, unsure whether she found pleasure or pain in his company, Bethany fell into step beside him.

"Several reasons. The first is selfish."

She glanced up, noting the smudges of fatigue beneath his eyes. "Such as?" Although he owed her nothing, not even an explanation for why he hadn't made it a point to see her since they'd slept together, she couldn't help goading him. The bliss they'd shared in the attic of Gray House had no strings, no obligations. She'd wanted it that way.

"I've wanted to see you. If it takes the form of problem resolution, I'll settle for that."

"Who said there's a problem?" The biggest problem in her life walked beside her. Ignoring the sexual tension coiling inside her posed new issues. Now that she'd tasted pleasure with him, she wanted more. Instead of abating, the need to touch him, to revel in his kiss, and feel him moving inside her, had assumed fresh urgency.

They walked in silence for nearly a block.

"About the other night . . ." Matthew started, his voice as tight as his looks.

"There's nothing to discuss. It happened. It's over. It won't happen again. You're in no danger of being anyone's daddy."

"It's not that simple."

A distant siren whined into a full scream. Everyone on the street froze.

"Son of a bitch," Matthew seethed.

"What? What is it?"

"Disaster."

Bethany instinctively scanned the empty sky for marauding airplanes. "What kind of disaster?"

"That's the Gray Wolf's siren."

The next thing she knew, Matthew took off at a run toward Ludden's livery, half a block away.

Whatever was happening, Bethany intended to witness it firsthand. "Wait for me!" she cried. Skirts hiked, she raced after him.

She caught him at the livery as he mounted his horse. "I'm going with you," she said.

"No."

"Every pair of hands helps if you have wounded." She clutched his leg. "You know I'm good in a crisis. Take me with you."

"What'll it be, Mr. Gray?" Oscar Ludden asked with a gap-toothed grin. "You want me to hold the little lady while you head out?"

Cursing, Matthew slid in a fluid move off his horse, picked her up and threw her onto the steed's bare back. He bolted up behind her. "I hope like hell you can ride, Miss James."

"I was born on a horse," she assured him. Catching the reins, she patted the chestnut's big neck. A firm nudge to his sides let him know it was time to go. "Which way?"

"South, through town. Give me the reins."

"Hold on and don't be a backseat driver."

With her bent low over his neck and Matthew conforming to the contour of her back, the big horse sensed the urgency of his riders. It galloped through town and toward the Gray Wolf mine. Almost every man in town seemed to move toward the same destination. Sirens screamed. Bells clanged.

Following Matthew's directions, Bethany let the horse out all the way.

They passed a buckboard with the Golden Nugget's markings on the sides. The hilly terrain barely slowed their horse. The closer they got to the mine, the louder the sirens wailed.

Not until they crested the last hill did Bethany glimpse the size and expanse of the Gray Wolf. Half a dozen large buildings jutted from the rocky land crowding the sea. A long, two-story barracks nestled against a line of trees. Smokestacks rose from what had to be the noisiest building on God's green earth. Dimly, Bethany realized it housed the ore stampers. A brick chimney jutted above another sturdy building.

Everyone's attention was focused on an odd, angular wood structure rising from the ground and towering over the rest.

Bethany reined the horse in that direction, slowing it to avoid the steel tracks leading to a building with a MAINTENANCE sign over the door.

Before she stopped the horse, Matthew slid off.

Dust billowed from the blown-out windows and open doors of their destination. As they watched, six coughing, choking men stumbled out. Two fell to their knees and hunched over in the clear air.

Matthew and three other men ran to help the rest of the miners escape the roiling, noxious dust cloud.

"Who else is down there? How many?" Matthew demanded.

"Five," said the nearest man between coughing jags. "Ellison, Lockner," he paused, coughed hard, then continued, "Craddock, Meeker, and the Russian in Tunnel Four. Don't know how many on the lower levels. We was in Tunnel Three."

The last vestige of color drained from Matthew's face, his hands balled into fists, and he swore. If looks could burn, the entire mountain would become lava running into the sea.

"There were men in Tunnel Five, too," said a smaller man wiping his eyes with his grimy sleeve.

People streamed up the slope. Most were on foot, but a few rode horses, and several came in wagons, including the Golden Nugget's buckboard. In open amazement, Bethany watched the chaos turn into what appeared to be a well-rehearsed drill.

Shouts from inside the mine house and the screech of metal on metal chased the dust cloud from the building.

"Clear the lines! Why the hell aren't the blowers running? Get clean air down there now!" Matthew barked orders and the men followed. "Why the hell are the stampers still running? Shut 'em down. Now!"

Thunderstruck, Bethany slid off the horse. Holding the reins, she watched a side of Matthew emerge that she'd barely glimpsed before. The man was a natural leader, and the miners looked to him for guidance.

The full impact of what was going on struck her like a physical blow. All she knew about mining were the images from educational channels on television, those specials on operations which were gargantuan open pits with trucks the size of buildings moving along roads cut into the earth.

Infected by the fear riding the air like a contagious virus, she led her horse to a small corral where three other mounts huddled around a water trough. As she did, she watched Matthew disappear into the open jaws of the mine house doors.

At last, electric lights brightened the interior through the thinning dust. The stampers broke cadence; the deafening noise slacked off as the mining operation shut down. The final sounds of the big rock crushers echoed between the mountains scraping the sky and patient, quiet sea.

Shouts and cries came from the opposite side of the building housing the Gray Wolf business offices. Bethany closed the corral and dashed toward the sound.

She was just in time to watch the last of a dozen wounded men being carried to the mine offices. She hurried to lend assistance.

One glance was all it took to let her know no one was in charge. The men carrying their coworkers had no inkling of what to do or where to put them.

"Where's the first-aid kit?" she asked the nearest man.

He looked at her as through she'd spoken Greek.

"Medical supplies," she reiterated.

He pointed to a cabinet in the room across the hall.

Within moments, the sheer number of suffering men daunted Bethany. Part of her screamed to run; the other part identified so intimately with these men's plight that she had to help.

She tucked up her skirts and knelt beside the closest victim. Even through the blood and grime he didn't look a day over sixteen. She touched his cheek; he didn't even shave yet.

"Am . . . am I gonna die?" he asked in a voice even younger than he looked.

"Not if I can help it," Bethany said with far more assurance than she felt. "You," she ordered the man standing beside them, tugging on his trousers to get his attention. "Get fresh water and clean cloths."

He nodded and started to obey. Bethany caught his trousers leg again. "Go outside and brush yourself off first, then wash your hands."

The man examined his filthy hands as though just discovering they belonged to him.

"Hurry," she encouraged gently, realizing he too was in shock. Then, "Where do you hurt?" she asked the boy in front of her.

The man she'd asked about medical supplies brought a box over. She gave him quick thanks, then another task. She needed to get these men helping each other!

"M' leg's broke. I ain't gonna lose it, am I?" asked the boy.

Bethany found a scissors in the medical supply box and cut the young man's trousers leg along the bloody seam. She intentionally avoided a close look at the sharp right angle of his heavy boot. She fought down the bile rising in her throat. "It's broken, all right." At least the bone wasn't poking through the skin. The majority of the blood soaking his duck trousers oozed from a wound higher up, on his thigh.

"What's your name?"

"Billy, ma'am."

"Billy Ma'am? That's an unusual name." She checked his left arm, which seemed fine. His right posed a new problem. A piece of wood protruded from his biceps. A quick swipe with the scissors opened the rent in the shirt wider.

"Edwards, ma'am. Billy Edwards from Choctaw Creek, Oklahoma."

She managed a smile while rummaging through the medical supplies. "I'd never have guessed you were a Southerner. I take it you're a tough young man."

"Yes, ma'am. Do what ya gotta do, and I'll be better for it."

God, she hoped so. Using alcohol and a sterile rag, she cleaned the area around the wound in his biceps. She met his trusting gaze for a moment, got a firm grip on the wood impaling his arm, and pulled it free.

To his credit, young Billy only closed his eyes and inhaled sharply.

"This needs stitching, Billy."

"Go ahead. I kin take it."

"I've never stitched anyone up before."

"*I'll* do it."

"Megan! Am I glad to see you." Relief flowed through Bethany at the arrival of her friends. At last, someone who knew what to do and how!

"The lad behind us is in need of attention," the Irishwoman commanded.

Nodding, managing a weak smile for Billy, Bethany turned her attention to the next man.

Doc Swenson thundered into the room several minutes later.

Bethany looked up from tending a man with a crushed hip and probable internal injuries. Her heart sank. She knew a drunk when she saw one and she didn't need to look closely at Doc Swenson to see just that. She smelled the sour stench of stale alcohol through the sweat, blood, and dust.

The bearded man she'd been helping shook his head in resignation and closed his eyes. A few minutes later, while Doc Swenson hustled, bustled, and bellowed, her patient stopped breathing.

Bethany moved on to the next man, and continued doing so until Paul Ryman, the Treadwell Mine's doctor, arrived and put her to work as his assistant. A short, pudgy, balding man whose glasses balanced on the end of his pug nose, Dr. Ryman set to work with a no-nonsense efficiency.

Shortly after midnight, Bethany settled on the bench outside the Gray Wolf offices beside Megan.

"How many dinna make it?" the woman asked.

"Three. Four more might not last the night. Dr. Ryman is tending them. Thank God he came."

"Amen," Megan agreed.

Noise and shouts erupted from the mining house. Someone yelled for Dr. Ryman, and the man appeared suddenly and hurried across the compound.

Bethany and Megan followed.

"What's happening?" Bethany asked when they reached the yawning doors.

"They're bringing up the rest of the men."

"Then we've work to do," Megan said, taking Bethany's arm and pushing inside.

The lift creaked and groaned. Though it cleared the ground, all six men on it looked dead.

# Chapter Nineteen

Although no one had expected Matthew to lead the rescue crew into the depths of the mine, guilt assailed him. The truth was, he couldn't force himself to get on the lift and descend into the inky darkness. Even if the blast hadn't taken out the lighting in the tunnels, the claustrophobia he'd developed nearly half a lifetime ago prevented him from entering that cramped darkness.

Every other man in the compound could and would search the tunnels for survivors, but not the owner of the Gray Wolf Mine.

No, not him.

Nothing—not guilt, shame, anger, or desperation—quelled the sweaty panic that damn near froze him at the thought of descending into the closed, confining darkness, that void in which the walls moved in until they slowly, inexorably squeezed the air from your lungs.

When he weighed his responsibilities, he found himself lacking. He was less of a man than any here. Regardless of how he tried to compensate, that reality hung over him like an anvil ready to drop and crush him.

The hardest to face were those close to the men who had died. Doc Swenson had brought the names of three miners who hadn't survived. Then, claiming the injured were in good hands and the dead beyond help, he returned to town and his unfinished drink.

Driven by anger at his own weakness, Matthew worked tirelessly to help the survivors.

He oversaw and set up a hospital ward on the first floor of the barracks. The displaced residents swapped out their belongings with those of the injured.

Worried about the condition of the remaining men, he checked the makeshift infirmary hourly. Each time, he saw Bethany grafted to Dr. Ryman's elbow.

Thank God Paul Ryman was both a humanitarian and a competent physician willing to cross company lines.

"Camden," Matthew called across the compound upon seeing the mine manager. He took a cup of water from one of the men, drained it, and tossed the tin cup back. "Where the hell have you been?"

"Doing my job." Camden whipped off his tie and stuffed it into his stained pocket. "We're going to miss our projected yield this shipment. We need to get the stampers going again and men into tunnels Two and Three. I understand they're undamaged."

Not quite believing he'd heard correctly, Matthew stopped in his tracks. "You want to resume operations?"

"We must—while we still have the chance to make up for the time lost."

The man had a heart harder than the quartz encasing the gold in a granite crust. "We'll resume operation when you've personally checked all the tunnels and we've made sure every man is accounted for." Anger and fatigue sharpened his already planted dislike for Camden. "I don't give a damn about quotas or shipments."

"You will when those loans come due."

"Men died down there today." Matthew had never wanted to hit a man as badly as he did at that moment. "Go count rocks, Camden. Stay the hell out of my sight. This mine doesn't open until I say."

"And when will that be?"

In the light spilling out of the mine house, Camden's dark eyes glittered with hostility.

"Maybe in a few days." If he had a choice? Never. "I'll let you know. Meanwhile, you get the rest of the statements and files I asked for. And don't tell me they're at Gray House. I've looked at every piece of paper there. We both know the Old Man never threw anything away. I'm out of patience and you're out of time." Seething, Matthew turned on his heel and stormed back toward the mine house.

"Comin' up," called a man from across the way. The cry continued throughout the complex and brought men on the run.

Inside the cavernous mine house rising nearly four stories over the shaft, the lift mechanism creaked. Timbers groaned.

The lift stopped at ground level. Six men lay against one another on the floor in a tangle of arms and legs. The fine powder of pulverized granite had turned shiny black where it mixed with their blood.

Dread ate at Matthew's gut. He waited for Dr. Ryman to examine the men. In the apprehensive quiet, the physician's softly spoken orders were followed without hesitation.

The sound of his name brought Matthew to the lift, which was closer to the black hellhole of the mine shaft than he'd ventured since men had dug him out years ago.

His gaze riveted on Bull Craddock's lifeless body on a stretcher, and he swore.

The last man taken from the lift was Dall.

With Bethany glued to his side, Dr. Ryman spoke quietly and used a thin rod to poke and prod places on Dall's legs. "Your back is broken, son," he finally said.

Matthew crouched onto one knee beside his friend.

Dall's pain-filled gaze met his for a long moment before flicking to Bethany and the doctor.

"Give us a minute?" Matthew asked them.

Bethany tucked her hand in the crook of Dr. Ryman's arm and tugged him away from the others.

Matthew put his ear next to Dall's mouth.

"Rotten timber," Dall breathed.

Matthew nodded, listening, watching Bethany's animated, private discussion with Ryman. The doctor appeared both interested and skeptical.

"Ellison knew. Camden. Son of a bitch."

Judging from Dall's increasingly laborious breathing, speaking taxed his waning strength.

Matthew raised his head slightly and watched Dall's eyes. "Camden told him not to replace the timbers?" he asked so softly only Dall heard.

His friend closed his eyes and nodded.

"Is that what caused the cave-in?"

Dall shook his head and tried to speak. All he got out was "Blasting."

Matthew's blood chilled in his veins. "Ellison was blasting with men in the tunnels?"

Bit by painful bit, Matthew extracted the bare bones of the events leading to the cave-in.

"I'll kill that son of a bitch," he seethed at last.

Dall caught his wrist in a surprisingly strong grip. His dusty head shook and the fire of revenge burned in his eyes. "He's mine," he croaked.

"Time's up, Mr. Gray. Miss James and I have plans for this man."

Bethany knelt beside the wounded miner and cradled his face in her small hands. "Will you trust me, Dall?"

"For what?"

"Son, your back is broken. I can't help you," Dr. Ryman said. "Miss James thinks she can, and I'm inclined to believe her."

The bottom fell out of Matthew's stomach. He heard nothing beyond his friend living in a wheelchair for the rest of his life. The threat of tears stung his eyes. When his vision cleared, Bethany was tucking blankets around Dall and forming a brace around his head.

"I need your best craftsman, a welder, and free use of the machine shop," Bethany said.

"Whatever you need, you get." Matthew barked orders in the otherwise silent mine house. Two minutes later, Bethany left with three of the best craftsmen the Gray Wolf employed.

"Stay with him, Mr. Gray. We don't want to move him any more than necessary, so until Miss James is ready, he'll stay here," Dr. Ryman said to Matthew, before addressing Dall. "You're in excellent hands. Do what she says. I'll check on you later."

Then the last rescue crew arrived, and he hurried off to attend his other patients.

Bethany awoke with a jolt. When had she dozed off?

Nightmares of men with crushed limbs and sightless eyes filled her sleep. She wasn't alone in her dreams, either. Mary Katherine Murphy held baby Patrick on her left.

The dead woman beseeched Bethany to care for her child and never allow him into the mines.

Laurie Craddock watched with sad blue eyes colored by loss and loneliness. Her small hands remained clutched in front her. Dream-Bethany felt the girl's longing to reach out and connect. The stoic child stood apart from everyone else, unaware of how to breach the invisible barrier and ask for what she needed.

Disoriented, Bethany sat up slowly on the wooden chair she'd pulled over to Dall Lockner's bed. She looked around and took her bearings. Sun streamed through the parted window drapery. These all-purpose quarters had become a hospital room.

Immediately, Bethany checked on Dall.

The traction device the woodworker and welder had constructed on Dall's iron-framed bed held him motionless. The deep rhythm of his breathing assured her that he slept soundly. Morphine and exhaustion had dragged him into oblivion.

She laid the inside of her wrist on his forehead. Satisfied he wasn't running a fever, she stood and stretched.

The sight of Matthew approaching with a cup of steaming coffee caught her with her arms raised and her mouth wide in the middle of a jaw-popping yawn.

"How is he?" Matthew asked in a low voice.

She took the mug he offered and settled back in her chair. "I'll have a better idea in a couple of days."

Zombies in a horror movie had a healthier pallor than Matthew. The dark smudges beneath his eyes weren't makeup, and two-day growth of heavy beard added menace to his appearance. Crazily, she found herself thinking he had the most patriotic eyes she'd seen in years: red, white, and blue.

"You've got him trussed like a Christmas turkey. He's going to hate being confined to bed."

"A year from now he won't care. This is his only chance at walking like he was yesterday morning, if ever again." The scant bit of restless sleep she'd gotten had left her more tired than when her eyelids had first drifted closed. "Great Gerty's Ghost, what time is it? I've got to get to school."

"School is canceled until after the funerals. Megan and Henry sent word to the families."

"*Laurie*. What will happen to her?" Bethany's heart

ached at the thought of the Craddock girl being alone in the world. "Is there any other family she can go to? Are there any relatives who'd be willing to raise her?"

"Not that I know of, but I've got people working on it." His gaze never left his friend. "What do you call that thing holding his head?"

"It's a brace to keep his neck and upper back immobile. I put his legs in a makeshift traction device to immobilize his lower back. The cradle holding his hips is for reinforcement. The welder is working on a rotator device; Dall has to be moved periodically so his lungs don't fill up and he doesn't get bedsores. If we have this figured out correctly, we'll be able to secure him as he is now, and move the entire bed so it'll be the equivalent of him lying on his stomach." God, she hoped this worked. During the construction, and later when the men laid Dall into the coffinlike niche of his bed, she'd prayed. Now, it was up to Heaven and Dall's recuperative powers.

"How did you know to do this for him?"

The simple question was anything but simple. She couldn't answer without opening the floodgate of her secrets. When he met her gaze, she knew everything had changed.

"You don't want an answer."

"The hell I don't. Ryman couldn't help him. How is it you knew what to do when he didn't?"

She looked away, not trusting herself to answer.

"Damn it all, Bethany! What's going on with you? What the hell are you hiding?"

She snapped. "That's it. I can't do this anymore." She started to rise, knowing if she didn't leave they'd both regret it.

Matthew's hand gently fell on her shoulder and kept her in the chair. "No one expects you to take care of Dall. You've done all you can for him." The edge of his voice fell away when he continued, "All I need are a few simple answers."

She drew a heavy breath. "I wasn't referring to Dall or anything else that happened last night." The shadow of senseless death crept across the bedrock of her soul. Lessons from the past rang in her ears.

Regardless of where or when she was, life was too short to live a lie. Somewhere in the midst of this tragedy, the great truth Bethany had learned two years ago resurfaced.

"You're a good man, Matthew Gray, with a lot on your mind and the weight of the world on your shoulders. You aren't ready to hear the answer to your question, so don't ask me anymore. I'm too tired to shine you on. In fact, I'm just tired of living a lie."

"What lie are you living?" He looked her in the eye. "Damn it, Bethany . . ."

Lord, she was tired. "Leave me alone, Matthew."

He repeated the question as his thumb moved slowly across her collarbone.

"One of normalcy. The truth can't help you or anyone else. Not even me." *Let me out of this chair. I'm too tired for sparring.*

"Why don't you let me be the judge of what I'm ready to hear?"

She grimaced against the fist of sorrow tightening inside her, but she had to go forward. "All right, Matthew. All right." She took another sip of her coffee.

"I know about broken backs because I had one. I laid in a contraption far more sophisticated than this one for three months. I had the best doctors, hospitals, and surgery procedures available.

"For two of those three months I had a lot of time on my hands. I wanted to know everything about the ramifications of the five surgeries I'd had, the pins holding my bones together . . ."

Memories of lying in the hospital day after day crashed

down on Bethany with the force of an avalanche. "I asked questions, studied the books and articles my sisters brought, and picked the brains of every doctor and nurse who walked into my room. I learned many things during those three months."

"I had no idea medicine had come so far," Matthew mused. "What kind of pins hold bones together?"

"Stainless steel. You won't see them in your lifetime, Matthew, because today's medical profession doesn't know anything about what I went through. They're only beginning to understand how to treat someone with Dall's injuries. He can feel his feet; his spinal cord is intact. Probably bruised, but that'll heal with time if the broken vertebra don't sever it. That's why he has to be immobilized."

"I don't understand. Tell me about how you got pins in your bones." His absolute stillness and the tone of his voice reminded her of a steel hand in a velvet glove. He wouldn't hurt her, but he wasn't leaving until she told him what he wanted to know.

"I was in car crash. Four people died. I was the only survivor, and more dead than alive when they cut me out of the wreckage. That happened November twenty-fourth, 1999. Two of the fatalities were my parents. Of the other two, one was a drunk; the other was his fifteen-month-old daughter."

Matthew's expressionless stare made her wonder if anything she said had reached him. It didn't matter. The floodgates had opened and her secrets were spilling out.

"We have vehicles; they're descendants of Henry Ford's cars. My mind is too fuzzy to remember when they became available." Was it 1893 or 1903?

"Whatever," she encouraged herself. "Anyway, it was a head-on collision at seventy miles an hour." She closed her eyes, remembering as though it had happened yesterday. Other than giving the facts to the police in the hospital, she hadn't spoken about the crash since.

"I didn't hear you correctly." Matthew rubbed his eyes with his thumb and forefinger as if awakening from a dream. "I thought you said seventy miles an hour."

"I did."

"Seventy miles an hour? More than a mile a minute? You must be mistaken. I can't fathom—"

"I'm not mistaken. Both my legs were broken. So was my back, and several ribs. But it was the internal injuries that damn near killed me. No one thought I'd live. Not even me. And there were times when I didn't want to survive. My sisters wouldn't let me give up."

"Slow down. Did you say 1999?"

"That's what I said, Matthew. Over a century from now, and coming up on three years ago for me." She almost felt sorry for him, almost. The night's events had necessitated tamping her emotions into an invisible bottle and hammering down the cork. If she let them out now, they'd erupt in all directions.

Unable to watch his struggle, she lowered her gaze and continued. "On June third, 2001, I sang at two funerals. The first one started in Drexel, Wyoming; the second service was your father's."

"That's not possible." Anger charged his voice.

She flinched, realizing she was destroying something precious—a trust she'd earned from him she might never regain. "Say what you like. Believe what you will. I don't have the luxury of denial."

"How could such a thing happen?"

"I was swept away by a phenomenon called the River of Time. Oh, I was warned. Yolanda D'Arcy warned me, and I heard her, but I didn't listen. Not really. At the time, I was too busy feeling sorry for myself because I'd survived death and paid a helluva price in the process.

"When I fell down that hill into your graveyard, I was coming from much farther away than Wyoming. I'd traveled over a century back in time. That's why I had no luggage, and why you couldn't find the name of the ship I arrived on. If I had the vaguest idea of how to get back, I'd go. But I don't.

"Now you can choose to believe me or not. That's out of my hands, too."

"You need some sleep, Bethany. You're delusional."

"Don't we both wish it was simple enough for a few hours of sleep to be the answer? But it isn't." She hadn't expected him to accept her fantastic claim.

"Come on, I'll get you home. After you sleep—"

"Nothing will be different, Matthew. I'll still be a stranded castaway on the River of Time." She handed back her coffee cup. "I am going home. Meanwhile, Dall shouldn't be left alone."

Before her spine turned to jelly, Bethany left. She couldn't bear looking back at Matthew. And when she closed the door, she knew the gulf between them was broadening with every step.

Why was the right thing to do always so painful?

"Ya havena been home yet, lass?" Jeb asked Bethany as she left the foreman's quarters.

Squinting, she lifted her hand to shade her eyes. "What are you doing here?"

"Deliverin' supplies. How's Dall? Will the man walk again?"

"He's sleeping. Matthew is with him. As for him walking, it's too soon to tell."

Jeb reached down from his perch on the buckboard. "Give me your hand. Ya look ready to drop."

"I am." She hiked her skirt, took his hand, and climbed up to join him. "Tell me you're taking me home."

"Aye, lass, I am."

"You're an angel." A stretch limousine couldn't be more welcome.

*"Bethany."*

She turned on the seat at the sound of Matthew's voice. Anguish pinched his features and blazed in his bloodshot eyes. She opened her mouth, but the words caught in her throat.

"We're not done talking," he called. When she managed a nod, he looked satisfied and returned to help his miners. The door closed slowly behind him.

"Ya both look like somethin' run over by a team of horses," Jeb said.

That was exactly how Bethany's heart felt.

# *Chapter Twenty*

As owner of the Gray Wolf, Matthew assumed responsibility for burying the five men who lost their lives in the bowels of his mine.

Over Camden's strenuous objections, he also assumed financial responsibility for the burials. Matthew had yet to determine how to compensate Anton Slokov's widow and one very stoic orphan. Their lives had changed forever in the blink of an eye.

Recompense of income was obvious, but restitution for a spouse was impossible. Nothing made up for the loss of a loved one's warmth on a cold winter night. Or a loving touch. A shared glance that spoke louder than words.

His gut churning with frustration and sympathy, Matthew assumed the grim task of arranging the services personally.

Fog shrouded the treetops climbing the mountains behind the cemetery. An unseasonable chill rode the early afternoon of the funeral. Most of the town had turned out for the graveside services; men from the Treadwell, Mexican Hat, and Bear's Nest mines crossed the Gastineau Channel to pay their respects.

Everything in Matthew stilled when he caught sight of Bethany at the foot of Bull Craddock's grave. Clad in black with a white diaper draped over her shoulder, she cradled Patrick in her left arm and held Laurie Craddock's hand with her right.

What was there about Bethany that attracted the bereft and wounded spirits—his own included?

A wiry Scotsman draped in a navy-and-green Campbell tartan stood on the hillside. The black ribbon of his bonnet hung at an angle and disappeared into his curly, shoulder-length hair. The sleeves of his blousy, snow-white shirt rippled quietly in the breeze as he played a dirge on his bagpipes. The mournful wail filled the air with sorrow. Beside him, a young miner in need of a haircut and dressed in his finest clothing, outgrown several years ago, harmonized on a harmonica. It was a strange amalgam of sound.

Father O'Sullivan gave a requiem for three of the men in Latin, then Reverend Pettis, pastor of the Anglican Church, prayed for the remaining two miners in English.

Matthew stood slightly apart from the others. He had a clear view of the five graves and the faces of the mourners. How in God's name had this happened? Why? He was prepared to beggar himself to compensate these people, to find the truth behind the cave-in. He took it upon himself to ensure there was justice for those burying loved ones today.

Again, his gaze settled on the trio at the foot of Bull's grave. The dry-eyed little girl damn near broke his heart.

When the time came for Matthew to deliver the miners' eulogy, he tried to clear the lump from his throat but didn't quite succeed.

He began with the miner's prayer he'd learned half a

lifetime ago. Next, he spoke about each man, his family affiliations, and acknowledged those left behind. Matthew cited individual talents, skills, and personalities, trying to keep them alive for another minute in the minds and hearts of those clustered at the graves.

"In finishing, I'd like to mention that the Gray Wolf won't resume operations until we've got the debris cleared from the tunnels and new timbers set. There will be other changes. I'll keep you informed as they're made." Most important, before work resumed, he'd have an open assessment from the miners who worked those tunnels. Camden's opinion on the operation wasn't worth a pile of sand.

"Thank you for coming," he said, "and may God have mercy on us all."

Before the buzz of conjecture started, Bethany began to sing "Amazing Grace." The bagpiper and harmonica players joined in a subdued complement.

The bundle of blankets in Bethany's arms stirred, but Patrick didn't cry. The baby was probably looking up at her with the same wide-eyed fascination with which Matthew regarded her. She was right, he realized. Patrick belonged with her. And he had no doubt she'd choose a good father for him when she was finally ready to wed.

A sudden shortness of breath caught him off guard. The idea of Bethany married to anyone else made him sick.

His throat closed at the sight of Laurie Craddock showing the first signs of emotion. The child clutched Bethany's hand in both of her own as though she would never let go. The two had become an island at the foot of Bull's grave. Tears rolled down Laurie's cheeks as Bethany sang.

Her lament chipped away the protective armor Matthew had constructed the last couple of days.

" 'I once was lost but now am found . . .' "

Matthew knew he himself was the wretch in that song—lost, but with not much of chance of being found.

Why had Bethany come into his life, only to make him so crazy?

She seemed so . . . normal. Perhaps fatigue had made her delusional the other morning. What other explanation was there?

" ' 'Tis grace hath brought me safe thus far, and grace will lead me home.' "

*Home.*

A simple word with so many implications.

A gust of wind sent Bethany's skirt billowing, and he recalled the clothing she'd worn the day he found her. The soft feel, the texture and colors that defied description . . . and her boots had been even odder.

Suppose she'd told the truth about where her home was? In that light, her explanation made perfect sense. The strange bits of knowledge she revealed like golden nuggets shining in the depths of a mine had originated in another time and place.

Matthew watched her at the foot of Bull Craddock's grave. She'd switched to "Ave Maria," and the harmonica on the hill cried in harmony.

*Home.*

*It isn't possible to travel through time.*

If she wasn't delusional, perhaps she hid a bigger secret. But he couldn't fathom what it might be. And he couldn't ignore the way she'd brought Mary Katherine Murphy back to life. Not when he'd seen it with his own eyes. Nor could he pretend the elaborate scheme she'd contrived for Dall was anything short of brilliant. And damn, it all made too much sense for him to doubt.

He wanted a simple, plausible, *different* explanation.

Listening to his songbird transition to "The Lord's Prayer," he admitted that nothing about her would ever be simple.

No one moved when she finished, as the final notes of the bagpipe and harmonica faded into stillness.

Matthew couldn't drag his gaze away. She evoked emotions he'd never thought to experience again. But allowing the resurrection of those tender feelings hurt like hell. He'd grown accustomed to the numbness of not caring after Victoria's death. For two years he hadn't allowed anything to penetrate his defenses. Nor had he afforded anyone the opportunity to try.

Yet, without even trying, Bethany had melted the shell formed by his pain and grief. And he wasn't sure whether he wanted the numbness back.

Surrounded by reminders of past tragedies, Matthew longed for the sense of connection he and Bethany had shared when they hastily made love in the attic. Frenzied and unrestrained, her need had rivaled his own. Then, as now, desire knew no master—particularly not discretion or caution.

"Excuse me, Mr. Gray."

Yanked from his reverie, Matthew turned his attention to the woman in front of him. "Yes, Mrs. Chester?"

"I don't mean no disrespect, but I can't keep care of Laurie much longer. It was one thing ta look after her for Bull while he worked. Now that he's gone, well, things've changed." With a chapped hand callused by too much work and too little rest, the woman tucked a drab brown lock of hair into her chignon. "Jody, my husband, he hasn't come back from his last voyage. Truth is, I don't expect him to. I got enough mouths ta feed. Laurie's a good girl, but I jest can't take her in permanent-like."

"I understand." Matthew reached into his pocket and brought out a pair of five-dollar gold pieces. "Thank you for taking care of her as long as you have. If you could do it a while longer, I'd appreciate it. Make sure she's fed, sheltered, and protected. If she needs anything, let me know. We'll work something out soon." Matthew sought the child who had listened to the news of her father's death without a sound, without a tear. She hadn't moved from Bethany's side.

"Fair enough and mighty generous of you, Mr. Gray." The Chester woman pocketed his coins. "Thank you." Head hanging, she joined the mourners near Bull Craddock's grave.

Matthew spoke to Anton Slokov's widow long enough to assess her immediate needs. Unlike his father, he couldn't walk away and leave the dependents of the mine's disaster on their own. He felt responsible.

He spoke with each of the men of the Gray Wolf and many of the miners from across the channel. After a bit, the graveyard emptied.

At last, Matthew stood with his hat in his hand at the foot of Victoria's grave. Their short courtship and marriage seemed a lifetime ago. He longed to bare his soul to her. Although she'd seldom offered advice, she'd been a safe harbor for his thoughts, hopes, and dreams.

"What a mess things are, Victoria," he whispered. The worst of it was Bethany, the woman he didn't want to love.

A short while later, he prepared to leave. The living needed him.

Half a dozen mourners remained in the graveyard. In the foggy afternoon, the only sounds were those of Mrs. Slokov's tears. How well he knew that only time could heal her.

When he looked around for Bethany, he saw her handing Patrick up to Megan. Jeb waved from the buggy seat. Once Megan and Patrick were settled, the Irish store owner rippled the traces and the horse began to move.

Bethany returned to the granite angel marking the Webster baby's grave and stared up the hill into the misty trees.

"Bethany?" If she became any paler she would fade from sight. "Are you ill?"

"No. I'm fine. You?"

"Great. Just great."

"Liar," she said without so much as a glance.

"What are you doing?" he asked.

"Listening."

"For what?" All he heard were the soft sounds of Elizabeth Slokov's sobs.

"The River of Time." Her tear-filled violet eyes looked over at him through thick black lashes. "This is too lonely, too painful. Right this minute, all I can think about is wanting to go home, Matthew. Back to the life I know and my sisters. Every time I hold Patrick . . ."

A stone fist slammed into his gut with the realization that her delusions of traveling through time persisted. "Would you feel that way if Patrick was yours?" He was careful to keep emotion out of his tone.

"This is his time and place. This is where he should grow up." Tears filled her lavender eyes. "Then there's sweet little Laurie Craddock. What will become of her?"

"Come on. I'll take you into town."

A sad smile tugged at the corners of her mouth as she turned away. "You haven't had much luck with schoolteachers lately, have you? The last one was a lecher who seduced an innocent fifteen-year-old student. Now you have me, whom you believe mentally unstable."

"I didn't say—"

"I see it your eyes, your expression, your body language. That's the thing about us twenty-first-century women. We're a lot more observant and less docile than our nineteenth-century counterparts."

He wasn't sure what to say. "I don't know what to believe." Placing his hand in the small of her back, he escorted her toward the road.

"For now, why don't you believe the children are in good hands with me as their teacher."

"Are they?" He wasn't sure of anything beyond his desire for her, anymore.

"Yes."

Silent, he helped her into the waiting buggy, and drove them back toward town.

As the buggy drew up to Gray House, Bethany could stand the silence no longer. "I was in the attic this morning," she said.

"What happened between us there—"

She lifted her hand to silence Matthew, loathing the possibility he'd regret what they shared. Under different circumstances with vastly different attitudes . . . "Things are as they are. Don't look back," she said. But what could she do with her own burning desire to strip him naked and make love with him in the sunshine?

"Do you regret it?" he asked, slowing the horse practically to a stop.

Bethany's breath caught in her throat, and she shook her head. "Not then. Not now. Not ever, Matthew. But it won't happen again."

"I'm not sure that's a comforting scenario, but it's the safest. If you were to have a child—"

"Don't worry, you're safe." *Very, very safe.*

He stopped the buggy in the middle of the street, braced his left foot on the kickboard, then turned toward her. "Damn right I am, as long as we don't make love again."

"I think I can restrain myself from attacking you." It would be tough, but he was making it increasingly easier. "Your virtue is safe around me. I've already satisfied my curiosity. What more could I want? An instant replay?" Well, maybe. *Or ten. In slow-motion.*

Other than visibly swallowing, his expression remained unchanged. He flicked the reins. The horse snorted, tossed its head as though to urge them to make up their minds, and continued down the lane.

"As I started to tell you, I was in the attic this morning, and it struck me there was something strange about it."

He sounded surly. "It's an attic. Like most attics, it holds useless stuff and pieces of the past someone didn't want to let go."

Watching Gray House loom larger, Bethany realized Matthew had no need for attics; he carried all his past around with him. "Okay, fine. You don't want to talk about the attic. And I don't want to talk about what happened between us there. I guess this conversation is over."

She'd had enough of him, this place, the raucous, roiling emotions he incited, and the physical ache of needing him to touch her. She bolted from the buggy the instant it stopped.

"Damn it, Bethany!" he called.

"Thanks for the ride." She dashed up the steps and into the house.

She didn't let the lump in her throat turn into tears.

The next morning, school began, but it seemed more like an extension of the funeral service. The children watched Laurie Craddock as though she were a stranger. For her part, Laurie sat like a mannequin, her hands folded atop the table, her face expressionless. Her sad, hungry eyes followed Bethany.

During afternoon recess the children were quieter than usual. The elder Bittlehorn twins had opted to remain in the schoolhouse and pore over algebra problems, a clarion call that something wasn't right.

Bethany rang the bell to call the children inside.

One by one they all moved to their places.

Instead of resuming the daily routine, she cleared off the edge of her desk and sat on it. "There's an elephant in the room," she said, deliberately looking at each child.

"He didn't come in during recess," Harvey Bittlehorn volunteered, looking around.

"This is a metaphoric elephant. It means everyone here has the same thing on his or her mind and no one wants to mention it." She had their undivided attention.

Hortense Bittlehorn raised her hand and stood up when Bethany called on her. "I think we was—"

"Were," Bethany corrected.

"We were wondering . . ." Her gaze roamed to Laurie. "We don't want her to go away."

Laurie turned on her chair. "I'm not going away, Hortense. Mrs. Chester says I can live with her as long as Mr. Gray pays for my keep. I'm gonna ask him if I can go to work for him so's I *never* have to go away."

"I'm sure you, as her friends, as a community, can come up with a good solution for Laurie," Bethany said, noting the relief on several of the young faces. "Take a look around you, children. Look at your neighbors. They are your support systems, your friends—even when you disagree on something. Every time you help each other, you help yourself. Kindness begets kindness. Don't be afraid to talk to one another and lend a helping hand or a friendly ear."

Twelve-year-old Hubert Bittlehorn raised his hand, then stood when called upon. "Every time I look at my neighbors, there're two of them."

Laughter trickled through the classroom.

"Laurie, how about you being my twin?" Hubert suggested.

"I'm too short."

"And you're a boy, Hubert," his sister Hortense said, then giggled.

Bethany sat back and smiled. At least the kids knew how to talk about the elephant in the room. Now, if only she and Matthew could do the same one day.

After that the afternoon passed quickly, the children exchanging ideas about *A Connecticut Yankee in King Arthur's Court.*

After class let out, Bethany watched Hubert wait for Laurie. It seemed the boy had found someone more alone in the crowd than himself.

Tears stung Bethany's eyes when she heard him tell the little girl he'd walk her home after school from now on, and come by for her in the morning. She needed a big brother, and he was it.

Bethany closed the schoolhouse door believing that overall, the day had ended well. Tomorrow, they'd wind up for the week.

She cleaned the blackboards, consulted her notes, and picked up a fresh piece of chalk.

First, she'd prepare for tomorrow's school day. Then, she'd work on her plans for the future. So much depended on Jeb's willingness to trust her. It was asking a lot, but he'd reap the rewards. Men would get their provisions for the long trek to the Klondike from the Golden Nugget.

When Canada announced the terms for gold seekers—provisions and money to last a year—everything would sell at a premium. The law of supply-and-demand would kick-start Juneau's growth and prestige into the twentieth century.

Thinking about the future history of the place, Bethany laughed aloud. The Yukon gold rush was coming. All she had to do was figure out how to capitalize on it and she would survive.

She opened the bottom drawer of the desk, withdrew several catalogues, and started a rudimentary list for next year's gold seekers.

If Jeb opted out and Matthew turned down her offer to buy Gray House on a deferred payment plan, she'd come up with another plan. But she wouldn't give up. She was a survivor.

As soon as she finished here, she'd visit another survivor, Dall Lockner.

Bethany entered the offices of Gray & Skinner Architectural Design and Construction. The dinner hour had lured everyone from the outer office. She approached Matthew's door and poked her head into the office.

Matthew's dark head was bowed over an enormous drafting board. Bins of scrolled drawings, a flat file, and bookcases covered the walls. The drafting table and a desk gave the space a cramped feel.

The tools of his trade lay on the large, tilted table and in a rectangular box holding flat the rendering on which he worked.

Clad in a white shirt stretching over his broad back and black trousers that hugged his thighs, Matt sat on a high stool. His heels hung on the lower rungs.

Oblivious to everything around him, he penciled a series of numbers. Tracks from running his fingers through his hair indicated his need for a haircut. His forelock curled over the arch of his left eyebrow.

He reminded her of a picture: Artist at Work.

She knocked lightly on the open door.

Startled, he turned from the drafting table. One foot thudded onto the floor. The glaze of concentration cleared from his eyes. And for a moment, she thought him genuinely glad to see her.

"Hi," she said, feeling the flush of desire course through her.

"Come in." He rose and reached for a chair. "Sit down."

"No, thank you. I can't stay."

"All right. What can I do for you?"

"Is there a glassblower in town?" Best to get right to the point, then leave. The impulse to put her arms around him strengthened in direct proportion to the amount of time she spent around him.

"Yes, down on the wharf. What is it you want?"

"I'd like him to make some straws for Dall. Just a straight straw or pipette won't do." She offered the wire template she and Dall had designed. "The straw has to bend and curve this way so he can drink without moving his head."

He took the wire and examined it with open interest. "You're incredibly inventive."

"Not really." If he liked this, he'd love the novelty section of Wal-Mart. "That's just a slight modification to a flex straw. Except it doesn't flex when made out glass."

"Flex?"

Preferring not to get into the time-travel topic, she said, "Glassblower? Dall hates dribbling down his cheek."

"Sure. I'll take you. The wharf isn't any place for you to go alone."

"That isn't necessary. I'll get the Bittlehorn twins—"

"Let's go." He handed the wire to her and picked up his coat.

"You're just going to ignore me and do what you want, aren't you."

"Hulda doesn't allow her children near the wharf."

The flat statement caught her off guard. "Oh."

"It's not far." He opened the office door for her.

"Nothing is far here."

He locked the office and escorted her onto the walkway. "I owe you an apology."

Because she could think of several things that easily fell under the apology umbrella, she asked, "Are you just going to owe me? Or is this the apology?"

The trace of a tired smile lifted the corners of his mouth. "You like things complex, don't you?"

"I thought it was a simple question."

"Two questions."

"Okay, answer them one at a time."

"No, I'm not going to owe you, and yes, this is an apology."

"Got it." She stole a glance at him before stepping down the wooden stairs to the lower walkway linking the buildings. "And you say *I* like things complex."

"You do."

"If I were psychic, I'd know what you were apologizing for. But"—she put the back of her hand to her forehead—"alas, I am not. So I haven't a clue, unless you decide to provide one."

"You started to tell me something on the way out of the graveyard, and I distracted you."

Little did he know how much or how often he distracted her. Like now. "You mean about the attic?"

"Yes."

"Have you ever looked into a room and known something was out of place?"

The skepticism she'd expected tensed his entire body. "Only from a design perspective. Walls, doors, molding, woodwork, flooring, that sort of thing."

"Despite the accumulated dust up there, the floor space was as neat as a pin. Dust cloths protected the upholstered furniture and most of the wooden pieces, too. The trunks were separate and easy to get to. The crates he put up there are stacked better than Martha Stewart's towels."

"Martha who?"

"Forget it. The point is, everything was neat as a pin, except the place where I found the box with the loan papers." She looked up at him. "I was right, wasn't I? Those were the loan papers, weren't they?"

"Yes."

"Tell me about them later. I think there are other things up there you need to look at."

"What?"

She slowed her step and swallowed her exasperation.

"I don't know. The area where I found the mother-of-pearl inlaid box was . . . out of kilter. Things weren't stacked neatly."

"You were damn lucky to escape without being seriously hurt."

"Thanks to you. When the furniture fell, it buried another box I'd swear was open. I couldn't lift the trunk." Caught up in her explanation, she stopped cold and gazed up at him. "That trunk was out of place. Every other one was at the back of the attic neatly placed against the wall."

He regarded her for a long minute. "Okay. I'll look at it soon. Have you any objection to my doing that during the school day?"

"None at all." Strangely, her sense of disappointment outweighed the practicality of not being alone with him in the attic again. Well, maybe it wasn't so strange.

He glanced over his shoulder. "Alfredo Stephini can make straws for Dall, and anything else you want out of glass."

For a brief instant, she wondered if Mr. Stephini could make a cold glass heart—one to replace the one feeling far too much for this man whose blue eyes were burning her to the core.

# *Chapter Twenty-one*

"I fired Ellison," Matthew told Dall the next day.

"He'd better be gone by the time I get out of this bed," his friend growled. "A week ago I'd have wanted to beat him to a pulp with my fists. Now I'd be content to shoot the bastard."

"I doubt you'll get the chance. After it came to light that he hadn't replaced the old timbers, none of the men would work with him. He's done here." Matthew opened the wooden box he'd picked up from Alfredo Stephini's shop hours earlier.

"The timbers have to be replaced before work resumes. And *no* blasting." Dall scowled, not hiding his anger.

"Who can I trust to make sure the job is done right?" Matthew put one of the three strangely formed straws into a glass of water and offered it to Dall. It worked perfectly. *Amazing*.

Dall gave him names and sent him to a drawer in the bureau across the room. He'd kept a daily journal of events. Matthew flipped through the pages, marveling at Dall's precision. Everything he needed, including timber dimension and rock types, was on the pages.

Mine business and planning with Dall—who insisted he could give orders flat on his back—consumed the rest of the afternoon, and before leaving the compound, Matthew appointed two new foremen. Both would start their jobs immediately by reporting to Dall.

Camden had made himself scarce since the night of the cave-in. He remained holed up in his office during the day and seldom left his quarters in the evenings.

Going there, Matthew pounded on the front door until Camden opened it. He didn't wait for the formality of an invitation to enter. Two partially filled crates sat in the middle of the parlor.

"Heading somewhere?"

"Preparing to do so, yes," Camden answered, unruffled. His impeccable attire bore no evidence of physical exertion.

Matthew moved farther into the spacious house. "Had you planned on giving notice?" Not that he cared too much about the loss of the man.

"Your dissatisfaction with the way I've run the mine is apparent. We have philosophical disagreements that interfere with me doing my job. You're here to terminate my employment, anyway, are you not?" Camden resumed wrapping several ornately carved walrus tusks in soft cotton bed linens.

"I've no intention of letting you off the hook so easily. You put men in danger by ordering Ellison not to replace all the old timbers in those tunnels. You skimped on their safety and caused the deaths of five men."

Camden stiffened, his jaw clenched for a moment before he spoke in a soft, deadly voice. "Those are serious charges, Gray. You'd better be ready to prove them."

"We've started excavation. The timbers will tell their own story."

"I don't see that they matter much. It sounds as if you've already taken Ellison's word, tried me, and found me guilty."

"Are you going to tell me Ellison failed to replace the timbers without your order? What could he possibly gain by putting himself and everyone else in jeopardy? Only you could make the risk worth his while." Matthew watched the tension build in Camden's face and the way he bunched his fists.

"I did what was *expected* of me," Camden said through clenched teeth. "I ran the mine and the operation the way your father wanted it done." He tossed a quilt over the clothes he'd just packed and glared at Matthew. "Don't blame me for his business tactics. And don't blame anyone but yourself for not knowing how he did business."

"You son of a bitch." Furious, Matthew took a step toward Camden. "My father was a bastard, a spiteful, vindictive man when it came to me, but not when it came to the men who worked for him. He'd never compromise their safety!"

"He was worried about the cost—"

"The hell he was," Matthew shouted. "He and I were nothing alike in temperament, but we were cut from the same cloth when it came to taking care of those in our charge." He spied a pile of papers beside the fireplace.

"You didn't even know him." Camden moved to block him. "You lived blocks away and never came to see him until he lay on his deathbed."

The urge to strike the man for telling the truth balled Matthew's hand into a fist. "I'll not be diverted from the real issue so easily." In a moment of clarity, he realized he'd become inured to guilt.

"Don't talk to me about the mine, Gray. You don't know the first thing about it."

"You are mistaken on that score." He crossed the room and picked up the papers beside the fireplace. "Ah," he said, flipping through the stack. "I see you found the bank statements and the missing invoice files. I'll take them with me."

"If I'm still running the mine, I'd prefer to keep them here."

"You're not fired, and you're not running the mine. I am. I'm taking these with me." He headed for the front door, then paused before turning the knob. "By the way, Camden, my father and I set the timbers in Tunnel Four together. Thirteen years ago, it was Tunnel Two. The boarded-up tunnel was Number One.

"I'll be by tomorrow morning. I want to see the shipment records and the smelting logs for the last two years. No delays. No excuses." Matthew closed the door behind him.

The sharp clack of the metal door knocker reverberated up the stairs and into Bethany's bedroom. She tossed the book she'd nearly finished reading aside, grabbed a blanket from the bed, and wrapped it around her. Barefoot, she hurried to the front door and nearly tumbled down the stairs on the way.

"Who is it?" she demanded during a break in the heavy knocking on the door.

"Matthew. Let me in."

Didn't the man have better things to do on a Friday night than beat on her door? A quick flip of the lock gave him entrance. She had to jump back to keep the door from scraping off the top of her toes.

He closed the door, slapped an envelope into her hand, and caught her in a hard embrace. Before she recovered, he kissed her.

In that instant, all reason and resolve disintegrated into lust. The envelope fell to the floor, and her arms twined around his neck. The blanket slid down to her ankles, leaving only her thin nightgown as a barrier between him and her naked flesh. Nothing felt better than being in Matthew's arms. She would pay the damn piper later.

For now, she drew Matthew closer. The male scent of him mingled with the fresh aroma of evergreens and filled her nostrils like an aphrodisiac.

She welcomed the intimacy of his tongue gliding along the edges of her teeth, the promise of his arousal straining against his trousers and her soft belly. She wanted more.

His hand closed around her breast and she breathed in sharply.

With a groan, he deepened the kiss. The sensation of his thumb and forefinger tweaked, massaged, and titillated her nipple until she was beyond control. She wanted those fingers in her, wanted *him* in her.

Naked desire plunged her into a frenzy, which spurred him to wilder depths.

As abruptly as he'd swept her into the carnal embrace, he reluctantly ended their kiss.

"What the hell am I doing?" he asked.

"I thought you were kissing me hello," she managed. Breathless, she felt the first tinges of embarrassment creep out.

"I want to make love with you so badly, it hurts."

"Is that a proposition, an excuse, or an explanation?" She pushed against his shoulders, he did not released her.

He rested his chin on the top of her head and stroked her back. Everywhere he touched became liquid fire.

"I don't want to get you with child. I won't get you with child! No amount of pleasure is worth the price of you dying in childbirth. I won't risk—"

"I'm *not* going to die in childbirth, Matthew."

"You can't be sure of that. No one can."

"I'm not Victoria or Mary Katherine. They were whole women." Her confession spilled out against his thundering heart. She'd never have said the words aloud had she looked into his eyes, but now that she'd started, she had to finish and move on. "I can't have children, Matthew. The car crash I told you about . . . the internal injuries . . . were severe. You might say they were life-ending, because . . ." She drew a steady breath. "I no longer have the physical ability to conceive a child."

This time when she pushed against him, he let her go. She immediately retrieved her blanket from around her bare ankles, busily adjusting it around her shoulders. She clutched it as though it were armor.

"Look at me, Bethany."

Slowly, she lifted her gaze. In the near darkness of the late twilight fading at the window curtains, she faltered. The gentle lift of the curled finger under her chin coerced her to comply. Tears stung her eyes. Would she ever get over her sense of loss?

"Since I was a little girl I wanted to be like my mama, to marry a man I loved more than life and have babies. My childhood dreams died with her. There *won't be* any babies. I can't even adopt one. . . ." A dizzying sense of grief expanded in her chest. Unable to tolerate the pity softening his features, she lifted her chin off his finger and turned away.

"Why did you come here tonight?" she asked bitterly. The question was far easier staring into the shadows than looking at him, touching him, feeling the erection she ached to have inside her throbbing against her belly.

"I could tell you a half-dozen reasons, and they'd all be the truth. But reason number one is that I've missed you. I wanted to see you."

"I think I'd rather hear reason number six."

"Number six, huh?"

It was easier to deal with him, with the situation, if she kept her back to him. "Yes."

"The attic."

Bethany closed her eyes. "You know where it is."

His arms draped over her shoulder, enfolded her. The tender contact put a hitch in her breathing.

"Ah, Bethany—sweet Bethany." His tortured whisper filled her ear. The feel of his lips on the crown of her head made her clutch tighter the blanket at her breasts. "What a complex woman you are. So full of secrets and sorrow."

"Don't forget scars," she added with false bravado.

"Are they the reason you turned out the light in the attic?"

She couldn't answer, couldn't move for fear of tripping over her own secrets in the darkness. Yet his insight seemed like a beacon illuminating all she ached to hide.

The touch of his lips on her ear was almost painful.

"You think I wouldn't desire you because of your scars?"

She squeezed her eyes shut and let her tears begin to fall.

"I'm not so shallow," he said.

She sniffed. "I've never thought you shallow, Matthew. Never."

"You have a beautiful, generous, compassionate heart to complement your intellect and delightful wit." He laughed softly, the vibration of his chest coursing through her. "Your beauty is a bonus."

"I'm no prize."

"But you are. You've driven me to the brink of madness, little songbird. Forgive me; traveling through time is incomprehensible to anyone who hasn't done it. It's easy to deny what we fear or don't understand. But I've decided there is no other explanation for the things you know how to do but yours. I saw you bring Mary Katherine back to life when her heart had stopped. None of us knew to do that. And Dall—he may walk again because of you."

Bethany's knees turned to jelly and she leaned against him. God, he was so solid, so strong, and so damn sexy. And he believed her! She cleared her throat, needing to say something, but at a loss for words.

"Shhh. I'm still working on accepting what I can't fully understand yet can't deny."

She let him turn her in his arms until she looked at him through the darkness. All she saw were his shining eyes.

"I brought you something."

"Wh-what?" Besides hope for something she'd thought as impossible as traveling through time.

"The deed to this house. I've had it transferred to your name. The Old Man didn't put it up as collateral for any Gray Wolf loans."

She felt her world drop away. "Why? Why would you do this?"

"Call it a show of faith. If you tell me you'll be able to pay the mortgage in five years, I believe you. Besides, you need a place of your own. I've no plans to live here."

His lips pressed to her forehead. "And now I'll go. Good night, songbird."

Dumbfounded, she watched him open the door. "Lock your house up after me," he said. Then he left.

The front door snicked closed.

She stared at the darkened doorway for a long time before locking it and picking up the envelope that held the deed to her future.

The depth of his generosity bordered on incomprehensible. His caring and thoughtfulness touched her heart with a poignancy that brought tears to her eyes.

He might not love her, but he cared for her. And he

believed her. The bitter-sweetness of the realization sent the tears over the dam of her lower lashes.

On her way up the stairs, Matthew's heartfelt declarations continued rattling through her head. What did they mean for their future?

# *Chapter Twenty-two*

Matthew showed the house plans to his new clients at their property on Saturday afternoon. The Maloneys had presented a challenge in that they knew what they wanted, but neither possessed an ability to visualize the plans on the land before them. This presentation had required numerous renderings.

All the while, Bethany filled his thoughts. The way she'd trembled when telling him that she could never have children had stayed with him. By opening the door on her painful secret, she'd opened the door to more than she imagined. More than he'd imagined.

He scribbled a note and had it delivered to her at the schoolhouse. Although class had finished for the day, he was quite sure she'd still be sitting at her desk, working.

They'd have dinner together this evening and he'd formally request permission to court her. Was that how things were done in Drexel, a hundred-plus years from now?

"Ah, hell." What if she said no? He entered his office building and found Randal Skinner winding up the weekly payroll.

"What?" his partner asked.

"Nothing. Just have a lot on my mind."

"You're about to have more." His thumb jerked toward Matthew's closed office door.

Had Bethany received his note already and hurried over? God, he hoped she was as eager to see him as he was to see her.

"The Maloney project is a go." Matthew withdrew a money transfer slip from the bank and the Maloneys' construction contract from his inside coat pocket. He gave them to Skinner. "I'll have the materials list for you by Monday."

His partner examined the transfer slip. "I'm impressed."

"They're in a hurry and willing to pay a bonus for us to finish before the heavy snow falls." Matthew juggled the two large scrolls of plans and his valise on the way to his office. "How are we fixed for crews?"

"We need a few more woodworkers and a couple of laborers, I think. Leave the plans with me. I'll have a better idea after I study them."

"Gladly." He'd had his fill of the Maloney project for one day. He left the drawings on Skinner's desk on the way to his office.

There was a woman waiting on the other side of the door, but not the one he'd expected. His first instinct was to turn around and walk away. Hell. Not walk. Run!

"Hello, Matthew. Have you missed me?"

Delphinia Crutchfield Moore—the first woman he'd loved, the last person he wanted to see, now.

She hadn't changed a bit in the seven years since his departure from Spokane. Her ivory skin was still flawless and accentuated her long, sooty eyelashes and perfectly arched brows. Just the right amount of color highlighted her cheeks and lips. Hazel eyes that had been enigmatic, knowing, when she was seventeen had lost none of their allure.

Her thick, golden blond hair was perfectly coiffed under a lace-covered straw hat. The flowers clustered along its side matched those embroidered into a long basque cinched at her waist with a satin belt and gold buckle. The tiny pleats of her underblouse rose to gather around her neck.

She was simple, elegant, expensive.

A dazzling smile revealed her perfect white teeth. "I see you are surprised. We're a long way from Spokane."

"You're right on both counts." He crossed the office and set his valise on the desk. "What brings you to Juneau, Mrs. Moore?"

"Mrs. Moore, not Delphinia? My, my, you've become formal." The ghost of a smile lingered on her full pink lips.

"I find it best to maintain a professional distance from my business acquaintances." He folded his arms over his chest and met her twinkling gaze. "Once again, what brings you to Juneau, Mrs. Moore?"

"I'm a widow now."

"My condolences. I trust your husband's death didn't come as a total surprise." How could it? Matthew mused silently. Moore was sixty-three and breathing hard at a standstill when he'd married Delphinia.

"Thank you, no. Archie had been ill for two years prior to his death." Her head tilted, catching the light from the window in a manner that enhanced her beauty. "I understand you married, too, but she did not survive childbirth."

He glared at her. "I'm assuming you have a point you're trying to make."

"Did you love her?" The softly spoken question held a

tinge of insecurity that he had not noticed seven years ago.

He opened his valise and removed the Maloney file to compile the materials list. "I ask again, to what do I owe this visit?"

"Of course you loved her. You were never motivated by anything else, were you, Matthew?"

"Are you intending to foreclose on the Gray Wolf's loans?" He had no intention of discussing his private life.

Delphinia sighed as she always had when ignored. "Must we talk business? Money is such a dreary topic."

"You didn't think so seven years ago when you married Archibald Moore. As I recall, you considered his money an aphrodisiac." He looked at her through the lens of time, distance, and the newer experience of being loved without condition or reservation. "Love never entered into your equation."

"I had a sick mother and two younger sisters to consider," Delphinia said, all traces of her wispy smile gone. "Archie wanted my youth, my adoration, and a trophy he could squire around town and flaunt before his cronies. I needed money and security for my family. Love never fed a family, Matthew. But it doesn't go away, either. I never forgot you or Dall, never stopped loving either of you. After Archie died, I'd hoped one or both of you would return to Spokane. But Dall walked out on his family, and you married.

"I wondered about your wife, if she reminded you of me. I wondered if you thought of me when you made love with her. I hoped you did each and every time. Did you?"

He looked her in the eye, this woman he'd once loved more than life. "No. I didn't think about you or Archibald Moore at all until I inherited the mine and found my father had taken out loans with Moore Mercantile."

She laughed softly. "So the Gray Wolf is finally yours."

"Unless you call in the loans. Then it's yours." The way things had gone lately, she probably wouldn't do him so big a favor.

"I'm not here to talk about how the Gray Wolf juggles accounts."

"Don't tell me you're here to promote tourism."

Delphinia laughed softly, her sparkling gaze roaming his body in frank assessment. "No. This is personal, very personal. For seven years, I thought about you and Dall. Neither of you answered my letters, so I stopped writing. But I didn't stop remembering. I'm here to discover if there's any feeling left between us."

The bold statement astounded him. "There isn't."

She moved toward him and placed her gloved hands on his chest. "My, but that was a quick answer, Matthew. How can you be so sure?"

"I'm sure." When she leaned forward, he caught her shoulders, intent on putting distance between them.

"In a couple of days we'll be tearing each other's clothing off just like we used to." As a reminder, she cupped the back of his neck and unerringly found his mouth with hers.

A faint knock sounded before the door swung open. Trying to disengage Delphinia, he glanced at the entrance.

Bethany's big violet eyes widened in startlement.

He pushed on Delphinia's shoulders, finally loosening her arms from around his neck. "Don't do that again, Mrs. Moore."

"Again, so formal!" The smile on her red lips faded at the sight of Bethany.

Shaken by the sight of Matthew kissing another woman, Bethany became rooted to the floor. Everything in her screamed *run*.

But she couldn't outrun heartache and knew better than to try.

Her chin lifted a fraction. The smile she forced felt brittle enough to fracture her face into a thousand pieces. "My apologies for the interruption, Mr. Gray. I just dropped by to let you know I can't make our meeting."

"Bethany—"

In the span of a heartbeat, she sized up the tall, glamorous woman with whom Matthew had shared a kiss. Fashionable clothing cut to perfection. Not a golden hair out of place. A flawless complexion with minimal cosmetics.

"Now that I have interrupted, I should introduce myself," she said. Her words held a graciousness worthy of an Academy Award for Best Actress in a Dramatic Debacle. "I'm Bethany James, traveling schoolteacher."

The woman had the audacity to smile with straight white teeth. "It's quite all right, Miss James. I'm Delphinia Moore, an old friend of Mr. Gray's." Her honey-hazel gaze darted to Matthew, then back. "And his banker."

"Perhaps we'll see one another around town. Unfortunately, Mr. Gray, Patrick awaits me." She turned to go, then paused and said, "Thank you for delivering Mr. Stephini's project."

With a dignity born of resignation, she walked swiftly from the office and away from Matthew.

She should have known better than to believe his sweet words spoken in the dark. The only thing more foolish was indulging in daydreams of happy-ever-after with the man she loved. Dear God in heaven, as much as she hated admitting it, she did love him.

Where did a broken heart hide? What place in the universe provided a haven for shattered dreams?

In a town hemmed in by steep mountains to the east and south, the vast Mendenhall Glacier on the north, and the Gastineau Channel on the west, running space was scarce. Worse, Bethany believed in running to something, not away from a difficult situation.

The stainless-steel rods holding her bones together were flimsy in comparison to the strength she'd found in her spirit. She was a survivor. She remained dry-eyed and walked with her head high.

Perhaps if she hadn't received that note asking her to have dinner with him, her self-deception might have been less.

*Fool,* she snapped. The note had merely bolstered her false impression of his feelings for her.

Now, she thought of a half-dozen reasons he might ask her to dinner, none of which had anything beyond a business implication.

Still, the scene she'd walked in on felt like a betrayal.

But it was not. What was there to betray? He'd promised her nothing. He wasn't responsible for her pie-in-the-sky dreams. If anything, his generosity and trust were far more than anyone had a right to expect. What else could she call his willingness to give her Gray House on wild, unconventional terms? No doubt people would believe him the crazy one for doing it.

Well, she had her pride, but not so much that she'd throw away a place to live and an opportunity to support herself after Phineas Montgomery took over the school.

"Bethany. *Miss James.*"

At the sound of her name, she slowed and looked around.

Jeb waved at her from the door of his store. "Have ya a moment?"

"Sure," she answered, turning back to the Golden Nugget. *Ten or twenty of them, as many as you'd like, thanks to Matthew.*

Jeb led the way behind the counter where his two clerks handled customers to the store's back room and storage area. She regarded the surroundings with interest.

Any diversion was a good one at this point.

"Please, come in." Jeb opened the door of a small office at the back and held it for her while he watched the doorway to the store. His furtive actions made her feel like a co-conspirator in some plot to overthrow the government.

"I'll tell ya up front, I spoke with Megan about your proposition. I figured she should know the risk I'd be takin', too." He left the office door open, no doubt for propriety's sake, but kept watching the main doorway as a precaution against being overheard.

"I see." The admission came as no surprise, considering the closeness of their marriage. "And what have the two of you decided?" Might as well get all the bad news in one day.

"We'd like to hear what you have to say and discuss the matter. Perhaps over dinner when it's convenient for you. Megan and I, we're behind ya, lass. You'll be telling us what to change and when."

Bethany's spirits soared. "That's wonderful, Jeb. I'd be delighted. I'm free right away."

Five minutes earlier, she hadn't thought anything could raise her spirits. Even the prospect of holding Patrick had held a bittersweet taste. Like Matthew, he wasn't hers. He never would be. But it didn't stop her from loving him—or Matthew.

But this was a ray of hope.

Damn and double damn!

Matthew again peeled Delphinia's arms from around his neck. "You and I said all we had to say to one another in Spokane."

"Not quite." Delphinia concentrated on straightening her sleeves and smoothing her basque.

Matthew wiped his mouth with the back of his hand. The fire he'd thought would never dim had turned as cold in seven years as the Mendenhall Glacier. He'd loved Victoria, and . . .

"I told you there would be a time for us when Archie died. It could be now, Matthew."

"No, Delphinia. Our time has come and gone. We can't go back."

"We're not going back. This is what we planned." Her chin lifted.

Despite the years, her mannerisms had not changed. He saw determination in the set of her jaw and the unwavering brightness of her eyes.

"Your plan, Delphinia, never mine. When I left Spokane, I left you behind forever. I wouldn't ever have married Victoria if I hadn't loved her."

She rested her hands on his folded arms. "Your wife is dead. Gone. Like Archie. You and I, we're here. Living. Breathing. We could be in love again."

"Everything you say is true—"

Triumph glowed in her bright smile. "You could fall in love with me all over again."

"I have fallen in love again, Delphinia, but not with you." He caught her hands when she reached for him again. "We've each made choices. Some good. Some not so good. As far as I'm concerned, the only commonality we share centers on the banking business."

Sophistication acquired as a banker's wife and society leader surfaced and asserted itself in her bearing. Delphinia assumed a regality that abolished any hint of uncertainty.

"Ahh. The traveling schoolteacher," Delphinia whispered, nodding. "There's nothing as all-consuming as a new love."

Matthew started toward the door, intent on finding Bethany and explaining. The shock in her violet eyes had certainly turned to pain by now. Delphinia's voice stopped him short.

"We do have business to discuss, Matthew." As he turned, her hazel eyes glittered. "We need to discuss the Gray Wolf's convoluted loans."

He opened the office door. "Yes, we do."

"I may be persuaded to consolidate and renegotiate the terms. Unfortunately, I can't forgive them."

"Nor would I ask you do. Make an appointment with my partner next week. He's usually in the outer office. Right now, I have more important things to do than discuss money." He opened the door wide. "After you, Mrs. Moore."

Unabashed surprise cracked her composure. "Very well. I'm sure we can arrange to discuss our business early next week."

He nodded and remained silent. They'd said everything there was to say.

The clack of Delphinia's heels on the wooden floor sounded like a hammer pounding the final nail in a coffin lid.

On the street, a young man climbed down from a buggy and offered to help Delphinia up. She turned to Matthew. "I have personal business with Mr. Camden. Am I correct in assuming he is still in your employ?"

"Yes."

"And Dall? Where might I find him?"

Matthew paused, debating how much to tell her. "They're both at the Gray Wolf compound. If you want to see Dall, he's in the foreman's section, the south cabin. You used to be good at making him laugh. Think you can give it a shot again?"

Delphinia straightened her skirts. "He made me laugh, too."

"His back is broken, Delphinia."

Genuine horror froze her. "Oh, dear God. What happened?"

"He was in the mine during a cave-in. He'll be glad to

tell you all about it." He turned to leave, intent on finding Bethany.

"Matthew?"

He looked over his shoulder at her, and she smiled sadly.

"Thank you," she said. "I'll visit Dall tomorrow."

# *Chapter Twenty-three*

The long summer day had yielded to a short, cool night. Clouds scudded over the treetops, unable to make up their minds whether to allow the moon to shine through or join forces and rain. A soft breeze carried the smell of the ocean, cooking fires, and damp wood through the night.

Matthew had looked everywhere for Bethany, some places twice.

At this hour, if she wasn't home, she was in serious trouble. Damn near anything could happen to a woman alone, and Bethany wandered wherever her whims dictated, taking too few precautions to ensure her safety.

Dappled moonlight lit his way through yards and down the streets to Bethany's home. Each step deepened his determination to find her and make her understand she hadn't seen what she thought. Well, she had seen Delphinia wrapped around him like a Maypole decoration, but the situation wasn't what it appeared.

For the hundredth time that night, he cursed Delphinia and lamented Bethany's rotten timing.

As he'd expected, all the windows were dark.

Knocking on the front door wouldn't do any good. If she was home, all the stubborn woman would do was take one look and then ignore him.

No, he'd not give her a chance to ignore him.

Matthew brushed his fingers over the frame above the back door. The dusty spare key remained tucked in a crevice.

A flicker of guilt twisted in him with the key in the lock. The house now belonged to Bethany, so his actions were no better than those of a common burglar. But the only thing he wanted to steal was her anger. What he wanted most—her heart—she had to give freely.

The door into the kitchen opened and closed without a sound. With forced patience, he remained still while his eyes adjusted to the darker interior. Rather than wend his way through the downstairs to the main staircase, he chose the direct route upstairs via the servants' stairs off the kitchen.

The carpet runner along the center of the steps absorbed the sound of his footfalls down the hall to her room.

Moonlight played peekaboo through the lace undercurtains billowing in the breeze, passed like a hand over the woman lying in the bed.

Relief that she was here and sleeping like a baby lifted the weight of worry from his shoulders.

Her head turned toward the door as he moved into the doorway. Quick as lightning, Bethany was out of bed and across the room, away from him.

"Bethany," he called softly. "It's me, Matthew. No one's going to hurt you." Damn, he'd expected her to be asleep. The hope of waking her with a kiss disappeared. He'd scared her, instead.

"Matthew? Wh-what are you doing here? How did you get in?" She remained in front of the open window as though still ready to make an escape.

He tossed his key onto the night table. "The old man kept a spare over the back door for deliveries and Doc Swenson's visits."

"Excuse me?" she said. She did not sound pleased.

"I used a key," he repeated softly.

"A key. How many more keys to this house are floating around town?" Her tone evolved from fear to anger.

"The old man liked his privacy. There were only two keys made. You now have both."

"Terrific." She paused. "Knowing where the second key was gives you the right to come in here in the middle of the night and scare me? At the risk of sounding ungrateful, the papers you gave me said this is my house."

"It is." He leaned against the doorjamb and folded his arms across his chest. He'd crossed some invisible line but didn't care. "You didn't answer the door the first time I came. Tell me, would you have answered this time?"

"No, and that's my prerogative, isn't it?"

His little songbird had the talons of an eagle. "Other than letting myself in, there was no other way to speak with you tonight."

"Frankly, my dear, I don't give a damn," she said haughtily. Then she laughed to herself, but it didn't change the look of annoyance on her face. The fickle moonlight broke the clouds and illuminated her silhouette, her fists on her hips and her wild hair an enticing halo fluttering with the breeze ruffling the curtains.

"I owe you an explanation." She sure as hell wasn't making it easy, either.

"The only explanation you owe me is why you couldn't wait until tomorrow to speak with me, Mr. *Gray*."

"We're back to formalities?"

"What do you want from me?" The softspoken question was wistful rather than angry.

He grinned in the dark, sure she had no idea of the provocative sight she presented in front of the window. "For starters, I'll settle for you climbing back into bed and listening."

"Is this going to take long?"

"That depends on how angry you are."

"You barge in here in the middle of the night—"

"That's not why you're angry and we both know it. Let's talk about the reason we didn't go to dinner tonight."

"Let's not." She approached the bed, then hesitated before she slid under the covers. "I don't have anything to say to you, Matthew. Please go. Lock the door on your way out." Making a show of adjusting her quilts, she turned her back to him. By the time she stilled, the covers were above her shoulders and the pillow was folded around her ears.

Matthew remained propped against the doorjamb, his gaze focused on the lump curled beneath the quilt and pillow. "I'm not leaving until we talk, Bethany. *Really* talk." He shifted his shoulder in search of a more comfortable position. "We can either discuss this afternoon, or I can stand here for the rest of the night and watch you sleep. Then, we'll talk about it when you wake up in the morning. Either way—"

"Go *away*, Matthew." After what seemed an eternity, she shifted and released the pillow.

He strode to the bed and settled at her side. He reached over, half-expecting her to cringe, and was relieved when she did not. The pillow had tangled the fine cloud of curly hair around her face. "I can't do that," he whispered. Tress by tress, then strand by strand, he moved her veil of tousled hair. All the while, her big violet eyes glistened as she watched him.

"Today, you saw the finality of something over and done with seven years ago. I was twenty-two, Delphinia seventeen. We were in love. I wanted to marry her; she wanted to marry money. She did. I returned to Juneau. End of story. If it hadn't been, I'd never have married Victoria."

"For love," she whispered.

He nodded in the dappled moonlight. "For love."

"Do you still love her?"

"Victoria?"

"Yes . . ." came the almost fearful answer from his songbird.

He leaned down on one elbow and stroked her hair. "A piece of my heart will always belong to her and Ethan, but they're gone. There was a time not so very long ago I believed there was no room for anyone else."

The way her cheek pressed into his hand as she closed her eyes drew him closer. "A violet-eyed vixen tumbled into my life and turned everything I believed in upside-down. I've done things I would never have before I met her. She awakened desires and emotions I'd thought buried in the graveyard." He kissed a line along her chin and jaw as he spoke. She smelled of lilacs and lemons, clean, fresh.

"I know she doesn't want to care for me." He ached to hold her against him and taste the sweet warmth of her bare skin. "I know she'll leave me at the first opportunity and go so far away I'll have no chance of holding her again."

He kissed the corner of her mouth and felt her bottom lip tremble.

"D-don't—" she started but didn't continue.

"Don't what, songbird? Kiss you?"

He stretched out next to her, allowing the barrier of the quilt for the illusion of safety. The moon's glow on her pale cheek and neck tantalized him with another taste of gold-limned skin. He traced her jaw with his lips, caught the lobe of her ear between his teeth, moved down her neck to the crook of her shoulder.

"Don't touch you?" He swept the quilt back, exposing her upper arm and the fullness of her breast beneath the fine lawn of her nightgown. He could never touch her enough. His fingertips slid along the curve of her shoulder, down her arm to her elbow, then up the seam of her arm and breast.

Her sharp intake of breath and sudden arch of her back might have been involuntary, but he smiled nonetheless. He continued his explorations over the top of her breast and along her collarbone, all the while kissing her temple.

She tasted like heaven and felt like salvation.

"Don't desire you?" he whispered into her ear.

He returned to her breast, unable to keep from sampling what he ached to possess. Need pounded in his temples. His arousal threatened to split the seam on his trousers. He knew he should stop, but the tremors running through Bethany and against his fingers promised ecstasy. If she allowed, he'd take her in a manner that left no doubt she was his.

"God help me, Bethany, I want you more than I want to see the sun rise." He caught her turgid nipple between his thumb and forefinger. Further proof of her subdued excitement came from the small sound she made deep in her throat, the slow, sinuous shift of her body stretching against his.

"I don't care where or when you came from. It feels right having you here—beside me now. Against me now." He found her mouth and brushed his lips against hers until they parted. "Damn, woman, you're a miracle and magic."

A light kiss brought her hand to his cheek. The reciprocal touch tested his restraint. *Slow and easy*, he reminded himself.

"Are you trying to seduce me?" she asked in a throaty voice.

"Do you want me to?" He traced the corner of her mouth with the tip of his tongue. If he didn't make love to her soon, he'd lose what was left of his mind.

Her head turned just enough for her to return the intimate exploration.

"You know I'll leave if the River of Time—"

"It's not here. I am." The prospect of losing her added an urgency to the heat coursing through his veins. "It might never come."

"I know." One-handed, she removed his tie. "Or it might come tomorrow."

One at a time, he toed off his shoes and let them hit the floor with muffled thuds.

"That leaves tonight."

"Just tonight," she echoed. Just a little more heartache to go with the memory they'd make in the dark. "No promises. No strings. No obligations." With each declaration, she released another button on his vest before starting with his shirt. "No tomorrows."

"Bethany, sweet Bethany," he murmured as though in disagreement.

Love and desire further crowded argument and anger from the air.

Matthew shed his shirt, vest, and coat as though they were a single item of clothing. If only he knew how sexy, how undeniably enticing he was in the moonlight. A well-defined pattern of dark hair grew on his pectorals and narrowed to a single line down his abs and disappeared beneath his waistband.

Bethany reached for his belt buckle. Whether by instinct or magic, her fingers freed the fastening on his trousers. The heat of his erection sent a thrill down to her toes.

"I want to see you, songbird." The sensation of the opening buttons on the neckline of her nightgown registered. Everything in her stilled. How could she have forgotten the scars still crisscrossing her body?

But before an objection reached her lips, his mouth captured hers in a slow, sense-stealing kiss. He took everything she offered and demanded more—and heaven help her, she gave it. All the reasons to protest melted away. Matthew Gray became her entire universe.

It was impossible to satisfy her voracious appetite for touching him. In rough, eager motions, she helped rid him of his trousers.

"Now you, sweet songbird," he breathed when they ended a slow kiss that had turned hot and ravenous.

She might have regained her senses and protested the removal of her nightgown, but the way he kissed her, teased her mouth, and used his tongue to fence and dance with hers, stole her reason.

The keen disappointment she'd experienced that afternoon evaporated. This golden moment with Matthew's naked, passion-heated body against hers became a reason for breathing. And her breath came fast with hungry anticipation of becoming one with him again. Of glimpsing heaven.

Just when the quilts and her nightgown ended up on the floor, she didn't know, nor did she care. The fire Matthew created with his mouth trailing along her throat forced her head back. Oh, yes—touching, being touched, being worshipped by this man she loved, his mouth, his hands, his entire body, was exquisite pleasure.

Caught in the heat of her desire, every nerve ending alive and singing in response to him, she forgot her physical flaws. Everything was right. He was right. They were right together.

"You're beautiful inside and out, songbird." His lips traced the scar running from between her breasts to her pubic bone. Dimly, she realized what he was doing but was helpless to object.

"What a passion for living you have." He traced the badges of survival on her flesh with his hands and mouth. The heat of his breath on the sensitive area above her hipbone made her writhe in anticipation.

"You look like porcelain, but you're Damascus steel—strong, resilient, beautiful. Nothing less could survive these injuries." The awe and tenderness in his voice made the breath catch in her throat.

Tears filled her eyes. The gentle yet erotic way he explored her hips and legs made him a magic and miracle she'd never have believed possible.

A hand skimmed over the juncture of her thighs, coaxing, stroking until her legs parted of their own accord. "Bethany," he said with a reverence that left no doubt he thought of no one else. His dark head lowered into the juncture. The sensation of his tongue sliding into her made her cry out.

The need pooling in her belly tightened almost painfully. How could anything feel so good, be so exciting, and become so essential to her next heartbeat?

Even now, surrealism clung to the carnal seduction of her soul, heart, and body. In that moment, they ceased being hers; she'd given them to him. And, dimly, she realized she had surrendered far more. She'd relinquished the fear of never knowing intimacy, of being viewed with revulsion. Matthew had beaten back the monster of her old fear, each kiss, each touch, a sword blow against it.

"Matthew," she whispered.

His body slid up hers. Lightning sparks of need shot through her with the contact. She caught his face in her hands and kissed him, tasting herself on his lips. It drove her wild.

He rolled her on top of him and slowly moved her down until his arousal throbbed at the entrance to her.

Moonlight revealed the intensity of his features and a wildness in his eyes.

"Take what you want, songbird." His voice was a growl.

Curling her legs on either side of his hips and bracing her hands on his chest, she scooted down and pushed up.

The sharp hiss of air he drew between his teeth matched her own.

"Oh, God," she whispered.

His hips rose and he slid into her.

The sensation of his hands gliding along her thighs, over her hips, and closing around her waist until they caressed her ribs helped her set a slow rhythm.

"Songbird," he rasped.

Her fingers pressed into his chest in search of an anchor, but to no avail. He filled her with long, slow strokes, again and again. Her back arched, thrusting her breasts toward him as he teased her pebble-hard nipples.

The hot yearning threatening to push her over the brink of sanity took control. The sounds of passion filled the night, and the fragrance of lovemaking floated in the air.

The glide of flesh over flesh built in desperate intensity until at last Bethany found fulfillment.

Groaning, Matthew held her hips and thrust hard. The sensation of his climax intensified her own.

She collapsed on top of him, more content than she thought possible, as his arms closed protectively around her. Their ragged breathing ebbed.

The thudding of his heart became a drumbeat on the march toward life and hope. Tears stung her eyes. Never in all her years had she dreamt such beauty existed in the world. She tucked her hands around his shoulders and smiled when he reached for a quilt and drew it over them both.

Tomorrow, they'd talk.

Tomorrow.

# *Chapter Twenty-four*

Bethany woke alone.

For a moment, she wondered if she'd dreamt the bliss she'd shared with Matthew. Then the morning breeze kissed her bare shoulders, and the tangle of quilts and sheets spilling across the bed and onto the floor assured her of the night's glorious reality.

Disappointment over Matthew's stealthy departure gave way to her practical nature. How would it look if he were seen leaving her house? Unlike Drexel, where folks gossiped for several days, then accepted an affair between two single, consenting adults, here, any kind of an affair was unacceptable. As the object of that kind of gossip, she might kiss any future opportunity to teach school good-bye and abandon hope of adopting Patrick—no matter what she managed to make off the Gold Rush.

Invigorated by the previous night, she bathed and washed her hair. Too bad the River of Time hadn't seen fit to sweep some salon hair conditioner or styling gel her way. Or a lion tamer, she thought, idly smiling. Her wild mane dried while she made the bed. The key Matthew had tossed onto the night table was gone. Smiling at the prospect of another midnight interlude, she dressed in a tailored white blouse and a Russian blue gored skirt.

The warm morning promised an even warmer afternoon and evening. The small hat she'd fashioned, out of felt discovered in a drawer and ribbons Mrs. Feeney had left for her, was anchored firmly to her unswept hair with combs.

"Gloves," she said. Remembering the little fashion necessities got easier with time.

After opening the upstairs windows for a cooling breeze, she checked the time and hurried a bit more. She had a great deal to do today, including taking Laurie Craddock to visit her father in the cemetery. There was no time to waste.

The sun shone brightly on the Gray Wolf mining compound. The silence of the stampers cast an eerie pall over the yard. Matthew knocked on the door of Dall's quarters. Twelve-year-old Hubert Bittlehorn invited him inside.

"Ma wants Dall to eat right and be taken care of," the boy explained. "If you'll be visiting a while, I'll run Mr. Lockner's linens down to the laundry."

Matthew dug into his pocket for a few coins. "This is for the laundry. Anything left over is yours."

"You don't need to pay me to help out Mr. Lockner."

"I know." Matthew smiled. Henry and Hulda had fine children.

"When can I get out of this bed?" Dall asked after Hubert left. He pushed away the book holder the men had fashioned out of wood and metal. "I haven't read so many books since we were with the Jesuits in Spokane."

Matthew perused the bedside stack of books. "This is a good selection. Some of these look familiar."

When Dall didn't respond right away, Matthew glanced over at him.

"Bethany brought them from your father's library. She was right about Jules Verne. He's a writer with a great imagination. I had no idea the old man liked that sort of thing."

"Lately, life is full of surprises." He tossed the book he'd picked up onto the stack. "I thought I'd better warn you about the one you'll be getting."

Dall raised an eyebrow and frowned. "I hate surprises."

"I know. But this one you may like. Or maybe not. Delphinia is here. She'll be stopping by for a visit with you," Matthew said softly.

"Son of a gun. She always did like seeing me at my best. Well, I hope she understands when I don't get up when she enters the room," Dall said wryly.

"I think she'll overlook your rock-quarry manners." Matthew noted the time and wondered if Bethany had awakened yet. What he wouldn't give to have watched her eyes open in the warm light of morning—but the reaction of his body at the thought promised they'd have done more than look at each other if he'd stayed.

"Delphinia is meeting with Camden this morning. I'll go see him afterward. I suggested she ask *you* whatever she wants to know about the mine."

"Is there anything you'd prefer to keep hidden?"

"No. Don't duck anything. She holds the paper on the loans. I've got nothing to hide, and I'm not sure Camden can say the same. Delphinia's coming here might help us get to the bottom of this fiasco—well, at least the mine's financial difficulties," Matthew concluded.

"Are you suggesting I charm the Delicate Delphinia? Make her take our side should there be any legal proceedings."

Matthew couldn't help grinning. "Make her laugh. You always could, regardless of how dismal the situation."

"I'd've rather made her breathe hard," Dall admitted. "Maybe if I tell her about my inheritance . . ." He trailed off.

Seeing his friend get maudlin, Matthew asked about the progress of clearing the debris from the tunnel. From what Dall had heard, at their present rate, the work crew would shift to timber replacement and reinforcement by Tuesday.

The rest of the morning passed quickly, as they reviewed the roster of injured miners, their progress in recovery, and the remaining work force. In another week they'd gain eighty-percent capacity.

A soft rap sounded at the door. "The next baby-sitting shift has arrived," Matthew told Dall. "I'll be back later."

He opened the door to find Delphinia. Elegantly dressed in a brown day dress trimmed in yellow satin, she smiled as though yesterday afternoon had never happened.

"Mr. Camden is not happy working for you, Matthew. I get the distinct feeling he doesn't think you trust him to run the Gray Wolf properly." She breezed into the room. To her credit, she didn't even slow when she saw Dall laid out in the mechanical contraption holding immobile his broken back.

"Care to dance?" Dall asked. "I'll let you lead."

"It's good to see you, too." Laughing, she bent and placed a kiss on his forehead.

Matthew slipped outside. Camden still owed him several records and answers, and it was time to get them.

Before seeking the mine manager out at his office or the superintendent's quarters, Matthew visited the locked records cabinet in the smelting building. The enormous brick ovens with their heavy doors still radiated heat. Before confronting Camden, Matthew would make his own comparisons of the shipping and foundry records.

* * *

Two hours later, Matthew found Camden cleaning out the desk in the superintendent's office. Although meticulously dressed and groomed as usual, his father's mine manager had an unsettled air. Bloodshot eyes and faint traces of discoloration below his lower lids were mirrors into his agitated state.

"I'm leaving, Gray. Have the lawyer release the funds your father left to me in his will." Camden collected the various pictures of his wife from around the office.

"Now why would I do that?" Matthew dropped the notebook with his findings onto the edge of the highly polished desk.

Camden reached for a packet beside the notebook. Matthew got it first.

"That's personal property," Camden challenged.

Matthew flipped the packet open with his thumb. The manager's talk about leaving wasn't a bluff. The ticket on the *Northern Lights* bore tomorrow's departure date.

"So it is." He tossed the packet on the desk. "I won't ask you to stay."

"I refuse to be a party to the financial ruin you've ensured by shutting down the mining." He reached for a ribbon-bound folio.

"Shutting down the operation while the men dig out the tunnels and shore up timbers you and Ellison skimped on is the right thing to do." Matthew took the folder and glanced at the contents. "As for the financial condition—"

"You can't lay the blame of what happened in the mine at my door, Matthew. If Ellison failed to carry out orders and replace the timbers—"

"If?" Anger bubbled up from the soles of Matthew's feet. "*If*? There is no *if*. Haven't you even bothered to look at the debris hauled out of the cave-in site?"

"Ellison's shortcuts came of his own volition." Anger flushed Camden's fair skin.

"You're the mine superintendent. If it isn't *your* responsibility to make sure the work is done, whose is it, Camden? What the hell have you been collecting a salary for the last three years?" The man's lack of conscience repulsed as much as angered Matthew. "Five men are dead. Seven are injured. Dall Lockner may never walk again—because those timbers weren't replaced and you ordered the men to blast in Tunnel Four anyway. Who is responsible, Camden?"

"You are. You're the owner. You're the man who profits from what they pull out of the ground."

With forced restraint, Matthew took a step forward. There was no talking with this man, and if he remained in the same room with him, he'd pull him across the desk and beat him into a pulp.

"You won't be sailing on Monday," Matthew said with a calm inverse to the violence roiling inside him. "If fact, Camden, you won't be going anywhere until the books balance and I've received a complete accounting. That includes the financial discrepancies and the reason our shipment amounts don't match the smelting and storage totals."

"Where the hell do you get off implying I'm a thief? Not once of all the time I've worked here have you taken the slightest interest in this mine. Not when your father became ill. Not when he became bed-ridden. I ran this mine the way he wanted it run." Fists balled, Camden leaned over the desk. "Now you want to lay all the problems at my doorstep? You miserable excuse for a son, he owed you nothing! Nothing! Which is just what you gave him."

"At least I didn't steal from him," Matthew said with a coldness he felt chilling his gut. "The sooner you provide a coherent, auditable accounting of the mine's financial condition, the sooner you can leave."

"I want what's mine, Gray, what your father left me in his will."

"I'll consider the terms of the will met when you provide what I've asked for." He retrieved the notebook, turned on his heel, and left Camden seething across the desk. If he stayed for another round, he'd attack the lying, thieving bastard. "Leave before you satisfy those minimal requirements and I won't sign off on the provisions clause. And I'll have you up on charges."

Camden was right about one thing: Matthew hadn't involved himself with the workings of the mine. He hadn't expected to inherit it, hadn't wanted it, and had no interest in how much money it made or lost—not until he'd become responsible for the Gray Wolf employees with one stroke of a pen.

Five minutes after leaving Camden, Matthew walked into Dall's quarters. Delphinia sat beside the bed. Both looked over at him as he closed the door.

"It's time for a little honesty," he said.

Bethany held Laurie Craddock's hand at the foot of Bull's grave. The clusters of wildflowers they'd gathered on the way to the cemetery framed the area where the headstone would rest when the stonecutter finished.

"What's gonna happen to me, Miss James?" the little girl asked.

Bethany squeezed her hand. "You're going to be fine. Your Mom and Dad are your guardian angels now."

"But who's gonna love me *here*? Mrs. Chester don't want me."

The question was haunting. Was there anything a child needed more than love? Even if Bull Craddock had been guilty of the abuse Bethany suspected he inflicted on his little daughter—something she was less sure of each day—the child loved him. He was all she'd had. Now, he was gone. From everything Bethany had garnered about the grieving man, he'd adored his daughter. Maybe Mrs. Chester was . . .

"Can I love you, Miss James?" Laurie asked, her small face lifted in solemn expectation.

Permission was only part of what the girl sought. Bethany realized the child was asking for what the James girls had taken for granted since birth—that someone would love them, that someone would care for and protect them. Laurie wanted the same thing. She had no one.

Or did she?

Bethany smoothed a windblown lock of hair from the child's hopeful face.

"Yes," she said. The child had already wormed her way into Bethany's heart. "Oh, yes, Laurie."

The consternation coiled in the child's small body visibly eased. "Are we gonna sing for my daddy?"

"Yes," Bethany agreed. The rightness of the decision to take on Laurie Craddock as a foster child settled more comfortable with each passing moment. She would take the orphans—the baby boy *and* the little girl. Love would make them a family. *Somehow*.

Soon, possibly as early as tomorrow, she'd speak with Matthew and find out how to become the child's guardian. She'd get the girl into a home where she would be loved. Perhaps the powers-that-be would be easier regarding a six-year-old than an infant. Lord, she prayed so. And once she proved herself a good mother to Laurie, maybe, just maybe, she could persuade those with the authority to let her have Patrick, too.

For the remainder of the day, Bethany concentrated on the emotion-starved little girl. They didn't return to Mrs. Chester's home until they'd had a full afternoon of exploration, some genuine laughter, dinner at the best café in town, and ice cream. No good outing was complete without the latter.

After, Bethany stopped by the Calahans' to give Patrick his evening feeding. The little guy seemed content and rarely suffered from colic. She and Sorcha sang to him, and encouraged the baby to smile.

The infant went to sleep and Sorcha said good night. *Little Women* waited beside her bed.

"You've a streak of melancholia about ya this evening," Megan said as Bethany came into the kitchen.

Bethany poured a cup of tea and joined her at the kitchen table. "I suppose I do, my friend. Sometimes . . ." She sat across the table from the Irish woman. "Sometimes I get to wanting more than I can have. Maybe old dreams take a long time to die."

"And maybe they change and become better. What're ya wishin' for, besides Patrick?"

"If I could find a way, I'd raise him as my own." She met Megan's patient gaze. "And I'd take Laurie Craddock to raise as my daughter."

" 'Tis not so complicated a ravel. Sounds ta me like all ya need is a man."

Bethany grinned. "Talk about complications!" Matthew Gray's suspicion, coupled with his inexplicable generosity, was the most complex conundrum of her life.

Megan's left eyebrow lifted sharply. "Men are no' complicated creatures. They're like potatoes. There're good ones, not so good ones, and rotters."

"You got a good one," Bethany agreed.

"Aye. And he indulges me shamelessly. Ya may not want ta hear it, but Matthew was the same way with Victoria."

Bethany's heartbeat quickened at the mention of Matthew's deceased wife. "Oh?"

"That woman was my best friend. She and her da came with us from Ireland, but he dinna survive the trip. He died a few days before we docked."

"What was she like?"

"Verra different from you in looks. She was a sturdy,

tall country girl with eyes as blue as the sky and straight hair as black and shiny as a raven's wing. Like you, she had a love for children. She and Matthew wanted a half-dozen." Megan squeezed Bethany's hand, then pulled free, folded her arms, and leaned back in her chair. "I couldna save either of them. I feared we'd lost Matthew, too, for a time."

The midwife paused, then went on. "The deaths of Victoria and Ethan changed him. He doesna want children, Bethany. You should know that."

"I don't understand. He wants Patrick."

"Aye. The wee lad is already here. He doesna have to worry the babe will die at birth and take his mother with him. 'Tis not the same at all. You and me, we're small women. Jeb and Matthew are big men. He is right to be concerned about a woman birthing his child. Ethan was the biggest baby I've ever delivered. Sweet Mother Mary, I donna think you or I could birth a babe his size and live."

Bethany closed her eyes and nodded. Small wonder he worried so. She felt a wave of empathy wash over her. When she opened her eyes, Megan was watching.

"Matthew is a good man. His heart is the size of the great ocean, Bethany. Speak with him about yer dreams of mothering the orphans ya love. It might help ya both find new lives."

"Oh, I've dreams and plans enough for two lifetimes," Bethany mused. "I'm working on making them come true. Will you help me?"

"With Laurie? Aye. All I can, for a body has only to look at the child when she's with you to see how much she wants to be yer daughter. Patrick?" Megan shook her head sadly. "I'll not involve myself. I love you and Matthew both and canna take sides."

Bethany finished her tea. "Speaking of Matthew, I have a few things to discuss with him tomorrow, and a couple of drawings to make to explain my points. I plan on turning Gray House into a boardinghouse."

"Ah, you are an ambitious one. And brave, if yer making drawings for an architect." Megan smiled wryly.

"I'm learning," Bethany agreed, carrying her cup to the sink. Before leaving, she checked on Patrick a final time for the night and placed a kiss on his head.

On the way home, her thoughts returned to the ramifications of becoming Laurie's guardian—or, in this case, single parent. Could she support the child?

She made some mental calculations. With the Calahans' agreement to her proposition, and rents from the rooms she let once the Klondike Gold Rush began; if she invested prudently . . .

It wasn't as though the Securities and Exchange Commission would pound on her door and demand to know about her inside information.

Yet the dominoes she placed side by side would topple if things did not fall into place as she anticipated. She needed to be sure so that she would offer the children a true home.

She moved through Gray House with an eye of turning it into a boarding establishment. True, Matthew hadn't built the place with the notion of making it a paying business. But it lent itself to just that, particularly if she and Laurie shared the room off the kitchen and she turned both studies into bedrooms.

She counted potential rooms on the first and second floors. With a bit of work, the attic lent itself to an open bunkhouse. From a practical vantage, four single beds with a small chest or trunk would fit. A heavy drapery would muffle sound and allow a modicum of privacy, without obstructing the airflow from the four gabled windows. She sat on one of the trunks and sketched out the potential use of space.

Space, she mused, would be at a premium once the

Klondike gold rush started, and more so after Juneau became the capital of Alaska Territory.

An upscale boardinghouse would do well, she decided. She'd speak with Doreen Feeney and see if they could reach a permanent working arrangement for Doreen to continue cleaning the place and perhaps share the cooking chores.

"Laundry and linens," she added aloud, flipping the pages of her tablet to add more notes.

She and Laurie could take care of the yard, particularly if Doreen agreed to cook the evening meals. She'd recruit the Bittlehorn boys to help build a playscape. Patrick would have his own little swing, one he couldn't fall out of, right beside Laurie's.

Lost in her daydreams for a self-sufficient future, Bethany secured the house, doused the lights, and retired to her room with her tablet and pencil. Stretched out on her bed, she began a new list of items she'd have to beg, borrow, or buy to transform the attic.

Time was on her side if she started now. After all, she had the entire winter to prepare. Even then, the northward-moving hordes would start slow.

She hugged a pillow and made a few more notes, vaguely aware that she was planning a future that meant staying in Juneau forever. Her mind spun with possibilities and consequences. For just a moment, she'd rest her eyes and slow her thoughts. Then, she'd get ready for bed.

How long the momentary rest lasted, she wasn't sure. Suddenly she was wide awake.

The sun had set.

Moonlight reflected off her closed bedroom door.

She bolted from the bed.

"Matthew," she whispered. Her questions and plans forgotten, she opened the bedroom door and dashed down the hall to the door leading to the attic off the back stairs.

Light spilled into the hallway, along with the noise of furniture scraping across the floor.

This was a heck of a time for Matthew to check out the attic, she thought.

She lifted the front of her skirt and hurried up the stairs, glad she hadn't changed for bed before she fell asleep.

"What are you doing up here? I thought—" The words died on her lips. The entire attic looked like a tornado had struck. Not a square inch of flooring showed through the papers, clothing, linens, and keepsakes of a past life.

Lawrence Camden stood in the mess, his eyes glistening, his hair wild, his tie gone, and the top buttons of his shirt open. "Too bad you aren't a sound sleeper, Miss James."

She turned to run, but before she reached the bottom of the stairs, he caught her by the hair and hauled her down the hall and into the Old Man's room.

Screaming, kicking, clawing at his hands, Bethany fought every inch of the way. Lawrence Camden had six inches and eighty pounds of advantage.

He backhanded her, splitting her lower lip.

The scream ripping from her throat melted into a moan.

He forced her facedown on the bed, stuck his knee in the small of her back, and pulled her wrists high behind her shoulder blades.

Dear God in Heaven, he was going to kill her.

# Chapter Twenty-five

Matthew unlocked the back door of Bethany's home. He should have left the key on the night table when he'd left this morning, but the prospect of another midnight rendezvous had proved an irresistible temptation.

Tonight, he'd see her again.

Tonight, they'd talk.

After they made love. After he stroked and tasted her delectable body and made her cry out with joy. After he buried himself in her and brought them both to ecstasy. After—

Something whacked his shin. He side-stepped to keep his balance and stepped on something slippery. Groping for a solid hold in the dark, he shuffled sideways and slammed into what felt like a chair in the wrong place. It tipped, bit into his other shin and nearly took him down. His foot came down hard on a round object at the same time he reached the hutch. Glassware toppled and splintered in the darkness.

"What . . . ?" He regained his balance and carefully made his way to the wall.

He lit a lamp and froze at the sight of the kitchen. In a single glance, he took in the sight of empty drawers overturned on the floor. Cupboard doors hung open, their contents pulled out or in total disarray. China and crystal were piled on the countertops and floor, some shattered, others neatly stacked beside a mound of unfolded table and kitchen linens. Cooking utensils, pots, and pans created a precarious mountain on the stove. Flour, sugar, coffee, and grain bags lay on the heap. Each bore the ravages of a knife blade, their contents spewed across the stone floor in a hodgepodge of grains and powdery flour.

"Bethany!"

Matthew bolted up the back stairs two at a time, rounded the landing, and banged the attic door shut on the way to her bedroom.

A pencil and tablet lay beside a bunched pillow in the center of her bed. The window was open, the screen intact, but there was no sign of Bethany.

Like a madman, he dashed from one room to the next, his fear for her growing with each breath.

No Bethany.

The contents of the bookshelves in the old man's study lay like broken soldiers on the floor. The desk and cabinets mirrored the ransacked condition of the kitchen.

Shouting her name, he looked into every nook, cranny, and closet on the second floor of the house before heading into the attic.

He swore at the ruin littering the floor. It took three minutes to check the trunks and dark crannies.

Fear overwhelmed him. His songbird was such a petite woman. How could she withstand the fury evident in this maniacal destruction?

He returned to the old man's room, which appeared only half destroyed. The intruder had pulled the big bureau away from the wall and left the closet untouched.

His roar of anguish reverberated through the room. Fear for Bethany's fate filled every cell of his being. The bloodstains on the white quilt covering the bed were all he saw for a full minute. A hank of curly auburn hair lay beside a crimson smear near the middle of the bed.

Bethany's hair.

Anger and fear combined to still his heart for several beats.

He touched the smudge, felt the cool dampness, and rubbed it between his fingers.

Fear turned to terror over what she was enduring this very second. Driven to find her, he dashed down the front staircase to the foyer. Nothing on the main floor had escaped the frenetic wrath of the intruder.

Matthew grabbed the front doorknob and turned. The door was unlocked. Had it been that way when the intruder arrived? Or had there been a third key?

Who would have had a third key?

Nothing of apparent value was missing. Polished silver glinted amid the ruin of the kitchen and pantry area. The gold candlesticks beside the Old Man's bed were untouched.

Who might have a key and not take—

Lawrence Camden?

Whatever the intruder had torn the place apart to find, he'd been desperate. And Bethany had gotten in his way.

He told himself that Camden hadn't killed her outright, or he'd have left the body behind. He forced himself to believe that. Where would the man take her? Where might he hide her where no one would look until Monday, when she didn't show up at school?

The answer rose out of Matthew's worst nightmares.

The mine.

The son of a bitch would use the mine.

The second shift had finished for the night, and no one worked on Sunday.

By the time the work started Monday morning, Camden and the *Northern Lights* could be a day out to sea.

Dogs barked as Matthew ran through yards and down streets to Ludden's livery. He didn't bother saddling his horse, just swung onto his back and headed for the Gray Wolf.

Judging by the dampness of the blood on the quilt in the Old Man's room, Camden couldn't be too far ahead of him.

He had to catch up before he took Bethany into the mine.

And if he didn't?

"Not an option," he seethed.

Matthew's heart quickened, and he began to sweat. His love was trapped in absolute darkness, in the cold confines of his mine.

Bethany's head throbbed and a fist pummeled her abdomen.

And she'd gone blind.

Panic almost overcame her. Then, *Not blind*, she realized with immense relief. She was blindfolded and gagged with a bloody rag. Soft fabric bound her hands behind her back.

God, Camden was carrying her over his shoulder like a sack of potatoes. No wonder her ribs felt as though they were a punching bag.

"Hold still," the mine manager growled. "Unless you want me to knock you out again."

Again?

No wonder her head felt like the bass drums of a rock band.

Where was he taking her? And what was he going to do with her once they got there?

She fought the instinct to struggle for freedom. He'd already proven he was bigger than she and had no compunction about knocking her around.

If he was going to kill her, why hadn't he done so?

As long as she drew breath, she had hope; escape remained a possibility. She tamped down the panic swelling her stomach. She couldn't see, but she could hear, so she listened.

Gravel crunched under her captor's feet. Several paces later, the ground became solid and his footfalls quieter.

Moments later, metal grated on wood. The squawk of nails being ripped from wood pierced the silence.

The smell penetrating the chaos of her senses had a familiarity. She knew that smell.

The mine. He'd opened the boarded-up adit. Once he replaced the boards, she'd never be found.

Oh, God, he *was* going to kill her. Or worse, hog-tie her and leave her in the depths where she'd die slowly. Panic tore away her fragile grip on discipline and she struggled with every ounce of strength she possessed.

Hoping against hope, Matthew made a slight detour around the superintendent's house. Lights from the compound reflected against darkened windows with open drapes.

A horse and buggy were tethered beside the mine building.

He slid off his horse and entered the building. A safety light glowed near the lift.

She was in the lower tunnels.

Or was she?

Through the frantic sound of his heart in his ears, he caught the silence of the cavernous building. The lift motor was not operating.

"Camden!"

The sound echoed in the spacious shadows.

Camden wouldn't have taken Bethany into the active part of the mine. Rather, he'd opt for the old tunnel Matthew had dug his way out of fourteen years earlier. The man had a sense of irony.

The pit of Matthew's stomach contracted, perspiration popping from his every pore. Still, his feet kept moving toward the old section. He found a miner's hat and several old-fashioned torches, the kind used when he and the Old Man had started the mine a lifetime ago. Unwilling to limit himself, he lit one and carried two others.

Boards that had covered the opening now stood propped against the rock wall. He extended the light into the darkest recess of his private hell. The firelight flickered on the walls, shook in his unsteady hand.

A single set of boot-sized footprints marked the dusty floor leading into the old tunnel. Camden was carrying her. How badly had he hurt her? Yet, he hadn't killed her. He hoped. *Please, God, let me find her alive*.

Concentrating on the footprints and images of Bethany, he forced himself into the tunnel. He held his light out and followed the trail in the brightest part of the sphere. His rapidly beating heart thudded so loud he heard it echo in the tomblike silence.

Forty feet in, the tunnel expanded to a lopsided Y. The dusty footprints led into the very passage that had collapsed on him so long ago.

Perspiration ran down Matthew's forehead and stung his eyes. Dry-mouthed, he struggled to take deep, controlled breaths.

Time contracted.

So did the walls.

How well he knew these rough-hewn walls, shadows trying to crush him with memories as heavy as the mountain that had nearly crushed him two days shy of his seventeenth birthday.

He raised the light and looked behind him. Sweat

stung his eyes. The last vestige of safety offered by the dim light at the mouth of the tunnel had disappeared around the bend. The surrounding darkness closed off his escape and thwarted him from moving forward. He focused on the circle of light surrounding him.

"Bethany." Her name felt like sandpaper on his dry throat. The vision of her in Camden's foul clutches got him moving again.

Camden could have only one reason for bringing her into the far reaches of the old tunnel. He surely meant to kill her.

New urgency battled old terror. All the while, he put one foot in front of another and kept the image of Bethany foremost in his mind.

Bethany laughing with the children, her violet eyes shining, her wild auburn curls slipping the combs holding them away from her face. Bethany, holding Patrick and singing a lullaby with a tenderness that burned his soul.

Bethany, railing at him in anger after he'd offered to buy her clothes.

And Bethany, clutching him in the throes of passion, her dilated eyes bright in the moonlight, her hair a damp halo, and her delectable body one with his.

Grit filtered from the ceiling into his head. He ignored it.

The walls narrowed with each step.

The darkness drank in the light.

The urge to run back to the entrance—before the wall, floor, and ceiling entombed him in utter darkness—swept through him in waves.

It seemed hours, maybe only days, since he'd last entered this old tunnel. He knew exactly where he was—just over a hundred yards from the entrance. The tunnel bent to the left again.

Where the hell was Camden taking Bethany? China?

Not much farther, Matthew assured himself. The tunnel turned twice more before fanning into a large area where they had completely lost the ore vein back in '89.

As he rounded the next bend, a board caught him with rib-cracking force across his abdomen. The impact knocked the air from his lungs. Doubled over, he didn't know what hit him until it struck again, this time knocking the light from his hand.

In the shadows illuminated only by the light from Matthew's torch, Camden ran past inflicting a final shove. Matthew fell to his knees.

Struggling for air, he knew he'd asked for exactly what he'd got. Carrying a light in a dark tunnel made him the perfect target. Ironically, his light guttered out.

Frantic for the light and wheezing, he groped the floor. His fingers caressed the fallen torch. He couldn't get the matches from his shirt pocket and light it fast enough. The darker it was, the faster the walls closed in.

Shaking, his breathing ragged, his ribs screaming in agony, he lit the torch and gathered up the other two as though they were long-lost children.

The bright flame stopped the walls from closing in.

He got to his feet, desperate to find Bethany.

Around the next bend he caught sight of a bundle of clothing at the fringe of his light.

*Bethany*.

God, she wasn't moving!

He rushed to her side and laid the torch down.

"Bethany, sweet Bethany," he whispered, removing the makeshift hood Camden had wrapped around her face. The bastard had blindfolded and gagged her, too.

"Matthew?" Her eyes fluttered open as he removed the blindfold.

"I'll kill him for this."

She struggled to sit up, turning to give him access to her bound wrists. "I'll help you."

A moment later, she was on her feet and lighting one of the spare torches from his.

Matthew wasted no time on words. Everything inside him screamed to get out of the tunnel, to get into the open space where there was light, where the stars and the clouds filled the sky.

Now that he'd found Bethany and knew she was safe, his claustrophobia returned with a vengeance. His legs felt like two-hundred-pound weights. Other than the coppery taste of blood, his mouth was dry, although perspiration dampened his clothing.

He held her hand and followed her lead, forcing himself to look only at her. She'd bring him into the open, into the light, into the clean, expansive air under an open sky.

It seemed an eternity until they turned into the final portion of the tunnel.

"There it is. The exit," Bethany said in a raspy voice.

They were within ten feet of it when an explosion from behind them brought down the mountain.

# *Chapter Twenty-six*

The rumble from deep in the tunnel struck terror into Bethany. She ran, her fingers entwined with Matthew's. She hadn't expected rescue, and right now she couldn't think what it must have taken for Matthew to enter the mine in search of her. She couldn't think about how he'd come for her; she could only see that if he hadn't, she'd be caught under the mountain crashing down behind them.

They raced toward the blessed light.

The ground shook beneath her feet. Small rocks, grit, and dust clouds rained on them from the ceiling. As the rumble grew louder, the debris increased in size and volume.

In the blink of an eye, Matthew was ahead of her, pulling her forward, urging her toward light and life. She dropped her torch, hiked her skirts, and ran for all she was worth.

They didn't slow until clear of the entrance. An enormous dirt cloud billowing from the old mine caught them before they made it out of the mine barn, but squinting and holding her breath, she blindly ran where Matthew led.

The rumble culminated in an enormous belch of dirt bubbling out of the building.

The mine's warning sirens blared an ear-splitting wail.

Cool night air filled her, and she coughed. Its cleanliness stung her lungs. All the while, she clung to Matthew as the tunnel protested its demise in a roar of rubble and rock.

Perspiration soaked Matthew's shirt and hair. The fine tremors of the terror he'd faced and conquered rippled on his skin, ghosts not quite yet put to rest.

Dust clouds belched from the mine house's shattered doors and broken windows. The few lights burning in the compound lost their illumination to the dust cloud spilling from the mountain. Then as suddenly as it had begun, the earth beneath Bethany's feet became solid and the mountain quieted.

Shouts from the miners rushing from their barracks mingled with the warning siren.

"Turn that damn thing off," Matthew shouted.

Two men instantly detoured to the mining offices.

Through the noisy chaos, Bethany caught sight of a buggy racing away from them.

"Camden," she said, peering into the dusty darkness.

"Stay here," Matthew ordered.

"Not on your life." They'd come this far together; they'd get that snake Camden together, too. She hurried to keep up with him as he rounded the side of the mine house.

Eyes wild from fright at the noise and dust, Matthew's horse danced at their approach. It tossed its head and pawed at the ground, eager to run.

Bethany caught the reins. When Matthew started to

mount without her, she held them away. "I'm going with you. I have a score to settle, too."

"This isn't the time—"

"You're wasting time, macho man."

She held the reins until at last he helped her onto the horse's back. Letting him have control after that seemed an equitable compromise.

Half-dressed miners raced about, trying to find and resolve the crisis. The siren had stopped, but the sound continued to echo in Bethany's ears.

"Jonathan, count noses," Matthew shouted. "If you're all here, stay out of the mine building until I get back."

"Right, boss," called back one of the miners.

"And get Dall to answer any questions that arise," Matthew added. Surely the man was, even now in his sick bed, demanding to know what was happening.

Their horse needed no encouragement to break into a full gallop. Bethany leaned over its neck and grasped fistfuls of mane. Matthew curled protectively over her back.

Fickle moonlight played with the clouds but allowed enough visibility to see the road into town, the way their enemy had fled. Despite the hazards, they didn't slow until reaching Juneau's limits.

Matthew seemed to know Camden's destination, which was more than Bethany did. They turned toward the waterfront, an eclectic arrangement of buildings, piers, warehouses, torches, and electric lights, and there all the activity focused on a single ship. As they neared, she was able to read the name: *Northern Lights*.

At the same time, she saw Camden approach the gangway as someone else drove away with his buggy.

"I see him," Matthew growled. "Take the reins."

She complied as the horse slowed.

They caught up with Camden as he dashed along the pier, valise in hand.

Matthew launched himself from the horse. His momentum brought both men to the ground in a rolling bounce that must have jolted Matthew's teeth, but thank heaven, he landed on top of Camden.

Bethany reined the horse sharply before turning him back. She wasn't going to miss a single minute of Matthew's retribution—or the opportunity to deliver her own.

Camden staggered Matthew with a powerful uppercut.

Sailors and stevedores ran down the gangway and the cargo area of the warehouse.

Bethany slid off her horse but kept hold of its reins. The clack of its agitated hooves on the wooden dock contrasted sharply with the sounds of impacting flesh and bone.

Matthew buried his fist into Camden's midsection and doubled him over. He followed with a rising knee to Camden's jaw.

Blood splattered on the dock.

Bethany picked up Camden's valise, held it high, and smiled.

Camden reached for the case.

"You don't touch her again, you son of a bitch." Matthew's fist caught Camden squarely on his bloody jaw. The once-dapper mine superintendent collapsed face-down on the wharf timbers.

"Don't get up," Matthew warned.

Camden started to roll over. Matthew's boot planted firmly on his neck thwarted the attempt.

"What's going on here?" demanded an officer from the *Northern Lights*.

"One of your passengers has just canceled his trip," Matthew said. "The only place he's going is to jail."

"What'd he do?" the officer demanded.

"He kidnapped and tried to kill me," Bethany said. "If Mr. Gray hadn't rescued me, I'd be in the back of the mine Mr. Camden just blew up."

As she suspected, her brief explanation engendered the wrath of both sailors and stevedores.

"String 'im up!" came a cry from the back of the gathering crowd.

"Turning him over to the authorities will be sufficient—for tonight," Matthew said.

"They're on their way," said the officer. "I suppose you'll want this man's trunks, too."

The two spoke of details, but all Bethany took in was Matthew, the way he stole a glance her way at every opportunity. This was the man she loved, the man strong enough to save her from physical and emotional death, the man trusting enough to allow her to save him.

Drawn by the realization that she loved him beyond measure, she closed the distance between them. He was her hero—as flawed and scarred on the inside as she was on the outside, but wonderful nonetheless. The River of Time had brought her here, to this place and time, to *him*. He was her soul mate, a man who accepted her as she was. Perhaps Yolanda D'Arcy had not warned her of this so many years ago, but promised her.

"Do you love me?" she asked softly.

Matthew stopped his explanation to the men hauling Lawrence Camden away in handcuffs and met her gaze. "I'd walk through hell for you."

"You already did." What it had cost him to enter the mine in search of her, she could only guess. "Will you marry me, Matthew?"

The sudden silence on the wharf became deafening. The sailors were surely shocked by her forwardness but she knew Matthew wouldn't mind. He had always understood before.

He thumbed a lock of hair from her cheek. "Are you going to stay around?"

"Yeah, I am." She nodded, remembering an old quote. "Home is where the heart is, and my heart is with you,

Matthew Gray. You're my hero." She grinned, and added, "The man I want to adopt children with."

She couldn't stop looking into his eyes. The love she saw there reached into her heart and soothed all doubts and fears. This was right. He was right. For her entire life in her time, she had needed her sisters—now she needed no one but him.

He gave her a wide smile. "In that case, it would be my great honor and privilege to be your husband, Bethany. The sooner, the better."

He caught her up and kissed her amid the dockside cheers. Bethany tasted of grit from the mine, but also the sweetness of love.

"You two had an eventful night," Dall said when Matthew and Bethany entered his quarters the next afternoon. "Is it true? Camden's going on trial for a list of crimes as long as my arm?"

"Yes," Matthew answered, bringing two spare chairs to Dall's bedside. "Theft, embezzlement, battery, robbery, kidnapping, attempted murder, and murder."

"Murder?" Delphinia asked from her chair at Dall's side, her gloved hand gliding over his shoulder. "He *killed* someone last night?"

"He's being charged with the deaths of the five men who died in the mine. The cave-in was a direct result of his collusion with Ellison to state the timbers were replaced, when in fact they were not," Matthew continued. "He dummied the timber and rail invoices, falsified the work reports to show maintenance never performed, and pocketed the money. He skimmed every way possible and was damned good at it. But his greed caused him to slip up.

"Tell me, Delphinia, how many loans did my father take out for the mine, and how many did Camden sign for as mine superintendent?"

"You father took out a loan for fifty-thousand dollars," she answered.

"The amount we found in his study," Bethany said.

"And the amount promised to Camden in the will, providing he remained with the mine until September or after familiarizing his replacement with the intricacies of the business," Matthew added. The entire picture began taking shape. "And Camden?"

"He signed on your father's behalf for half a million dollars." Alarm widened her hazel eyes. "If you're looking for a way out of those loans, Matthew, I'm afraid there isn't one."

He laughed, as did Dall.

"Knowing you, Delphinia, I'm sure you didn't lend Camden a nickel on behalf of the Gray Wolf without a fully documented authorization from the Old Man."

"Nice to see you haven't forgotten my thoroughness. Actually, the main reason for my visit here was to discuss those matters in person with Mr. Camden. He transferred almost the same amount into his accounts last month. One of our bright young tellers noticed the drastic change in his financial affairs when Mrs. Camden attempted to withdraw an amount much larger than their previous balance."

"Did she receive the money?" Dall asked.

"No. The teller thought it was a mistake and notified me immediately."

"But there was no mistake," Bethany murmured.

"No. I have seen shenanigans before. I didn't want the bank involved. Lawrence swore he had a letter of authorization from George Gray. Until I saw it, and compared the signatures—" Delphinia shrugged and cast a skyward glance.

"He had a letter signed by the Old Man, but the ambiguous wording must have given George pause, because he hid it after he signed it. According to Camden, your father died before Camden could convince him to give it to him. Your persistence and questions made him desperate."

"He'd booked passage on a ship that sailed this morning," Dall said in amazement. "He nearly pulled this scheme off. Once he presented the letter to the bank—"

"We would have given him what he asked for," Delphinia finished.

"He turned the house upside down searching for that letter," Bethany said. "I got in his way. After he found the letter, rather than take a chance, he decided to put me in the back of the old mine shaft, set a charge, and hightail it to the ship. That way, I'd be missing and no one could prove I was dead."

She shivered, and Matthew tightened his arm around her.

"Why did he do it? Greed?" Delphinia asked.

"Love. Insecurity. Mr. Camden's wife is accustomed to a lavish lifestyle," Bethany explained. "Regardless of what he earned, it would never be sufficient to satisfy her tastes. They wanted to travel abroad and live large. He'd known about the bonus in Mr. Gray's will for a long time, but even that wouldn't be enough."

"Live large," Delphinia repeated. "What a unique turn of phrase."

"We looked at the books this morning," Matthew continued. "The *real* books. Camden was taking them with him in his valise. No doubt he'd planned on tossing them overboard once the *Northern Lights* reached the high seas. He couldn't risk anyone here finding them."

"How much trouble is the mine in?" Dall asked.

"It isn't, or at least it won't be once we work out all the details of Camden's embezzling. And that shouldn't be too difficult, considering we know someone with authority at Moore Mercantile." Matthew gave a sheepish look at Delphinia.

Apparently, his old lover held no grudges. "As far as I'm concerned," she said, "that's Gray Wolf money. Any time you want to pay off the loans, you're free to do so."

"Do you still want to sell the mine?" Dall asked. "Now that it'll be profitable again?"

"Believe it," Matthew said, surprised by the question.

Dall gave a small smile. "It's about time I settled down. Besides, I can't get any more tied down than I am right now. Things can only get better."

Delphinia stood, her back to everyone else as she faced Dall. "I was thinking of selling the bank and relocating."

"Juneau's a good place," Dall proposed.

Bethany stood. "Keep the bank, Mrs. Moore. Open a branch up here and oversee it yourself. Trust me, you won't be sorry."

Everyone looked at her, and Matthew grinned. "Listen to her. She won't steer you wrong."

"What an interesting prospect."

Matthew grinned, knowing Delphinia was already calculating the logistics of a new branch.

"On a more pleasant subject, rumors say you're getting married. Any truth to that?" Dall asked.

Matthew laughed. "Beats me how you know what men are saying on the wharf when you're flat on your back up here."

"I have my sources."

"Apparently so."

"Is it true?" Delphinia asked. Her apparent nonchalance at the news made both Matthew and Dall blink in amazement.

"I asked him to marry me, and he said yes." Color rose in Bethany's cheeks, and she smiled over at him. Matthew's heart leaped with joy. In a couple of weeks they'd be married and get a ready-made family with Laurie and Patrick—provided the circuit judge agreed.

"Congratulations, Matthew." Delphinia rose from the

chair beside Dall's bed. "You've got a good man, Bethany."

Matthew found himself pleased by his one-time beloved's change. It boded well for the women. But even more, what made him happy was his future wife's, "Thank you, I know." And then Bethany's fingers tightened on his.

# *Epilogue*

On a clear, late-summer morning two weeks later, Matthew held Patrick. He stood beside Bethany and Laurie at the foot of Bull Craddock's grave. Bethany had just sung "Wind Beneath My Wings" and they'd said a prayer.

"It's not that I don't love you, Daddy," Laurie said. "You'll always be my daddy, but now you've got Mommy. And I've got another family to love me, and a baby brother. His name's Patrick. He's Irish." The little girl paused.

"I won't forget you or Mommy. I promise." She looked up at Bethany. "Can we sing again?"

"Sure. How about one of my sister Caitlyn's favorites. It's called 'Pie Jesu'."

Once again she heard her sisters' voices harmonizing in her memory. The only difference was that this time, she sang the lead instead of Caitlyn. God, how she hoped her two sisters would find a modicum of the happiness she herself had found with this man and these children she loved.

"Gosh," Laurie said, awed.

"Excuse me." The voice belonged to a tall, slightly built man. He stood with his hat in his hand, though his stance exuded a commanding presence. Deep, weathered wrinkles troweled his face. The breeze caught wisps of his thinning gray-brown hair. Brown eyes twinkled beneath his thick, gray eyebrows.

"That song. Where did you learn it?" he asked.

"In Wyoming. My mother taught it to me," Bethany answered. Laurie wrapped her arms around Bethany's waist and stared at the intruder. "Why?"

"Your eyes. They're lavender."

Matthew straightened Patrick's blanket and gave the child to Bethany.

The man laughed and raised his hand. "I'm Alphonse Wardel, the circuit judge. I've heard you sing in this graveyard."

"From whom?" Astonishment raised Bethany's voice half an octave.

"People here in town. But I've just come from a place you might find it beneficial to visit—Sitka." With a wry smile and merry eyes, he gave her a half-bow and put on his hat. "You might ask for Caleb Marker's wife, Alicia. She, too, is a lavender-eyed woman, and she sang for my daughter at *her* grave."

"My sister? Alicia is in Sitka? She's married?"

"Yes, yes, and yes," Judge Wardel said with a laugh. "I suppose so. She asked me to keep an eye on for you—or another sister."

"No." Joy danced through her, along with shock.

"Yes."

"Thank you! Thank you, Judge Wardel. From the bottom of my heart, thank you. This is the happiest day of my life. All my dreams are coming true today." And maybe Caitlyn was here, too. She'd have to search for them. Everything looked like it would be all right.

"Do I have an aunt?" Laurie asked.

"Sounds like it," Matthew said. "And an uncle."

"And a cousin." Judge Wardel turned to go. "I'll see you at the Gray Wolf Mine. I've never married anyone in the best man's sick room, but I'll manage." He wandered off.

The trio stood in silence for a few moments, but it was soon broken off by the sound of rushing water.

"Son of a gun," Matthew whispered.

Shock froze Bethany's ability to speak.

"What is that?" Laurie pointed to the trees.

Fog was sweeping through the green boughs on an invisible current. The sound of water running the rapids of a mountain creek flowed from the trees even louder. Distant chords of laughter and tears wove through the sound. Hues of color danced through the swirling fog, confined neatly between invisible banks.

Bethany kissed Patrick's covered head and gazed over at Matthew. "It's a river."

"A river of fog? I didn't know there was such a thing," Laurie said, her hand slipping into Matthew's.

"There is, sweetheart," Matthew assured their new daughter. "And sometimes it's magic."

"Wow."

"Yeah, wow," Bethany agreed. It had finally come back for her, but there was no longer any reason to go. She was content here, in her new time, in her new place, in her new family. "Let's go get married and sign adoption papers," she said.

"How about a family honeymoon in Sitka after Phineas Montgomery arrives next week?" Matthew suggested.

"Can we? I mean, can you manage that with your work?"

"For you, I can walk under a mountain. I love you, songbird."

*And she loved him.*